A Defiant Gaze—
and a Shock of Desire . . .

So she thought he should show her mercy? After the hours of humiliation she'd put him through? His eyes swept down, paused on her lips, then on the smooth column of her neck. He wanted to push the coat and dress from her shoulders, dip his head, and have a taste. She was a savage, but she was also more striking, wrapped in her fur, than any woman dressed in silk or satin and adorned with glittering jewels. Still, her beauty and her meek look wouldn't make him forget the way she'd treated him.

Her eyes flashed. "Do not look at me that way!" she gasped, stepping away from him.

He couldn't help a mild grin. His look alarmed her—because of how it made her feel, because for a second or two, she had allowed herself to enjoy it . . .

* * *

More praise for
Teresa Warfield's *Cherokee Rose:*

"A story that glistens with tears and shines with heartwarming tenderness, a story that will touch your heart . . . Ms. Warfield fills the pages with intense emotions and blazing passion. *Cherokee Rose* is a gem of a book, a real jewel to add to your keeper shelf!"

—*Affaire de Coeur*

Also by Teresa Warfield

CHEROKEE ROSE
PRAIRIE DREAMS
SUMMER STORM

Teresa Warfield

JOVE BOOKS, NEW YORK

CHEROKEE BRIDE

A Jove Book / published by arrangement with
the author

PRINTING HISTORY
Jove edition / June 1994

ISBN: 0-515-11390-5

A JOVE BOOK®
Jove Books are published by The Berkley Publishing Group,
200 Madison Avenue, New York, New York 10016.
JOVE and the "J" design are trademarks
belonging to Jove Publications, Inc.

PRINTED IN THE UNITED STATES OF AMERICA

10 9 8 7 6 5 4 3 2 1

For Tom Marlin and Kathy Fischer-Brown
who share my love and sympathy
for all Native Americans.

May the Cherokee prosper,
may the Shoshone prevail,
may the Seminole gain exclusive rights
to their ancestral tribal name ...

ACKNOWLEDGMENTS

No book is written alone, and I like to give credit where credit is due . . .

First, to my immediate family: You're the best for tolerating the moodiness of this author. Tanya, Stephanie, Kimberly, Jonathan, Melissa, Jack . . . thanks for your endless patience and understanding. Without you this book would not have been written. (Or at least improved.)

Big thanks must be extended to Debbie Krauss, who read a big chunk of the first draft. (What a brave soul!) Debbie, your criticism was right on. Laurie Miller, Rhonda Hermes, and Beverly Shippey: thanks for muddling through the original first three chapters.

Thank you, Judith Stern, for having faith, for having tact—and for being a totally cool editor.

The core participants of *Historical Fiction* . . . You know who you are: Kathy, Tom, Barbara, Bev, Sherrilyn, Roger, Kay, Charlotte, Carol, Tanya, John, Dakota . . . I'd better not be forgetting anyone. To any *Historical Fiction* bulletin-board personality who ever chatted with me . . . I love you all. You're wonderful. Writing this book would have been hell without your support.

Ginny: Your ear is always available. I'll pay the insurance premium, my outstanding friend.

To the '93–'94 Northeast Ohio Romance Writer's group—thanks for supporting me through thick and thin.

Prologue

EARLY SUMMER 1807

WITH WATER FLOWING AROUND her thighs, Danagasta paused in the Tennessee River and glanced excitedly up at the clear Skyland. From there she turned her gaze and a smile to Kayini, her close friend, who stood nearby. Kayini grinned and lifted the fish she had just speared. But her grin was not prompted by the catch she had made; it was prompted by what Danagasta had told her during their walk to the river only a short time ago.

Danagasta eased a hand down over her belly. *"Usdiga,"* Kayini said, watching her.

Danagasta smiled. "Yes . . . baby."

Right before she and Kayini had started off to fish, she had realized . . . She had been thinking about the odd way she had been feeling, that her breasts were swollen and tender, and that nearly every morning now she drank soothing tea to calm her stomach. Then she realized that she had not gone to the menstrual hut last moon . . . last month.

Danagasta clutched her sharpened stick—used to spear fish—and marveled again at the fact that she was with child.

Kayini opened the pouch resting at her side and plopped her catch into it. "Your husband and his brother will raise the baby to be a powerful hunter. He will be tall and strong, and Losi will insist that he be covered with a wolf-skin during sleep so he will grow to be swift and clever."

"He?" Danagasta remarked, amused. She had married Losi only three seasons ago, and he had talked many times of them having a child. He would be thrilled when she told him she was pregnant. But how could anyone know if the baby was a boy or girl child?

"It is a boy," Kayini responded. "I know already."

Danagasta laughed, but seconds later she sobered as Kayini twisted around in search of more fish. More than the stomach sickness caused by her pregnancy had been bothering Danagasta today. "Losi and Sequatchee took whiskey with them on the hunt," she said. "The white man's brew makes them crazy—they should not drink it while hunting. Only last night Losi was drunk and did not know me."

Sequatchee was Losi's younger brother. Two seasons before, he had introduced Losi and Chief Doublehead, one of their closest friends from a neighboring village, to whiskey. Then he had told them that some white settlers would trade flasks of the drink for trinkets and for the soft, odd-colored stones the Indians often found floating in their rivers and streams. Ever since, Losi had not been the same. Danagasta had told him that she did not like the way whiskey affected his mind. She had said nothing to Sequatchee, however, and had not spoken of her concern about the men's drinking to Kayini, who had loved Sequatchee since her childhood. But today . . . the time had come for her and Kayini to band together to try to make the brothers realize that whiskey was not good for them.

"You should not worry, Danagasta," Kayini said softly. "Our men are wise. Surely they will not drink much today."

"Before today, they never took it with them during a hunt," Danagasta responded. "I do worry, and you should worry, too. Finally Sequatchee has decided to court you. Surely you want him to live a long life with you."

Kayini's gaze shifted to the water. She was eighteen winters, and she had loved Sequatchee for many seasons and did not want to be critical of him. "You sound angry."

"I am becoming so."

"At Sequatchee? Danagasta—"

"He told Losi where he could trade for whiskey."

"You have caught no fish," Kayini said. "We cannot stay long. My parents will be angry if I am gone long."

Danagasta sighed. "Do not act as though their drinking is not a problem. Do not ignore it. I have not wanted to speak with you about this, but when I realized that Sequatchee and Losi were taking their whiskey flasks with them today . . . I have had a terrible feeling in my stomach. Like something is not right."

"You said your stomach has bothered you for many days."

"This feeling is different, and it is not only in my stomach. My heart feels different. It feels heavier."

In the distance, a branch cracked. Danagasta glanced about—to their peoples' side of the riverbank, then to the whites' side. Sometimes the white settlers called foul names across the water, and sometimes they scrambled into their boats and approached, shouting insults. They wanted to claim more Cherokee land, and frightening Indian women and children who were fishing or gathering cane was only one of their tactics.

Seeing no danger, Danagasta speared a fish and put it into the buckskin pouch she had slung over her head and shoulder and brought to rest on her hip before leaving the settlement. Then she and Kayini stood still and silent, waiting for more fish to appear. Three finally swam close by, and Danagasta and Kayini caught one each.

A breeze rustled tree branches and low-lying scrub on the river's east and west banks. Danagasta glanced about again, studying the scrub, her nostrils flaring, her body tensing.

"What is it?" Kayini inquired softly.

"Something . . . I do not know. We should return to the town."

They turned and neared the bank.

"There!" Kayini pointed north. "The men return from hunting already."

Danagasta's heart seemed to stop beating. Yes . . . *already*. Hunting parties traveled many miles and often did not return for several days. This party had left only this morning, and the fact that they were returning so soon meant something was wrong.

She forced herself to look in the direction Kayini pointed, and she spotted a small group of men approaching along the water's edge, small game dangling from their waists. Two men pulled a litter bearing a large deer. But there were only five men—half of the original party. Losi was not among them.

"Where are the others?" Danagasta whispered, scanning the trees for glimpses of more fringed and beaded buckskin. "Where is my husband?"

Water dripped from Kayini's dress as she mounted the slope and walked toward the group. As she neared, the men halted, looking shocked and sad. Danagasta had to order her feet to rise and fall and carry her forward. Catolster, one of the men, said something to Kayini, and she shook her head, denying his words. He took her by the shoulders and pulled her aside just as the rest of the original party emerged from between trees up ahead.

There were only four in this group . . . *four*—and another litter. The disquiet Danagasta had felt all morning turned to icy alarm and slithered like an evil snake through her body.

"What is it?" she asked, stopping near Catolster and Kayini. Neither of them responded. Danagasta glanced at the other men. "Shutegi? Otter? Whitetree? What has happened? Someone tell me." She would not become crazy and shout . . . She would *not*.

"I am sorry, Danagasta," Catolster said. "He is . . . Losi and Sequatchee . . . They like the whiskey. Losi ran in the way."

Danagasta stared at him for a long moment. Then she demanded, "Where is my husband?"

Catolster glanced over his shoulder.

Danagasta forced herself to look at the second group. She scanned the tight expressions, not seeing Losi.

"He is on the litter," Catolster said quietly, regretfully.

"He is hurt?" she heard herself mumble. "You will tell me he is only hurt? That we will take him to the healer and he will live?" The strap of the pouch in which she had put the fish ran diagonally from her shoulder to her waist, cutting between her breasts. She rubbed it rapidly, scarcely aware of what she was doing. "I caught fish. He likes fish more than venison. I ground acorns and made bread . . . I picked squash from the field and . . . he is alive! I know he is alive. You will tell me he is alive?"

Catolster shook his head. "I am sorry, Danagasta. I cannot."

She put the back of a hand to her mouth. "It is not so! You will tell me—"

"It is so. Losi is dead."

"No!" she whispered.

"Yes."

Somehow she moved her feet in the direction of the second group. Seeing her, the men lowered the litter they had been pulling and stepped back.

Her footsteps slowed. She squeezed her eyes shut, not wanting to see Losi lying lifeless. They had been married such a short time, and she had not even had a chance to tell him that they were expecting a child. No—this could not be!

She opened her eyes and saw the blood staining his chest. "No . . . no. Oh no!" she cried, smoothing the black hair from his brow.

"He was drunk," Talalah said. "We aimed for the deer, but he was there."

Drunk . . . he was drunk—on the white man's poison!

Over the sickly sweet smell of blood Danagasta smelled the brew that had helped kill Losi. She saw the leather-encased tin still tied to the belt she had woven for him, and when she glanced up, she saw Sequatchee, her husband's brother, with a flask of whiskey dangling from his waist.

She fumbled with the ties binding the tin to Losi. They

finally slipped free, and she threw the flash at Sequatchee, hitting him in the chest. He stumbled backward, sorrow and fear glazing his eyes. "You did this!" she shouted through her tears.

He shook his head. "No, Danagasta, I did not make him drink it. I did not make him run—"

"You did, you did, *you did*! You told him of the whites who come through with it!"

He rounded the litter and reached for her. "Danagasta—"

She pushed him away. "I will rid the land of it! I will stop you, do you hear? You will make no more trades with white whiskey peddlers! You have killed him . . . my husband."

Her voice broke with her last two words, and she sank to her knees beside the litter . . . beside Losi's body.

Chapter One

NOVEMBER 1807

DANAGASTA LED HER HORSE alongside the great river, picking her way through trees and brush, recalling the many times she had hidden among them as a child. She remembered well the days when her people, settled in a number of towns and villages around Chickamauga Creek, a tributary of the Tennessee, had battled encroaching whites. Cherokees in many other settlements had wanted peace—at the expense of land. And they had gotten it. Too many times Chickamauga towns and villages had been burned, rebuilt, and burned again. Finally the creek people had been forced to make peace and accept the loss of some of their mountain homeland.

Things were much different now than when she had been a child. They were better in some ways; worse in others. The whites across the river had not attacked in many seasons, though some were still hostile. A number of them had ventured, without permission, to the Cherokee side of the water to settle. Because many of the Indians feared the United States military, they left the whites alone. But that did not mean they were friendly with them.

What will happen to us? Danagasta wondered desperately as she rode along, her bow and a hollowed gourd filled with arrows slung across her back, over her wolfskin coat. *The whites will soon take every mountain and valley we hold dear.* Sharing was impossible. Too many whites hated Indians. They complained to their government that the Indians occupied land they needed, and their government sent men to negotiate for land. When that did not work, soldiers came to kill and burn.

But it was not just the whites who took the land. Not anymore. This morning Danagasta had finally become brave enough to ride to the mouth of Chickamauga Creek and see the iron foundry the Cherokee National Council had given the whites permission to build. The foundry was located no more than a mile from her peoples' settlement of Big Water. The whites had even built homes around the foundry, on Cherokee land! How soon before their village grew and grew? How soon before it approached the palisade surrounding Big Water and her people were told to leave—again? The Council did not have the right to give away Chickamauga land. Many people in Big Water felt the same outrage Danagasta did.

At the foundry she had reined her horse on a crest and had sat for a long time looking down at the iron place and the houses. The whites had stopped walking between their homes to stare at her. Finally she had kicked her horse into a trot, riding defiantly down the slope and right through their settlement, scattering chickens and shocking people. She had seen a white man lift a rifle and she had ducked low, clinging to her horse's neck, kicking the rifle out of the man's hands as she passed. She had ridden on, faster and faster, finally slowing when she realized her horse was tired and that she was safe. And now here she was, near the rapids.

Since Losi's death, she had occasionally watched the Tennessee River for white whiskey peddlers. But this time she had wandered farther than she had in a very long time. Farther than was wise, she was certain.

Shouts arrested her attention. She peered out over the churning rapids and sighted an approaching flatboat. It twisted and turned, rose and dipped, then the water caught it, drove it past her, and sent it spinning beyond her vision. She squinted, trying to catch sight of it again. Instead she spotted a dark-haired man in the rapids, fighting to keep his head above the froth. Some of her people traversed the river in flatboats—boats with cabins built into them—but most had the sense to know that an awkward flatboat might not survive the rapids!

Danagasta jumped from her horse, dropped her bow and gourd of arrows, pushed her way out of her coat, and hurried toward the churning river.

Once in the cold water, she fought the current, knowing the man would have been driven in this direction against his will. Her hand closed around a pole. Then she spotted the man up ahead, going under, and she pushed the stick away and struggled toward him. Her hand finally closed around his upper arm and she fought the current and swam for the bank, ending up a good distance south of where she had entered the river.

Once ashore, Danagasta and the man collapsed on the grass. She turned onto her back, coughed, and managed to catch her breath. Then she rose slowly to her knees, shivering as the wind drove through her wet dress. Beside her, the man tried to get up.

He was a white man . . . she had saved a white man! She had not been thinking. She had not looked closely. She had seen what looked like someone drowning and she had run into the water.

He was dressed in buckskin, which meant he could be a "white" Indian—he could be from one of the Cherokee villages or towns upriver. Could be . . . He also could be a hostile settler from the opposite bank.

She bent beside him, tossed his arm over her shoulder, and began forcing him to walk with her back up to the spot where she had left her horse and belongings. Once there, she released him. He stumbled around, appearing confused. Then he fell over, unconscious.

Danagasta shed her wet dress, grabbed her coat and slipped it on. She pulled arrows from her gourd and broke them in two, thinking they would serve to build a small fire until she was warm enough to search for dry twigs and wood. She cleared a place on the ground and stacked the kindling, then took stones from the leather pouch tossed over her horse's back and began rubbing them together until she produced a spark. Beneath the spark, the broken arrows soon began smoking and caught fire. Warmth drifted up, heating Danagasta's face.

Glancing at the man she had rescued, she saw that his breath was shallow. She approached him, hooked her hands beneath his arms, and dragged him toward the growing flames where she began removing his wet clothes. A leather-covered flask tied to his waist caught her attention.

When she untied the belt cinching his shirt, the tin slipped free. She worked the cork from it, then brought it to her nose.

Whiskey.

She had smelled its sourness enough times on Losi's breath. She wondered how much whiskey the white man had had on his flatboat, and why.

She recorked the container, walked over to her horse, and hid the flask in her leather pouch. Then she returned to the man and tugged his shirt and boots off. Straddling his legs, she unbuttoned his breeches and pulled the buckskin down over his narrow hips and thighs, peeling away woolen stockings, too. She would finish undressing him, then cover him with the animal hide draped over her horse's back.

Grant Claiborne drifted somewhere between extreme sleepiness and heaven. He was incredibly cold, and the hands working at his clothes were warm in comparison. His eyelids fluttered, and he glimpsed orange flames in the darkness that swirled around him. He heard a roar, watched a dark figure struggle with his breeches. What—?

He fought blackness, had to have a better look . . . Who in God's name was undressing him?

The woman's skin was the color of copper, her hair blacker than midnight. Feathery lashes touched high, wide cheekbones, then fluttered up, and for a few heavenly seconds Grant stared into eyes the color of rich coffee. Then his head dropped back weakly, and he drifted again, giving himself up to the angel's care.

He woke, unsure of how much time had passed. The woman had built a larger fire and had spread a thick animal hide over his body. She now stood on the other side of the flames, clad in a thick coat, struggling to push a branch into the ground. She was definitely an Indian. But was she Cherokee or Creek? Both tribes occupied parts of the Tennessee River. He knew that from the few briefings his father, President Jefferson's secretary of war, had given him before he'd left Baltimore to embark on the long journey. Pines, hemlocks, and a host of other trees mingled behind the woman, climbing blue-green hills and snow-topped mountains.

Grant remembered the flatboat dipping as he tried to control it with the pole. He'd lost his footing on the slippery deck and had gone off into the river . . . into the roaring rapids. Who the hell knew what had happened to his companions—his friend, Luke, and the men from Virginia they had hired to help guide them into the Cherokee Nation. He had vague recollections of the woman stumbling up onto the bank, slipping his arm around her neck, helping him walk . . . undressing him.

She had pulled him from the rapids.

She finally finished whatever she was doing with the branch, then lifted articles of clothing from the ground and began draping them on various small arms protruding from the limbs. Up went his shirt, then his breeches, then both gray stockings.

"Osiyo," she said in a breathy voice, and he realized that her dark eyes were fastened on him.

He met her gaze, having no idea *what* she'd said exactly. And he had no idea what to say back to her. She might not even know English.

She crouched, then straightened and draped a brownish-yellow dress over another arm of the branch, never taking her intense eyes from him. He tried to shift his position and found that he couldn't, not very easily anyway. "What the . . . why are my hands and feet bound?" he demanded.

"You survived the rapids, Tsuwa," she said in a breathy voice, "and now here you are—with me."

Apparently she not only understood English, but she also spoke it fluently. Grant tried to wriggle his wrists against what felt like brutal strips of rawhide. They creaked, but gave little. "Untie me. This is not something you should—"

Holding a knife in front of her, point out, she neared, giving him a cold look that made him wonder if she wasn't about to draw and quarter him—or at the very least, scalp him.

She sank to her knees beside him and traced his entire jaw, from one ear to the other, with the deadly tip of her blade. He hadn't shaved since yesterday, and the knife made a scratching sound as it moved along. Grant wanted to jerk away from it but forced himself to lie still and look straight into the woman's eyes. Better to show courage than fear in the face of a threat.

"Did you have whiskey on your flatboat?" she asked sweetly.

"Yes." He was courageous but not stupid; the woman was beautiful, but the look in her eyes . . . She'd rather slit his throat than wait one or two seconds for a response.

A smile touched her lips. She sat back on her heels and studied him. Grant tightened the muscles in his stomach and jerked his shoulders, trying to sit up. She thrust the blade beneath his nose, her dark eyes glittering with warning. Her lips, the color of fine Madeira, came together in a thin, angry line.

"Do not think to run away, Whiskey Man. If I do not stop you with this knife, I will stop you with an arrow."

Whiskey Man?

Grant tilted his head, moving it away from the blade. "How can I possibly run away? I'm only going to sit up. Why am I tied?"

Instead of answering the questions, she gave him another infuriating smile. "Rest and try to warm yourself. When you are strong again, we will travel."

Then she stood, turned, and walked away.

* * *

Danagasta's dress dried quickly, and she slipped it on behind the cover of a thick cluster of trees. She put her coat back on, then approached the white man and slit the leather binding his feet. She did not want to risk untying his hands. He was tall and slightly muscular and could probably overpower her. So she slid his stockings and breeches on, feeling his eyes on her the entire time she worked. She pushed the first boot on him just as he asked her name.

"Danagasta," she answered, seeing no harm in telling him. The harm came when she glanced up and his gaze caught and held hers. His eyes were as blue as the Skyland on an uncloudy day. She had never seen eyes so blue. Eyes in which she could lose her soul, or at least her determination, if she looked into them for long. They were fringed with dark lashes and hooded by thick brows. Chestnut hair spilled gently over his forehead and waved over his ears, ending just below his broad shoulders.

"Are you Cherokee or Creek?" he asked.

She tore her gaze from his and struggled to work the second boot onto his foot. "Cherokee. You are not helping."

"Should I? Where are you taking me?"

"To Big Water. It is a town—"

"Near the mouth of Chickamauga Creek."

She glanced up again just as he cursed under his breath. So he had been through the Nation before . . . He probably knew all the right places to go to sell his poison.

"Danagasta, I should warn you that—"

"Do not warn me about anything, *yun wunega*. Push your foot into the boot!"

He did, then she took him by the arm and helped him stand. He was slightly taller than she, and he stood so close she felt his warm breath in her hair. Stepping away, she smothered the fire with the wolfskin she had used to cover him earlier, then she settled the hide around his shoulders. She put her head and one arm through the leather strap attached to her container of arrows and felt the gourd fall to rest on her back. She carried her bow, wanting it in her hand in case he tried to run away. Pulling an arrow free and settling it in the weapon would take only a second.

A click of her tongue brought her horse. She took the reins and jerked her head, indicating that the white man should go first. He began walking. She followed.

Grant wanted to curse aloud as they walked through the forest. Before leaving Baltimore, he'd been briefed about the Chickamauga faction. While the rest of the Cherokee seemed peaceful, the creek people were known rebels and had to be watched. They were notorious for being brutal, and damn if he hadn't landed right in the middle of them, or at least in the lap of one who seemed cold-blooded and true to Chickamauga nature. He gave brief thought to telling Danagasta exactly who he was, but he wasn't fool enough to do that until he learned more about the current political position of her people. The journey from Baltimore to the Cherokee Nation had taken months, and a lot could have changed during those months—he could very well have arrived right in the middle of another Indian uprising, and if that were the case, Danagasta would undoubtedly want his scalp. She would want it a hell of a lot more than she'd want any other white man's.

Dry leaves and twigs crunched beneath his boots, but she somehow walked softly, hardly making a sound. The forest smelled of decay and of pungent pine. Saplings and bushes mingled between towering trees, and the last shreds of summer and fall clung to wild blackberry and strawberry bushes in the form of shriveled fruit. Birds fluttered on the naked branches of dogwoods, poplars, chestnuts, and oaks. The wild rhododendron, azalea, and yarrow had ceased flowering long ago, but the latter still exuded its strong scent. The botanist William Bartram was right: Something about these mountain forests cast a spell on a person. No wonder the United States Government wanted the land.

Grant slowed his steps, enjoying the scenery, and she prodded him in the back with her bow—a rather insolent thing to do. He quickened his pace, but not enough to suit her; she prodded him again, harder this time, enough to make him fight the urge to wince. "Keep that damn thing away from my back," he growled through gritted teeth, unable to bite back the words.

She prodded him again. "Walk faster."

His rising temper got the better of him. "I'm walking as fast as I plan to. Don't touch me with that bow again."

"And if I do, Tsuwa?" Her voice was soft and low, breathy. It sent a shiver of desire through Grant, and he treated himself to images of her bending over him, murmuring words, her long velvety black hair hiding one side of her face as it spilled down to brush across his naked chest.

"If you do . . ." he responded huskily, feeling his breeches grow tight. "Suffice to say, I *will* get untied at some point."

She laughed, but he thought he heard a bit of nervousness in the laughter. "We shall see . . . My father is the chief of Big Water. Two seasons ago, I vowed to rid our land of whiskey. You, *yun wunega*, have whiskey in your flask."

Grant glanced down at his waist. She hadn't bothered to put his shirt back on him. She was carrying it. But what about his belt on which he had tied his flask? He couldn't recall seeing the container since before he had been washed over into the rapids. He *hadn't* seen it. Obviously she had it.

He didn't drink whiskey much, but it was about all they had had to drink, besides water, on the boat. He'd only tied the tin to his waist so he could have a drink now and then while working the oars. But damn if she wasn't planning to hang him by his vitals for carrying the whiskey with him.

A cold wind shuddered through the boughs of hemlocks and pines, and cut through Grant with icy vengeance.

Chapter Two

THE MOON WAS JUST beginning to appear in the sky when Grant spotted what appeared to be a tall enclosure surrounded by gardens and pens holding horses and cattle. Someone whistled. Danagasta turned her head to the left and whistled back, then again prodded Grant with one end of her bow. He was just jittery enough, nervous about what fate might be awaiting him, that he stopped cold and turned a glare on her, something that was most definitely not a wise thing to do. But he'd had more than enough of her treating him like an animal.

He held her dark gaze, then his eyes dropped to her bow. "I said don't touch me with that thing again."

A gate creaked open in the enclosure, and an Indian man appeared to take Danagasta's horse. She lifted a long-handled pouch from off the horse's neck, then the man took the animal away. Danagasta jerked her head toward the gate. "Will you go calmly, Tsuwa, or must I call for people to drag you inside?"

He turned and went calmly.

As soon as they passed beyond the gate, he began spotting cabins. Torches burned near most of them. In the distance, dogs barked. Scores of men, women, and children began drawing forth, emerging from lodges and from the shadows, it seemed, their expressions hostile. They weren't all Indians; there were a few white men in the crowd. Some of the people wore colorful woven clothing, some wore stitched animal skins, and some wore precious little of anything. Silver ornaments dangled from the ears and noses of many older adults.

Grant concentrated on the path ahead of him. Danagasta prodded him again with her weapon, and he swore under his breath—swore that as soon as he got untied, he'd grab that damn bow and snap it in two.

"Walk faster, Whiskey Man."

"You keep calling me that—that and that other name," he said irritably. "Choo . . . What does it mean?"

She laughed.

He suddenly didn't want to know. It couldn't mean anything good, and he already wanted to choke the woman for the way she'd driven him for the last hour or two.

A Cherokee man stepped into their path. Grant stopped short, expecting to be prodded with the bow again. He braced himself, waiting. But the irritating jab never came.

Danagasta stared coolly at Sequatchee, the man who had stepped in front of her prisoner.

"What are you doing, Danagasta?" Sequatchee asked in Cherokee. "This man harmed you in some way?"

"No," she responded sharply. "He was bringing whiskey into the Nation. I am taking him to my father."

"Danagasta—"

"Is he one of the men you trade with?"

Sequatchee flinched. She would forever blame him for telling Losi where he could get whiskey. Trying to honor the ancient custom that a man should marry and care for his brother's widow, he had devoted himself to her since Losi's death. Regretfully he had given up his courtship of Kayini to try to convince Danagasta to allow him to court and marry *her*. But she had refused the three bowls of hominy he had placed on her doorstep; she had refused his three requests to court her.

She gripped her captive's elbow. "I must see my father. I must speak with him."

"Danagasta . . . Are you sure? You are still vengeful. As long as men like whiskey, you will not succeed in ridding the land of it. Stop this! Your father grows impatient with your bitterness."

She stared coldly at him.

Sge! If only he could soothe the hatred from her eyes! If only he could relive the day Losi had died. He would hide the flasks, then he and the men would hunt. They would kill many deer, then return to Big Water, clean the meat, and put it on racks to dry or store it in the smokesheds some whites had taught them to construct. Danagasta would fry the fish she had caught, bring out the bread she had made, and she, Losi, he, and Kayini would sit together and eat.

None of that could be. Losi's death had changed everything . . . *everything*. Most important, it had changed Danagasta. She was no longer filled with sweetness. She was filled with fire.

"Stop watching me all the time, Sequatchee!" she snapped. "I do not need your protection—and I do not want your bowls of hominy."

He inhaled deeply, then released his breath in a rush.

"My father—"

"Your father sleeps, Danagasta. I must wake him."

"Then do."

Nodding sadly, Sequatchee turned and led the way to the chief's cabin.

Inside his lodge, Hanging Basket stirred when a hand touched his shoulder. He had been dreaming again, the dreams of an old man with many memories. In his mind, he had been a young warrior, fighting white soldiers in the river, then gathering what was left of his people and drawing them back into the mountain forests for protection. So many had been slaughtered. So many . . .

He was glad someone woke him.

He rolled onto his back on the thick animal-skin rugs laid over cane mats, and squinted weary eyes at the figure standing nearby. Finally recognizing the man, he blinked and spoke to Sequatchee in their native tongue: "What has happened?"

"Danagasta has captured a white man she claims was bringing whiskey into the Nation."

Hanging Basket groaned. Danagasta. She always made trouble. Since her husband's death and the miscarriage of her child shortly afterward, she had become difficult. Losi's death had been unfortunate, but why could she not go on and be happy? Sequatchee had made clear his desire to court her, and he was good and strong. He would be a fine husband.

Hanging Basket wanted to leave the decision of whether or not Danagasta should marry Sequatchee to his daughter, but since late summer, her increasing determination to stop the trade of whiskey in their Nation had begun to irritate the chief. Earlier this evening, again finding her gone from Big Water when he wanted to talk to her about her husband's brother, he had decided to *order* her to marry Sequatchee. He felt certain that Sequatchee had not drunk whiskey since Losi's death. Once married to Sequatchee, Danagasta would have the responsibility of keeping their lodge, of cooking for her new husband . . . Perhaps they would soon have a child, and that responsibility would help calm her, too. At least she would not have time to roam the banks of the great river in search of whiskey peddlers.

"She brought the man here?" Hanging Basket asked, sitting up.

A nod of Sequatchee's head confirmed the chief's fear. Hanging Basket drew a hand over his wrinkled face. He had told her to stop watching the river for whiskey traders. "It is not only the whites," he had tried to explain. "Some of our own people now brew the poison. The only way to stop anyone from making it is for people to stop wanting it." He had thought Danagasta would heed his words. She had not.

"Bring her and the man," he told Sequatchee. "Bring George Dougherty, too."

Nodding, Sequatchee turned, lodged the torch he carried in a hollowed hickory stump, and exited the cabin.

Moments later, a white man with dark hair entered the lodge. Danagasta followed, nudging the man's back with her bow. In Cherokee, Hanging Basket ordered her to lower the weapon. Then, sitting up, he leaned against the wall in the corner where he had been sleeping, and studied his daughter and her captive while waiting for George Dougherty and Sequatchee to return.

The second she stepped through the cabin opening, Danagasta felt and saw her father's anger. The air was thick with it, and he did not greet her with a soft "Hello, my daughter," the way he usually did. Flickering shadows deepened the lines on his face. His black eyes shifted slowly and deliberately between the white man and her, and she grew more uneasy, wondering if she had stretched her father's patience for the final time. Sequatchee had warned her, but she had not listened. Since Losi's death, her ears had often heard only grief.

"*Edoda* . . ." She spoke the Cherokee syllables for "father" softly, hoping to coax Hanging Basket into listening to her. If he would only listen! She had the man's flask—she had stuffed it in her pouch. She fumbled with the bag's flap, and tried to explain: *"Tsi ga ta ha—"*

"Elowehi!"

His order of *"Quiet!"* silenced her. She swallowed. Her confidence had faltered some when she first entered the lodge and saw him regarding her fiercely. Now it melted around her feet. He would not listen. He had ordered her to stop hunting for whiskey men, but she had persisted. Now perhaps he would do some horrible thing . . . He would not speak to her again. Or he would send her from her people—banish her. She had seen such things happen to those who committed great wrongs or dishonored the tribe.

If he banished her, she would die. She had spent her life on the banks of the creek and the great river. She loved her father and her people.

Grant shifted his stare from the man to her, surprised by the apprehension that tightened her jaw and flickered in her dark eyes. Her obvious fear gave him a ripple of pleasure. After all, she'd spent hours prodding him, treating him the way she might treat the cattle in the fenced-in area outside the enclosure.

"Is he your father—the chief?" Grant asked her.

She nodded. "Chief Hanging Basket."

"You're afraid of him, Dana?" Grant couldn't resist taunting. "But I thought—"

"Shut up, *yun wunega*! And do not shorten my name. Say it right or do not say it."

"Does he speak English like you?"

"I speak English," the chief said.

Grant turned his gaze fully on the man. "Are your people at war with the United States?"

Hanging Basket tipped his head. "We are not. Have you come to make war?"

"You're peaceful?" Grant wanted—*needed*—to be sure.

"We are peaceful. You have nothing to fear unless you were bringing whiskey to sell in our Nation."

"I wasn't. There's only the one flask." Though there had been others on the boat. But he didn't have to say that. He'd already told Danagasta that there had been, and that was when she had turned really cold. He wasn't about to condemn himself any more than he already had. "It was tied to my belt," he said. "I wanted a drink now and then while rowing."

"Are you from the other side of the river?"

"What . . . ? No." Grant remembered what his father had told him, that the Tennessee River was the western boundary between the Cherokee Nation and the United States.

The chief continued to watch him, and Grant studied the man right back, deciding that the time had come to play his cards . . . take a chance . . . be burned or scalped, possibly tortured in some fashion.

Or set free.

He breathed deeply. "I am a United States official,

Agent Meigs's deputy." He waited for any indication that the chief recognized Meigs's name.

Hanging Basket's eyes flickered. Beside Grant, Danagasta gasped. "You lie . . ." she whispered, obviously not quite sure.

Grant turned a hard look on her. "No, I don't lie." He shifted his gaze back to her father. "I believe the official title is deputy agent."

The chief's gaze shifted, narrowing on Danagasta. She flinched, and Grant almost laughed aloud. Dear. The brave Dana just might be in deep trouble, in dung up to her chin. Grant released a long breath, beginning to feel something other than the apprehension that had gnawed at him ever since he'd realized he was tied. He felt a slight surge of confidence.

Danagasta felt that the walls were beginning to close in on her. *United States official? Deputy Agent?* No . . . It could not be! "My father, he admitted that he had whiskey aboard his flatboat! Look . . ." She fumbled with the flap on her pouch, this time drawing out the rawhide-encased flask that had been tied to her captive's waist when he had gone down in the rapids.

Grant shook his head in angry disbelief. *Devil take the woman!* He had already admitted to having the tin. Why the hell did she feel the need to produce it? What in *God's* name was driving her? Her father's gaze was hard and biting, but it didn't contain the absolute dislike for him that hers did.

Grant's attention was snared by the entrance of the Indian man who had led him and Danagasta here, and by another man—a tall, burly-looking white man with dull reddish-blond hair. The two crossed the cabin and sat on either side of Hanging Basket, folding and crossing their legs. The chief spoke to them in Cherokee, motioning to Grant and Danagasta now and then. Danagasta lowered her thick lashes to study a dark spot on the leather covering the flask her father had ignored.

In the orange-yellow light, her skin glowed like polished copper and appeared baby smooth while her blue-black hair waved over her gray coat and tumbled down her back. She raised her lashes, and Grant held her dark, pleading gaze.

So she thought he should show her mercy? After the hours of humiliation she'd put him through? His eyes swept down, paused on her lips, then on the smooth column of her neck. He wanted to push the coat and dress from her shoulders, dip his head, and have a taste. She was a savage, but she was also more striking, wrapped in her fur, than any woman dressed in silk or satin and adorned with glittering jewels. Still, her beauty and her meek look wouldn't make him forget the way she'd treated him.

Her eyes flashed. "Do not look at me that way!" she gasped, stepping away from him.

He couldn't help a mild grin. His look alarmed her—because of how it made her feel, because for a second or two there, she had allowed herself to enjoy it.

Hanging Basket watched his lovely daughter and the white man from the corner of his eye while telling Tsatsi—George Dougherty—how Sequatchee had awakened him to tell him that Danagasta claimed to have captured a "whiskey man." He saw the look of desire that passed between Danagasta and her captive, and he wondered at it. Before now, he had not seen her look at any man but Losi with want, and he considered her interest a good thing.

Not all whites were bad. A number of them had married into the tribe, and now lived with the Cherokee. Hanging Basket could not believe that any man claiming to be deputy to Agent Meigs could be fool enough to sell whiskey in the Nation. The white man's government would not tolerate such a thing. The man would be removed from his position and thrown in what the *unegas* called a jail.

Sequatchee spoke English to the white man: "Why did Meigs not send word that you were coming?"

"I was supposed to report to the agency at the Tellico Blockhouse, but a storm drove the boat downriver to the rapids," the man responded. "Meigs didn't send a message because he didn't expect me to end up here."

"What is your name?" Hanging Basket asked.

"Grant Claiborne."

"We do not want whiskey in Big Water. We do not want it near Big Water. We do not want it in our Nation."

"I understand, and I'll respect that. I wasn't bringing it here. As I said, I was supposed to have reported to the agency. I believe the blockhouse is located outside the territory."

Hanging Basket nodded, then looked at the light-haired George Dougherty—or Tsatsi—who also had questions for the man. Only Tsatsi, a Scotch-Irishman by birth, directed his words at Danagasta: "Did ye manage to bring back any o' the whiskey, girl? Anythin' to prove yer claim?"

She stepped forward and handed him the flask she had wanted to hand Hanging Basket earlier, then she stepped back. Tsatsi twisted and freed the cork, lifted the flask to his lips and tipped it. He swallowed, ran a hand over the back of his mouth, and glanced at Hanging Basket. "Whiskey. There's more, Danagasta?"

"No. But—"

Hanging Basket held up a hand to silence her. "One container . . . did you see him trying to sell it to anyone?"

"No," she admitted truthfully.

George Dougherty began speaking Cherokee, his adopted language, telling her what she had been told many times: that to act on her accusation, they must have proof that the man had been trying to sell the whiskey. If this man *was* Meigs's deputy, her actions might offend Meigs and the United States government. The Chickamauga people had survived, though they were not the warring people they had once been. Her persistence in trying to capture white "whiskey men" could again put their peoples' lives in danger. Her abduction of this man could cause hard feelings, if not outrage. Then the whites might send soldiers again. Tsatsi talked softly and sensibly; he was the wise man all the people of Big Water had learned to love and trust since he had married into the tribe long ago.

When he finished, Danagasta hung her head. She looked as if she might cry, though Hanging Basket knew her pride would not allow her to cry before them. He felt a surge of pride that in that way she was like her mother, whom he had loved more than the ancestral mountains. But his love alone could not teach his daughter a lesson, could not heal her inside and protect their people.

He told her in English, for he wanted the white man to hear too, that he would send a message to Agent Meigs telling of Grant Claiborne's arrival. If the man was not who he claimed, Meigs would send word. Until a message came, her prisoner would be allowed to roam freely in Big Water. "Untie him, my daughter," Hanging Basket ordered in Cherokee. "If Agent Meigs is displeased and you have put your people in danger . . . If there is war again, your punishment will be to leave our settlement."

She glanced up at him, pleading silently. He turned away and reached for his pipe. She thought him cruel. She did not realize how punishing her in such a way would wound him. But he had to consider all the people, not just her. He had to consider that she did not listen to him anymore. That she did not heed his warnings.

He watched from the corner of his eye as she moved behind Grant Claiborne and freed his hands. The white man rubbed his wrists, then raised his hands before his chest and turned them back and forth as if to show her that they were free. She glared at him. He leaned toward her and whispered something Hanging Basket could not hear; his ears were old. But the chief watched Danagasta step back, watched her breath quicken and her gaze fall to rest on the man's lips. Then she swallowed and fixed her eyes nervously on her bow.

The *asgaya*—man—pulled at the woman in her. *Ha!* He did . . .

Sequatchee issued a low animal sound and started to rise; apparently he, too, saw the look of desire that passed between the white man and Danagasta. Hanging Basket spoke Sequatchee's name softly but firmly, and Sequatchee paused, then settled again.

"Your desire to marry her is noble," Hanging Basket said quietly in Cherokee. "But she has never looked at you in such a way."

Sequatchee's brow tightened. "You cannot think to encourage the man to—"

"I will put them together and watch what happens.

Whatever happens, it will at least keep my daughter busy for a time. It will keep her from searching the riverbank."

A dark look passed over Sequatchee's face.

Hanging Basket spoke in English again so the white man would understand, too: "You brought this man to Big Water. He will share your cabin and your food. I put him in your care. You will cook for him and draw his water."

Danagasta's eyes widened, then glittered with fury. Hanging Basket did not doubt that once she left his lodge she would rumble like Thunder.

"My father, my husband built the lodge for me," she dared in their tongue, perhaps so Grant Claiborne would not have the satisfaction of understanding. "It is my property! Only I should say who may be allowed in it."

"I have spoken, my daughter. Now I will smoke, then sleep."

Huffing, Danagasta spun and hurried through the cabin opening, not daring to object more. Hanging Basket waved Grant Claiborne after her, exhaling with relief once they had both gone.

"I have tried to court your daughter for two seasons, my chief," Sequatchee said. "By ancient custom, a widow should be allowed to marry only her husband's brother. Yet you have put her in the hands of that white man! What if he *was* bringing whiskey into the Nation? What if he is not deputy to Agent Meigs? You may have placed your daughter in danger. In the hands of a dishonorable man!"

"You question my judgment?" the chief challenged. "She is my daughter—and the ancient customs are changing. You have acted honorably toward Danagasta, but I believe that more than blaming you for Losi's death keeps her from marrying you. I do not believe she desires you. I did not smell the scent of a lie on the man. I do not believe he is dishonorable."

"You act on his *scent*? I am her husband's brother! I—"

"Losi would want someone for Danagasta whose heart and will are as fierce as hers. She has always been stubborn. She has always been quick to anger. I have said how things will be."

Sequatchee rose and left the cabin.

"He has much to learn, that one," Hanging Basket commented wearily.

"I, too, wonder about putting that man in Danagasta's lodge," Tsatsi said. He spoke his adopted language well, and most always when advising the chief. "The people will not be pleased. He is a stranger in Big Water. Danagasta has not been nice to anyone since Losi's death and the loss of her unborn child, but the people will not hesitate to defend her if they feel the need."

"They will not go against what I say will be for her—I am her father, and they will respect that."

Tsatsi grunted, agreeing.

"Tell them who he claims to be, that they should not hurt him. That I want him for my daughter."

"I will. But when they hear that, they will want to know if he has courage and strength, if he is worthy of her. They will provoke him."

"I want to see those things for myself," Hanging Basket said, stuffing his pipe bowl with tobacco. "But no gauntlet. Provoke him, but do not give him wounds that could kill him. Meigs will understand that it is our way, and he will not be offended."

George Dougherty's eyes shifted to the cabin opening. Like Sequatchee, he was unsure about the man Danagasta had brought to Big Water. He knew she still grieved for Losi, who had died a tragic, needless death. He, Sequatchee, and many of the townspeople did not want to see her hurt ever again.

Chapter Three

OUTSIDE, DANAGASTA WALKED QUICKLY between widely spaced cabins, hurrying by many people who stood talking near torches and cabins. She felt the white man's presence behind her, and she smelled his male scent though smoke twisted above many lodges, filling the air with the essence of hickory and pine. She did not want to smell him, but her senses had always been as sharp as finely chipped flint. His scent was that of a *yun wi-usga se ti*. Dangerous man, terrible man. She wanted to put an arrow in her bow, turn, crouch, and shoot it at him. Drive him away. Defend herself.

She could not.

Unbound, he frightened her. *Sge!* He stirred fear beneath her skin like no man ever had. He was angry about the way she had treated him. And now she would be alone with him! What would he do? Not hurt her, surely. Her father and the people would not allow him to hurt her.

He was to share her cabin. *Share her cabin!*

Why? Because she had plucked him from the great river and forced him here? Because Hanging Basket and

Dougherty felt she had unjustly accused him? Her father would subject her to Grant Claiborne's stares, perhaps even his touch? Force her to share her lodge with him? Force her to cook for him and draw his *ama*?

Ha! Sge! She knew of no greater humiliation!

She swept past Catolster and Whitetree where they sat on stumps sharpening some young boys' arrows. The boys—Wadigei and Cullowhee—sat on the ground before the men.

"Danagasta—you are ill?" Catolster asked.

"No," she responded, hurrying on.

She was worse than ill; she was frightened. The white man's hands were no longer bound . . . And she remembered his words: "I *will* get untied . . ." She recalled the heated way he had looked at her, and a shiver of something akin to desire coursed through her. She fought it, refusing to lie with a man who had brought whiskey into the Nation. She quickened her steps, suddenly wanting to protect from the white man the lodge she had shared with her husband.

Grant followed at a slow, steady pace, planning to simply watch which cabin Danagasta entered, then join her there. He felt his chin jutting out, his head tilting back, his gaze burning down his nose. He was driven by his inherent, aristocratic Claiborne nature, a disposition he couldn't always seem to control while he was angry. A disposition he didn't *want* to control right now. He opened and closed his unbound hands, stretching them, feeling stinging sensations as blood flowed freely in them. The leather had cut into his skin in places, and the raw flesh burned. Without looking, he knew his back was bruised where she had jabbed him with the end of her bow. Damn the woman! All over one flask of whiskey! When the chief and his advisors had pointed out to her that she was wrong to condemn him without proof, she hadn't even apologized—she had run from her father's lodge. If things had gone her way, he'd be tied to a stake and burning right now.

He hadn't expected to convince Big Water's chief so easily that he was Meigs's deputy, that he had innocently brought whiskey into the Cherokee Nation. In retrospect,

Hanging Basket had seemed irritated with his daughter even before she opened her mouth. And now . . . now she couldn't lift a weapon against Grant since he was clearly under her father's protection during the remainder of his stay in the town. Now she would answer for prodding him with that bow when he had told her to keep the damn thing away from him.

Grant watched her shadowed figure as she passed cabin after cabin, the bow at her side. She soon disappeared beyond a piece of pale hide hanging in a lodge doorway.

A man stepped into Grant's path. Another approached from the right. Some twenty feet to Grant's left, a boy who couldn't be more than ten years old lifted a bow, drew an arrow back in it, and aimed the thing directly at Grant. Behind Grant, someone shouted. Grant didn't dare move; the man in front of him had produced a knife and was waving it slowly. He looked past Grant as another shout rang out.

The man with the knife hesitated, then stepped aside. The boy lowered his arrow. The man on the right backed off. Grant turned around to see who had stopped the assault, and he watched the white man from the chief's cabin approach.

"No one'll stand for ye hurtin' her," the man told Grant in a low, raspy voice.

"I've never hurt a woman," Grant responded rather indignantly.

"Remember what I said. Convincin' her to lie with ye is one thing. Hurtin' her is another."

Nodding slowly, Grant took the four steps separating him from Danagasta's cabin. He pushed aside the deerskin flap that hung in the doorway and entered the lodge.

He faced near darkness. There were no windows, or if there were, they were covered or closed. Moonlight trickled in through a hole in the roof. He heard her fumbling around. Tins clanged. He turned toward scratching noises, thinking she was rubbing something together.

Moments later, flames appeared to one side of the cabin. The fire she had built lit her face and cast an orange glow about the lodge. She watched him from the corner of her eye.

He took a step forward. At last, they were alone—and his hands weren't bound. He moved to the right, touching a number of foreign-looking objects dangling from wooden hooks protruding from the carved walls.

"Do not touch my things!" she said, almost hissing at him.

He lifted a brow. "Bothers you, does it? Me, touching your things? Moving them about . . . *Prodding* them . . . Me, invading your cabin? And with your father's permission. I daresay this is the first time a father has encouraged me."

She did not respond.

Wooden spoons and ladles swung and collided as he brushed them. A tin flask fell, landing on one of many furs laid over mats—as in her father's cabin. A number of furs were stacked in one far corner of the lodge. Grant's right foot collided with a large hollowed gourd, knocking it over. Water poured over a hide. Danagasta's eyes shifted to it, then back up to Grant's face, narrowing at the affront. He merely walked on, pleased that she obviously felt violated. He gave only passing thought to the men who undoubtedly lurked right outside the doorway flap.

From a hook he snatched what appeared to be a dressing robe, made of rough red cotton with blue borders. He shed the wolfskin she'd draped over him near the river, and replaced it with the robe. He fiddled with a bunch of turtle shells strung together, and listened to them rattle. Fingering a stone pipe on which the figure of a squirrel had been carved, he accidently knocked over two long sticks that were looped and netted at one end. When they clattered together beneath his feet, Danagasta leaped the fire and came at him.

Grant caught her wrists and forced her arms down. He held his breath, waiting for her to scream and for her protectors to flip aside the deerskin. She only glared at him, breathing heavily.

"Now, now, Dana. Temper tantrums lead to trouble," he chided.

She struggled, but succeeded only in twisting herself around, pulling one arm over her head, and enabling him to lock the other arm behind her back. A mere inch separated their bodies. Her hair brushed his chin, her buttocks teased his groin. His right forearm settled just below her breasts and pressed up against the firm mounds. She struggled again.

He used his chin to nudge the hair from her left shoulder. Then he nipped at her earlobe, bit lightly at the smooth column of her neck, and worked his way down. She smelled of smoky elm, of pungent pine and sweet birch; fresh like the river, wild like the wind that had whipped it. "That's it, Dana," he murmured as she wriggled against his groin. "Stir things up. Just the sight and smell of you is enough, but all that movement helps."

She stilled.

He planted a kiss on the curve of her neck and shoulder. She yelped, then struggled harder. She was strong, but he was stronger. Still, she managed to twist around again, then they both lost their balance and stumbled to the floor.

Grant quickly threw a leg over her and pinned her to the mats. She almost succeeded in scooting away, but he grabbed her arms and held them over her head. Panting, she glared up at him.

He glared right back.

He lowered his head to kiss her, but she turned her face to the side, denying him her lips. He nipped at her jaw. She stiffened more, if possible, but didn't resume kicking and flailing. He again pushed her hair aside and touched his lips to her neck, whispering that she smelled like the land. She uttered a low cry of frustration and denial as he kissed his way up to her jaw and rubbed his rough cheek against her velvety hair.

She cried out again, a soft sound, almost a moan. Then she turned her face back to his.

Grant lifted his head to stare down at her. Her eyes had turned hazy, and her lips had parted. He gazed hungrily down at them . . . then claimed them.

He drove his tongue into her mouth, dipping and tasting, suddenly filled with the fury of not being able to get enough. She opened to him, urging him, tempting him . . . He released her arms, lowered a hand to the pounding pulse at her throat, then to her arching breast.

She tore her lips from his. *"Tla no!* I cannot stop you, but I will not honor this in my mind. I will not! I will not like it!"

"You do like it," he murmured, massaging her swelling breast. He'd been with enough women to know the signs.

"I do not! *Tla no!*" Tears welled in her eyes, then slid down her temples. "Please . . ."

A chill went through Grant. *Bloody hell.* He'd never used sex as a weapon, and though he seemed to have no other recourse for the hours of humiliation she'd put him through, he wouldn't start now. He wouldn't force her to submit to him.

She turned her head and mumbled, "Losi."

Grant took her chin in hand and made her look at him. She swallowed, appearing harmless and demeaned, appearing frightened. He knew her pride by now, so he knew she undoubtedly despised baring weakness. He ought to feel satisfied. Instead he felt ashamed that he'd let his temper get the better of him. "I—I won't hurt you," he stammered.

She shook her head. "*Tla no* . . . Please—off."

He reluctantly removed his hand from her breast, brought it up to the curve of her shoulder, then slid it down the length of her arm. He caressed her fingers, then rolled away and stared up at the hole in the roof.

Sitting up, she scooted to a far corner, a wounded animal seeking dark shelter. Silently cursing himself, Grant rose to straighten the gourd and the sticks. He tidied other things he'd disturbed, too, then turned around to face her shadowed form.

"I suppose we . . ." He rubbed his forehead. "It seems we're stuck with each other for a time. I'm tired. It's been one hell of a long day. Where can I sleep?"

A moment passed, heavy and silent. "The . . . the skins," she finally responded.

He approached the pile of furs and pulled two from it.

To one side of the fire, he spread them atop the mats, then, with the sweep of one hand, he motioned her to them.

"Tla no!" she said for what seemed like the hundredth time. The word was obviously a negative response. She thought . . .

Sighing in exasperation, he took two more skins from the pile and spread them on the opposite side of the fire. Then he grabbed another to cover himself, and he settled on the two he had just spread, again motioning Danagasta to the others.

Her lashes swept down, then up, as if she were still unsure about approaching the hides.

"For God's sake, I'm not going to bite you! I won't touch you. Come and lie down. I'm not the son of a bitch you seem sure that I am!" He raked a hand through his hair. Hell . . . why should he care what she thought of him? He had been sent to the Cherokee Nation to help Agent Meigs negotiate for land. He had to please the chiefs, Meigs, his father, and the United States Government, that was all. He didn't have to please her.

He settled on the skins, turned his back to her, and shut his eyes.

Danagasta watched him, shuddering at the fact that she had been willing to give herself to the white man. His hot breath on her neck had put fire in her blood and made her heart pound with desire. His lips had been soft and coaxing, his tongue warm and caressing, his hand on her breast large and warm. *Sge!* She was ashamed that she had wanted to part her legs and welcome him—a man she felt certain had been bringing whiskey to sell in the Nation. And he claimed to be an agent . . .

Why would the white man's government send another agent? She did not want to believe he was who he said he was. She did not want to believe because of what she knew believing would mean—that the United States Government wanted more Cherokee land.

She could not sleep. She snuggled against the furs, feeling the fire's warmth on one side of her face. She smelled the man's alien scent as she stared at her husband's ballplay sticks, their ends curved and netted. She shifted her gaze to Losi's pipe bowl, then reached for the leggings she had stitched for him. Drawing them to her breast, she buried her face in the hides and let her tears flow.

Chapter Four

When Grant woke, soft morning sunlight was spilling into the cabin from the hole in the roof. There were two windows over which hung hides. Danagasta slept soundly, wrapped in wolfskins, her features smooth and unmarked by anger or emotion. Grant sat up and studied her for a few moments. Her lashes rested softly on her high cheekbones, and her dark lips were parted. Her black hair cascaded over one shoulder. Some sort of buckskin garment, not exactly breeches or pantaloons, lay beneath one of her hands.

He rose and stretched, then shivered and glanced hopefully around the cabin for wood to build another fire. Seeing none, he quietly lifted a hide and draped it over his shoulders. He rounded the blackened spot where she'd built last night's fire, and headed for the lodge opening.

He heard children's laughter and light chatter just before he pushed the deerskin flap aside.

Through the hazy morning light he glimpsed a group of young girls, some clad in red, yellow, and green woven dresses, and others wearing brownish-yellow buckskin.

They paused in weaving little baskets to watch him cautiously with their dark eyes. Shivering beneath the cold morning breeze, he wondered why the children weren't more warmly attired. A quick glance at the adults who mingled around other lodges revealed that, just like last evening, no one was warmly dressed. But Danagasta had had her coat . . . Grant wondered if they only dressed warmly when leaving Big Water.

Like the girls', the men's and women's clothing was a mix of woven material and animal skins, and some garments were beaded and fringed. Some feet were bare while others were covered with moccasins or pliable boots resembling Danagasta's.

Now that the light of day allowed for better vision and now that he wasn't so worried about his fate or so angry at Danagasta's treatment of him, Grant took a few moments to observe the cabins.

Of the many he saw from here, eight in the row before him and eight in the row behind him where Danagasta's was located, some were built of logs, carved at the ends and fitted snugly together; others had outside walls crudely constructed of what looked like a mixture of dried clay and grass. Roofs were covered with pieces of bark, and over the slopes facing him eight logs were laid in patterns that created three rows of squares. Strips of hide, wound and tied, held the logs in place. Chimneys rose from some lodges, skins hung over windows, and the few doors Grant spotted were constructed of planks held together somehow and tied in place with more hide strips. The lodges were fascinating. They weren't elegant by any means, but more planning had gone into them than Grant had thought savages, as his father called the Indians, capable of. Danagasta's was built of logs but had no door.

Another cabin rose above and behind the row in which hers sat. A woman was backing down a ladder propped against the side of the raised lodge. She held a basket filled with what looked like potatoes on one hip. Grant stepped forward, wondering if the cabin was a granary—a storehouse.

A child shrieked behind him. Grant spun in time to

watch one of the girls fly off in a flurry of pumping legs and spraying mud. Some five cabins down the row, she threw herself at a woman who, holding the girl's face to her stomach, stared at Grant.

In fact, everyone seemed to be staring at him now. The girls, who held small, half-constructed baskets. A number of buckskin-clad boys, large and small, who apparently had been shooting arrows at trees inside the settlement. Other women, who had paused in the middle of a variety of tasks—washing clothes and other articles in tubs, cooking over outside hearths, using small logs to work something in hollowed stumps, molding pottery . . . One man stopped milking a cow that was tied to a post before a lodge, and stared. Another man had given up chasing several hogs from sniffing around a barrel in favor of watching Grant. And a number of other men who had been sharpening spears and the ends of smaller sticks were now headed this way, their black eyes fixed coldly on Grant. One man was the Cherokee who had stepped in front of him before Danagasta's cabin last evening. A night's sleep had evidently done nothing to improve his disposition.

Grant gave serious thought to simply fading back through the doorway to Danagasta's cabin. But what good would that do? The Indians might come in after him. Where was the chief now? he wondered nervously. And the other men who had been with Hanging Basket last evening? As Grant watched the crowd of men, he spotted the Cherokee who had led him and Danagasta to her father's cabin. But *he* had heard Grant tell who he was! He had surely seen the chief's alarm, and he'd definitely *heard* every word that was said. Unless he *couldn't* hear, something that Grant didn't believe.

Danagasta would like this hostile scene, no doubt—her people against him. It was what she had hoped to accomplish when she'd forced him into Big Water.

He thought the men might at least stop and question him before deciding to do anything to him. But no . . . Two marched right up to him, each took one of his arms, lifted him off the ground about three inches, and carried him off.

He wouldn't panic. He would not. He'd tell the men who he was, why he was here, and they would let him go, simple as that.

Other men, women, and children flanked him and his captors, pointing and chattering excitedly in Cherokee. He couldn't be heard above the din. Or if they could hear him, they either couldn't understand him or were pretending they couldn't understand him. The children threw rocks while some of the women reached between men and poked him with sticks. They'd seen whites. He *knew* they had seen whites. There had been a white man with the chief last night, and there were even a few white men in this crowd. So why the devil were they acting so hostile?

They passed a circular lodge, then approached a wooden fence containing a large, square field that had obviously been one of their gardens. Grant had spotted others outside the palisade as he and Danagasta had approached Big Water last evening. Tall browning cornstalks flapped and rustled in the morning breeze. A variety of vegetables had grown here; the food the Indians had not used for whatever reason lay scattered about the ground: five large pumpkins bearing dark spots, a number of squash and corn that had been picked at by birds and other animals . . .

The men lifted Grant over the fence and dumped him in the muddy plot. He tried to land on his feet, but fell on his back instead, scowling when laughter rose from the crowd.

A solidly built man leaped the fence, turned and caught two long poles someone tossed him. He whacked Grant across the stomach with one, then dropped it on him as Grant grimaced in pain and struggled to catch his breath. The man backed up, feet apart, dark eyes searing, a sneer crossing his lips. "Up, white man. You will fight."

An arm protectively clutching his belly, Grant managed to sit up. "No, you don't understand. I'm—" The pole lashed, this time across his side.

Pain shot through him. Nausea rose in his throat. *Bloody hell,* they were going to kill him. If this man didn't, two dozen others were waiting to take his place, and the majority of them held those ghastly looking spears.

"Up," the Cherokee repeated.

Grant was reaching for his pole when the man started at him again. He shielded this blow by tipping his stick. The Indian's pole met his with a resounding crack, and surprise flickered in the man's eyes.

Grant climbed slowly to his feet, trying to ignore the agony in his stomach and side. "You're going to have to work to kill me," he vowed under his breath. The others couldn't hear him, but his opponent did.

Laughing, the man glanced off at his friends. "He say Kaloquegidi must work at killing."

The others laughed, too, and Kaloquegidi took a moment to joke with them in Cherokee.

Grant struck, driving his pole into the man's belly. Kaloquegidi doubled over in pain, dropping his stick. Grant hit him across the shoulder blades, driving him to his knees. A blow to the head knocked the man unconscious, and he fell facedown in the mud.

With much effort and pain Grant shoved a boot beneath the Indian's stomach and flipped him over to keep him from suffocating.

Silence ensued, marred only by the sound of dogs barking, hogs snorting, and cows lowing. Grant stood, glaring at the crowd from beneath his brows, daring any of them to jump the fence. Weapons or no weapons, they *would* have to work at killing him—and they now seemed to know that.

The man who had stepped into his path in front of Danagasta's cabin last night started over the fence, unarmed, but Grant stepped back and squared off anyway. This man *would* kill him. He would have killed him last evening if the white man from the chief's cabin hadn't intervened.

The Indian landed on his feet, untied a white belt from around his waist, and held it out to Grant, saying, "White is good. White is peace. You come. Wash in the creek. Then we will talk. You will tell how you came to be in Big Water."

Grant cautiously took the belt, wondering if the man was tricking him. Then three women and the boy who had aimed the arrow at him last night joined them in the garden.

One of the women walked right up to Grant and put a hand on his pole. "I am Kayini. They are Sali and Ewi," she said, her eyes sparkling as she glanced at her companions. "Kaliquegidi likes to fight. You are a good opponent for him."

"You enjoyed the attack," Grant accused breathlessly, pain searing his side.

"No . . . You must prove worthiness. You lay with Danagasta?"

Grant put a hand over his ribs, fighting the urge to heave. "Lay with her?"

"Mate," said one of the other women. "You mate with her?"

"Mate?" So that was what this was about. "No, I didn't ma—share her bed . . . skins! She pulled me from the river. I only slept in her cabin. Your chief wants me to stay there."

A slow smile spread over Kayini's lips. She glanced at her friends and mumbled something in Cherokee. They nodded and smiled.

"Come," Kayini said, wrapping a hand around the pole. "You will wash."

Grant pulled the stick out of her hand and glanced at her friends, then back at her. "If you don't mind, I'll keep this with me," he said, indicating the pole with a jerk of his head.

Her smile still in place, she nodded. "I do not mind. But they will not hurt you now. You quickly defeated Kaliquegidi, a fine warrior."

Grant wasn't sure he believed they wouldn't hurt him.

She helped him climb the fence, then Sali, Ewi, the man, and the boy hurried after them.

Kayini led the way, Grant and the entire crowd of people following, and growing, as other people apparently heard of his appearance in Big Water. There were a few whites and even blacks among them, dressed in Indian garb.

They walked beyond the fenced garden to the gate in

the palisade wall. Kayini lifted a looped piece of hide from a carved hook, pushed the gate open, and stepped outside the settlement onto grass still sparkling with dew. A valley lay ahead, nearly shrouded by fog.

Grant followed her through a forested area, populated with stately trees, all slightly hidden behind the mist that thickened lower down and floated on the forest floor, hiding the scrub and swirling like thin smoke. The vapor smelled of mold, pine, and a freshness Grant couldn't identify. Birds chirped, and somewhere in the distance a woodpecker knocked. To the left a rustle of foliage sounded.

"Awi," Kayini said, smiling again, the lower half of her body nearly lost in the mist.

Grant stared at her, wondering what she'd said.

"Deer."

"How do you know?"

"I smell them," she said. "The smoke comes most every morning except during winter. If you stand on the hillsides, you can see it rise. When Grandmother Sun lifts high in the Skyland, the smoke leaves."

Grant wondered at her referring to the sun as if it were a living relative. While his father had briefed him about previous Cherokee wars, he hadn't said a word about the customs and beliefs of these people. In fact, he had told him that Meigs would inform him of anything else he needed to know.

Behind Grant and Kayini, children jabbered and adults conversed in Cherokee. Twigs snapped beneath Kayini's moccasins. Grant brushed by a tall fern, its foliage dappled with dew. They approached the low bank of the creek. In the distance Grant thought he heard rushing water, and he cocked his head to the right curiously.

"A fall," Kayini explained. "*Ama* rushes from the hills and mountains and flows into this creek, then into the great river. Wash the mud from yourself. I will hold the pole."

Grant looked down at the stick, considered it, then he handed it to her. If the Indians were going to send someone after him again, they could have done it while they walked behind him.

He sat on the grass and removed his boots, aware of the many people watching. For God's sake, were they all going to stare at him while he washed? He ought to be beyond caring, after having been subjected to Danagasta's many humiliations. But he wasn't.

Nevertheless, he stripped off his clothes. But knowing the water would be icy, he didn't look forward to this dip.

He stepped into the creek, shivering immediately, and forced himself to lie back so the water flowed over him and washed the mud away. Then he sat up and rose, thinking that though the trail back to the town wasn't a long one, it would seem long as he walked, wet, through the forest.

A woman came forward, holding out a warm-looking coat made from buffalo hides. Grant took it, draped it around his shoulders, and thanked her. She nodded, then stepped back and faded into the crowd.

Kayini knelt near the creek, dipping his clothes in the water to wash them. Then she draped his shirt, breeches, and stockings over a forearm.

"Tell me something," Grant said, following her back along the path to Big Water. "Why aren't you, and they—" he jerked his head toward the crowd—"wearing coats like the one that woman gave me?"

"We sometimes do. For now, we are not cold. We have cabins, but we spend much time outside. It is not so cold today."

"It's cold to me."

Amusement tugged at her lips. Seconds later, she sobered. "You have brought no wife? No children?"

"I don't have a wife and children." He wondered why she asked. He noticed that a few men had moved up closer behind them and were listening. Was she trying to trick him into saying something that would condemn him in their eyes?

"You have come to trap animals?"

"No."

"Then you have come for the bright stones we sometimes find in our streams?"

"No," he said loudly. "I've come to talk about the problem of whites settling on your land. I'm Agent Meigs's deputy."

The men whispered behind them. More whispers rose behind the men, then waves of murmurs rose clear to the back of the crowd.

Kayini stared at the man, wondering if he was sincere. With good reason, she and her people did not trust many whites who came through. "We have heard who you think you are. But some of us . . . Some of us are unsure of things. The white settlers are a problem. They do not ask if they can build homes on Cherokee land. They build them and they bring their families and trap the animals in our forests. Sometimes they come from across the great river to hunt. Sometimes they simply kill the animals, take the hides, and leave the meat to rot. Now an iron foundry has been built at the mouth of the creek. When will it end, we ask. But there is no good answer, no truthful answer. There is fear among our people that someday there will be no more animals to hunt, no more water to drink, no more fields on which to plant. We have asked to be left alone, and still we are not left alone."

"There's a place where you'll be left alone," Grant said, sensing the crowd press up behind them.

"More white man's promises, made to be broken?" Kayini asked. "Promises to be ignored despite the wampum belts offered by our fathers as signs of peace and honesty? You must understand—"

"You must give me a chance," he countered. "Give me an opportunity to talk. The place I mentioned has hills and valleys like these where animals run wild."

"You will have a chance to talk," the man who had leaped the garden fence said from behind Grant and Kayini. "You will smoke with us and speak of the hills and valleys in this new land. You will tell if there are fields where we can plant, forests where we can hunt. You have not come bringing gifts?"

Grant kept his eyes on the path. "I wasn't aware that you required gifts."

"We do not. Agent Meigs brings looms and farming tools and talks about land. He insults us by offering these things and 'money' for our hills and mountains here. He says nothing of where we will go if we trade. So we do not trade."

"There's a place west of here, land near a river called the Arkansas . . ." Grant said, glimpsing the palisade through the thinning vapor. He wanted to free a breath of relief; he seemed to be saying and doing all the right things. But he still felt an almost tangible tension between himself and these people.

The man grunted. "I am Catolster. The women will dry your clothes. You will come with me and other men and speak of this place."

Catolster led the way back to the cluster of cabins in which Danagasta's was located. Grant spotted at least three other groups of lodges along the way. Some four cabins from Danagasta's, Catolster paused to push open the door to a lodge. Then he stood aside from the door and allowed Grant to enter the cabin first.

Inside, Catolster said something in Cherokee to a woman and a small girl who sat before a fireplace working what looked like dough in bowls. Nodding, the woman took the girl's hand and left the lodge. At least ten men poured in and either stood near the walls or sat in rickety-looking chairs and on stools.

"It is our way to offer food to visitors," Catolster said as he handed Grant a bowl filled with chunks of dark bread.

Grant took the bowl, thanked him, and ate several chunks of the sweet bread while Catolster moved to the hearth, where he fitted what looked like an intricately carved pipe bowl onto a long hollow stick. He stuffed the bowl with dried and shredded tobacco, then used two long flat sticks to lift a glowing ember from the fireplace and light the tobacco. As he puffed on the pipe, smoke swirled up around his head. Moments later he held the pipe out to Grant, who took it without hesitation, just as he'd taken the bowl.

One of the men stepped forward and said something in Cherokee. Catolster responded with softly spoken words, his eyes never leaving Grant: "He is Whitetree," he told Grant. "He says, 'no more welcome.' He wants to hear about the Arkansas land. We all do. We grow weary of whites who bring their families and settle in our Nation. Last winter they received permission from our National Council to build the iron place at the opening of our creek. They built it, then they built houses around it. We do not like seeing what looks like a village of white people settled so close to our creek. Soon there will be more and more houses closer and closer to Big Water. We will be forced to fight again for our home if we do not find a way to make them leave, or if we cannot settle the land problem peacefully. Tell about the Arkansas land."

Grant exhaled tobacco smoke. "It's west—"

Murmurs went up from the gathering. Eyes widened. Several men headed for the cabin door. Sharp syllables from Catolster made them turn back.

"To the west is darkness," he said, fixing a cold gaze on Grant. "Your government would send us to the land where souls go after death? When we are not dead?"

Grant tensed. He hadn't expected to encounter such a belief. If they were frightened of the west, how could he convince them to go there? "No, it's . . . when there's sunlight here, there's sunlight in the west," he explained.

"You lie, *yun wunega*," said the Cherokee who had led him and Danagasta to Hanging Basket's cabin last evening. "The Nightland is in the west. Is the Arkansas land the Nightland?"

The small crowd bristled again.

"Sequatchee says a wise thing," someone remarked in English.

"Sequatchee is jealous that the white man spent the night in Danagasta's dwelling!" another man said.

Sequatchee folded his arms across his muscular chest and tipped his head calmly but angrily as he leaned against the fireplace. Grant met the Indian's searing gaze head-on, realizing that when he'd stepped beyond the deerskin hanging in Danagasta's doorway last night, he had acquired an enemy. Sequatchee's obsidian eyes warned that he was a far more dangerous foe than Kaliquegidi had been. Grant knew that if Sequatchee ever tossed him a pole and squared off, the fight would be to the death.

"Let the agent-man speak," Whitetree said, stepping forward.

"You have no proof that he is an agent," Sequatchee argued. "Even if he is, Meigs brings us looms and plows, but we do not trust him when he talks about land. Why should we listen to this man more than we listen to Meigs?"

Whitetree glanced at Sequatchee. "You are not forced to listen." His eyes shifted to all the men, one at a time. "*No* one is forced to listen. I will listen because I grow tired of worrying about our women when they go to the river to collect water and cane. I grow tired of other things, too. My grandfather once went hunting with parties that struggled to bring back all the meat they had collected from the forest, so much meat that the people celebrated and feasted for many days. Game is not as plentiful now. We still hunt, but we must also raise cattle, the white man's buffalo, and hogs. Like Catolster, I worry about the *unegas*' houses coming closer. We closed Big Water off with our palisade, but have we removed ourselves from the threat of white men who hate us? I say no, we have not! If we fight, our women and children will not have homes—the whites will burn them. Going to a different land may be our only choice."

Rumbles of agreement went up from the gathering. Sequatchee leaned toward a younger man standing next to him and said something. The man turned and started toward the door, where another man stopped him and called to Whitetree and Catolster.

"He goes to alert the chief that we are talking about trading land," the second man said. "Sequatchee sends him."

Whitetree, Catolster, and many others turned hard gazes on Sequatchee.

"Hanging Basket is our representative," Sequatchee said. "If you plan to talk about trading land, he should be here."

"Like some people in other settlements, our chief does

not want to talk about trading land," Whitetree said. "But the whites are closing in around *all* villages and towns. I say we *must* talk about the new land! And I say do not bring the chief." More cries of agreement went through the cabin.

"Like some people . . ." Sequatchee laughed in apparent disgust. "He does not want to leave the land of our fathers because the thought pains him. Is that not how many of you feel in your hearts? Can you honestly say no?" His harsh gaze scanned the crowd. "Hanging Basket is wise. He will look beyond his feelings and consider what is best for our people. He will not let fear of white settlers force him into a quick decision, one that he, and all of you, may regret."

The cries died down. Guilty looks flashed on a number of faces—even on Whitetree's. "We are not letting fear rule us," he objected.

Sequatchee uncrossed his arms, approached him, and spoke softly: "You are. Fear makes you consider being disloyal to a man who has served his people for years. If you want a different chief, choose a different chief. But be honorable enough to *tell* him you have elected someone else. Do not gather secretly."

The crowd of men began murmuring. "We want Chief Hanging Basket here!" someone said. Others agreed.

A nod of Catolster's head freed Sequatchee's messenger. The man opened the cabin door and slipped outside, then closed the portal behind him.

Sequatchee said something to Whitetree, but his voice was so soft this time that Grant heard only a few Cherokee syllables. Whitetree nodded, not looking nearly as insulted or indignant now. He approached Grant and stared down at him. "If you lie, *yun wunega*—"

"I'm not lying," Grant responded, holding the man's gaze. "My government offers a fair trade—your land here for land in the west. You'll be supplied with necessities during the journey, and we'll help get you there."

Catolster drew close, his voice low and threatening: "But *if* you lie about the Sun being in the west at the same time it is here, you will not live to see our bright grandmother climb the arch again."

Grant nodded, understanding the message behind the words: The man would kill him if he lied. "I'm not lying," Grant said again.

Catolster nodded slowly, then withdrew.

Chapter Five

WHILE THE TOWNSMEN GATHERED with Grant in Catolster's cabin, Kayini and Sali sat on stools in front of Sali's lodge. Finger looms—frames made from sturdy branches—stood before the women. Sali worked at weaving a belt she had begun days ago. Kayini tied numerous red threads to her own loom and began weaving them the way she had been taught by her aunt and mother when she had been a young girl.

"Look," Sali said.

Kayini glanced up, following Sali's gaze. It rested on a man hurrying from Catolster's lodge—the fourth dwelling to the east on the opposite row.

"They should not be meeting to discuss the land without Chief Hanging Basket," Kayini said nervously.

"My husband feels the chief does not want to trade land. Whitetree feels the iron foundry the Council allowed the whites to build is a sign: We should leave these mountains willingly, before the white man's government forces us out."

"We are allowing the settlers to create division among our people. Whitetree has always been loyal to our chief."

"He is only concerned."

"I know. Still, the division makes me worry. Together perhaps we can fight the settlers. Divided . . ." Kayini shook her head.

"We tried fighting, and we were defeated. We should not fight again."

Kayini sighed. "You are right. Many people died."

She and Sali wove in silence for a time.

"The stranger is tall and handsome," Sali remarked presently. "Tsatsi says Danagasta took him from the river and that the man is not to be hurt."

Kayini nodded. There was much to worry over this morning—all that George Dougherty had told a group of them last night. "She claims the white man was bringing whiskey into the Nation. He says he did not bring it in to sell. He says he is Agent Meigs's deputy. She says he is not. Who is to be believed?"

"We will not know that for some time. Hanging Basket will send a messenger to the agency," Sali said. She was quiet for a moment. "The white man looked angry and determined last night when Catolster stopped him before Danagasta's dwelling. I wonder what happened during the night while they were alone inside the lodge."

"He said he did not lie with her."

"And you believe him?"

"Yes."

"He could have lied."

"He did not," Kayini responded with conviction, though regretfully. "I would have seen the lie in his eyes. Besides, I do not believe that Danagasta would lie with a man she believed was peddling whiskey."

Sali smiled. "Ah, but Kayini . . . Danagasta *might* have. Sometimes the body is stronger than the mind. I often forget that you are young and have not been with a man yet, my friend. After a woman lies with a man for the first time, she grows hungry for—"

"How do you know I have not been with a man?" Kayini had stopped weaving to stare at Sali, who lifted her composed smile to her friend. Beneath the woman's knowing gaze, Kayini felt her face warm. She glanced away, and saw Chief Hanging Basket, Tsatsi, and Ewi—Danagasta's aunt—walking between the rows of cabins. "Look, Sali."

Sali looked, and sighed. "I imagine they are going to Catolster's cabin. I hope my husband has not caused too much unrest among the people." She went back to her weaving. Kayini did the same.

They worked again in silence. Then Sali continued the conversation they had been having before Kayini had spotted Ewi, the chief, and Tsatsi: "A woman sometimes grows hungry for the attention of a man. And it does not always matter who the man is."

"Danagasta would not lie with a man she does not trust, one she thinks has done a dishonorable thing," Kayini disagreed.

Sali fell silent again. "Perhaps you are right," she said finally. "As long as she believes he did such a thing, she will not allow him to touch her."

"Do you . . . Do you *hope* she will lie with him?"

"Yes. Then she will realize only one of the things she is missing by not taking another husband."

By not taking another husband . . . Sequatchee? He was the only man who had expressed interest in Danagasta since Losi's death. No matter how often Kayini told herself that she wanted Sequatchee's and Danagasta's happiness, the pain that clenched her heart when she thought of him marrying someone else was nearly unbearable.

"You should hope, too, Kayini," Sali said. "You admired Sequatchee when you were a child not much older than Awe-ani-da, but now you love him. You remember the day he rescued you from the forest, from the animals there? That was the day it began."

Kayini wanted to leap up and run away, but she would not do such a childish thing. Of course she remembered that day! How could she forget, though she had been very young indeed. It had begun when she had decided not to heed the warnings given by many adults—that she should never go beyond the enclosure alone . . .

Ever curious, she had seen the opening in the palisade and had slipped out, escaping observation. Time passed while she wandered, exploring. The Sun began lowering over the jagged tops of distant trees, casting an orange haze on the forest and flickering red on a stream by which she stopped to rest. She should go home soon, she thought. Her parents and other adults would be angry. But oh, what a day she had had!

Soon afterward she realized that she was lost, that she had wandered too far and might never get home, and she grew frightened. She would eventually be eaten by some animal—a wolf or a mountain lion perhaps. She wondered if her mother and father roamed Big Water, calling for her, wringing their hands with worry. She had done a terrible thing, and the angry Spirits would surely punish her.

Hearing noise in the trees and scrub behind her, she had frozen, waiting for the wolf or mountain lion to strike. She yelped when it did, when it grabbed her shoulders and growled low, telling her she would never go beyond the town gate again, that everyone was frightened for her, for the life of sweet Kayini, whose laughter and smiles warmed Big Water, whose curiosity prompted many of the old people to gather the children around and tell the ancient legends over and over.

But wolves and mountain lions could not speak! Not unless . . . Like Bear, had they once been man? Had one of them turned back into a man, knowing she was lost and that she needed guidance?

She had dared a peek over her shoulder, needing to know . . . and stared into Sequatchee's sparkling eyes.

"You are frightened?" he had asked softly.

She had not answered at first, only looked ahead at a cluster of trees. Then she had nodded slowly.

He had urged her to sit, then he had sat beside her. She had expected him to scold her more for leaving the protection of the palisade. Instead he had told her how the sons of Kana'ti and Selu, the first Cherokee man and woman, had been filled with curiosity about where their father found all the game. The boys followed Kana'ti into a swamp one day, where their father lifted a large rock, revealing a hole. A buck ran out from the hole and Kana'ti shot it and carried it home. The boys' curiosity was a good thing, Sequatchee said, for they knew where to find game. But they learned quickly that too much curiosity was not good: They returned to the swamp days later, made arrows from reeds, and lifted the rock, letting all the animals out. Not just deer but raccoons, rabbits, and all the other four-footed animals. Many birds escaped, too, darkening the air like an angry cloud. The boys were so disturbed, they could not think to cover the hole. Kana'ti came, found all the birds and animals gone, and told the boys that he could not just come and get a turkey or deer for their mother to cook anymore; they must learn to hunt and hope they could find meat. But that day they could find none—and so they went hungry.

With dusk settling, Kayini and Sequatchee had walked back to Big Water.

"You do remember, I see." Sali inclined her head at Kayini now in a knowing way. "You will never forget."

"Stop," Kayini objected.

"Neither will you forget the years after that. The years you spent waiting for your body to mature, for Sequatchee to notice you."

Kayini squeezed her eyes shut. It was true. She had waited. And waited. And waited. After that day in the forest, she had seen Sequatchee frequently. He often called at her family's lodge, offering to answer her questions about animals and plants and many other things, and he always spoke gently to her in the square when the townspeople gathered for dances and festivities. She finally became a young woman, filled with different feelings and sensations whenever he neared. She hoped he would soon think of her as more than an overly curious child. But even though she hoped, she was not blind. Nor was she deaf.

Many townspeople whispered about him. He was in love with his brother's wife, they said, with Danagasta, the very person with whom she had formed a close friendship over the years. Danagasta never spoke to Kayini of Sequatchee's affection for her, but Kayini saw the love in his eyes whenever he looked at Danagasta.

Then a wonderful day came, a day of awakening. Sequatchee hugged her close as he sometimes did, only this time the embrace was brief and when he withdrew, he stared at her in an odd way, then walked off mumbling to himself. He returned days later, and again the conversation was awkward and forced. Finally he remarked that she was growing up, becoming a woman, and her heart raced with joy.

For days and days, he did not visit. Then one morning she found a bowl of hominy on her family's doorstep and when she lifted it and glanced up, there stood Sequatchee near a lodge across the way, waiting . . . The hominy was from him—he was asking her permission to court her. Smiling, she wrapped her arms around the bowl, held it against her breast, and withdrew inside the cabin to tell her grinning parents the news.

"You are cruel today, Sali," Kayini whispered, opening her eyes. "I do not want to remember."

Sali leaned forward. "You *need* to remember, my friend. You should not act so—"

"I worry for Danagasta. What do we know of the white man except what he has told us? Danagasta must be frightened with the stranger in her dwelling. Ewi has been talking to Hanging Basket. Perhaps she has something to tell us. We should learn as much about Grant Claiborne as we can. Learn what kind of a man—"

"Kayini," Sali scolded gently. "Danagasta holds the devotion of the man you love. Yet you try to go on as if nothing has happened, as if he has not been taken from you. You protect Danagasta. I do not understand why."

"She does not ask for Sequatchee's devotion," Kayini mumbled. "She does not hold him to the old custom that a man should marry his brother's widow. Sequatchee holds himself to it."

"She holds him through guilt."

"She does not mean to. She still grieves."

"She holds him. She cannot accept that Losi is responsible for his own death, so she blames Sequatchee—and anyone who brings whiskey through the Nation." Sali's voice had risen, and it now contained a sharp edge.

"That does not mean we should stop caring about her."

"No one has stopped caring about her. We all want to

find a way to help her through her difficult time, but we worry that she will cause trouble for our people. Perhaps Hanging Basket thinks that putting the man in her cabin will help. Ordering such a thing is better than him telling Danagasta she *must* marry Sequatchee."

Kayini froze. She glanced up at Sali. "The chief has not said she *must* marry Sequatchee!"

"He had planned to. He told Tsatsi, who told Whitetree, who told—"

"You?"

Sali nodded. "He is tired of her roaming the riverbank in search of white men who sold Losi whiskey. He wants another husband for her, but one that *she* wants. Danagasta looks at Grant Claiborne with desire in her eyes, I am told."

"Tsatsi said that, too?"

"Yes. So you see . . . This man could mean the chance for you to recapture Sequatchee's interest. If Danagasta—"

"We do not really know him!" Kayini objected, trembling.

"Kayini, my hope is that he brings her to life again. She needs to realize that she has grieved long enough, that she should take another husband, burn Losi's things, and fill her home with children's laughter."

"But only two seasons . . . And my grandmother believes a woman should marry only once."

"So Danagasta should never find happiness again? *You* should never find happiness again? You are confused. You try to pretend that you want Sequatchee for her—"

"I do not want her to marry a man we do not really know! That is all!"

Sali shook her head. "That is not all. Besides, I did not say she should marry him. Perhaps he will stir her desire for another husband, for another man to live with her. Then she will choose from our men."

She will choose Sequatchee, Kayini thought, going back to her weaving with quaking hands. Sali was right: She did not really want Sequatchee to marry Danagasta. In truth, she longed to have him turn his desire back to *her*. Yet she had given up hope—she truly had. Sequatchee's noble loyalty to Danagasta was like the hardened clay that made the cabins sturdy; Losi's death had molded it and dried it in place. Losi had died the day after Sequatchee had offered Kayini the bowl of hominy, and Kayini's hope that Sequatchee would someday ask her to marry him had perished, too.

So had her close friendship with Danagasta, it seemed. Because Danagasta was so bitter toward and angry with Sequatchee, she and Kayini had not spoken much since Losi's death. Kayini felt bad that her friend had lost her husband, and she felt even worse that Danagasta had miscarried her unborn babe, but she did not feel that Danagasta should blame Sequatchee for anything that had happened. Many times since that fateful day last summer she had wondered what would become of the woman with whom she had spent many childhood days, laughing and talking and learning essential skills.

"Perhaps she will choose someone else, and Sequatchee will be free of his duty. Then you and Danagasta can become close again," Sali said, seeming to sense her thoughts.

"It is all very sad," Kayini whispered. "I do not want to speak of it anymore."

But Sali refused to let the subject rest. "I am told you accepted Talalah's hominy."

Kayini's fingers slipped on the thread she was weaving. She would not allow herself to become bitter like Danagasta had become. She would not snap like the box turtle at her friends and relatives because she had lost the man she loved. "Yes, I . . . Having a family . . . bearing children is important to me. I want to marry and have a lodge of my own to keep. I will not have that if I keep waiting for Sequatchee—something I have done for many seasons. So, yes, I accepted Talalah's request to court me. I took his bowl of hominy."

"Oh, Kayini."

Only yesterday morning Talalah, a man who had given Kayini many admiring looks, had placed the bowl beside her family's door. She had stooped and lifted the bowl—accepted it—but not in the joyful manner she had lifted

Sequatchee's. She had pressed Sequatchee's against her breast and smiled at him where he stood watching in the distance, then she had withdrawn into her family's lodge and eaten every morsel of the hominy. She had put Talalah's bowl aside, but this afternoon, she would walk with him in the forest . . . She would allow him to take her hand if he wished to do such a thing. Perhaps she would imagine that it was Sequatchee's hand.

She scowled at herself. That would not be fair to Talalah.

"The white man *must* be an agent. Why else does he talk of trading the land?" Sali wondered aloud. Kayini was grateful that she did not speak more of Sequatchee's devotion to Danagasta or of Talalah's courtship of *her*.

"But he brings no gifts," Kayini remarked. "If he is an agent, he is a strange one."

"He has courage, yes? How Kaliquegidi's head and pride must hurt!" Sali laughed. "I could not believe the white man beat him. And so quickly!"

"He is not so strong, I think, as smart."

"Talalah will be jealous of your admiration of the man."

Kayini smiled. "Then perhaps Talalah should fight him with poles and *win* my admiration."

"I will tell him," Sali said lightly.

"You will not! I was teasing."

"You will marry Talalah soon?"

"When I am ready." Kayini felt Sali's long look.

"*If* you become ready."

Kayini concentrated on her weaving, knowing she did not fool her friend. Sali knew she still loved Sequatchee.

Ewi, Danagasta's aunt, approached with a colorful woven blanket tossed over a forearm; Hanging Basket and Tsatsi had gone into Catolster's cabin. Sali stopped working to move her stool over, giving Ewi room to spread the blanket on the ground in front of the loom in the event she wanted to weave, too. Ewi sat on her blanket, and smiled up at Kayini and Sali.

"You do not seem disturbed by your conversation with our chief," Sali observed.

"Hanging Basket does not think that Grant Claiborne

was bringing whiskey into the Nation to sell," Ewi explained. "My brother put the man in Danagasta's lodge because, as Tsatsi said, he saw desire in their eyes when they looked at each other. We are to watch and listen, make certain the white man treats her well. We are to learn more about him if we can. Hanging Basket plans to ask Agent Meigs if he will permit the man to stay in Big Water during the winter."

Kayini shook her head. "No one should force a husband on Danagasta! Not even her father."

"Hanging Basket is not forcing a husband on her," Ewi said. "He is making it possible for the desire to grow between them. Then we will see what happens."

"I will tell my young son to aim no more arrows at the new white man," Sali said, smiling. "I will tell Cullowhee and his friends to watch him and tell us what he does, how he treats the people. Tonight I will ask my husband how he feels about the stranger, whether or not Whitetree feels that the white man is honorable."

"What if Whitetree will not talk about him?" Kayini asked.

Sali grinned like the sly Fox. "He will talk. I know how to make my husband talk."

Ewi giggled. Kayini could not restrain a smile or the warmth of embarrassment that crept up her neck. "You are sometimes more naughty than your young son," she teased, shaking her head. "I now know why Cullowhee behaves so shamelessly sometimes."

Sali simply went on with her task, her grin wider than ever.

Moments later Cullowhee and his good friends, Wadigei and Inoli, approached from the left. Sali called them over and began telling what she wanted them to do.

A woman brought Grant's clothes, which were still slightly damp, and he dressed, feeling eyes on him and listening to the men talk. Catolster indicated that they wanted to talk among themselves now, so Grant stood and walked, untouched, to the door of Catolster's lodge. Once outside, he turned his face upward, felt the day's promise of sunshine, and thanked the heavens he was still alive—and essentially unharmed. His ribs still hurt like hell, but he considered the injury minor compared to what the Indians might have done to him. He wondered what other surprises the remainder of the day would bring. Or perhaps he shouldn't wonder . . . He started off down the wide path between rows of cabins, intent on Danagasta's lodge, thinking he would lie down again for a while. The morning had been entirely too eventful.

Her cabin was the last at the end of this row. As Grant passed lodges, a number of men, women, and children stared at him. But none stared more intently than the three women who sat weaving colorful strips that hung from the crossbars of wooden frames. Three boys hunched near one side of a nearby cabin, chipping at wood or something. One of the women was Kayini, who had led the way to the creek earlier. One of the boys was the lad who had jumped the fence with her—and aimed an arrow at Grant last night. The boys went into the lodge and quickly reappeared carrying baskets. To Grant's surprise, the lads approached him.

They asked in English if he wanted to play with them. Grant tipped his head to one side and regarded them suspiciously. The baskets looked harmless, but he couldn't figure out why the boys wanted *him* to play with them. "You were going to shoot me with an arrow last night," he told the one boy.

"I am Cullowhee," the lad responded, grinning. "I thought you would hurt Danagasta."

Grant almost asked, "How do you know I didn't?" Instead he said, "I can understand why you would think that. I must have looked angry."

"You did."

"She pulled me from the river and tied me up. Then she poked me countless times with one end of her bow."

"Danagasta's husband died. Since then, she is not always nice."

"Is that so?" Grant said, becoming interested.

Cullowhee nodded, and suddenly Grant found that he wanted to know more about the woman. Cullowhee might just have some answers. "If she's not always nice, why do you protect her?" Grant queried.

"Because I feel bad for her. She is still sad about Losi."

"Losi . . . Her husband?"

The boy nodded.

Wincing at the pain in his side, Grant hunched to Cullowhee's level and studied the coppery face and the dark eyes. The lad's hair was cut at an uneven angle across his forehead and down either side of his face. In the back, it fell well beyond his shoulders. A woven belt secured a cloth arranged around his privates, and a knife sheathed in animal skin dangled from the belt.

"Do you know those women?" Grant asked, jerking his head toward Kayini and her two friends. "One led the way to the creek earlier. I know her. The others . . ."

"Ewi is Danagasta's aunt. Sali is my mother," Cullowhee said. Then he tipped his chin. "Whitetree is my father."

Grant lifted a brow. "Is he? You sound proud of him."

"I am. You will play the game with us?"

"As long as you don't aim another arrow at me—or accidently poke me in the ribs. You'll show me how to play? And you won't cheat?" Grand added playfully.

"Cullowhee does not cheat," the boy said, grinning slyly.

Grant chuckled. "Now . . . I imagine you're an expert at cheating."

Cullowhee laughed, then turned to lead the way to an open area on the other side of Danagasta's cabin. There Grant sat crossed-legged like the boys.

At first he just watched what Cullowhee called the "basket-dice game." But soon Cullowhee handed him a basket with carved dice resting in the bottom of it. Another boy offered Grant a small, hollowed gourd containing some sort of drink; a sweet, woody-tasting brew. Grant liked it. Cullowhee introduced his two friends as Wadigei and Inoli, then the game continued.

Grant watched the dice, encouraging the whooping Cullowhee when he apparently got the right combinations of numbers. Several times the dice flew a few feet away, and Grant retrieved them. Finally Cullowhee handed him the basket and encouraged him to compete with Wadigei and Inoli. Trying to get a good combination of numbers, enough to beat the others', was no easy task. When Grant didn't get a good combination, he made faces; when he did, Cullowhee scowled.

"How long was Danagasta married?" Grant asked casually.

Wadegei answered: "Not long. Three seasons."

"My mother says four," Inoli said.

Cullowhee shook his head. "No—three."

Grant glanced among the three of them as Cullowhee began counting the marks carved into the turned-up sides of his dice. "A season . . . is that a year, or is that like spring, summer, fall, or winter?"

The boys glanced curiously at him. "Spring, summer, fall, or winter. Seasons are seasons. Even the whites know seasons," Cullowhee said.

Grant remembered the one white man's presence in the chief's cabin last night, and he remembered the handful of white men he had spotted in the crowd earlier. "I thought your seasons might be different. Do you learn a lot from the white men in Big Water?"

"Sometimes," Inoli said. "How to speak English. How to count far—"

"That the white settlers who do not like us want to take our homes," Cullowhee interjected. "I do not want to be sent away."

Grant felt a stab of compassion. He was here to encourage the Cherokee to leave. "Are there a lot of white settlers who don't like you?"

"Too many, and more all the time," Cullowhee answered sharply.

Grant decided to change the subject again; Whitetree had obviously instilled in his son his resentment of white settlers. "So Danagasta was married three or four seasons . . . and now she lives alone."

"She is still angry," Inoli said. His hair was cut in the same fashion as Cullowhee's—across the brow, angled around the edges of his face, and allowed to grow long in the back. Wadegei's hair was cropped to just above his small shoulders.

"She's angry . . . that her husband died?" Grant pressed.

Inoli nodded. "She is angry that Sequatchee told him where to trade with white men for whiskey. He became drunk and was killed during a hunt."

"His death was an accident?"

"Yes."

Grant glanced off at Danagasta's cabin. The logs were carved and fitted together, and the cracks were filled in with a mix of grass and dried clay. A dark skin hung in the one window on this side. Grant rubbed his rough jaw. If what these boys said was true, no wonder Danagasta was so hostile toward him. Her husband had been accidentally killed while he'd been drinking whiskey while hunting, and she suspected *him* of bringing whiskey to sell in the Cherokee Nation. No wonder.

"Your turn," Cullowhee said, handing Grant a basket—for at least the fifth time.

Grant took the basket in both hands and gave it a jerk that sent the dice flying up. They plopped back into the basket. Grant looked down, laughed in disbelief, and mumbled, "My friend Luke would be proud. I believe I have the highest number."

"That means you lost," Cullowhee said, grinning.

Grant scowled playfully. "Oh, are you suddenly reversing the object of the game?"

" 'Object of the game?' " Cullowhee asked in bewilderment.

"What the player must do to win."

"I am doing what I must do to win."

"You little scamp . . ." Grant laughed. The boys laughed, too.

Kayini, Ewi, and Sali approached, smiling and commenting in English that Grant was playing a child's game. Grinning, he said it was interesting when one never knew what rules would govern the next round. As he went on playing, the somber-looking girl who had been in Catolster's cabin when Grant had entered walked up to Cullowhee and plopped down beside him. She couldn't be morc than four years old. Something beige-colored was smeared on her chin and on one cheek. Smiling at her, Cullowhee pulled the thumb from her mouth. She swiped at him playfully and popped the thumb right back in.

He grinned. "She is Awe-ani-da. She likes to follow me. Her father is Catolster."

Grant nodded, acknowledging the information, then his stomach growled loudly. Now that he wasn't worrying that these people might burn him, scalp him, or drive a spear or pole through him . . . now that he wasn't worried that he might offend Catolster or Whitetree by saying the wrong thing, he had time to be hungry. He had eaten the bread Awe-ani-da's father had offered, but bread alone wasn't enough. He wondered if Danagasta stored food in her cabin.

Talking among themselves in Cherokee, the women wandered off. Grant played a few more rounds of the game with the boys, then glanced up to see the women coming back this way. They were carrying baskets covered with woven cloths.

Danagasta's stomach rumbled, waking her. She rose to fetch some wrapped corncakes she had placed on a shelf carved into one wall. Turning back the cloth, she sat on the skins and ate.

Tsuwa—Grant Claiborne—was gone. The skins on which he had slept were still there, but he was not in the lodge.

She stood again, but this time she moved to the hide covering the doorway. She swept the skin aside and stepped outside.

There were the usual sights: men and women gathered in various places, sharpening weapons, talking and laughing, molding pottery, stitching beads . . . weaving. Children played around the two rows of cabins in this section of Big Water. Danagasta heard whoops coming from somewhere nearby. She turned her head to the right . . . and gaped at the sight before her.

With a buffalo coat draped around his shoulders, Tsuwa was seated on the ground, cross-legged, in the children's play area. Cullowhee, Wadigei, and Inoli were gathered close, playing the basket-dice game with him. Grant Claiborne shook the woven, oak-splint basket he held, then jerked his hands to make the dice fly into the air. They plopped back into the basket. Studying them, he tipped his head, then said something about God being against him this day. He wrinkled his face and pronounced Cullowhee the winner. Cullowhee grinned, and the other boys laughed as Grant Claiborne ruffled Cullowhee's black hair.

Danagasta frowned. Cullowhee was her friend. She would tell him she did not trust the white man, that she suspected him of terrible things, and Cullowhee would not act so friendly toward him anymore. But it was not just Cullowhee who was acting so friendly . . . Wadigei and Inoli were smiling and laughing, too, and Awe-ani-da, who would soon be four winters, drew close with her thumb firmly lodged in her mouth—as always. Around her thumb she smiled at Tsuwa's playfulness.

The last thing Danagasta wanted to see was him charming her people!

She wondered if he was hungry. She was responsible for feeding him, after all. She would use food to lure him from the children. She would cook some of the venison she had salted and stored in the small smokehouse behind her lodge only yesterday morning. She would make frybread, and the smell would make him come to her cabin.

Just as Danagasta started to turn away, Sali, Ewi, and Kayini approached Grant Claiborne, carrying baskets covered with loosely woven cloths. Sali drew forth a mound of frybread, offering him it and the cloth. Smiling, he took both items, turned his dice-basket over, spread the cloth on it and placed the bread on the cloth. Kayini handed him a piece of cooked meat. Ewi produced an ear of corn and spoke in Cherokee, telling him she liked his play with the children, whose faces beamed as they looked up at him. He appeared at ease with all three items spread before him, with the women and the children regarding him warmly.

Danagasta shook her head, as if trying to rid it of bad

images. How had Tsuwa accomplished this? While she slept half the day away, he was being welcomed by the women and children! She glanced around at the many cabins, wondering about the men . . . whether or not they welcomed Tsuwa, too. Catolster, Whitetree, and a number of other men were walking this way from Catolster's lodge. The group broke up: Catolster and Whitetree went to sit on stools before Sali's lodge, three of the men wandered between cabins and disappeared, and Sequatchee and the others began tossing blunt sticks at trees with a small gathering of boys. Awi-gadoga, Catolster's wife, sat showing a group of girls how to make corn dough. She glanced up and called to her daughter to come back and watch, but Awe-ani-da ignored her mother.

Danagasta stomped toward Grant Claiborne, unsure what she meant to say to him. She was shocked that he seemed to have eased into the lives of her people. How had this happened? How? The men acted as though they did not notice the newcomer, and newcomers were normally noticed very much! Kayini, Ewi, and Sali made him feel welcome with their offerings of food. And Cullowhee, Wadegei, and Inoli . . . playing with him! He was a *stranger*! What was the matter with all of them?

She cut between Cullowhee and Wadigei, grabbed the ear of *selu* Ewi had handed the white man, and sent it spiraling some distance away. It landed in a crop of tall brown grass near one side of her cabin.

The boys and Awe-ani-da scooted away. Ewi tossed Danagasta a startled look. In Cherokee, Sali said, "Danagasta, he is hungry." Kayini fixed an irritating stare on Danagasta, who stared right back. Finally the women took the boys by the hands and walked away, leaving Danagasta with the white man.

"Why did you do that?" he demanded, folding his arms.

"Why are you taking their food?" she shot back.

"I was hungry. I still am. They offered it."

"Did they? And do they know what you are trying to do?"

Afternoon light glinted in his eyes. "What am I trying to do, Dana?"

"My name," she said, breathing deeply to calm herself, "is Danagasta. Do not shorten it!"

He placed his upturned basket to one side, unfolded his legs, and came slowly to his feet, looking calmly down on her. "Very well, *Danagasta*. I haven't eaten much of anything since yesterday afternoon. Get the corn, wash it, and bring it back."

Danagasta inhaled deeply, lifted her chin, and stood her ground.

"Danagasta . . . the corn," he warned softly.

She refused to move.

His glittering eyes raked slowly down over her form, then lifted lazily to rest on her lips.

The heated gaze made her gasp and step back put more distance between them. A grin slanted his mouth. He seemed to know she was remembering the way he had kissed and touched her last night.

She spun to go get the corn, knowing she had already said too much, and knowing she could not risk an unfavorable report to Hanging Basket. She grabbed the *selu*, turned around . . . and found that he had moved up behind her.

She looked up into his blue eyes and was suddenly unable to move; she was unable to take even a single step backward this time. Shimmering chestnut hair tumbled carelessly over his forehead. His nose was chiseled to perfection. Dark whiskers peppered his jaw and the area between his upper lip and nose, and his breath, smelling of woody sassafras, fanned her face. The buffalo coat he wore gaped in front, exposing his solid, linen-covered chest. She knew the lean, hard feel of his body—he had pressed it against her last night—and she suddenly longed to feel it again.

She finally forced her feet to move her away from him. But she stumbled foolishly, and his firm grip on her upper arm was the only thing that saved her from falling down.

"We don't have to fight like this, Danagasta," he said huskily. "I'm not the man you think I am. I wasn't selling whiskey to anyone."

"But you at least admit to drinking it!"

"I like the taste of it sometimes—but I can live without it. And I damn sure don't drink it when there's important business to be done."

"Important business . . . The land?"

"Yes, the land."

He released her arm, took the corn from her hand, and returned to where he had been sitting.

Sequatchee stepped up beside Danagasta, looking as though he wanted to kill the white man. His tone was menacing: "Do not touch her again, *yun wunega*."

"I prevented her from falling," Grant said.

"You have a way of looking at her that I do not like."

Tsuwa merely stared at Sequatchee as he bit into his corn. The man had courage that Danagasta admired, that she did not want to admire.

"Do not make trouble," she told Sequatchee in Cherokee. "I have not asked for your protection."

Then she turned and walked back to her cabin.

Chapter Six

MUCH LATER, DANAGASTA STOOD near the stone hearth to the left of her lodge, stirring corn and ashes in a pot. Once the corn was parched she would sift the ashes away. The nutty-tasting *gahawi sita* would keep well; it was the very food the men often took on hunting expeditions.

She recalled her mother standing near a stone hearth much like hers, patiently stirring corn and ashes. The woman wore a deerskin dress, close-fitting, stitched with sinew and belted with a colorful woven strip. A chemise knitted from wild hemp peeked from beneath her dress, and bear grease made her straight-hanging hair appear glossy and pretty. She looked plain but beautiful without fringe on her clothing, bells on her buskins, beads around her neck, or metal dangling from her ears.

The sweet smell of the parched corn drifted up, making Danagasta's mouth water. She reached into the pot, snatched up a piece of *gahawi sita*, and popped it between her lips, sucking air in and out of her mouth to cool the food. Her mother had often scolded her for her impatience.

"It will lead to failure, my little Eagle," Cornsilk, or Seluunenudi, had frequently said, shaking her head.

Tsuwa was moving among the people again, near the council house, near the large hothouse, where many went to warm themselves during the height of winter, and near other distant rows of cabins. Danagasta even spotted her father and George Dougherty with the man and his small crowd of people.

Earlier she had left Grant Claiborne with his corn while she went back inside to straighten her lodge. Then she had gone to the smokeshed behind her cabin to get meat. Finally she had come here to cook and eat, wondering if her father would come or send someone to see if she had cooked for the white man. But no one had come, and soon she had spotted Tsuwa talking with Whitetree and others near the tall protective fence surrounding the town. The men were sharpening sticks that would be used to spear fish.

The white man moved again, this time to the corner of a lodge to talk with some women who were weaving thread into cloth on looms. Kayini was with them, and Tsuwa laughed at something she said, then he straightened, stepped forward, and bent to touch the strands folding in and out of a loom. He flashed his smile, and Danagasta watched the Sun glint off the women's hair as they dipped their heads, laughing beneath the man's charm. Doubtless they would soon rave to their husbands about him.

Danagasta had wondered if he claimed the title of deputy agent only to protect himself. But he *acted* like an agent, mingling with the people, and he had admitted that his business was the land. Besides, if the great white chief in the place the *unegas* called Washington wanted more Cherokee land, would he not send someone who could charm the Principle People the way Tsuwa was charming them? Would he not send someone who could talk them out of the land before they knew what they had done? Even if her father and many other people did not wish to give up land or accept farming tools, looms, and other things from Agent Meigs, some of the people did, and more might be convinced. The chiefs were elected, not given office by birth. They were representatives of the people, and if Grant Claiborne convinced the people to sell their land or accept more tools, Hanging Basket could not speak against their wishes.

A chill crept up Danagasta's spine despite the warmth of Grandmother Sun. Her heart beat fast as she watched Grant Claiborne work. He was like a predator, disguised and walking with the unsuspecting herd. He conversed, laughed, flirted . . . She closed her eyes, smelling him for what he was, but they . . . many of them did not.

What would make him leave this settlement? What? Oh, *what*? He must be made to go, she suddenly realized.

She finished parching the corn, then she made bread by forming corn dough, putting the loaf on the hot stone hearth, and covering the loaf with an earthen dish. Both the bread and the corn would keep, the bread for days, the corn for moons. By keeping the food in ready supply, she would not be faced with the white man ever accusing her of not cooking for him, and of her displeasing her father again. Last fall, she had gathered many hickory nuts—out of habit because Losi had liked them—and she still had many in a hollowed stump. She would pound the meats and place them in cold water, making a delicious drink. She would keep her water gourd filled, too, giving Tsuwa no reason to complain.

During ensuing days, more children than just Cullowhee, Wadegei, and Inoli began gathering around Grant for the basket-dice game, and for pony races through a large field located clear across town from the cluster of cabins in which Danagasta's lodge was located. He was invited to accompany Whitetree, Catolster, and a number of other men, who were still coolly receptive, in driving the small herd of cattle through the forest so the animals could drink from the creek. The Indians had fastened rattlesnake "bells" to long strips of leather and tied the leather around the animals' necks. If a cow or bull wandered off, someone had only to mount a horse and ride through the forest, listening for the rattle.

There were seven gardens outside Big Water's palisade,

and Whitetree explained that the ones located inside near each of the four clusters of cabins—one near each wall of the rectangular enclosure—were there to ensure that the people would have food if the gardens outside were burned. A storehouse—a lodge built on eight-foot poles—was located near each garden. Hogs were housed in a pen outside the western wall of the town palisade except when they were brought inside to be butchered. Grant spotted a number of dogs roaming freely inside the settlement.

Kaloquegidi, the man Grant had fought with poles, approached Grant one afternoon as Grant was helping Kayini bring baskets of corn and squash down from the storehouse. Kaloquegidi lived with his wife and three children in a cabin in the same row in which Danagasta's lodge was located, Kayini had explained only that morning when Grant had spotted the man and unconsciously rubbed his side. "He is not so fierce," Kayini had said. Grant had seen the man a number of times these past days, but Kaloquegidi had scowled and turned away every time.

Now the man halted before Grant, grinned sheepishly, and mumbled something about Grant being a white warrior. Kayini broke into a smile. Grant couldn't help a chuckle. Kaloquegidi held out a basket containing chunks of bread and something else . . . Grant lifted a pipe bowl on which was carved the figure of a bear.

"I am from the Bear Clan," Kaloquegidi said to explain the figure.

"How do you make something like this?" Grant asked in amazement, inspecting the pipe bowl. The bear was crouched. Even its small face was perfectly carved. Every edge and curve was smooth.

"I will show you. Can you come?"

Grant glanced at Kayini. "Two more baskets," she'd said just before Kaloquegidi had approached.

"Go," she said now. "I will get Sali or Ewi to help."

Grant started off with Kaloquegidi.

Inside the lodge every evening and night, Grant tried his best to stay clear of Danagasta. She often went off and returned a short time later with her hair wet. She carried her clothes, so he guessed that she was naked beneath her wolfskin coat. He always left the cabin for a time to give her opportunity to dress and do whatever women—even Indian women, he supposed—did during their toilet.

One morning, he asked if she knew where he might get a razor. The ever-increasing growth of hair on his jaw and above his upper lip was a scratchy nuisance, and he wanted to shave. Danagasta merely shrugged, then went on attending her thick ebony hair with what looked like a comb carved from bone.

Undaunted, Grant went to Kaloquegidi and asked about a razor. Kaloquegidi explained that Cherokee men normally plucked out any hair that grew on their faces. Grant winced. Grinning, Kaloquegidi said he would ask one of Big Water's white men about getting a razor for Grant.

Near dusk that evening, George Dougherty appeared at Danagasta's lodge. Without a word, he handed Grant a length of thin flint, cast an imploring look Danagasta's way as she sat weaving cane with a sharp-pointed tool, then turned and left.

Grant held the flint out and examined it curiously. Then he glanced at the doorway where George had disappeared. "Now, why do you suppose—"

"It is a razor," Danagasta said in her usual cool tone.

"Ah." Grant examined the thing more closely. The sharp edge was clean enough, he supposed. Not too deadly looking.

"He chips at the edge, then takes sand from the riverbed and rubs the edge until it is sharp but smooth."

Grant turned an uplifted brow on Danagasta. "You're certainly accommodating this evening."

She rose and started toward the lodge opening. "Your wounded flatboat could not have stayed afloat for long—if it even managed the remaining rapids. Perhaps your flasks containing whiskey are scattered about the riverbank."

Devil take the woman. She was hell-bent on continuing the nonsense about the whiskey.

Three strides put Grant between her and the doorway. He braced a hand high up on the frame, leaned into it and glared down at her. "If you find any flasks filled with whiskey, there's no way you can prove they're mine. And if you somehow manage to do *that*, there's no way you can prove what you want to believe—that I was selling them."

"I will find a way. I will drive you from our land."

"You'll find *trouble*, Danagasta. Why don't you stop—"

"Perhaps."

"Definitely."

"I want to go outside," she said, lifting her chin. The fire she had built shortly before George Dougherty had appeared leaped in her eyes and cast an orange glow on her hair and on the shoulders of her buckskin dress.

"Do you?" Grant had grown tired of her menacing looks, of having to endure her angry quiet every night. And he was sick of the whiskey business.

"One scream would bring some of the men. You know that, white man."

"White man . . ." Grant shook his head. "You take words that sound fine coming from most people and make them sound ugly."

"Move," she ordered.

"You won't scream," he responded softly, his gaze falling to rest on her full lips. *The color of fine Madeira . . .* And how he'd like a drink . . . "If I tried to kiss you, you'd fight, but you wouldn't scream. You have too much pride to scream."

Danagasta stepped back. What was he doing? *What? Was* he going to try to kiss her again? She would not let him. He was right—she would not scream. But she would *not* let him kiss her.

"What is it, Danagasta? I haven't even moved."

She did not answer.

"Cullowhee tells me you were married."

Her eyes flared. "Cullowhee talks too much!"

"What happened to your husband?" Of course, Grant knew what had happened to her husband, but he wanted to hear her say, "He was drinking during a hunt, . . ." He wanted to hear her blame her husband for the hunting accident; he wanted her to realize that just because he'd had a flask of whiskey on him when she'd found him didn't mean she should take her anger, frustration, and grief out on him.

"That is not your business!"

"I'm curious."

"Curiosity can be a bad thing. Curiosity lures animals into deadly traps."

Lowering his hand, he stepped toward her. "Danagasta," he said in a tone of mild anger, "I believe you've just threatened me."

Backing up two more steps, she grabbed a knife from the top of a nearby stool, crouched slightly, and held the blade out in front of her. "You have a weapon. I could say you tried to hurt me."

He cocked his head . . . and realized he still held the razor. He dropped it.

"I could still say you tried to hurt me."

"*Damn*, but you're vengeful!" he exploded. "Can't you see you're not getting anywhere? That you're only hurting yourself? You're so angry no one wants to be around you."

"That is not true."

"It is true. Kayini's your friend, isn't that right? Or at least she was. Has she been here to see you of late? Does she approach you when you walk through Big Water? Does anyone?"

"They did before you came."

"Oh, that's my fault, too?"

"I have become angrier since you came," she accused.

He took another step toward her. She thrust the blade forth. He didn't flinch. "You won't touch me with that knife."

"You say that," she said, seething, "but you worry."

"What happened to your husband?" he persisted, taking another step.

"He died. Stay back!"

Grant regarded her closely. "Calm down, Danagasta. I'm not going to hurt you. I only want to talk. Put the knife down."

She shook her head.

He took more steps toward her. She kept backing away until finally she glanced around frantically, finding herself trapped in a corner. He reached out, planning to grab her wrist and take the knife. She again thrust the blade forward, and this time it hit its mark—it sliced into his forearm. Gasping, she dropped the weapon and clamped a hand over her mouth.

In shock, Grant stood staring at the blood soaking his shirt sleeve. As the pain began, he put his hand over the wound and issued a string of curses. "Shit! Son of a . . . What did you . . . *Damn!*" He backed up, staring at Danagasta in disbelief and anger. The wound began to throb.

"Sge!" she whispered in horror. "I told you stay back. I—I will stitch it!" She scrambled past him and fell to her knees near a basket containing pieces of woven material, animal skins, thread wound tightly into balls, and various other items. "Carved from bone." She lifted a needle to show him, then her trembling hands fumbled with something else—one of the balls. "Thread," she mumbled, holding it up. "I can stitch . . . I am sorry . . . Please—do not go out . . . do not tell my father!" She dropped the needle and the ball of thread, and twisted her hands together.

Still holding his arm, Grant neared Danagasta and lowered himself to the floor beside her. Her horror at what she had done was real, not pretense for his benefit. Her lips quivered; her breath came fast and shallow. His anger had lessened as he watched her desperate actions and listened to her plead with him not to tell her father. "I'm not going anywhere. Calm down. It's not entirely your fault. I shouldn't have provoked you. I have a temper, too, you see."

She glanced up at him, then back down at her hands. She reached for the needle and thread again and began unwinding the ball.

"No, Danagasta."

"B-but it will need to be stitched! It is deep . . . I know."

"You're not stitching it until you're calm. Put the needle and thread down."

Danagasta did as he said, still not believing she had cut him. She had thought he would back off! She should have known that he would not. His stubbornness was like hers, too strong at times, too powerful for his own good.

She reached for a cloth from the basket, then she brushed his hand aside and held the cloth to the wound, not daring to look at his face. "Why will you not tell?" she asked quietly, trying to keep the tremble from her voice.

"Because I once lost someone who was very close to me and I know the anger you feel over your husband's death."

She looked up in surprise.

"Yes, Danagasta, I know about the hunting accident. I know your pain. You think I'm a monster, but I'm human."

She searched his eyes, then whispered, "I wish you would leave Big Water."

"You brought me here," he reminded her.

"I will take you to the agency. When I brought you to the settlement, I did not know that you were Agent Meigs's deputy!"

"I thought about telling you while we were at the river, but I figured you'd scalp me rather than listen to me."

Her heart began pounding again. "*Sge!* I have never scalped anyone!"

"But I imagine you've killed a few people."

She shook her head adamantly. "Only one—in defense! When I was nine winters. The white man was trying to hurt me in a bad way . . . I did not understand. I was frightened. They had come to set fire to Big Water again. They . . . soldiers were everywhere. People were screaming. I—"

"Danagasta. Hush. I understand. And I believe you." He had lifted his hand to put a finger to her lips. But upon noticing the blood on his fingers, she winced and withdrew. He lowered his hand.

She could not believe what she had just heard. "You believe me when I refuse to believe you—that you were not coming to the Nation to sell whiskey."

He smiled weakly. "You haven't given me any reason to doubt you. You don't have scalps hanging around your lodge. I don't see bodies dangling from overhead beams."

She continued to stare at him.

"What bothers you more—the fact that you think I was bringing whiskey to sell in this nation, or the fact that I'm Meigs's deputy?"

"Deputy . . ." she mumbled, briefly closing her eyes. "That means you are Meigs's helper, and to help him, you must destroy my people. You must take the land and give it to the white settlers. They do not love these mountains where Kana'ti, the first Cherokee man, lived and hunted, where Thunder watches and *Nunda sunnayehi* peers down from the night sky with silver eyes. Where the mist rises from valleys created long ago by the wings of the mighty Buzzard. The white settlers cannot love this land the way my people do because they do not understand it. These mountains are my peoples' ancestral home—and it is a home we love."

Grant sat in stunned silence, wanting to pass a soothing hand over his face from forehead to chin. Her words unnerved him because he realized how heartbroken she would be if she were made to leave her "ancestral home." Moments passed. They seemed like an eternity as he sat looking into her eyes.

He spoke finally, but his voice was thick and strained: "What if . . . What if someone offered you land in another place? Land with hills and valleys and forests like the ones here?"

"There can be no other forests like the ones here. I would not go," she said simply.

"But what if there were?"

"There is not."

Sighing, Grant gently lifted the cloth from his arm and found that the bleeding had slowed. "Let me see your hands."

"My hands? Why?" she asked.

"Hold them up."

She did.

"Good. You've stopped trembling. Do you have any candles? I saw some of the women making tapers . . ."

"Yes. Why?"

"I want more light so I can be sure you can see what

you're doing when you stitch this cut. I like needles about as much as I like knives, and I don't want you to do any more stitching than is necessary. Perhaps after you light a candle and start stitching you can tell me about all these things lying around your cabin."

Danagasta's breath stopped in her throat. "Why would I want to do that?"

"Don't start looking frightened again," he said. "I haven't threatened to set fire to your husband's things."

"How do you know they are his?"

"Pipe bowls, breeches, leggings like the townsmen wear. Ballplay sticks like Kaliquegidi's . . . I've been busy since coming to Big Water. I've talked to people, asked questions . . . Cullowhee told me how your husband died. I'm sorry."

"Cullowhee, Cullowhee! *Hiwonihi!*" She glanced away, then looked back at Grant. "Why do you ask questions about me?"

"A man has to know a little something about his enemy," he answered softly.

"If I am your enemy, why will you not tell my father I cut you?"

"Because after spending a number of days in Big Water, I realize that although the people who reside in this cluster of cabins protect you, their protection stops at your father. If he decides to punish you, that punishment will stand because that's how the family structure here works—the father has final say except in deciding whether or not a daughter should marry. That's the aunt or mother's responsibility."

He had learned a lot in the short time he had been in the settlement. How many days ago had she brought him to the town? Eight, nine days . . . surely no more than ten. She had brought the enemy among her people, and he was not only making friends with many of them, but he was also learning their ways. Her stomach felt sick; she wanted him gone from Big Water. He was too smart for her to fight.

He shifted his position, drawing up the knee farthest

from her. "I don't *want* to be your enemy," he said, as if reading her mind. "*You* want to be mine."

She moved away to fetch a candle from where she kept three in a chest pushed against a far wall. He was a good talker, the white man. For a second she had almost believed him.

She gathered the candle, lit it from the fire, then went back to him to stitch his arm. She would work in silence, not responding to anything he said to her, and not looking at his face. Then she would make a healing balm from the dried herbs dangling from long pieces of sinew tied to overhead rafters, and apply it to his wound. She would not be mean or spiteful . . . or anything. She would show no emotion. And if that angered him and he went to Hanging Basket when he had promised he would not, she would be brave when her father punished her.

Chapter Seven

Some days Danagasta took her bow and her gourd of arrows and went hunting, enjoying rides through the forest and near the creek and the great river. She was surprised that no white men had come from the foundry to complain that she had ridden through their settlement terrorizing the chickens and a few women.

Some evenings she joined her father, the townspeople, and Grant Claiborne in the large square located near the western part of Big Water. The people often met to roast meat, eat grated corn wrapped in husks, and share conversation and stories and legends that had been handed down through generations, most of which Danagasta had heard many times but enjoyed hearing over and over. Kayini had always loved to repeat the legends, and one evening she told how, when the world was made, the animals wanted to come down but the earth was dark so the conjurers put the Sun in the Skyland, lifting it handbreadths at a time. Finally, at the seventh height, it was no longer so hot. Every day the Sun traveled under the arch the conjurers had created, returning at night to the starting point. At first only a brother and sister lived in the mountains and valleys, until the brother struck the sister with a fish and told her to multiply. Seven days later she produced a child and every seven days thereafter, another child, until the Principle People grew very fast in numbers.

"In the beginning," Kayini said another evening, "the world was cold, and the Thunders, who lived in *Galun lati*—the Upper World—sent lightning and put fire in a hollow sycamore tree. The animals saw smoke coming out of the top of the tree, and they were anxious to have the fire, so they sent the Raven to get it because he was large and strong. The heat scorched his feathers black, and he returned, frightened. The little Screech-owl went, and returned with red eyes because a blast of hot air came up when he looked down into the hollow tree. The Horned Owl went for the fire and returned with white rings around his eyes from the blinding smoke and the ashes carried by the wind. Other animals tried to get the fire: some Snakes and then the Water Spider, who wove a bowl and fastened it to her back. She finally returned with a small coal of fire."

There were legends about where certain game came from—how the first boys raised a rock and a deer came out, and from the hole made by the deer came many other animals and birds. Many times Danagasta observed the fascination on Grant Claiborne's face as the stories were told and translated. He often sat with the children, pulling them onto his lap and teasing them, making them laugh, and making their mothers smile with adoration.

There were dances, some done with masks and feathers and poles, and sometimes Danagasta glimpsed Grant among the people, writhing to the wild beat of drums and rattles. The people pulled him into circles they formed, and into the lines they made for shuffling. During one dance—the friendship dance—Danagasta stood watching from one edge of the field. Grant's eyes met hers, their gazes locked, and soon he came over and offered his hand. A refusal issued from between her lips, but her hand went out to join with his, and he pulled her into the dancing.

They moved, dancing around each other, twisting their

bodies and alternately lifting their legs and arms. The glow given off by numerous torches lodged in various places around the large field flickered in his eyes, catching her in a pleasurable, breathless spell. Suddenly he stopped dancing, though the drums and rattles continued their magic. His eyes urged her to him, and she went without question.

His fingers brushed like a feather on her hand, on her arm, dancing up to her neck, sliding beneath her hair, pulling her closer. His lips touched hers, briefly, lightly, then they withdrew and she wanted them to come back, to caress hers with sweetness and fire and healing power—like the balm she had spread on his wound. A tingling began in her breasts and ran a heated course to the delicate female flesh between her thighs. She stared into Grant Claiborne's blue, blue eyes and wondered how she could ever deny him anything. If he wanted her, she would give herself. If he wanted the land, she would give that . . .

Shocked at being so caught in his spell, she gasped and turned away, touching a hand to her lips as she raced from the field.

Near an edge of the field, Kayini and Sali sat watching Danagasta and her "whiskey man," observing the way Danagasta was drawn to him, the heated way they gazed at each other, the deep desire that was so obvious between them.

"They will lie together soon," Sali remarked. "If they have not already."

Kayini was scarcely aware that her breath had caught in her throat while she watched them. She observed Danagasta running off, looking distraught, and she wanted to race after her friend and somehow comfort her. She moved, but Sali's hand, gently placed on her forearm, stilled her. Sali shook her head.

"She's so frightened!" Kayini whispered.

"Because she desires someone other than Losi. It is good for her. Or will be once she stops fighting herself inside."

"I hope you are right."

"I *am* right. And you . . . perhaps you can start thinking

of Sequatchee again soon and stop pretending with Talalah."

"Perhaps," Kayini said quietly. Then she put her fingers to her mouth, wondering if she was a fool for allowing herself to dream again. To even think about hoping.

The following day, Grant observed Danagasta take a bundle of belongings and walk off between lodges. Curious—wondering if he'd frightened her so badly last evening that she was moving from her own lodge—he followed, hanging back some so she wouldn't notice him. Near one far corner of Big Water she went into a cabin he'd seen some of the women disappear into for days at a time.

An hour passed, and Danagasta didn't come out. Finally Grant went off to play with Cullowhee and his friends.

She never showed up in the cabin that night. By the next morning, with curiosity, worry, and irritation gnawing at Grant, he walked up to Sali as she sat molding a pitcher outside her family's cabin. He asked what the women did in the thatched lodge in the northeast corner of Big Water.

Sali's brows lifted. Then she smiled sheepishly. "The women go to the hut during their bleeding time."

Grant stared at her for a few seconds, feeling his face warm. "Oh. Well, I suppose I deserve some embarrassment for my extreme curiosity. Danagasta went in yesterday and hasn't come back out since. I was worried, you see."

"You miss lying with her?" Sali asked boldly.

"I haven't 'lain' with her." His tone was more sharp than he intended. "I'm sorry," he said quickly. "I don't understand why you and Ewi seem to need to know now and then if I've slept with Danagasta. It seems to me that it's no one's—"

"Like you, we are curious." She was still smiling.

Shaking his head, he walked away, not wanting to offend her.

Days later, Danagasta returned to her lodge, looking tired. Grant thought about asking if she was feeling better, then decided he shouldn't. He wasn't sure about the Cherokee customs surrounding women's menstruation, so he didn't know if asking such a question would be proper. Even if it *were* proper, it still might embarrass her.

That same day, the messengers Hanging Basket had sent to alert Agent Meigs of Grant's presence in Big Water returned with a missive from Gideon Blackburn, the Presbyterian minister who oversaw the mission school at the agency. Yes, Grant Claiborne had been appointed deputy agent. Meigs was attending business in southern Georgia right now, however, and would return in a few weeks, Blackburn said, but Mr. Claiborne was welcome to come to the Tellico Blockhouse.

Grant considered the offer of hospitality, and the fact that some of Big Water's people were becoming more and more receptive to the idea of a land exchange. Right now he could accomplish far more if he stayed here. When he asked Hanging Basket if he could stay in the settlement longer, the old chief smiled eagerly and nodded. Grant wondered aloud if some townsmen might be sent to search for the other men who'd been on the flatboat, and again Hanging Basket nodded. Grant began to wonder if there was anything the chief would *not* try to do for him.

Rain came and went, lasting an entire day, mixing with tiny slivers of ice that melted within minutes of hitting the ground. It did little to hamper the activities of the townspeople, but Grant sought the quiet and warmth of Danagasta's lodge. He awoke to sunshine the following day, and afternoon brought an archery-lesson invitation from Cullowhee and his friends.

He should have known they were up to mischief; he couldn't recall too many times when they weren't. Along with Awe-ani-da, the quiet girl with the thumb-sucking habit, they took him to a far corner of the town, laughing when he handled Cullowhee's small bow awkwardly. The string was drawn tighter than Grant expected it to be, and he could barely position an arrow in the bow, much less send one of the sharply pointed sticks sailing in a straight pattern. At one point he aimed at the trunk of a tree, released the arrow, and watched it veer right, piercing a deerskin water bag hanging from a wooden hook beside the door of a nearby lodge. The heavy portal cracked open, and an old woman peered out, chattering angrily in Cherokee.

Grant tried apologizing, but he couldn't speak her language, and she apparently couldn't understand English. He glanced around for his little friends, thinking Cullowhee could interpret for him, but the boys and Awe-ani-da had disappeared.

He found them later, all three boys, seated and conversing pleasantly on several tree stumps near the fenced garden. He tapped Cullowhee on the shoulder, then folded his arms and waited.

Cullowhee glanced around, saw Grant, clapped a hand to his mouth and giggled. Grant noticed a bowl of dark bread resting on the boy's lap. Grinning, he reached around and snatched it, holding it just beyond Cullowhee's grasping hand. "You talked me into learning to shoot an arrow, then you ran off and left me at that woman's mercy," he said playfully. "And here you are, calmly eating bread while I'm trying to defend myself!"

"She chased you, Agent-man?" Cullowhee teased, standing on the stump and reaching for the bowl. "She called the evil Uktena-serpent to come for you?"

Grant poked the boy's belly with a forefinger. "Jester. She's chased you before, hasn't she? You knew what to expect, that's why you took me there! She threw the skin at me and pointed in the direction of the river. But the pouch won't hold water anymore. It has a hole in it! And you think this is funny."

Cullowhee's dark eyes sparkled with laughter. He grinned his little rogue's grin that Grant found endearing, and said, "*Gayewisdodi yvgi*. You will need . . . *Gayewisdodi*."

Inoli and Wadigei snickered.

Grant lifted a brow and peered down at Cullowhee. "Tell me what you said—if you want your bread."

"He said needle . . . Sew," Wadigei said shyly.

But there was nothing shy about Cullowhee. He put his hands together, and pretended to be holding something with one hand while making motions with the other. Grant realized he was pretending to sew, putting a needle in and pulling it out. "Like a woman," the boy taunted.

Eyes narrowing on Cullowhee, Grant handed the bowl to Wadigei. "I'll count to two," he told Cullowhee. "Then I'm coming after you."

Giggling, the lad twisted away, leaped from the stump, and tore off. Grant raced after him, laughing, unable to remember the last time he'd had such unrestrained fun. The cold wind whipped through his hair and chilled his face, but inside he felt warm.

They raced through a maze of cabins, around and around the large round hut that Grant now knew was the council house, and through another maze of lodges. Grant recognized Danagasta's by the deerskin flap. He chased Cullowhee around her lodge, noticing that a number of women and men had appeared to point and laugh at them.

Still giggling, Cullowhee tore around one corner of Danagasta's cabin. Grant tore around the same corner—and stopped short at the sight of Danagasta standing angrily over Cullowhee as the boy stooped to gather pieces of cane that were scattered over the grass. Cullowhee's grin had been replaced by a scowl.

Speaking angrily in Cherokee, she motioned wildly with her arms.

"We'll get more cane, Danagasta," Grant said, out of breath. He hurried to where Cullowhee hunched and began helping the boy.

"Pick it all up," she ordered as she folded her arms in front of her. Cullowhee paused to glance up fearfully at her. She waved an arm at him, her eyes glittering with rage. *"Wi di tsa lv wi s da si!"*

Cullowhee winced and worked faster at gathering the cane.

Grant straightened. He didn't know what she'd said to the lad, but Cullowhee didn't scare easily, and Grant didn't think she had good reason to chastise him. The boy had apparently run into her while they were playing, that was all.

"It was an accident, Danagasta. A mistake," Grant said, his voice low. She seemed forever unapproachable, forever angry, and he was tired of her wallowing in self-pity and fury at the world.

"We teach our children—"

"What do you know about teaching children?" He was amazed at the fury *he* felt. He probably knew as little about teaching children as she did, but he couldn't stand anyone intentionally hurting a child's feelings or being overly critical of a child. His mother had always been overly critical of *him*, and he knew exactly how small Cullowhee was feeling right now. "Don't be a shrew," he advised Danagasta as some of the women behind him began to murmur.

Danagasta's hands went to her hips. "What is a shrew?"

He leaned toward her so she would hear him well. "A vixen, harridan, madcap, siren, witch . . . bitch. A shrew is an evil person. You might be pretty—beautiful, in fact—but you have a cold heart sometimes. Answer the question. What do you know about raising children?"

The small crowd quieted. Even Sequatchee stood still, watching in silence from one edge of the gathering.

"What do you know about *me*?" Danagasta demanded softly, suddenly looking as if she might cry. She wrinkled her brow, pursed her lips, shrank back, folded her arms protectively across her chest, and disappeared around the back of the cabin.

Grant helped Cullowhee gather the scattered cane.

Later that day, the many enchanting colors of the Sun began spreading over distant hills and mountains, and Brother Moon, the *Nunda sunnayehi*, or "The One Dwelling in the Night," peeked down on the land of the Principal People. Wind rose from darkened valleys to the east, stirring like brew in a cauldron and rushing up and over the sides, sweeping through Big Water with icy vengeance. Huge, cottony-looking clouds pressed against distant slopes. The air held a crisp freshness that Danagasta knew foretold the coming of the white powder.

Greatly troubled, she wandered away to bathe; even during winter her people bathed in the great river or in the creeks and streams, breaking the ice when necessary. Cleanliness had always been stressed among the Cherokee.

Shrew.

What were the other words Grant Claiborne had called her? "Vixen," "siren," "mac" . . . "madcap," "harri-con" . . ."don"? She could not remember some of the names, but she knew they were all bad. All names used to describe a not-very-nice person. A mean person.

She pushed through a brake of pale winter cane, swept aside browning reeds, and shivered when the frigid water closed over her calves, thighs, buttocks, and back. She forced herself to dip down into it, to immerse her head, to *hide*, then she rose again and washed herself with her hands.

She remembered the frightened look on Cullowhee's face as she lurked over him, and she covered her face with her open hands. She had been so *mean*. Cornsilk would not be proud of her. She should apologize.

Danagasta immersed herself in the water again. Then somehow—oh somehow!—she came up to face the world again: the Thunderers, the Moon . . . the Wind that rattled the cane.

Shivering, she headed back toward the riverbank where she had left her clothes. She trembled with cold as she dried herself with a woven blanket, then slipped a cotton chemise, as George Dougherty called this type of garment, down over her head, arms, and legs. Feeling somewhat better, she slid her arms into her wolfskin coat and held the garment shut with one hand while carrying the blanket and her buskins—soft animal-hide boots, or moccasins wrapped to the knee—in the other. She walked quietly back to Big Water.

She had built a fire in her cabin before going to bathe. When she entered the lodge, she found Grant Claiborne holding a long-handled pot over the flames. One of the women had apparently given it to him; Danagasta did not recognize it as one of her own.

"I'm warming water," he said to explain.

"Put it on the cooking hearth outside," she suggested.

"That fire went out."

"Build another."

"You'll most graciously tell me where to find the kindling to start one?" he snapped, his eyes flashing at her. "And the wood to feed it?"

She flinched. "I was not trying to be smart. There is a pile of dry sticks and wood inside the smokeshed behind the cabin. I will dress, then show you how to make sparks with stones."

As she moved to a corner, Grant watched her turn her back and push the coat from her shoulders and arms. He ought to leave for a while and give her the privacy he usually tried to give her, but tonight was too damn cold, and he didn't want to walk around town in the wintry air. *I'll turn my back in a few moments,* he thought, watching her.

"I was bathing in the river," she said.

She wore a white chemise, in stark contrast to her ebony hair, and she lifted it to just above her knees. She sat, untying the drawstring that shaped the neckline of the garment.

Grant knew he shouldn't watch. Though he was regarded as something of a hellion by his father and many people in and around Baltimore, he was a gentleman at heart, and he shouldn't watch whatever she was about to do.

"Did you gather more cane while you were at the river?" he inquired in a mockingly nice tone, still not turning his head.

She did not respond for a moment. Then: "No. I—I am sorry that I shouted at you and Cullowhee."

"Apologize to Cullowhee."

She did not reply. She pushed the chemise down over her shoulders, clear to her waist.

At the sight of her smooth back, her shoulder blades clearly outlined despite the only light being the glow from the flames, Grant inhaled deeply, coughing as smoke seared his lungs.

The noise startled her; she grabbed the front of the chemise at her waist and pulled it up in front, glancing over her shoulder at the same moment.

The firelight cast an orange glow on her sleek hair, enhanced her coppery skin . . . danced red in her otherwise dark eyes. She stared at him momentarily, looking apprehensive. Then she turned back to her corner.

She reached for a small pottery bowl and worked with it. He couldn't tell what she was doing, but an instant later she put it down and began rubbing something into her skin.

She began at her stomach and worked her way up, her head tilted down. From the bend of her left elbow and the position of that forearm, he could tell when she reached her breasts. He imagined her fingers working over, under, and around each one, and just knowing what she was doing unnerved him. He *couldn't* look away now.

Heat stung his arm, and he dropped the long-handled pot he had been holding forth above the small fire. During the distraction she presented, he'd gotten a little too close to the flames, and now the ends of some of his forearm hairs were singed and frayed.

"Something is burning?" she asked, her movements pausing.

"Burning? No." He cleared his throat. Then louder: "No." Lord, he wanted her to resume what she had been doing. But this time he intended to put a little distance between himself and the fire, more distance than the pan's handle provided. He again thought about looking away, then, since she didn't seem to care whether or not he did, he decided to be true to his reputation and disregard decency for a few moments longer.

Putting the pot aside, he stretched out onto his left side, watching her.

She smoothed the ointment—or whatever it was—over her arms, between each finger, up and down, around every curve, in every valley, over every hill. Firelight flickered in her hair with each movement of her head. Wind whistled around the cabin eaves outside. The flames popped. She scooped more balm from the bowl, and reached over, then around, struggling to coat her entire back.

Grant moved soundlessly, rising from his place near the fire to approach her from behind. He meant to offer his assistance, but when he neared, she clutched the chemise up over her breasts and froze again.

"What are you doing?" she demanded, as skittish as a virginal debutante.

"I thought I might help."

"No. *Uyo i.*"

"I won't do anything but rub the ointment on your back, Danagasta," he said, noticing the sheen on her left shoulder where she had applied some balm but had not rubbed it in entirely.

She made no effort to flee his nearness. "No. Go back to—"

But his fingertips were already on her shoulder, swirling slowly, spreading the ointment. It was thick, and it smelled of something wild . . . of some animal. The small amount was enough to cover one entire shoulder and blade.

He reached around her for the bowl, glancing at her face as he did. Her lips were parted, her knuckles were nearly as white as the garment they gripped, and she stared down at the bunched lower half of the chemise that covered her thighs and folded legs, refusing to look at him.

Some sort of grease half filled the little earthen bowl. He scooped a small amount out, placed the dish to Danagasta's right, and rubbed his hands together to coat them with the substance. Then he began a slow massage at her shoulders and worked his way down her back.

Her skin shimmered beneath his hands. He felt every vertebra, every rib, the narrowing of her waist and the flare of her hips. He made his way back to her shoulders, working the taut muscles beneath his finger and thumb tips until they relaxed.

Then he withdrew to the fire.

She didn't move for the longest time. She sat very still, holding the chemise to her breasts and staring down at her lap, her back and arms glistening with the oil. Finally she inhaled deeply and put her arms, one at a time, into the chemise sleeves. She pulled the rough material up over her shoulders, then worked the drawstring, gathering the neckline well above her breasts and tying it together. As if to protect her body from him.

She was more discreet about rubbing the balm on her legs, reaching up under the garment instead of raising it.

Grant never took his eyes off her, and he did not fail to notice her trembling hands when she again lifted the pottery bowl.

"I'll get the wood," he said as she pushed the chemise down well over her calves.

She nodded slowly.

He half wanted to tell her that he wanted to give her time alone to compose herself more than he wanted to fetch wood from the smokehouse, that he knew she was disturbed . . . unsettled by his touch. That he knew he should have gone earlier. That he really wasn't Satan in the disguise of a man.

"The word . . . 'shrew,' " she murmured. "It is not kind."

He worked his jaw back and forth. "No, it's not." *But bloody hell if I'll apologize,* he thought, remembering Cullowhee's frightened look.

One of the men had given him a carved pipe and some tobacco. Grant grabbed the items along with the buffalo coat the people had given him, stood, and moved to the cabin doorway, glancing over his shoulder at Danagasta as he swept the flap aside and stepped out into the night.

To keep him fed well, Danagasta spent days making certain she had dried or smoked meat, bread, and parched corn stored on a shelf in her lodge. A hickory-nut drink was kept in a pottery pitcher, covered with a woven cloth and placed in a far corner. The water gourd sat nearby.

The nights became long, filled with Grant's soft snoring and with the talking he did during sleep. He sometimes mumbled things about "Charles" and "Randolph," and once he said something about "bringing wood to build . . . to build" . . . Then his words became whispers, and the whispers became mumbles again. One night Danagasta caught herself listening closely, making out the words "Baltimore" and "clipper." The next night he called for someone named Emily, crying *"No . . . No!"* He wanted to hold Emily. *"One . . . time . . ."* he pleaded, over and over, tossing his head back and forth.

Startled, Danagasta caught herself moving his way. She stopped short, reminding herself who he was and that if she crossed the cabin to the side where he slept, there might be no return. Then he cried out again, and she was unable to help herself. She went to him, dropped to her knees, smoothed the damp hair from his brow, and whispered his name and comforting Cherokee words.

He woke and stared up at her, his eyes glistening in the dying firelight. She would go into his arms if he tugged her down to him. She would comfort him more . . . She would warm him, draw his head to her breast . . . She would lie with him.

He sat up, ran a hand from forehead to chin, and muttered something about needing a drink and a breath of air. Then he went to the water gourd, drank, and soon after left the lodge.

Chapter Eight

DAYS LATER, GRANT AGAIN played the dice game with some of the children, only this time his group gathered on tree stumps and logs on a hill overlooking the river where their mothers were cutting cane. Farther behind the stumps and trees was the forest, and a quarter mile beyond and to the south of it, tucked in a large clearing, was Big Water. Upon leaving the town, Grant had watched several women lift flintlocks to take with them to the river. Though he had wondered why—he'd witnessed no hostile actions from white settlers since his arrival in the Cherokee Nation—he had said nothing.

He shook his basket, then jerked it, sending the dice flying up in the air. They landed back in the basket with a soft *plop!* and he groaned at the number of carved holes staring up at him.

He wrinkled his nose at Cullowhee, who was currently his partner. "No winner."

Shaking his head, Cullowhee plopped down on a log, leaned forward, and lodged an elbow on his knee, his chin in his palm. He scrunched his nose and lips, then sighed. "*Sanela.*"

Grant had played this game enough times with the children that he now recognized the Cherokee words for various numbers. Cullowhee had said "nine" rather regretfully. "Yes . . . nine to our four. Another round?" Grant asked his and Cullowhee's two opponents. He suspected that this particular game had been going on for nearly an hour, and he didn't especially want to continue, but he would if the children wanted to.

"*Uyo i,*" Cullowhee said, glancing up at him with reluctance and amazement. "Six times they have won, Agent-man!"

"You're right," Grant responded hesitantly. He looked back at the others. "No more?"

A number of scowls and mumblings, some English, some Cherokee, rose from the gathering of eight children. Grant had always liked children, but the Indian children were the cutest he'd seen. Some were stark naked beneath a motley array of stitched-together furs. All had large, shimmering dark brown eyes. Some faces were wide and appeared flat while others were rotund. He enjoyed the smiles that frequently flashed his way, the occasional rounds of giggles, the way they called him Agent-man. The boys' hair resembled little black caps, while the girls wore theirs long, with grease and a reddish-clay substance worked in.

"All right," Grant said, unable to resist. The two boys holding baskets and standing before him tossed their dice up the same instant he did.

A musket shot split the air.

The women screamed. The children scattered, some fleeing back between trees, some rushing from the tall covers to their mothers down in the canebrake.

Cullowhee sought inadequate shelter behind some low-lying scrub near Grant. Awe-ani-da, from whom Grant had finally coaxed a charming smile days ago, stumbled, crying, toward Cullowhee. The bright boy had the good sense to pull her down beside him, then she popped her thumb into her mouth.

But the scrub was so thin, only half covered with snow . . . Cullowhee's and Awe-ani-da's dark fur-coverings stood out against the white, making them fine targets for whoever had fired.

Another *crack!* sounded. Grant jerked.

"Outta the river, Injuns!" a white man shouted from the opposite bank. "Outta Tennessee!"

Two figures dressed in fringed and sashed buckskin raced along the opposite bank, pushed a small, hollowed-out boat into the water, and jumped in. They grabbed oars and rowed this way, yelling as they came. "Squaws! Injun squaws!"

Outraged and still stunned by the attack, Grant glanced at Cullowhee and Awe-ani-da, who both stared at him with wide, fear-filled eyes. Something akin to a riled serpent uncoiled and slithered beneath his skin. During his days in Big Water, he'd come to know some of the women well, and he now adored the children. He cursed, watching his friends scramble for safety. Some women lifted their skirts and fled the brake—escaped the white men coming after them. Some sank down and hid in the stalks. Only one woman managed to escape back into the forest, and Grant hoped like hell she would run to Big Water and bring back help.

The men continued rowing and shouting.

Cursing under his breath, Grant jolted into action, racing down the hillside, not knowing what he would do if faced with the hostile whites, but knowing he'd do something. He wouldn't stand and watch while the ruffians harmed innocent women and children.

Ewi, fleeing up the hill past him, thrust him a flintlock. Grant grabbed the weapon, becoming more and more furious as the men closed in. They were damn close now—at least in the middle of the river—and coming this way fast. What exactly they intended to do he didn't know. And he sure as hell wouldn't wait to find out.

One man dropped his oar in the boat, lifted a musket, and fired just above the brake. A shot whizzed by Ewi's head. She yelped, dropped the cane she'd gathered, stumbled, and lay whimpering in the snow.

The flintlock felt cold and awkward in Grant's hands, but he barely noticed. He swooped down, planted his feet near the first stalk, lifted the weapon, aimed, and fired.

Pure luck drove the ball. It hit the man who was still rowing, and he grabbed his arm and fell over.

"Tsotsidanawa! Tsotsidanawa!"

Grant felt something tug at his buffalo coat. He glanced down just as Kayini thrust out another flintlock from the brake. Grant threw the old one down and grabbed hers. Then Kayini hid her head in her hands and shrank back, but not before Grant got a good look at the fright in her eyes.

The skiff neared the stalks.

"Gonna get me a squaw. Make 'er pay in blood for shootin' me!" the injured man whined in agony.

"It's jest a little place, Daniel!" said the other. "Have some red meat first."

The laughter that followed fed Grant's fury. He lifted the fresh weapon to his shoulder, leveled it, and his glare was just as cold as the barrel of the weapon. "You'll float back across that river if you come any closer! I'm deputy agent to the Cherokees," he said, "and you're encroaching on their land."

Both men froze.

"Squaw shot me," Daniel blubbered, holding his arm.

"*Woman,*" Grant corrected icily. "*I* shot you. And I'll do it again unless you turn that boat around."

"This's part of Tennessee," Daniel's companion snapped. "Falls under state—"

"This is the Cherokee Nation, and you've come to harm. If you step out of that boat, I'll have to kill you."

The men studied him, trying to measure whether or not he was serious.

Finally Daniel's friend, eyes narrowed on Grant, laid down his weapon, took up his oar again, and began turning the boat. "Help me, Daniel," he said. "C'mon."

"I can't!" Daniel wailed. "My arm!"

Grand heard Awe-ani-da whimper. A cold breeze swept through the brake, rattling the stalks. Scattered female voices rose here and there in shrill tones, and somewhere in the distance behind Grant, an older child cried. All the women and children were frightened, and his sense of honor was the only thing that stopped him from shooting both men even as the skiff moved back across the rippling water. He moved his hand off the trigger, back toward the butt of the weapon.

Presently, when the boat neared the opposite bank, the low rumble of male voices rose behind him. He turned his head and saw that a number of Big Water's men had appeared and formed a queue along the crest overlooking the bank. Arrows were drawn back in bows, while flintlocks were aimed at the two white men.

"They're going back," he said loudly enough that all the men could hear. If they felt anywhere near as angry and outraged as he, they were giving serious thought to retaliating. And wouldn't that be wonderful? He was sure those two white settlers weren't the only ruffians on the other side of the river. If they brought back others, he might have a war on his hands.

"Tlanuwa! Tlanuwa!" cried a female voice behind the men. "Agent-man, Tlanuwa!

Other women joined in, and soon the word "Tlanuwa" filled the air. Grant turned, not especially wanting to put his back to the two whites, but he was amazed by the chant. Women and children had popped up in the canebrake and all over the hillside and were emerging from the trees. Grant's heart beat fast from the chilling knowledge that if he hadn't been here some of them might have been killed.

"They'll not be back," George Dougherty said, lowering his bow and arrow. His narrowed green eyes shifted to Grant. "They're callin' ye Tlanuwa for the great hawk that swoops down on its prey. 'Tis an honor to be titled so."

Giving Grant a hard look as if he wasn't quite sure he considered him worthy of such a title, George dislodged his arrow and settled his bow on one shoulder. Then he turned and headed back up the hillside, sunlight glinting off his reddish-blond hair. He passed Sequatchee, another man Grant knew didn't trust or like him.

The other men gathered around Grant, breaking into

smiles of relief, uttering English and Cherokee, all words of gratefulness, Grant thought. Little did they know they needn't thank him. He would have gladly killed those men.

Sali hurried down the hillside, crying *"Wado! Wado!"* And Ewi closed in on the right, throwing herself against Grant's feet, mumbling indecipherable words.

Tlanuwa. They had given him a Cherokee name, a much better one than Tsuwa, the one Danagasta had given him the day she had pulled him from the water.

She had raced to the river behind the men. Though there had been only two white settlers, she did not doubt that had they put their hands on even one woman or child, blood would have been spilled; bodies would have been violated. She had seen and known too many horrors as a child not to fear what could have happened.

He had swooped down the hillside with much courage, Kayini said later, once everyone was safely back inside Big Water's palisade. He had shot one man, showing no mercy or fear. Then he had ordered them to go back to their side of the river, had said that if they did not, he would kill them.

"He is a good man, Danagasta," Kayini said in Cherokee, after approaching Danagasta where she stood alone near a chestnut tree.

Her throat and mouth dry, Danagasta turned and sank back against the trunk. "He is here to take our land, Kayini. That is his only reason for becoming friendly with the people. And now . . . now we are in his debt."

"He does not talk of *taking* it. He talks of *trading* it."

Danagasta pursed her lips. "And you believe that? He works for his government, a government that has taken and taken from us! Our people once held lands clear to the Wabash, Ohio, Kanawha, and Cattawba rivers. If you take a huge bowl filled with beans and lift only a handful of those beans, that handful will be the lands we now hold! The rest of the beans . . . what we once held. That is why my father does not like the idea of talking to the white government men. They make promises they do not keep—

and they take our lands! *That* is why he has come, Kayini. Do not fool yourself into thinking anything else."

"No. You are wrong. He told the Tennessee whites that they were on *our* land, in the Cherokee Nation. That they had come to do harm and that he would *kill* them if they did not leave. He meant it. He did not act just so he could talk us into trading."

Danagasta closed her eyes. "He is the enemy. I brought him here. I brought him among our people, and now—"

"No. He is not our enemy," Kayini said. "He is our friend, perhaps our only friend in the white man's government. I know that in my heart. I would not lie to you. I tell the truth about what happened. Ask any of the other women. I do not like the way you blame Sequatchee for showing Losi where he could get whiskey, but—"

"He did show him," Danagasta snapped, flashing a heated look at Kayini.

"I am your friend and I do not lie," Kayini continued, undaunted, as if she had not heard Danagasta's last words.

Danagasta did not respond, but Kayini was right—she did not lie, and so her words put doubt in Danagasta's mind, doubt Danagasta wished she could rip out. She did not want to trust Grant. He worked for the white man's government, therefore no Cherokee could afford to trust him.

When night descended on the mountains and valleys, Danagasta noticed that Grant was not about, not with the women gathered around a large fire in the center of the town where they sat grinding corn and making bread, and not with the group of men gathered around another fire some ten cabins away. She did not know where he was.

She went to the fenced area outside the palisade and milked a cow, thinking she would make butter, something Tsatsi had shown her people how to do. "White people like to smear it on bread," he had said. She liked the taste of it, but she had not made any in at least two seasons.

When she returned to her lodge, she draped a woven cloth over the ewer of milk she had collected from the cow, and left the ewer sitting near one wall of the lodge. Later she would skim the cream from the milk.

She went outside and sat on a stool positioned near the cabin door, smashing hickory nuts by the light of a greased torch lodged in a hollow stump to her left. The cold was severe this night, but her work warmed her. She liked watching Brother Moon peek from between distant hills, moving silently and bewitchingly across the deepening sky.

She would not make her nightly excursion to the river. The episode with the settlers had scared her more than she liked to admit. Would they make terrible trouble again? She had heard of trouble with whites settled near other Cherokee towns and villages, but for some time the people of Big Water had been left alone. Painfully she recalled the fires of long ago, the shouts and shots, the scrambles through the forest . . . She remembered being reunited with her people, then returning to Big Water, thinking she would be safe again within the lodge Hanging Basket had built for Cornsilk. Only it no longer stood . . . Where it had been, there was a pile of ash—and her mother was dead, killed by a white man's musket ball.

Would the whites come again with their fires? Would they attack and kill until every Cherokee was dead?

Please . . . no. Danagasta's hands stilled as she glanced off in the distance and closed her eyes, whispering passionately, "*Asga-Ya-Galun-lati!* Protect my people!" She did not want to see any more lying dead, as she had seen her mother that horrible day.

She worked more, trying to put fears from her mind. Soon she took her pestle and mortar and went inside her lodge, finding it cold. She built a fire, then repeatedly poured water from the gourd into her cupped hands and washed herself.

She dried her body, and reached for the little bowl containing the bear grease she applied daily to help keep her warm. Kneeling beside the fire, she looked down into the dish, remembering the evening Grant had applied the grease to her back.

Tlanuwa. The people loved him, trusted him. *She* had loved his touch.

His fingers had felt warm and comforting, swirling on

her shoulders, sliding slowly down her spine, pausing at the flare of her hips, then slipping up her back. His touch had felt achingly sweet. Her only defense had been the chemise held over her breasts. The thought that he could have tugged it away with one finger because she had felt so weak made her breath catch in her throat.

He *was* a white government man, and she had best remember that since no one else in Big Water did anymore.

She applied the grease, then pulled the chemise down over her body. After skimming the cream from the milk, she placed the ewer outside, knowing the cold would keep the contents from souring. Then she returned inside, wrapped herself in several wolfskins, lay beside the fire, and tried to sleep.

She could not.

She wondered where Grant was. She listened for his soft snoring. She listened for his voice, too, as she always did now. She had begun listening more intently of late, wondering what had happened to the woman called Emily whom he spoke about in his sleep. Something tragic and unfair? Who were the Charles and the Randolph he mentioned? And what would they build with the wood he talked about?

"Danagasta," called a soft voice from just beyond the deerskin covering the doorway.

She sat up. "Tsatsi?"

"Vv."

"Come in," she said in Cherokee. A pleasant surprise, Tsatsi visiting her.

The flap was pushed aside, and the light-haired Tsatsi entered the cabin, his gaze resting fondly on her as it often did.

She smiled. "Come. Sit by the fire."

He approached, his yellow hair glowing reddish-orange. Taking a place beside her, he pulled his legs in and folded them, then he glanced over at her and spoke in his adopted language: "He treats you well, Danagasta?"

"We are only together at night," she answered reluctantly, knowing he referred to Grant.

A brief pause ensued. George rubbed his jaw. "And at night?"

"He treats me well." She was thinking again of Grant—Tlanuwa—rubbing the bear grease on her back, of his hands moving expertly, fingers massaging slowly . . . She was scarcely aware that her breath quickened.

"You have lain with him?"

Her eyes flashed to the Scotch-Irishman's rough features. "No." But oh, how she had wanted to lie with the deputy agent! And how ashamed she was!

Tsatsi's gaze shifted to the fire, where it hardened. "Ye've wanted to, lass?" he asked, changing languages, obviously disturbed.

"I am often lonely," she admitted hesitantly. "In the way of a woman needing a man. I am . . . not proud. I do not want to forget my husband, and I do not want to forget the fact that Grant Claiborne is here to take our land."

"Ye need another husband. Sequatchee . . . He's wantin' to take care o' ye."

"No. I do well alone."

He turned to her again. "Do ye?"

"Vv."

"If ye want, I'll ask yer da's permission to build Grant Claiborne a lodge. One where the agents an' other guests to the town cin stay."

She considered that. If Grant did not leave her cabin soon, she *would* lie with him. Her need was growing. She could no longer deny the attraction between them, not even to herself. "Will you?" she said, her voice a near whisper. If Grant were gone she would not be fighting her need. She would not be waiting, listening for him to enter the cabin. She would not lie awake, straining to hear the words he mumbled during sleep.

"Aye. Consider a husband, Danagasta. If na Sequatchee, then me," Tsatsi said softly.

Her gaze whipped to his. George's Cherokee wife had gone to the Nightland at least four winters ago, but Danagasta had not realized that he thought of marrying *her*. "Tsatsi, you—"

The deerskin covering was swept aside again, and in

walked Grant, his gaze darting between her and George. "I didn't mean to interrupt."

"Ye're na interruptin'," Tsatsi responded. The glitter in his eyes told Danagasta that he was annoyed, that he felt Grant's entrance *was* an interruption. It was, but one for which she was thankful. She could not bring herself to marry George. She could never think of him as a husband, only as a friend.

"I came for my pipe," the deputy agent said, moving across the cabin. He hunched near a wolfhide, unfolded it, and rummaged through a pile of belongings, mostly trinkets the women and children had given him. A moment later, he straightened, his pipe in one hand. "I'll be in Hanging Basket's cabin," he said, looking straight at Danagasta.

She nodded.

"I'll go with ye," Tsatsi said, standing. He did not bother to look at Danagasta again; he headed toward the doorway, leaving her with his gentle suggestion.

Later, Danagasta lay awake, again listening for Grant's soft snoring and for his voice. These past days, she had watched him with the boys as he played the basket-dice game and a game called hoop-and-pole, flashing his crooked grin even when the children defeated him. Only yesterday, he had twirled Awe-ani-da until she giggled and squealed. Danagasta had fought a smile at the sight and sound of such delight, then she had frowned. He was very good with the children. Better than she wished him to be.

Wind whistled around the cabin roof. The deerskin over the doorway flapped. Danagasta tensed, thinking the hide would be swept aside and he would enter.

It fluttered, then stilled.

She shut her eyes, trying to force sleep.

She smelled him. The thick, heavy, distinct scent of the buffalo coat he wore, and his own musky scent beneath—the heady essence of man. She had always had keen senses, sharp enough to smell out a deer or wolf or bear. Her ability had never annoyed her. This night, it did.

She soon rose, pulled on and laced her warm buskins, then slipped out of the lodge.

Big Water was dark but for the torches outside her father's lodge and the one still lit outside hers. She wondered if she had unconsciously left it to guide Grant's way. She scowled, thinking she should go back inside and try again to sleep.

Instead she wandered the way of Hanging Basket's cabin.

She paused just outside the buffalo hide hanging over his doorway, listening to her father's laughter that came from within. Then she heard Grant's voice talking about a ship . . . him being a young boy . . . off the coast of a place called England . . . pouring whale oil on the deck . . . watching the crew scramble about, lose their footing, fall on their backsides. There was more laughter, even Tsatsi's deep chuckle this time.

Sequatchee asked in his contrary way what that had to do with Grant's appointment as deputy agent. "Two days ago, a report came from Long Town that some whites came during the night, killed the village dogs and left them hanging in the trees. There have been reports of stolen cattle and horses, of settlers who shout foul words across the river. What will be done about these hostile whites?"

"I'll suggest that Meigs ask for troops to be sent to control them," Grant said without delay. "The attack I witnessed was unprovoked. The settlers are the aggressors." Hanging Basket mumbled an agreement.

Danagasta wondered how long the men would talk and when Grant would return to her cabin. She shivered, unable to remember the last time she had felt so cold. Her last thought before she turned away was that Tlanuwa sounded so sincere . . .

Chapter Nine

THE FOLLOWING AFTERNOON, DANAGASTA sat on a stump near a small fire behind her lodge and forced herself to work moist clay into a pot. She had not worked with clay since the day before Losi's death. He had sneaked up from behind, slipped his arms around her, and put his hands over hers, helping her mold a bowl while they talked and laughed.

She felt so alone, doing this again. She should push the clay aside, throw it. But she would not. She could not go on anymore feeling so twisted inside. She had loved her husband, but she wanted to smile and be happy again, not spend season after season being a shrew.

Someone touched her shoulder. She needed an embrace, a tender touch . . . She turned, seeking warmth . . . and went into a pair of waiting arms.

Grant held Danagasta against his chest, stroking her sleek hair, enclosing her in his arms, running his hands up and down her back. What the hell—? She sighed against his chest, clinging to him, smelling like the hickory wood that crackled in her fire. He placed an open hand upon her cheek to hold her head against him, and he found the skin there soft and pliant, silky from the balm she worked into it most every evening after she bathed in the river.

He knew she didn't want him among her people because of who he was. But this morning she had calmly entered Hanging Basket's cabin where Grant was eating roasted venison and talking with her father, George Dougherty, and Sequatchee, and she had quietly, *humbly*, thanked him for saving the women and children.

Another sigh went through Danagasta. Grant kissed the top of her head, wondering what was going on inside of it. He had approached her from behind, hunching down to where she sat on the stump, wanting to have a closer look at what she was molding. She'd turned and tossed herself at him so quickly he hadn't had a chance to say anything. Then her arms had slid inside his coat and around his waist, and she had leaned against him.

"Danagasta," he whispered against her hair. "Is something wrong?"

Her breath caught. Slowly her hands slid from his back around to his stomach, then splayed across his chest. Withdrawing, she gazed up at him with her almond-shaped eyes, eyes as dark and mysterious, as distant and strange, as the forest at night. Her hands slid a little lower, a little lower, then side to side across his belly, then back up to his chest.

What was she doing? Caressing embers, fanning sparks that might burst into flames . . . Then she would run again, as she had that night in the field when he had pulled her into the dancing and kissed her.

"Stop," he ordered, low and gruff, grabbing for her hands. "Stop, Danagasta, before I take you inside and ravish you." Her brow wrinkled as if she didn't quite understand. He leaned forward. "Ravish you . . . make love to you."

Her eyes flared, but she made no effort to withdraw more.

"Do you want me to?"

Her breath quickened. So did his. He thought she might

say yes. But she said "no" very quietly, then turned back to her clay.

Working his jaw back and forth, Grant stared at her back for a few moments, then stood and walked away. It didn't matter that she had said no. He was better off. She was a distraction he didn't need, and he had to keep his mind on what he had come to the Indian Nation to do.

That night, Danagasta lay awake again, feeling more tense than ever, wondering if and when he would come to the lodge, knowing she could not continue like this. She wondered if Tsatsi had asked her father if they could build a visitors' lodge, and if Grant could move there. Surely Hanging Basket would feel she had been punished long enough, that she had provided food, water, and shelter long enough for the man she had pulled from the river and taken captive. She had not wandered off to search the Tennessee for white whiskey men since the day she had brought Grant to Big Water, and she would not do so again.

By the dim reddish-orange light of her fire, she huddled deep within her wolf hides. But soon she rose and walked to the deerskin flap, pushed it aside, and wandered outside. This night she had not bothered to remove her buskins. She would do anything to warm herself. Anything.

Few torches glowed near cabins. Big Water was quiet. *Where is Grant?* she wondered. *With my father again?* She walked toward Hanging Basket's cabin and was not far from it when Sequatchee stepped into her path, his eyes glowing.

"You do not rest well lately, Danagasta," he said in Cherokee. "I sometimes follow your prints between your cabin and your father's."

"You are right, I do not rest well," she responded. "I worry about my father. He is getting old."

He studied her, seeming to know that she lied to him. She averted her gaze, looking at the ground instead of at him. "And when your father dies, who will be your comfort then? It is natural for a woman to rely on her husband's brother if something happens to her husband. By old ways, I should—"

"I rely on no one."

He sighed. She glanced up at him, finding his expression unreadable in the dark shadows. "You sometimes make me feel unlike a man, Danagasta."

"I do not want you to feel you must marry me."

"It is our way," he said, stepping closer. She felt his warmth. "Marrying me would be right and good. I will hunt for you, build you another lodge. I will live for you." He lifted a hand to caress her cheek. The touch was comforting, so she leaned into it, knowing she should not, knowing Kayini would be heartbroken. But she was so cold and lonely, she could not help herself.

She smelled the rich, sweet aroma of tobacco, and at first she thought the smell was in Sequatchee's bearskin. But he dropped his flintlock, and his arms came around her, clutching her to him. As he leaned down, meaning to kiss her, she smelled something more—the thick, heady scent of buffalo hide, wafting on the cold night air.

She tore away from her brother-in-law and glanced around, feeling a surge of heat, wondering if she was, perhaps, smelling the hide that hung in the doorway of her father's cabin. But no . . . that was not so. Sensing another presence, she whispered, "Tlanuwa."

Sequatchee stepped up beside her. "Danagasta . . .?"

A tall figure emerged from around the far corner of her father's cabin. The figure did not need to speak, did not need to step into an area where Brother Moon shone brightly. Danagasta knew the person's identity by his smell and by the way he carried himself, slow and easy.

"A fine evening for a moonlit rendezvous," Grant said, his voice raspy and strained.

Danagasta felt Sequatchee stiffen. "Go back to your business, *yun wunega*," he growled.

Tlanuwa laughed under his breath. The sound, so utterly masculine and pleasantly disturbing, sent a ripple through Danagasta, a want so fierce it was agony—a passion she had been searching for and had not found with Sequatchee. A sweet, healing passion she desperately needed.

Asga-Ya-Galun-lati, give me strength against this man!

she thought—pleaded—desperately. She had none. Or what little she had was being quickly destroyed by her body's need. She could not even remember Sequatchee's smell, was not aware of it. But *sge*! She smelled the buffaloskin! She remembered Grant's heady, musky smell. It was almost like the forest after a rain: pleasantly pungent.

"I don't think you want to make me feel unwelcome, Sequatchee," Grant warned in a low tone.

Sequatchee's glare could be felt, even if it could not be seen. The night was cold, but the space between Sequatchee and Grant sparked with tension that might quickly develop into more. Danagasta realized that both men were jealous. But how strange that Grant's jealousy made her feel comforted somehow, satisfied that he had not enjoyed his time away from her lodge.

"He was not trying to make you feel unwelcome," she told Grant as she clutched her coat above her breasts. "Please . . . both of you, go back to your cabins . . . to the place you plan to sleep this night." She watched the glitter of Grant's eyes.

"You were in Chief Hanging Basket's cabin," Sequatchee said to Grant. "Return there."

"I was only visiting." Grant's response was just as cold. He stepped forward, until The One Dwelling in the Night shone brightly down upon him, until he was no longer a shadow. Then he paused to look hard and long at Danagasta.

His gaze found its way into her soul. She felt breathless, suddenly wondering if he knew her every secret, if he knew her every thought and need. She knew he guessed the truth: that she had come looking for him, that if they walked back to her lodge and he invited her into the circle of his arms, she would go this time without question or objection.

"Do you even know what you want, Danagasta?" he growled. "Damn you!"

Sequatchee lurched forward. Danagasta had the sense to grab his arm and whisper his name. She did not understand Grant's anger. Was he curious because she had withdrawn from him after he had comforted her when she turned from molding the pot? She had not realized who he was, and he had not seemed angry when she pulled away.

"Do not protect him!" Sequatchee raged. "You are driving me mad!" He turned and stalked off, disappearing into the deep shadows before she could speak another word.

She turned, thinking Grant was still nearby. But he had gone, too, taking his scents with him, leaving her standing cold and alone in the night.

She returned to the cabin, not finding him there.

She lay down, but did not sleep.

Cursing himself, Grant withdrew into the shadows behind Hanging Basket's lodge. He shivered despite his warm coat, and cringed when he thought of how like a jealous schoolboy he had acted. All because Hanging Basket had told him earlier this evening that Danagasta wanted him gone from her lodge.

"I had hoped that she would realize . . ." Hanging Basket had begun, but he'd waved away the rest of the sentence. He had talked to George Dougherty earlier, he said. Danagasta had spoken to Tsatsi and pleaded . . . George had made him see that Danagasta was miserable, that she had withdrawn further and further from the people, even from Kayini, her closest friend, and that she would feel better once Grant was removed from her lodge.

Grant had listened in silence, but a slow anger had crept over him. How many times had he tried to help her? He hadn't told her father that she had cut him . . . He'd drawn her into the dancing that one evening, knowing she wouldn't participate unless he did. He had held her after she'd turned from molding her pot . . .

He wanted her, but she apparently didn't want him, at least not as much as he had let himself believe that she did. The woman was driving *him* mad, too. Coming into his arms, then pulling away. Going into Sequatchee's arms, then giving *him* a look of longing that had sent shards of heat straight to his groin. He had told himself again and again that she was a distraction he couldn't afford. Still, he wanted her.

He had been walking and smoking when he'd come upon her and Sequatchee together, and he couldn't deny that he had wanted to rush forward and yank her away from the man. How many times had he wanted her and either resisted the urge to seduce her or been turned away? To find her in another man's arms . . . Seeing her with Sequatchee had made him angry and jealous. Damn the woman, playing with his mind and body!

So she wanted him out of her cabin, did she? Well, fine . . . He'd really act like a temperamental schoolboy. He'd ask to sleep in Hanging Basket's lodge until George Dougherty, he, and some of the other men built the "visitor's" cabin. Danagasta could be as alone as she wanted to be. He would do just fine without her. He would do *better* without her.

Three afternoons later, Danagasta observed Grant's naming ceremony from the cover of trees on the hillside. She watched the old turbaned priest sprinkle him with river water, and she smiled to herself, wondering if Grant had talked his way out of being immersed. He was very good at talking his way out of and into certain things—and hearts. She whispered his Cherokee name as the people chanted it—"Tlanuwa, Tlanuwa!"—and when the priest nodded, indicating the ceremony was finished, she watched the men, women, and children surge forward to speak their approval. She smiled as Tlanuwa reached down, scooped little Awe-ani-da into her arms, and embraced the girl. Innocent and serene, the child turned her head and laid a pudgy cheek upon his breast as his hand stroked her back. Danagasta forced herself to look away, feeling as if a hand squeezed her heart.

The day after seeing her with Sequatchee, he had come to the cabin to gather his things; he would be staying with her father for a time, he had mumbled. And that same day, he and others had started building the new lodge. With many men working on it, the cabin would be finished soon. Then Grant could move in.

Danagasta withdrew farther back into the trees, again

telling herself that if he stayed in another lodge, she would feel better.

But in her heart she no longer believed that. In her heart she knew—and feared—the truth. The last two nights had been long and incredibly lonely, and she wanted him to stay with her.

The following day, as the light of Grandmother Sun dimmed, Danagasta sat in her cabin. Her bleeding time had come again. If her husband were still here or if Grant were still living in her lodge, she would go off to the menstrual hut to spend these days. She was glad she could stay in her own cabin, where everything was more familiar, where she could be more comfortable.

She dipped water from a gourd, poured it into a bowl, and dropped a softened piece of buckskin into the water to wet it. She cleaned herself with the piece of hide, thinking that when she was finished here she would brew a soothing tea from herbs she had gathered and dried last summer.

A knock sounded from outside the lodge.

She jerked. "Go away. Unclean," she said in Cherokee.

"Danagasta. It's Grant. I left a blanket Sali gave me."

She knew about the blanket. It smelled of him, so she had slept with it last night, and she did not want to give it up just yet. She answered in English: "I will wash it and bring it . . . soon."

He was silent. The fire popped.

"Could I get it now?" he asked. "I didn't realize it was missing until Cullowhee asked—"

"No, I will wash it. Soon."

"*I'll* wash it. Why does it need—"

"*Tla no!* It cannot be touched!"

"Are you well?" he asked impatiently.

A twinge of pain cramped her belly, and she could not help a slight groan. The flap in the doorway gaped open, and to Danagasta's horror, Grant dipped his head and entered the cabin.

"Tla no!" she whispered, dropping the piece of buckskin and shrinking back into a corner. She grabbed a nearby wolf hide and pulled it up over her legs, clear to

her waist. He was a crazy person, coming in here during this time!

"Danagasta," he said, his eyes narrowed. "Are you ill?"

"Go away, go away!" was all she could say as she stared at him. Not only was she unclean, but also she did not want him seeing her this way. "Go!" she gasped. *"Uyo i! Agehya!"*

He walked toward her, his head tilted to one side as he regarded her. "If you're ill, let me help you. Let someone help you. Bravery is a great thing, Danagasta, but there's nothing wrong with admitting that you need help."

Another ache seized her, and she grimaced. He took two more steps, nearing her fire. He could not touch things . . . No! he could not.

He walked around the fire, nearing the gourd, the cup in which she had poured water, and the softened piece of skin with which she had washed. It was now bright red in places. He stared down at it, and she looked away. He should not know this! He should not be here!

"Tla no . . . Go away!"

"You're bleeding," he said stubbornly. Closing the distance between them, he knelt at her side.

This was a horrible thing. He should go! His business would not do well! Nothing he touched would prosper! But that was what she wanted, wasn't it? For him to fail.

"Did you cut yourself? Where are you bleeding, Danagasta? I'll take you to the healer."

"Bleeding time! No cut. *Sge!* Go or you will be unclean. Tlanuwa . . ." she whispered, looking down at his hand touching the wolf hide—which touched her. "You already are."

She gripped the skin. He pushed it aside, though she grappled for it and shrank farther back into the corner. He did not know what he was doing, and no man, *no one,* had ever come to her like this during her time. She was so shocked, she could not utter many of the words flitting through her head. The women were supposed to be alone, to themselves. Even in the menstrual hut they stayed in their own areas. This was not a good time. Afterward she would wash all her clothes and belongings, everything in her cabin.

He touched her leg, and his hand stilled when his fingers met dampness. She whimpered. He pulled his hand away, looking at it, and released a long breath. "Danagasta, I'm going to get the healer."

"No!" she cried. She could not let him bring the healer or possibly some of the townspeople. She would be humiliated, more than she already was, and they would be as horrified as she.

He started to stand and turn away. She grabbed his arm, pleading with her eyes. "If you're hurt, you need help," he said, not understanding.

"No—I am not hurt! I will . . . explain. I will try. I—am—female. Bleeding . . . Woman . . . *Agehya.*" She released his arm, shrank back again, and looked away, feeling embarrassed. "Every moon . . . I do not have to go to the women's hut this time. You moved. I thought I could be alone."

She felt his intense stare. The flames leaped, flickering shadows about the cabin. Finally he sat back on his heels and exhaled heavily.

"Oh. Danagasta, it's . . . Damn! I feel like a fool." Shaking his head, he straightened her wolfskin, as if to restore some of her dignity. Then he ran a hand from forehead to chin the way she had seen him do many times when something disturbed him. "That's what you were doing. I'm sorry. I'll get your water. Your cloth—"

She did not look directly at him, though his obvious embarrassment and compassion touched her. Instead she watched him from beneath her lashes. "You are unclean. Surely you have seen the women go off alone! Yet you came here, touched my things! Touched me. Blood . . . on your fingers. Go to the river and wash. Wash your clothes. Wash long!"

"That water's freezing!" he objected. "It was bad enough having it sprinkled on me."

She forced herself to look at him, needing to let him know the seriousness of this. "Heat some. Wash," she ordered. "The people will blame you if harm comes to them or to the town—if they learn you have been here during this time." She shook her head. "I do not know why I protect you. Go now."

Her gaze held his a bit longer, then he nodded, withdrew, and finally hurried from the cabin.

Danagasta leaned back against the corner, hoping he would do as she had told him.

Her time ended days later.

She wondered how he was faring in his own lodge. The man had not even known how to build a fire when he had come to live in her cabin. She wondered if he was warm, if he was eating well, if he had all the provisions he needed. She wondered if he had washed. If not, and if some unfortunate thing befell him, she would blame herself. She had had such a difficult time making him understand that he should not be near or touch a woman during her time.

Gathering courage, she decided to go see him.

She carried a basket of fry bread and a small pottery bowl filled with *kana talu hi*—hominy cooked with walnut kernels. If he liked it, she would bring more. In a long-handled pouch draped across her breasts, she carried dried venison and pumpkin seeds. She also brought beaverskin; if he wanted, she would make him moccasins to warm his feet. Smoked over a fire, they would warm him better than his boots.

His new lodge was located at the far end of the same row in which hers stood. She approached it, nodding at other women who worked outside. But only Sali and Kayini returned her greetings.

She had become an angry person, a "shrew" to many. Losi's death and the miscarriage of her child . . . her mind had been very troubled these past seasons. She had been so angry, so *blind* with bitterness that she had not realized how she had set herself apart from her own people, how they did not seem to know her anymore—or want to know her.

She approached Cullowhee and a group of older children where they played in the path between cabins, gathering snow and throwing it at each other. Upon seeing Danagasta, they paused and sobered. She smiled weakly, but they turned and walked away, as if to escape her, as if not finding her smile genuine. She started to call an apology to Cullowhee for the way she had shouted at him about the broken cane, then she closed her mouth because he was nearly running. She feared she had waited too long to apologize.

She neared the end of the row and saw that, beyond the line, some men were throwing spears, then measuring off the distances. Only one man of the six dared a look her way—Catolster, with whom she had pleaded to tell her Losi was not dead. He inclined his head and continued watching her. A breeze shuddered the branches of trees to her right and blew snow in her face. Cold crept beneath her coat, and she shivered, knowing her trembling was not so much from the cold around her as the cold inside of her.

At last she reached Grant's cabin.

They had built a door in his rectangular lodge. She knocked on it as he had knocked near her deerskin covering. Then a thought occurred to her, and she almost shrank away: What if people were with him? Some townspeople who had become his friends? She would most surely not be welcome. She did not want more severe looks and rejection.

She would go away now, leave—avoid them. She would gather her things and go off into the mountains to live alone. And there she would die alone.

Turning, she took the first step. Behind her, the door creaked open. "Danagasta?"

She froze, looking down at her basket of split cane woven in a checkerwork pattern; it peeked from beneath her coat. She had placed a piece of softened skin over the bread and tucked it in at the edges to protect the food from snow. The bowl containing hominy and walnut kernels sat in the crook of one arm, resting on the draped beaverskin. She had tried to creep away, but she felt Grant's gaze on her back and knew she could not escape.

She started to turn back, but he walked around to face her. There did not seem to be anyone with him.

"Hello," he said softly. "*Osiyo.*"

Her lashes shot up; he had learned the word for greeting someone! She was pleased, but she had the brief thought that he had certainly not learned it from her. She suddenly wished she had been the one to teach him the word.

His appearance was startling. His face and form were the same: Chestnut hair spilled over his forehead. Eyes as blue as the clear Skyland watched her. Whiskers peppered his jaw—so firm and proud—and when his head tipped, his nose tilted up in a way that could be considered arrogant. He was clearly a white man. But in dress right now, he looked very much Cherokee.

He wore the skin of the brave mountain lion, cut and stitched so that it hung to mid-thigh, and it was belted by a broad strip of tasseled brown and yellow cloth. Beneath the shirt he wore buckskin leggings. She knew the dress of the Cherokee men, so she knew that over the leggings, he doubtless wore a breechclout consisting of two aprons, one in the front and one in the back, both drawn up between the legs and tied together with a thong. The leggings and the breechclout would be held up by a narrow belt. Beaverskin moccasins, wrapped to his knees, sheltered his feet and calves.

"*Osiyo,*" she said in return, not wanting to stare at him but unable to help herself. She felt startled, yes, but also embarrassed by the thought of the skins tossed over her arm, and what she had wanted to do with them. She stared at the more than adequate buskins covering his feet and calves, and her eyes filled with tears.

She wanted to throw everything she carried at his feet and run away. It had taken so much courage for her to come here. Yet she found that he did not need her to make coverings for his feet and legs. He was very well dressed. Doubtless the townspeople were making certain he was very well fed, too. She should leave before he ordered her to leave, and with good reason—she had never been nice to him.

Grant had seen a lot of emotions in Danagasta since meeting her. He'd seen anger, rage, sorrow, and most recently, horror and embarrassment. But he'd never seen her look regretful and startled, so much so that she seemed about to bolt.

He hadn't seen her since the day he'd gone to her cabin to fetch the blanket. What an awkward episode that had been. He had left feeling like an idiot, as if he couldn't do anything right where she was concerned, so he had elected to stay clear of her lodge. He'd bathed in the icy river just the way he had promised her he would. (He must be mad!) He'd even scrubbed his clothes. When the chief had needled out of him why he was washing the articles, Hanging Basket had had the women make him the ones he now wore.

Grant felt he had done a fine job of staying away from Danagasta. But now, here she was, looking for all the world as though she needed a friend. Just one. Just someone to care, even if only for a short time. He'd always had one hell of a time turning his back on her, no matter how shrewish she could be.

Upon opening the door and seeing her glossy hair spilling over the gray fur, he had felt a surge of longing. What was she doing anyway, knocking on his cabin door, then trying to run off? Why had she come in the first place?

He was truly glad to see her, bulky as she looked in her coat. She hid things beneath the wolfskin, he thought. And she looked sad, more so than usual.

He touched her jaw, gently urging her head up, and his eyes narrowed as his hand slid up to brush a tear from her cheek. "Danagasta, what is it?" Pushing a hand beneath her hair to touch the back of her neck, he drew her head to his chest.

Danagasta did not hesitate. Despite the bowl and the basket between them, she turned her head and laid it upon his breast. She thought of him holding Awe-ani-da after his naming ceremony, and she knew why the girl had shut her eyes and looked content. Because he was *warmth.* The warmth she needed.

"Let's go inside," he suggested, and she turned with him, letting him lead her into his new home.

Chapter Ten

A FIRE BLAZED IN the center of his lodge. Hides hung over the three windows. Danagasta spotted at least three stools in various locations, one near an array of domestic utensils—earthen pans, mugs, pots, wooden dishes, and buffalo-horn spoons—another near a hemp carpet elaborately painted with a figure and laid over cane mats on the ground, and yet another near a wide bed at the back of the cabin. She had never slept on a bed, but she knew Tsatsi and some of the others did, and if she ever decided to sleep on one, she would certainly choose one like Grant's.

The bed stood on timbers that lifted it to slightly less than Cullowhee's height, but the boards continued up until they were topped by an overhang of stitched-together buffalo hides, tossed up like a flap. Another hide covered the "tick" that, she assumed based on other ticks she had seen, was made of cane splints.

"You like it?" he asked from behind her.

"It looks warm," she said, managing a smile.

He neared her back, reached around her shoulders, and lifted her covering up and off. She stood very still, enjoying his closeness, wanting to sway back against him. He stepped around her, crossed to the bed, and her coat joined his on the tick.

Her eyes widened.

Suddenly she realized how warm the lodge was, how inviting the bed looked, that their coverings were now joined . . . She remembered that he had helped build this cabin, and that he had invited her in. All that remained was an exchange of food, from one to the other, and a joining of bodies. Words were not always necessary to bind a woman and a man.

Why had she not thought of this before, during the days he had spent in her cabin? Her mind had been on the whiskey business, on Losi and her lost child, and on the land. Why had she not thought of it when she had thought of lying with him? Because more was involved in a wedding than just mating.

"Do you know Ewi?" she asked.

Grant approached, rubbing one side of his jaw. "Ewi . . . She made the carpet."

"*Sge*," Danagasta said breathlessly. "To give such a fine gift, she must like you very much."

"She seems to—yes." Smiling, he shook his head. "Danagasta, you always confuse me."

"I . . . Ewi is my aunt." *She approves of you.*

Danagasta turned toward a chest made of clapboard bound to crossbars with rawhide. She placed her bowl and basket there, thinking she should lift them, take her coat from his, and flee his lodge.

"You seem well," he ventured, almost cautiously. "You're feeling better?"

She turned, sneaked a glance at him, then quickly looked down at her clasped hands. "Better . . . yes. You washed?"

"I *immersed* myself in that cold river."

His response was so emphatic, she could not help but laugh just a little. Being unclean was *not* something to laugh about, but he sounded so indignant. She was still somewhat embarrassed that he had come to her cabin during her bleeding time, and she would not hold his gaze.

But his words, and the image of him *immersing* himself in the frigid river, was amusing. "Tsuwa," she murmured, watching him from beneath her lashes. "Water dog."

Folding his arms, he gave her a stern look. "Oh, is that what that name means?"

She nodded, smiling. "Yes. Tlanuwa is more favorable."

"I think so." He quieted, and for long moments there was awkward silence. Then he spoke again, and there was tenderness in his soft tone. "Your laughter is a good sound, one I've not heard. Even if it's at my expense."

She was not sure what that meant—"at his expense"—but he seemed amused, too, so she flashed him another smile, a longer one this time. He continued watching her, his arms folded, his head tipped, hair tumbling over his brow, his clear blue eyes assessing her. Admiring her, she thought.

But perhaps she was wrong.

"I'd brave that frigid river again if you'd give me another smile like that," he murmured.

Her eyes widened. She now regarded him openly, wanting to throw herself into his arms and thank him. For her, for another of her smiles, he would brave the cold river again?

She started for the bed, meaning to collect her coat and be gone. She could not stay. If she stayed, she would surely find her way into his arms and become his wife.

"What did you bring?" he asked.

She hesitated, then turned back.

"What's on your arm, Danagasta? What's in the bowl and basket?"

She looked down at the beaver hide draped over her arm. She wore a yellow deerskin dress this day, and its long sleeve extended past the rough edge of the beaverskin and ended just beyond her wrist.

"It . . . it was for moccasins," she said softly. "I brought sinew to stitch . . . It does not matter. You have some. Fine ones. Bread in the basket. Hominy in the bowl," she said, motioning toward the chest. She touched the strap of the pouch that cut at an angle between her breasts, then one hand slid to the wide pouch. "Venison and pumpkin seeds . . . But they have given you everything. There is nothing more you need, Tlanuwa. I will take my things and be gone."

She spun away, walked to the bed, and lifted her coat, parting it from his. Turning, she collided with him.

He tugged the coat from her hands, coaxing her: "Stay, Danagasta. Stay, I need much more than food."

She shut her eyes, smelling him. His scent was like the wild tobacco today, fresh like the forest, sweet like spring. If she had not just come from outside, had not just walked through the snow, tasted its iciness and felt its bite, she might believe the warm season was upon them.

She felt the fur brush her arm as he swept her coat around and tossed it back on top of his. Her jaw soon rested in his large hands, and he tipped her face to his and stared down into her eyes. "I'm glad you've come. I want you to stay. I was about to go out. I was playing Cullowhee's chess game by myself—a ridiculous thing to do—and feeling a bit lonely."

"Chess game?" she mumbled.

He nodded. "I put it away under the bed. I'll show it to you. One of the Englishmen carved it for him."

"A white man's game?"

"Yes. But don't turn your nose up."

She wrinkled her brow, unsure what he meant.

"Don't frown at it before you've played it."

"I was not frowning. I did not mean to 'turn my nose up.' "

Her hands felt cold. He seemed to sense even that. His hands slipped down to hers, caressing, enveloping them in their heat. He led her to sit with him near the fire.

He lifted the pouch from her waist, then over her arm and head, his eyes never leaving hers as he did. He unwrapped the leather strip she had used to bind the pouch, opened it, and peered inside.

"Surely you have much food," she said nervously, glancing between the pouch and his face.

He smiled. "But no one's come to share."

He reached inside the pouch and pulled out a handful of seeds, opening his hand and inspecting them.

"Roasted on the hearth," she explained. "If you do not like them—"

He popped some in his mouth, and she heard crunching noises as he chewed. "Good," he mumbled, swallowing.

Joy tugged at her mouth.

His chewing slowed, and his gaze shifted between her eyes and her smile several times. She lowered her lashes.

"I've missed you, Danagasta." He laughed, as if in disbelief.

She blinked. Someone had missed her? Someone noticed when she was not present? Looking off at his fire, she fought tears. "I do not know why. I am a shrew."

"You don't have to be. Like right now . . . you're not."

"I . . . walking here. Women ignore me. Children run. Men wear faces of disgust. I am . . . very cold inside, I feel."

Despite the crackling flames, she heard the wet sound of his lips parting, and she turned in time to watch his tongue emerge to lick first the top lip, then the bottom. He was savoring the salty powder she had sprinkled on the seeds. It was an unconscious act, but one that excited her.

She moved forward, touched his full lower lip, dipped the tip of a forefinger into his mouth, then withdrew it, brought it to her lips and tasted him. He was good. Fresh. Salty. She eased closer, meaning to kiss him. He grasped her shoulders, holding her back, and she gazed up at him in confusion.

He did not want to lie with her. Not anymore. She had turned him against her, too. Glancing down at her hands, she felt more tears well in her eyes.

He took her face in his palms, tipped her head, and said, "Not like this, Danagasta. I'm not sure you know what you're doing right now. You're upset. Distraught. We'll sit and eat together. I'll show you the game. We'll talk if you want to."

"I do not want to talk," she responded. "Talking . . . many things hurt."

"If you don't talk about them, if you don't get the anger and the grief out, it will kill you."

She stared at him, not feeling as though she could tell

him the many things that clouded her mind. Losi's death, losing her unborn child . . . the distance that had come between her and Kayini. What a fool Sequatchee was—devoting himself to *her* when Kayini loved him.

"What do you want, Danagasta?" Grant asked. "Why did you come here?"

She shook her head. "To be warm. To feel wanted. To bring you food."

"You missed me?"

"I . . . the lodge was quiet." She shifted. What was he doing? Trying to force her to admit that, yes, she had missed him?

He released her and sat back on his heels. "You could have invited Sequatchee into your lodge."

She shrank back. "Sequatchee? No. You do not know . . . You do not understand. Kayini would be hurt. I do not want Sequatchee."

"You looked content in his arms that night."

"No . . ."

"Then why? Why were you there?"

"He was in the darkness. He told me to marry him. I wanted warmth. I cannot forget . . ." She turned away.

"Your husband?"

She did not answer.

Grant caught her by a forearm and turned her back. He knew she was still bothered by her husband's death—or by her memories of the man. He wasn't sure which. If she was still bothered by her husband's death, he wanted to comfort her, encourage her to forget and go on. If she *missed* her husband . . . he was amazed by his need to drive the man from her mind, but he didn't necessarily want Sequatchee to take Losi's place.

"Dammit, don't withdraw into yourself! You came here . . . Talk to me. Why can't you forget him?" Grant demanded, barely aware of his tight grip on her arm.

"It has been only two seasons! Let go!" she cried, struggling.

Grant pulled her against him, held her tight, and stared down at her. "Why keep everything he owned? The red robe . . . the netted sticks, the blowgun? Why keep them?

By keeping them you keep him in your mind all the time. You don't allow yourself to forget."

"Let go!"

"No, Danagasta. You have to get through the grief. You have to put him from your mind and go on. You have to stop being so angry at people. He died, and his death was an accident. A horrible accident. But no one is to blame, not Sequatchee for telling him where to trade for whiskey, not me for landing in the river with a flash tied to my belt, not anyone but Losi. He drank the whiskey and ran in front of the men when they aimed for that deer!"

Her eyes had grown wide. "Do not—"

But he wouldn't stop. He had been where she was . . . and he wouldn't stop. "You're young and beautiful. You could have children. I see you watching Awe-ani-da. You're wasting your life."

Her eyes filled with tears, and she began uttering words, some Cherokee, some English, some indecipherable: "Do not. Losi—*uyehie! Gi gv. Gi gv!* I . . . *usdiga . . . tsilvquodi. Uyo i! Diniyotli!*" Her voice quivered and fell with the last syllables, a word Grant recognized as "children," then she went limp with cries that trembled out of her.

He bent and scooped her into his arms. She had a handful of his shirt on one side and a grip on his shoulder on the other, but he didn't wince. He carried her to the bed, turned around and scooted up onto it, planting his back against the wall and cradling her.

She sobbed, crying quietly and uttering more words. He didn't think she knew all that she was saying, but there was something about a baby, Sequatchee, and Losi. And he heard *diniyotli* over and over.

She eventually cried herself to sleep, and Grant slipped out from under her, lowering her head gently onto the tick. Moving from the bed, he went to feed the fire. Then he sat staring into the flames.

He had never seen Danagasta reduced to such a state.

He went back to the bed, sat on the edge, and stared down at her, knowing the pain in her heart. She had no way of knowing that he knew—he hadn't told anyone in Big Water about Emily, his wife . . . about her death.

Soon Danagasta turned onto her stomach, and, through the threads of dark hair spilling across her cheek, he glimpsed her black lashes resting peacefully against her copper skin. Her back rose and fell with her breath. He wanted to touch her dusky lips the way she had touched his lips, press a finger between them, wet it with her saliva, and taste. He wanted to cradle her against his chest and protect her from the ugliness and pain of grief.

He raked a hand through his hair. How many years had passed since Emily's death? Nearly three? Yes, she had died in March of 1805, after they had been married only a few months. It had taken him at least two of those years to stop blaming people—God, himself, Emily's mother for spoiling her daughter as a child . . . Grant shook his head, remembering the ridiculous accusations he had concocted because he'd been so grief-stricken. He had ranted and raved at Douglas, Emily's father, for buying her the temperamental roan she'd fallen in love with on sight at that Maryland plantation. He had thought the animal was too spirited for her, and he'd told Douglas that, but damn if Douglas hadn't bought the horse for her anyway. Of course, Grant had finally realized that Emily would have the animal even if that meant going behind his back to make the purchase.

He moved to the chest and uncovered the bowl Danagasta had brought. It contained a pale substance mixed with small clumps of walnut kernels. He took a horn spoon from near the fire and tasted the food. It had a gritty texture and tasted bland, as most of the Indian food did, but he was hungry so he ate.

"You have not eaten for a long time?"

He glanced over his shoulder. Danagasta was now awake and sitting up on the bed. He wanted to ask her about the baby she had cried for. Cullowhee, Kayini, Sali, Ewi, Hanging Basket, and the many other people who had answered his questions about her these past weeks and months had said nothing about a baby. He decided to delay the question, not wanting to see her distraught again.

He grinned. "I was eating a bit fast?"

She dipped her head and nodded. Then she smiled back at him, and his heart skipped because she was so beautiful, peering at him with her coffee eyes through the strands of hair that slipped from her shoulder to create a black-velvet veil across part of her face. It draped over one breast and ended at her waist.

"I tend to forget manners when I'm alone—or when I think I'm alone," he said. "Are you hungry?"

"Vv."

He dropped the spoon in the hominy, lifted the bowl, carried it to the bed, and placed it in her lap. She looked at him with apprehension in her eyes, as if she doubted whether she should eat the food.

"What is it, Danagasta? Did you poison it?" he teased.

"No. I—"

"Eat."

He went to the hollowed, water-filled gourd he kept in one corner and dipped an earthen mug into it, filling it with water. Then he returned to the bed and found that she had not eaten a bite, that she'd been watching him.

"Am sorry for my *tsugasawody*," she said softly, looking away. "Tears." She looked sad again all of a sudden.

"Don't, Danagasta. Eat. We won't talk about it again tonight. We'll talk tomorrow."

She nodded and lifted the spoon, taking a small bite of hominy. He offered her the water, and she put a hand over his on the mug. She then withdrew with the mug in her hands, closed her eyes, and drank thirstily.

"I have become a shrew," she said, looking down at the bowl. "So bitter . . . I shout and cry and frighten people."

"Stop calling yourself that. You're not being a shrew right now. You're being civil. You're being a lady."

"A lady . . ." She glanced up. "It is a good thing to be?"

"It's a very good thing to be," he said, laying an open hand on one side of her face.

She shut her eyes, seeming to savor his touch. Then she turned her head and kissed his palm.

Sparks leaped up Grant's arm. He drew a sharp breath as her lips worked their way up his fingers, caressing the tips, then worked their way down again. He felt her hot breath on his sensitive palm, heard the fire hiss and the winter wind whip around the cabin, flapping the hides covering the windows. The buffalo coat was bunched around her waist, and he suddenly wanted to crawl under it with her, draw her close and—

"Danagasta," he grated. "Eat the food."

She lifted her head and looked at him as if he had startled her. Then she released his hand and went back to taking small bites of hominy.

He returned to the fire to heat coffee made from the beans one of the white men had given him. It soon sizzled in the pot. He poured it into a wooden mug and sipped the warm brew.

"I sometimes think I have no honor," Danagasta said. "I want to lie with you."

Grant coughed, sputtering coffee. Yes, he knew she wanted to "lie" with him, as much as he wanted to "lie" with her, but he'd never met such a blunt woman. Well, perhaps in a few taverns up north, but the wenches just gave a man a look from the corner of their eye, they didn't announce what they wanted to do. Not with words anyway.

"I startled you," she remarked.

"Why is 'lying' with me a matter of honor?" he felt compelled to ask.

"You are an agent—"

"Deputy agent," he corrected. "And I really do want to help your people, not hurt them."

She nodded. "It is hard for me—in my mind."

"And will that stop you?"

She stared at him.

Now why the hell had he asked that? It almost sounded like a challenge. He had come to realize these past days that keeping some distance between himself and her would be better. He wasn't planning to stay here forever. He had asked his father for this appointment after seeing Meigs's request for help in the Cherokee Nation lying on his father's desk. He had wanted to leave Baltimore for a time because he hadn't been able to walk the streets of the city without seeing Emily in his mind. He had wanted something to do that would be incredibly different, incredibly time-consuming and challenging. Something that would completely occupy his mind. But when the task was finished, he planned to go home.

But hell . . . he damn sure didn't get on his feet and run when Danagasta put the bowl aside, slid from the tick, and started his way, her hair again partially hiding one side of her face. His eyes feasted on the movements of her breasts and hips beneath her plain dress. Some of the Cherokee women stitched colorful beads on their garments, wore bells on their buskins and silver earrings on their ears. They adorned themselves, and they were lovely. But Danagasta didn't need to adorn herself. Her hair was enough, the firelight flickering off her skin was enough . . . her dark eyes regarding him intensely beneath black brows were enough . . .

Grant's heart threatened to pound right out of his chest.

Chapter Eleven

He watched her drop quietly to her knees beside him and dip her head to smell the coffee in the mug he still held. She put a finger in it, then put the finger to his lips. He wasn't sure what she was doing or what she meant to do, but he could stand no more temptation; he took the finger in his mouth and suckled every drop of dampness from it.

She gasped.

He somehow managed to put the mug down near the fire. Despite warnings in his head, he drew her close and captured her lips with his.

He immersed his tongue in her moist, hot mouth, probing, exploring, feeling an urgency he'd not felt in a good, long while. He tasted the grit of the hominy, and the nutty, rich flavor of the walnut kernels; the hint of coffee mingled therein. Her lips were soft, pliant, full, swelling quickly beneath his, opening wide with a sigh; a rush of her breath filled his mouth. Having her willing and wanting in his arms . . . the excitement he felt was like none he'd known.

His hands slid over her shoulders, then down her back.

Their arms tangled. Then hers slipped around his neck, and his moved around her waist, drawing her close. He cupped her buttocks and pressed her to him, groaning when their hips touched.

He was no longer thinking, not really. He vaguely remembered that he hadn't wanted this to happen, that she was distraught and that he never took advantage of distraught women; that she was a distraction and that he ought to keep some distance between them. But devil take his good intentions—a man could endure only so much temptation.

The deerskin she wore felt soft, and her body felt firm and lean beneath it as his hands whispered over her, up her back, around . . . over her breasts. Her fingers slipped into his hair, caressed the back of his head. Her tongue flitted hungrily around his. Beneath his hands, her dress slid easily up her shapely thighs.

Danagasta nearly burst with want when she felt the dress moving up. As weak as he had seemed when she had pulled him from the great river, she had always known he would be a passionate, masterful lover. He had had a look about him, an experienced way of raking her with his potent eyes, of stripping her of her clothes without ever touching her. She had feared him once his hands were unbound, and this was why. She had known their power, the power to make her pant, arch, cry and grapple for more of their touch.

Her hands went down, down . . . over his strong chest, splaying over the soft yet fierce skin of the mountain lion, fumbling with the woven strip at his waist, finally loosening it. It slipped away and the skin parted, baring his chest to her. She ran her fingers through the mass of dark hair there, marveling at it, at the wiry, tantalizing feel of it. She tipped her head beneath his and opened her mouth, whispering his Cherokee name, then his English name, and that she had never felt such incredible heat—it burned her yet made her want more. She wanted to touch the flames, feel them leap around her; she wanted to feel them lick at her body, singe her in places . . .

Her fingertips explored his sinewy chest, his shoulders,

his upper arms, then they stole up to touch his jaw and his lips. She felt his wet tongue surge forth to taste hers, diving in and out of her mouth in a dance she longed to have their bodies do. She could almost hear drums pounding and gourds rattling, as they had pounded and rattled the night Grant had kissed her on the square in front of everyone. She had wanted to give herself to him that night, right there on the field. *Sge!* She had. She still did not like the idea of him trying to talk her people into trading land, but he offered a passion she could no longer fight. A passion she no longer *wanted* to fight.

Her hands crept down over his chest again. She heard him growl her name just as she touched the thong ties that secured the belt holding his breechclout and leggings in place. She untied them, and pushed the breechclout and leggings down over his hips, imagining him hard and ready—and free. Then . . . *sge! Asga-Ya-Galun-lati!* He *was* free.

She took his shaft in her hands, feeling its thickness, length, smoothness, every ridge and the swollen sac beneath. He groaned as she caressed him. *"Asgaya,"* she said softly, desperately.

"Danagasta," he whispered, his breath hot against her hair as she slid her hand up and down his length.

"Asgaya. Tlanuwa," she whispered back.

He had lifted her dress nearly to her waist now. He slipped a hand between her thighs and stroked her, stoked the flames, gliding fingers back and forth, then into, her wet, throbbing flesh.

"No quo!" she pleaded, stroking him faster.

He groaned and grabbed her hand, stilling it. He tipped his head back, toward the ceiling, cursed, and squeezed his eyes shut, fighting what she knew was forthcoming. What she wanted—inside of her.

"Now. *Now,*" she cried again, but softer this time as she gently pushed him onto his back. He straightened his head to look at her, breathing rapidly, his eyes glazed, his hands moving on her thighs again, squeezing. She parted them wide, eased forward, and straddled him.

She thought to take him inside her, to lower herself onto

him, but he drove his own way in with a mighty upward thrust, filling her, evoking a cry that rose from the very pit of her being, swirling upward and driving from her mouth. He held her on the peak, clutching her . . . then he rose and pushed her gently onto her back and began a low, achingly sweet rhythm.

The ache grew and grew as he repeatedly withdrew and filled her. The mountain-lion skin was open, and she slipped her hands beneath it, cupping his buttocks and pressing him deeper. The hide draped on either side of her, enveloping her in it—his—strength and warmth, and when the explosion finally came, deep and exquisite, she heard a growl rise from far down in his throat. It mingled with her female cries in a mating song, fierce and sweet . . .

They lay side by side, staring at each other, still panting. *I should tell him,* she thought. Their coverings had joined, they had shared food, even intimate words, and finally their bodies had joined. Danagasta knew that marriage did not always require a priest speaking words.

They were husband and wife.

She swallowed. He had made love to her, but she did not know if he wanted an Indian wife. Not many white men did. If she told him, he might be angry. He might deny the marriage. He might reject her.

She deceived him by not telling him that they were now married, but she was too frightened to tell him; she was too fearful of the possibility that he would withdraw his warmth when she had finally claimed it.

Sge . . . she was a coward. Like the Terrapin, she liked the quiet of her shell.

"I love you," she murmured, startled that the words slipped from her.

He inhaled deeply, then released a long breath and withdrew from her. She watched him sit up and pull his leggings and breechclout up, then search around for the thongs that had held his belt. She lifted them from near her head and handed them to him. He issued a quiet "thank you," and began threading them into the small holes on his belt.

Fighting tears, she turned onto her side, putting her back to him. She stared at his trunk of domestic things, breathing slowly and deeply. He did not want her to love him.

"Danagasta," he said. "It's very soon after your husband's death. You're vulnerable. You're a woman who's been loved by a man once and . . . Damn, I'm not saying this very well!"

What was he *trying* to say? That she had lain only one time with a man? That was not right. *"Tla no,"* she said. "Many times with Losi."

"That's not what I mean. He loved you. You loved him. You're trying to replace that love. You don't really *love* me. We were just together. We've wanted to . . . *lie* together from the moment we saw each other. But, Danagasta, what we just did . . . It was not love. It was sex. Don't confuse the two."

She closed her eyes. "You speak as if you have known love, Tlanuwa."

He released another ragged breath. "I have. I was married, too. My wife died after being thrown by a horse."

She rolled onto her back and watched him as he rose and left the cabin. She wanted to follow him, but she sensed that doing that would only make him withdraw more.

"Uyehi," she murmured to the shadows flickering on the wall. She had known that *something* troubled him, but she had not known what. Now she did.

Much later, when she had tired of watching the moon through the ventilation hole in the roof, she went outside. He sat on a chair near the door, his hands clasped in his lap as he seemed to study the stars in their bed of black velvet. He glanced up at her when she stepped away from the cabin. Their eyes locked.

"If I disturb you, I will go back inside," she said.

The chair creaked as he leaned over, took her hand, and tugged her toward him. He sat her on his lap and pressed her head to his chest. "You're not disturbing me. I'm sorry for running out. It's cold out here but it's pretty. The moon is almost full. The stars seem brighter tonight."

She listened to his soft breathing and his strong heart-beat, and she knew that she could fall asleep like this—sitting up, wrapped in the strength and security of his arms.

"There was a period . . . perhaps more than a year—four seasons—after my wife died that I wanted someone else in my life," he said. "Desperately."

"A wife?" she asked.

"Yes. Before Emily and I married, I had never known that I could live almost completely for another person, that I could think of someone so much. That I could be so happy. I wasn't unhappy before, but something about the companionship of marriage was . . . good. After she died, I wanted to recapture what I'd had."

He laughed, and the sound held a faraway edge. "I must have been after every available woman in Baltimore. Then one day I realized that I couldn't go in search of love. It had to just happen again—if it was meant to happen again. If not . . ." He shrugged. "I tried putting my mind on other things, then decided I needed to leave home for a while. I heard Emily's laughter in every room. I saw us together on the streets, in friends' homes . . . everywhere."

"So you came here?"

He nodded. "I thought I'd go to England—across the ocean. But—"

" 'Ocean'?"

"You don't know what an ocean is?" he asked in wonder. "None of the white men in Big Water have told you?"

She thought very hard, going back over the many seasons that had passed since she had seen her first white person—to the time when she had been four winters like Awe-ani-da. She said the word again: " 'Ocean.' Perhaps once . . . water. Huge. Deep . . ." She saw a white man squatting between two heavily dressed trees, sharpening a hatchet on a stone, talking about places . . . lands across large water—across an ocean.

"Yes," Grant said, and she thought she sensed a smile. "God, I love the innocence I've found here. Sometimes your people seem untouched by the world, untouched by the stiffness of propriety. No polite smiles over goblets of wine. No formal greetings in entryways. No having to attend this affair and that affair. There's no pushing boys into breeches when they're a certain age. And the girls—they aren't stuffed into corsets and made to sit properly. The women don't spend hours before looking-glasses, getting this and that curl exactly right. The men don't gather in confining libraries for political nonsense."

Danagasta had lifted her head to gaze at him curiously. A slow smile spread over his face. He laughed and said, "The ocean . . . I was talking about the ocean."

"You speak of strange things, Tlanuwa."

"Yes, I imagine they are strange to you. Absolutely foreign."

"You use words I have not heard. 'Propriety,' 'corsets,' 'looking-glasses,' 'libraries' . . ." She shook her head, feeling as though he spoke of another world. The white people had introduced new things to her people—smokesheds and cattle, coffee and chemises . . . She had even been told that horses had not always been among the Indians. But he spoke of things she had never heard mentioned.

"I don't want to overwhelm you. In time I'll explain what all those things are," he said. "Right now, the ocean . . . You're right—it's huge and deep. But there's more than one ocean. They are vast bodies of salt water. The land called England lies on the other side of one."

"I have heard of England," she said, sitting up as a vivid memory flashed in her head: an old man telling of some chiefs journeying far away, to another place—and that place was England. "Something about ki . . . king? A great white father in England."

Grant nodded. "Yes. The king is a leader—like your father. Except with far more power. I crossed the ocean to England once with my mother and swore I'd never make the journey again. We encountered a fierce storm. Wind and rain and huge waves—water slapping the ship around. I've never been so frightened in my life, and I didn't want to brave the ocean again when I decided to leave Baltimore for a while. I've spent years helping my father build ships, but as far as getting on one again and venturing out onto the ocean . . ." He shook his head. "I liked the countryside in England, but I don't have the courage to face the open sea—ocean—again.

"My father works for our leader—President Jefferson. I went to my father's home to visit one morning. I was told that he was gone riding for a while—as is his habit before noon—so I waited in the library. There was a letter on the desk. I shouldn't have read it, but I did. It was from Agent Meigs, requesting help here. There were more white settlers coming into the Nation and . . . Well, I talked my father into sending me. Becoming a delegate to Indians was something I had never done. God's truth, I'd never seen . . . I had never been to an Indian Nation. It would be a different place—a different land—"

"Without memories of your wife," Danagasta said.

"That's right. Emily's not here. And I didn't have to cross an ocean to escape—though I faced one hell of a temperamental river. I don't suppose I have much luck where bodies of water are concerned."

She smiled. "The Tennessee is not so bad."

Shuddering, he slipped a hand beneath her hair to the back of her neck and urged her head back to his chest. "You're forgetting that I'm the one who nearly drowned in the rapids."

She snuggled against him again, hearing the cattle and the horses stir, lowing and whickering. In the distance, wolves howled. "Will you return to the place called Baltimore someday?" she asked suddenly.

He did not answer for a time. He became very still, though his heart quickened. "Yes, Danagasta, I will. My family is there—my mother, father, sister, brother. As much as they annoy me sometimes, I miss them. As you would miss your father if you went away, even though he's been angry with you."

"I do not think he is angry anymore."

"He's unsure about you—what will become of you. He loves you very much."

She lifted her head again to look at him, to search his face. "He told you he loves me?"

Grant nodded. "He's never told *you*?"

"He has, but sometimes I am not sure about his love."

"I'm not a father, but I can understand why a parent has to be gruff sometimes. I think that having to be that way hurts them inside, too, as much as it hurts the child."

Danagasta again laid her head against him. "I once thought of going away. Right after . . ." She swallowed. "Right after my husband died, I thought of going off alone, back into the mountains. But these are my people. We survived the great fires and many attacks and still we are here—on the banks of the great river and near the creek. I have lived here, hidden here . . . survived here. I will die here."

Grant held her, admiring her pride and her strong will, the very attributes that often caused her trouble. There was something undeniably commendable about the qualities. Something undeniably . . . engaging.

I will die here. He wondered if she knew that he had nearly talked her father and most of Big Water's people into trading their land. Did she know that the attack by those Tennessee ruffians had badly scared Hanging Basket and the people and made them ripe for the promise that if they moved to the Arkansas land, they would not be troubled by whites?

No, he didn't think she knew. She knew he was *talking* to them, but he didn't think she knew how close he was to accomplishing what he had set out to do, what he had been sent to do. If she knew how close he was, she'd be greatly upset. She wouldn't have come here this evening. She wouldn't have let him make love to her, something he suddenly wanted to do again and again.

He glanced down at the shadowed swells of her breasts pressing up against her soft dress. Their coupling had been swift and urgent, filled with desperation. He hadn't made love to her properly, he suddenly realized.

"I've never met anyone like you, Danagasta," he murmured, caressing her arm. "Anyone with such"—he searched about for the right word—"consequence."

She smiled against his body. "I do not know 'consequence.' "

He couldn't help but smile back. "Pride. Though I didn't think 'pride' was a strong enough word."

"You have consequence."

Sighing, he glanced off. "You're right. I do. Which is possibly why we butt heads so much. Let's go back inside," he suggested, kneading her shoulder.

She lifted her head. "The night is—"

"The night is getting very cold. But there's a warm bed inside."

They stood and entered the lodge.

Grant pulled the door shut behind him as she strode to the bedstead, her hips swaying slightly beneath her dress. It wasn't until she sat on the edge of the frame, bent, and began unlacing a buskin that he realized she was being deliberately provocative. Her long, slender fingers deftly worked the ties, pulling them, loosening the soft leather boot. Then she slid it off, baring a smooth, shapely calf, ankle, and foot. He stood watching her, a hand against the doorframe, an appreciative grin touching his lips. She glanced up, gave him the most sensuous smile any woman had ever given him, then went to work on the other boot, her one bare leg hugging the wooden frame.

Remembering the feel of her limbs around him, Grant moved to feed the fire that had died to a low flame in the center of the lodge. He glanced over his shoulder and saw that she had stopped working on the second buskin. He grinned again, knowing she wanted him to come and help. Desire warmed his blood and pooled in his groin as he slowly made his way to the bed—and to her.

He knelt before her, holding her gaze with his for a few seconds. Then he sat back on his heels, brushed her hands aside, and worked loose the ties on the second buskin. He folded the soft animal hide down from her knee, his fingertips grazing her satiny skin, and he eased the moccasin over her ankle, then off her foot. It dropped.

He admired her foot, the fine, delicate-looking bones, though he knew this woman was anything but delicate. She could be savage, like the rapids; she could be the very storm that had ravaged the flatboat. And storms frightened him. Storms sometimes scared the living hell out of him. Other times they fascinated him to no end.

Danagasta watched him bend his head to her foot and

kiss it, his lips so gentle, so very, very tender. His hair appeared baby-soft in the dancing firelight, and she reached out and pushed her fingers into it on either side of his head, reveling in its feel—as thick and smooth as a wolf's winter coat—as his lips moved up her foot, then tickled her inner ankle. His fingers advanced lightly up the outside of her calf while his tongue skimmed its way up the inside, forcing a moan from her when it licked teasingly behind the knee. She planted her open hands on the tick and leaned back just as he began pushing her dress up over her knees, then up over her thighs. His lips followed.

He nipped, kissed, licked . . . His fingers found her woman's flesh, still wet from their earlier joining. The heat from her enhanced the smells, making her light-headed; his gentle strokes provoked soft whimpers.

She somehow managed to plant her feet on the floor and raise her hips so he could push her dress up further. Then she reached behind and loosened the garment's ties. She crossed her arms, grasped the dress, and pulled it up and off. Grant's smoky blue gaze immediately shifted to her full, aching breasts, and his hands rose between her thighs, traveled over her belly, and around to her upper back, urging her up to him. His mouth closed tenderly around one of her peaked nipples.

"Uyehi," she whispered, her hands in his hair again, cradling his head as he suckled. His lips were so soft; his tongue flitting around the tip was hot. And when he lifted his head slightly, the breath he blew on her was cool. But his mouth took the chill, drank it, consumed it. She bent her head to his, whispering his Cherokee name. He changed breasts, suckled the other, teased with his tongue while his free hand slid between her thighs again.

"Tsilvquodi, tsilvquodi," she murmured, wondering if this torment would end—not wanting it to end.

And then it did. He withdrew and removed his shirt and buskins. Then he began untying the thongs on his belt.

"You do not have the coloring of a warrior," she said, admiring the sight of his bare upper body, "but you fit the breechclout and leggings well."

He chuckled, a low, rich sound that brought her much

pleasure. Then he sobered as his eyes raked over her body. "You're beautiful, Danagasta. Beautiful."

She stretched seductively. "You take a long time undressing."

"I'm savoring," he said, grinning. "As you know."

The belt came apart in his hands, and his breechclout and leggings dropped. Her eyes went to his stiffened manhood, and she felt a surge of pride, of *consequence*, that she was the cause for such need in him, that the sight, feel, and scent of her had made him ready.

He stepped out of the clothing, and joined her on the bed, stretching out beside her and drawing a buffalo skin up over their hips.

"They're strong, the *yunsu*," she whispered, tracing his mouth with a finger. "My aunt says one gains the strength of the animal whose skin he uses to cover. The mountain lion—it is fierce and greatly respected."

He drew a hand down her arm, slowly, then his fingertips retraced the path, causing a shiver to race up and down her back. He traced her shoulder, then ran his fingers up and down her neck, working his way to the inside. His open hand slid down to touch her breasts. His palm grazed a nipple, and she gasped and tossed her head back.

He nipped at her neck, his tongue pausing on the pulse, then moving on, up to her jaw. *Sge!* She had never felt anything so wonderful! Fire flared low in her belly, shot down, then spread to every part of her body. She arched to him, against him, entwining her legs with his, feeling his hardness press against her thigh.

But though she squirmed, he continued his slow torture, kissing her, dipping his tongue into her mouth, then withdrawing it, dipping again and withdrawing again. He licked her jaw, ear, neck, shoulder . . . tasting her as if he could not get enough. He kissed his way down to her breasts and drew a straining nipple into his mouth. She writhed beneath him, wanting fulfillment, wanting him to thrust up into her. She heard her sighs and moans, and the many words she uttered as the tension grew and grew; she felt her muscles tighten and release, again and again. A torrent of fire built inside her, needing escape.

When his head dipped to her belly, nudging the buffalo skin aside, and his hands gripped her hips, she cried his name, "Tlanuwa!", and raised up on her elbows. His dark hair was tousled, and when he glanced up at her and she saw that his eyes were aglow, she marveled that he looked like a beautiful, captivating animal hovering hungrily over his prey. But *ha!* she was his *willing* prey, wet and open, wanting to feel the strike.

He came up to her, growling low, gliding into her with a smooth stroke. He ground his hips against hers, and pulsed in and out, in and out, eliciting cries and groans. Her body surged up to his, wanting more, and he began an urgent rhythm that built and quickened. Pleasure seared through her. She tossed her head back, released more cries, and somewhere in the bliss she felt him swell more, stiffen . . . then flow into her.

She wrapped her legs around him and murmured her love—in Cherokee this time—against his hair.

Chapter Twelve

GRANT JERKED AWAKE, WONDERING what the devil had startled him. Danagasta's warm body was bundled with his in the animal skins. She stirred, then quieted. Sometime during the night, one of them had pulled the flaps down around the bed, casting them in darkness. The fire had died; the tip of Grant's nose felt like someone had rubbed it with ice, and the rest of his face was cold, too. He worked the stiffness out of his jaw and tried to blink the sleep from his eyes.

Someone pounded on the cabin door.

Groaning, Grant rolled onto his back—not especially wanting to be roused from sleep and the warmth of the bed just yet.

The pounding came again.

"They will not go away," Danagasta said sleepily. He thought she sat up. "I will go see."

Grant reached out for her, found her arm, and pulled her back down. "No. I'll go."

He pushed aside the flaps and rolled out from under the coverings and off the tick. Fumbling around in the dim light shining in through the ventilation hole in the roof, he located the long shirt the women had made for him, and he slipped his arms into the sleeves and belted the garment at the waist. It reached mid-thigh and would have to be good enough for now. He started across the cabin just as someone pounded again.

"I'm here," he grumbled, lifting the leather latch and pulling the thick door open.

Bright sunlight poured in, glittering off the snow. Grant squinted, thinking he should have lit a torch or one of the candles one of the women had given him; some whites, married to tribal members, had taught them to make tapers from tallow and beeswax.

When his eyes finally adjusted to the brightness, they focused on Sequatchee, who stood just outside the cabin door.

Grant thought of Danagasta, lying in his bed, and he pushed the door shut to a crack, mumbling that the sun hurt his eyes. He heard children's laughter and one of the town dogs barking, and, not seeing the sun to the east, he wondered if he and Danagasta had slept till noon.

"Some village chiefs have come to speak with you," Sequatchee said, his expression stoic as usual.

The children's laughter became louder. Grant heard Cullowhee chattering in his excited way at someone. Another child shouted at him, and Cullowhee giggled, obviously bent on yet another prank.

"I'll get dressed," Grant told Sequatchee.

Behind Sequatchee, there was suddenly a blur of bodies and puffs of light snow. Two figures barreled up to the lodge, around Sequatchee, and into Grant and the door. Grant reeled backward, lost his footing, and landed on his rear.

The door jerked wide open, and a body flew into the cabin, sprawling with a rush of air on the floor near Grant. There was a groan, then a shadow fell across Grant. He glanced up and saw a bulky boy standing stock-still in the doorway, glaring, his fists clenched at his sides. From beside Grant came another groan. Grant, confused by the flurry of activity, peered over at a balled figure.

"Cullowhee?" he sputtered, scrambling up to have a look at the lad. Though Cullowhee's face was twisted and red, there was no blood, at least as far as Grant could tell with a quick glance. "What the devil have you done now? Here, can you sit up?"

Cullowhee struggled to sit up while the larger boy in the doorway stepped forward menacingly.

"That's enough," Grant said, rising to his full height and standing between the attacker and Cullowhee.

The large boy glared more, then hunched and grabbed a pouch Cullowhee must have dropped on his flight in—it hadn't been there moments ago. The boy straightened and angrily shook the pouch. *"Daquasany.* He take. Mine! He run!"

Grant had no idea what the pouch contained, but obviously Cullowhee had taken it from the boy and run with it. The boy still looked as if he wanted to kill Cullowhee; his eyes were slitted, his lips taut.

Grant stepped up to him. "He shouldn't have. But you have it back now. I'll talk to him. It won't happen again."

"Danagasta!" came a loud whisper from the doorway. Grant's gaze whipped that way. Sequatchee had stepped up and was now staring past Grant and the feuding boys, his eyes hard and glittering.

Planting a hand on Cullowhee's attacker's chest to keep him from the smaller boy, Grant followed Sequatchee's gaze to the bed.

Danagasta had pushed aside a flap to view the skirmish. Her hand held a buffalo skin up over her breasts. Her shoulders were bare, her hair was mussed, her eyes were glazed with sleep, and her lips were still swollen and deeply flushed from the night's activity.

"Agent-man!" Cullowhee whispered loudly, having caught his breath. "This is not good."

Grant glanced at the boy and found Cullowhee's eyes darting between Sequatchee, him, and Danagasta.

"Sequatchee want Danagasta in his bed since the day Losi died!" Cullowhee said.

Grant gave brief thought to telling Cullowhee to be quiet—an eight-year-old boy wasn't supposed to talk about a woman being in a man's bed! Instead he glared at Danagasta, hoping the glare would be enough to make her shrink back behind the hangings.

It wasn't.

Sequatchee seethed; Grant heard his hissing breath as he stared at Danagasta, searing her with his condemning gaze. She tipped her head, staring right back—the normal Danagasta, defiance intact. Grant thought of the fact that she blamed Sequatchee for her husband's death because Sequatchee had told the man where to trade for whiskey. Grant wondered if she derived pleasure from the hurt look on Sequatchee's face. She certainly seemed to.

The day is beginning fine. Absolutely fine, Grant thought caustically.

He eased Cullowhee's assaulter back. "Go. You, too, Cullowhee. Leave each other alone. Go, Sequatchee. I'll dress and be along."

"Guque will hurt me, Agent-man," Cullowhee said.

Exhaling heavily, Grant looked down at the boy, who was now getting to his feet. "Cullowhee, you can't hide behind me. Go. You and Gugue stay away from each other."

Sequatchee had disappeared from the doorway. And *now* Danagasta withdrew behind the bedding.

Devil take the woman.

Guque turned and left the cabin next. Then Cullowhee, casting an admirable pout Grant's way—to which Grant merely shrugged—shuffled along behind the older boy.

Once the boys had gone, Grant took wood from the pile near the right of the door and went to the center of the cabin where last night's fire had burned. There he stacked the wood, picked up several stones and sat, shivering but rubbing them together rapidly.

"Get dressed, Danagasta. You're going with me."

She peeked out from between drapes. "Where—?"

"I said get dressed," he snapped. "I don't want you staying here alone."

"Sequatchee is not so angry that he would hurt me, Tlanuwa," she said softly. "I am still the chief's daughter."

Grant threw the stones at the wood and fixed an angry

gaze on her. "You enjoyed that, didn't you? You enjoyed letting him know we spent the night together. Damn you, Danagasta, I will not involve myself in your need for revenge! In your game!"

She winced. "I do not play a game."

"Why didn't you stay behind the hides when you heard his voice?"

"I heard others . . . Cullowhee and Guque. I was curious."

"But you saw Sequatchee and you didn't get back. You wanted to let him know you and I had . . ." Grant ran a hand through his hair. "The boys saw you, too."

Her lashes lowered. "You are ashamed of what we did?"

He stood and moved toward the bed, grabbing his leggings and breechclout from the floor. "I'm not ashamed. I just don't want to be the source of trouble. If you came to me last night, thinking to use me for revenge—"

"I came because I was lonely," she objected, looking straight at him. "*Uhi:so?di.* I came because I missed you, because I wanted—needed—your warmth. I do not play a game!"

"Me thinketh the lady doth protest too much," he said dramatically. He knew he was being cruel, but he was still startled by the rude awakening and by the fact that he thought she was using him. He yanked his clothes on, holding the breechclout and leggings in place with one hand while working the belt around his waist with the other. But he couldn't find the thin leather thongs again. *Damn.*

Danagasta slipped from the bed, lifted something from the floor, moved close, and swept his hand aside, working a thong into the holes on one side of the belt.

"*Uyehi,*" she murmured, tying the strip. "I will help."

"What does that mean?" he demanded, trying to ignore her nakedness. "You mumbled it a lot last night."

She lifted her lashes to regard him warmly. Coffee eyes . . . Inviting. Tempting. Despite being annoyed with her, he wanted to ease her back onto the bed and ravish her.

"It is . . . affection," she said.

He didn't feel she was telling him the truth. He brushed her hand away, finished tying the thong, then said, "I think you should return to your lodge."

Hurt leaped in her eyes. She turned away, gathered her dress from the floor, and slipped it over her head.

He'd wounded her and he wished he hadn't. But hell, better she be hurt now than months from now, after he had worked through the land trade and decided to return to Baltimore. He pulled his other moccasin on and laced it in silence. Then he stood, grabbed his coat from one end of the bed, and crossed to the cabin door.

Moments later, Grant entered Hanging Basket's lodge and found Danagasta's father surrounded by George Dougherty, Sequatchee, and three older men. A grin pulling at his mouth, Hanging Basket looked Grant straight in the eye. With a wave of one hand, he bid Grant to come and sit with them near the fire. Feeling thirsty, Grant shifted his gaze toward a nearby gourd, and the perceptive Hanging Basket nodded him that way.

Kneeling beside the gourd, Grant swished water around in his mouth, wishing he could clean his teeth with the quill bristle back in his lodge. He drank three mugs of water while the men conversed, laughed, and glanced his way. Of course, Sequatchee wasn't laughing—he was glaring; and George wore a grin that didn't quite reach his glinting green eyes.

When Grant finally joined the men, crossing his legs and sitting to Hanging Basket's right, Big Water's chief handed him a bowl of chestnut bread.

He'd taken two bites and was still chewing the last when Hanging Basket asked good-naturedly, "You rested well during the night, Tlanuwa?"

One of the chiefs said something in Cherokee, and the others—and Hanging Basket—grinned again. Sequatchee stiffened.

"I rested well," Grant said, taking another bite of bread. They apparently all knew that Danagasta had spent the night in his cabin—in his bed. Not that he minded them knowing. What he minded was them making a joke of the fact.

"That is good. You eat," Hanging Basket said. "Then we will smoke and speak of the Arkansas land."

Grant ate, wondering if Danagasta's father would broach the subject of his daughter later. He had dealt with querying fathers before, but he wasn't quite sure how he would deal with this one. He would have to be very careful. He suddenly realized that the difference in dealing with *this* father might just become a matter of whether or not the Indians would trade their land.

How do I make him want me again? Danagasta wondered frantically.

Perhaps to act very, very good. To act unlike a shrew. To not accuse Sequatchee anymore. To be kind to people. She would try hard to be a suitable wife to Tlanuwa during the remainder of his stay in the Nation. She would learn to use the looms brought by Agent Meigs. She would put the whiskey business from her mind. She would spend more time stitching and cooking. She would do whatever Grant required.

She had heard Sequatchee tell Tlanuwa: "Some village chiefs have come to talk to you."

She did not like the apprehension that prickled her skin. He might be her husband now, but he was still Meigs's deputy. He was still here for the land.

She pulled her soft leather boots on and began lacing them, thinking she would go grind acorns into flour and make bread. She borrowed one of the buffalo hides from his bed, not wanting just yet to part her coat from his coverings, and she tossed it over her shoulders and left the lodge.

She walked through Big Water toward her cabin, noticing the many stares she drew and wondering if Cullowhee and Guque had told some of the people that she had been in Grant's bed. The boys must have. She had not drawn so many looks in a long time. Of course, she wore the buffalo hide, too, and usually she wore her wolfskin coat. Sali, Kayini, Ewi, and other women stood near lodges, staring. Still others worked at looms while young children scampered around in play, and older ones stood watching her.

A group of men cleaning flintlocks paused in their work to follow her progress with their eyes.

She built a fire in the hearth outside her lodge, then she went inside to get her pestle and mortar and the pottery bowl of dried and hulled acorns she had gathered last fall.

Back outside, she brushed snow from the stump near the hearth, sat down, and began working.

After grinding each acorn, she dumped the flour into the bowl. She worked and worked, pausing now and then to watch Cullowhee and his friends practice with their bows and arrows a short distance away. They were very good, hitting their target, a slim tree, every time. But while one took aim, the others were quiet, and she had to wonder if they could shoot and hit amid distraction. She thought about advising them, but worried that they would run from her.

As she ground more acorns, her thoughts turned back to Tlanuwa. She wondered if someone would tell him that, though there were a number of different ways to wed according to Cherokee custom, some that involved families agreeing to the joining and others that involved a priest and speaking words, all that was truly required in Big Water was the approval of the woman's aunt, and certain symbols—the bringing together of coverings, the exchange of food, and her sharing his bed.

She should tell him. She should gather her courage and tell him.

Kayini's hopes had returned in force. Shortly after Danagasta had exited Tlanuwa's lodge and walked through this section of Big Water toward her own cabin, Kayini and Sali had left Ewi and gone into Sali's lodge to grate corn. Moments ago, Cullowhee had burst into the cabin, his face bright, his eyes sparkling. He had immediately begun chattering about how he had snatched turnips from one of the older boys and run to the agent-man's cabin, knowing the boy would beat him if he caught him.

Cullowhee snatching the turnips and running did not surprise Kayini or Sali; he was always up to mischief. But what he said after telling about the turnips and the older boy chasing him certainly arrested the women's attention: "Danagasta spent the night in Tlanuwa's bed. Sequatchee is angry."

Sali promptly dropped the ear of corn she held, then she stood and caught her son by the shoulders. "Tell us how you know this."

"Sequatchee stood in the doorway. I flew past him into the cabin . . . and fell on the floor. Danagasta's head came from between the bed hangings. Only a buffalo skin covered her. Tlanuwa's hair was . . ." Cullowhee paused to muss his hair.

Kayini nearly took off the end of a finger on the wooden grater. Could it be? Could it really be? Had Danagasta really lain with Tlanuwa? Had they exchanged food and brought coverings together? Had they married?

"Agent-man slept with Danagasta," Cullowhee said. "Maybe he has given her another baby? That will make her happy again."

Sali's grip tightened on Cullowhee's shoulders. "Are you sure of this? All that you have told us?"

He nodded.

"I do not know if he has given her another baby."

Sali and Kayini exchanged glances. Kayini suddenly needed a drink of water to wet her parched mouth and throat. Sali scolded her son: "You should not have taken the boy's turnips and burst into Tlanuwa's lodge."

He pouted. "He was not nice to me."

"You did a bad thing."

"I only took turnips."

"And ran into Tlanuwa's cabin."

"Ran for my life!"

"Someday someone you have offended will catch you, Cullowhee," Sali warned. "Then you will learn a lesson."

His scowl deepening, he shuffled off, perhaps to find more trouble, Kayini thought. "I cannot grate more today," she said, putting the grater aside and dropping her ear of corn in a bowl near her feet. She whispered: "What does it mean, Sali? Oh, what does it mean?"

"It means we find out more—exactly what happened

between Danagasta and Tlanuwa last night. It means . . . they are probably married."

A bundle of taut nerves, Kayini hurried to the water gourd resting in the far corner.

". . . ranges of mountains and low valleys, much like these," Grant told the chiefs an hour or so into their meeting. "There are oak trees, hickory, maple, pine . . . many of the same trees and plants you have here."

The assemblage had passed a pipe around a number of times as well as a small hollowed gourd containing *conutche*, a nut-flavored drink. All the chiefs could speak English, and one called Yonv-galegi had begun talking about the Tennessee settlers, how they sometimes came to his village of Long Town during the night and took hogsheads of dried corn and baskets of squash, pumpkins, and other vegetables. They also took dried meat and cane. They slaughtered the cattle and hogs and sometimes wild animals that roamed close to the village. Yonv-galegi felt the settlers were not necessarily in need of anything, but wanted to drive his people away. The people were willing to go to new land if, as the deputy agent promised, they would not be troubled by hostile whites. The other chiefs—Tahlonteskee and Goingback—voiced some of the same complaints.

"There are few whites in the new land," Grant said.

The chiefs began talking amongst themselves in Cherokee, sometimes motioning with their hands and fingers. Grant smoked more, puffing from the long, ornately carved, hollowed pipe stem and watching the glowing tobacco in the stone bowl just beyond the carved miniature of a bird.

Presently the chiefs, George Dougherty, and Sequatchee quieted, and Hanging Basket looked at Grant. "We would like to talk to your great white chief in the place called Washington."

They meant President Jefferson. "I'll send a message to Agent Meigs and see if that can be arranged," Grant agreed.

They wanted to talk amongst themselves more, Hanging Basket said. Grant interpreted the man's words as a polite dismissal, so he put the pipe down, stood, and left the cabin.

Outside he started through the maze of lodges toward his, briefly stopping numerous times along the way to talk with people he knew.

Kayini sat on a stump, working dough in a large wooden bowl. He greeted her with a nod of his head. Then, not two feet away, he hunched near Sali and Ewi, who kneeled on a decorative mat before a finger loom, and he commented favorably about the bright yellow and green items they were creating. The articles were long and partially woven, with numerous threads still dangling down beneath the women's hands, and Grant thought they might eventually be belts. The Cherokee loom was constructed of two thick parallel branches of equal height lodged in the ground approximately three feet apart. The branches were forked at the top, and a pole secured with strips of hide sat in the forks. One end of the many pieces of thread were wrapped around the pole, and the weaver began working near the stick. Sometimes two or three works were in progress on one loom. The women might work on one the first day, another the next, and yet another the next. Eventually all projects were finished.

"I scolded Cullowhee earlier," Grant told Sali.

Smiling, Sali nodded. "Cullowhee is bad sometimes. He told me he took Guque's turnips."

"Is he angry with me?" he asked.

"He is pouting. He likes to pout."

"And he likes to talk," Kayini said. Grant glanced over at her and found her smiling at him.

Kayini hoped more than anything that Danagasta would be happy with him. If Danagasta was happy with him, Sequatchee would give up trying to marry her, and perhaps he would look at her—Kayini—seriously again. "Danagasta—"

"Danagasta what?" Grant said, stiffening. He noticed that all the women were smiling now, too.

Sali spoke Cherokee words that silenced Kayini and made her look down at her bowl. But her smile didn't fade.

"Danagasta is troubled," Sali told Grant. "You are good for her—and Ewi likes you."

Ewi nodded eagerly at that. Grant's brow tightened.

He remembered Danagasta, too, asking if Ewi liked him. This was significant . . . this thing about Danagasta's aunt liking him. He thought over what he had learned about the tribe since coming to Big Water, what significance there might be in Ewi's liking him. Fathers and mothers both disciplined, though fathers had the final word. Descent was matrilineal—a woman's children were considered part of her clan. Mothers and aunts were important, having final say about certain things. About certain . . . men?

He was tired and couldn't seem to remember why the fact that Ewi liked him might be so important, if he had even been told. But he didn't like the conclusion to which his mind was leading him. He rubbed his forehead, hoping Danagasta was gone from his cabin, because if she wasn't when he returned there, he was going to sit her down and demand answers to the questions flitting through his head.

"Did you join coverings?" Sali asked.

He nodded, though reluctantly.

"Did you share food?"

Grant tipped his head to one side, uncertain whether or not he wanted to hear any more of what she was obviously trying to tell him. "A bowl of hominy. I ate some, then she ate some. What does—"

"You laid together?"

He wanted to lie, but he wouldn't. "Yes!" He apologized for snapping at her, then rubbed his head more. "I'm tired today."

Sali's smile turned into an outright grin. "I know. Danagasta's *uyehi*."

He studied her. "She kept saying that word. What does it mean? I asked her, but she didn't tell me."

" 'Husband,' " Kayini said excitedly. "You are Danagasta's husband."

Grant lowered his hand over his face, muttered *"Shit,"* then turned and walked off. Danagasta had better be gone from his lodge. She had better be . . .

Chapter Thirteen

DAMN HER! SHE'D TRICKED him. *Danagasta had tricked him!*

"She knew," he whispered to himself as he walked. He remembered her reluctance to stay in his cabin last evening. She had glanced uneasily at the bed where he had thrown her coat on his, and she'd wanted to leave. She had been reluctant to eat the hominy, too. But she *had* eaten it, and later she *had* encouraged him to make love to her.

"The marriage will be good for you and Danagasta," Kayini said, following him.

"Every one of you knew," he grated incredulously, spinning to face her. "I can't believe . . . You *all* tricked me!"

She winced. "We did not trick you."

"You just didn't warn me, is that it?"

"You are not happy with her?"

"I didn't come here to get married."

"Did you think there would be no price for the land we hold dear? None?" Kayini asked softly. "Yes, the white settlers frighten us, but it will take more than fright to tear us from our homes."

He had thought his disbelief couldn't grow anymore, but it just had. "Damn you all," he muttered. "If I didn't care what could happen to you, if I didn't worry that the settlers might come in and slaughter you all, I'd leave right now. This was supposed to be land for land. That's all! Your tribe will even be paid—"

"You are not happy?" Sali asked, approaching.

"You will divorce?" Kayini inquired, looking almost distraught.

A snort issued from Grant. "Such a simple ceremony that anyone could be tricked into, *and* you have divorce?"

Both women shrank back.

He closed in on them. "How does one divorce?"

The women exchanged nervous glances. Ewi approached and joined them, her alarmed gaze darting between him and her friends. They didn't want him to divorce Danagasta.

"What choice will I have in the end? I didn't come here to live, don't any of you realize that?" His tone had risen. Other townspeople were drawing close. He struggled to regain his composure, struggled to remember his father's words about Jefferson wanting the land badly. The President wanted the Indians convinced to move west. Conflicts between them and white settlers could be avoided. Grant thought he had convinced the Chickamaugans to move, but they comprised only a handful of all Cherokees. Besides, if he stopped negotiating with them now, if he angered them by divorcing Danagasta, they might not move. All the work he had done these past months would unravel very quickly.

"The husband and wife agree to divorce," Kayini said in a low voice, her dark eyes holding his. "That is all. He leaves the lodge, and it is done."

Grant shook his head. "So I lose my cabin, too?"

"You are only visiting, remember?" Sali said, tipping her chin. "Besides, if it was yours, it is not now. It is Danagasta's. It belongs to the wife."

Grant wanted to kick snow in the woman's face. Instead he turned and walked off.

* * *

Not long afterward, he was asleep on his bed when another knock woke him.

Wondering what he would be faced with this time, he stumbled from the bed to the door, lifted the leather strip off the wooden hook, and pulled the portal open. There stood Danagasta, her brow knitted.

"We must talk," she said softly, glancing over her shoulder at the townspeople who had gathered and were peering curiously at them from cabins not far away.

"You're sure as hell right." He stepped aside, allowing her to enter.

She strode past him to the wooden stool near his array of domestic utensils, all provided by Big Water's women, and there she sat, hands clasped in her lap, eyes fixed on them. He shut the door.

"Sequatchee told you?" she asked.

Wondering what she could possibly have to say in defense of her deception, Grant leaned back against the door and rubbed his jaw. "The women told me. You tricked me."

She winced. "I did not come to trick you. I was so lonely. I tried to leave once, but you would not let me."

"Don't lay the blame on me, Danagasta."

She glanced up, then back down. "I am not laying the blame on you. There was no time to tell you."

"No time to tell me?" he said, holding his voice down. He folded his arms across his chest. "What about when I handed you the bowl of hominy?"

"I could only stare at it and think how much I wanted you."

He moved from the door, rubbing one side of his rough jaw, and hunched near what remained of the fire he had built after returning to the lodge earlier. He fed the small flames and watched them lick at the piece of wood he piled on the other charred pieces.

The fire popped embers on the colorful carpet, and Danagasta jumped from the stool, raced to the carpet, and stomped the embers. Grant stared at her in surprise.

She straightened and ducked her head in embarrassment. "I hate *atsla*. It warms me, but I hate it." She shuffled back to the stool, saying, "So much *atsla* when I was a child . . ." She glanced up, fear sparkling in her eyes.

Despite being angry with her, he wanted to take her in his arms and hold her. He wanted to press her head to his chest again, tangle his hands in her thick black hair and soothe her. He had always sensed so much pain in her, and he didn't want to be responsible for hurting her more. But, dammit, he hadn't come to the Cherokee Nation to marry, and he hated having been tricked into the marriage!

"I'm Meigs's deputy, Danagasta, and you should remember that. I take my assignment very seriously. I'm here to talk your people into trading their land. That's the only reason I'm here."

Knowing how Danagasta felt about the land, he expected to be lashed verbally, even attacked with fists, with a bow, or with a knife. But that was ridiculous; she hadn't come here with either weapon, unless she hid a knife under the skin she wore. She had long ago laid down her weapons against him, knowing they would be ineffective.

She closed her eyes and breathed deeply, her lips thinning to a tight line. "I know why you are here. You do not need to remind me. Only a short time ago, I saw the chiefs who came to speak with you and my father."

"Hanging Basket, the majority of the people of Big Water, and the visiting chiefs feel a trade will be in the best interest of the tribe."

"You have talked well, *Agent-man*," she said scornfully. He realized he had wanted to make her angry, as angry as he felt inside. Telling her that her people had agreed to the land exchange had done exactly that.

"Did you realize that you're part of—"

She stood again, her eyes open now, but this time she walked with determination toward the door. "The chiefs cannot pretend to represent the entire tribe, only villages and towns along the great river! There are many more!"

Grant straightened, feeling a slither of apprehension, never knowing quite what to expect when Danagasta was angry. "Where are you going?"

"To my father, to tell him and the others that they are traitors to their people!"

She put a hand on the door's leather latch. Grant raced over and grabbed her arm. She breathed quickly, her lips thin, her eyes flashing. He pressed her against the portal, holding her in place with his shoulders and thighs.

"Bloody hell! Settle down!" he ordered. "You can't march into Hanging Basket's lodge and call him a traitor. Think about what you're doing. Don't just fly off in a temper! I know your father mentioned banishing you at one time. Is that what you want? Is it?"

"Yunwi-usga seti!" she hissed. "No matter what you say to me, no matter that you hold me and speak tender words, you are a white government man! Worse than any I have met! I thought I could trust you!"

"Don't talk to me about trust. You tricked me into marriage! Did you think I'd given up on the land exchange just because you offered yourself?"

"*Tla no.* I did not trick you. I did not think such a thing! We will divorce. You will leave. You will be free . . . free of a woman you hate."

She stopped struggling. He breathed deeply and leaned his head against hers. "God, Danagasta, it's not that. I don't hate you. I don't understand why you did this after what I told you last night—that my family is in Baltimore and that I'm going back there once the land deal is final."

"It was done when you told me that. We had already wed. I am sorry. I . . . did not have the courage to tell you."

She was right. They had already made love by that time. They had already brought "coverings" together. They had already shared food.

"We will divorce," she said softly.

"No. Listen to me. I came here and tried to sleep after I talked to Sali, Ewi, and Kayini. I didn't realize these past months that everyone has been wanting us to marry. I know that now, and I now know why I was accepted in Big Water so easily. But that doesn't change the way I've come to care about everyone, especially the children. Together we must think about what's best for your people. Kayini implied that they've been so agreeable to hearing about the land because they wanted you and me to marry.

It will be better if your people move, as much as you hate that idea. Think about the white settlers on Cherokee land, the Tennesseans attacking the women and children, ruffians killing village dogs and stringing them up in trees. What will be next—the *children* with their bellies cut open and their tongues hanging out? Think! What—*who*—will be next? They hung the dogs by their front legs, Danagasta! Then they—"

"Tla no! Elowehi!" She panted, intermittently squeezing her eyes shut, as if fighting images.

"You want me to be quiet?" he demanded, recognizing her last syllables. "I will if you promise to stay in this cabin the rest of the day. Don't fly out of here in a temper and say things to Hanging Basket and the other chiefs that you haven't thought out. Go back and sit on that stool and *stay there* until I'm certain you're calm."

Her lips snapped together as she struggled to slow her breathing. "They would not do that to the children. *Tla no!* Awe-ani-da. Cullowhee. They would not!"

"I don't want to believe they would," he whispered against her hair. "But, Danagasta, if I hadn't been at the river that day, some of the women and children might be dead right now. The women were so frightened they couldn't think to fire their flintlocks."

"I would have killed those men!"

"I'm sure you would have. And with just cause. Then other men would have come across the river, and maybe they would have burned Big Water. How many times did you watch towns and villages burn during the Chickamauga Wars? How many times? Is that why you hate fire?"

Silence, then: "Many, Tlanuwa. *Sge!* Many," she said, her voice a low wail.

"Yes, many. Too many to count. You must have been horribly frightened, Danagasta. Perhaps you ran from the soldiers and settlers. Perhaps you were separated from your parents. How old were you during the last fire?"

Her breath became fast and erratic again, and he suspected she was reliving the fire as it licked and consumed cabin after cabin, raging through the town, driven by the wind. He loosened his hold on the back of her head, and she turned her face to the door.

"I was . . . I was seven winters!" she cried, trembling, her voice muffled.

"A year younger than Cullowhee. Three years older than Awe-ani-da. Oh, Danagasta," he said, stroking her hair, "do you want them to witness the same horrible things that you surely witnessed?"

She shook her head, then slowly turned around. He backed away. She swiped at tears on her cheeks and said, "I will not go to my father's cabin."

Grant ran a hand along one side of his face, from brow to chin, and exhaled with relief. Turning away, he neared the fire where he placed in the flames a pot containing sassafras tea he had made earlier.

"I'm not a horrible white government man," he said. "I want to see your people live in peace."

"We could move back farther into the mountains."

"The settlers are everywhere. You know that."

"Ask your government to send soldiers to get them out!"

He glanced at her, wondering if she was about to rage out of control again. "I plan to do exactly that. But with a war brewing between my country and England, I doubt that troops will be sent here."

"You do not believe in your government, in your great white chief!"

She meant Jefferson. Grant eyed her. "Calm down. I didn't say I didn't believe in my government. I'm trying to make you realize that other matters will be considered more important than protecting Indians."

She lifted her chin, her lashes still damp with tears, her mouth a tight line. "*Anything* is more important than protecting Indians."

"Go sit on the stool, Danagasta," he said, tensing more. Any second now, he expected her to fly off in a temper again.

"No one orders me!"

Grant stood, narrowing his eyes. "I said go sit on the stool. I'll put you there if I'm forced to."

She glared at him for another moment, then wisely lowered her chin and shuffled across the lodge, finally settling quietly on the stool.

Grant ran a hand through his already tousled hair. "I'll do what I can to get soldiers here," he promised, settling near the fire again.

He lay back on the carpet, entwining his fingers behind his head. Moments later he heard the tea sizzling in the pan and he sat up, wrapped a piece of hide around the pan's handle, and poured the tea into a nearby mug. He took the mug to Danagasta, holding it out in offering. "I'm sorry I shouted at you."

She stared at the mug. Then, glancing up at him, she accepted the token of peace, and sipped the hot brew.

"You do not wish to be married to me," she mumbled as he stood watching her.

He wanted to rub his forehead and his jaw again, rake his hands through his hair again. He didn't want to have this conversation, not really.

"It's not you. I'm not ready to be married again yet—to anyone. And as I said, sooner or later, I'll be going home."

"You are right," Danagasta responded. "I should have told you that joining our coverings, sharing food, and being together would mean . . . would be . . . We will divorce."

"Would you stop saying that? Divorce would not be the best course of action right now—that is, if you really care about your people."

Her chin shot up again. "I care about my people."

"Think about the settlers and about what life for your people will be like if they stay here. I don't believe everyone's willing to move, but that doesn't mean some of you can't. It doesn't mean the Chickamaugans can't."

Danagasta closed her eyes. Tlanuwa was right. She could not fly off in a temper to her father's lodge and accuse Hanging Basket of being a traitor. He was also right that her people could no longer live in peace in these mountains, and that it was doubtful that the white man's government would protect the Cherokees. She did not want to leave the land of her ancestors; every time she thought about leaving she cried, and her temper flared. But she could not continue to act like an angry child. She must be strong and face the change she knew was coming. She must stop being a shrew.

"I know we must leave, but I am afraid," she whispered, staring up at overhead poles.

"I know, Danagasta." Grant stepped forward and gently urged her head to rest against his stomach. "Change is frightening."

She clung to him, inhaling the wild scent of his mountain-lion shirt, and listening to his breathing. She could not afford to drive him away. He possessed inner strength she did not believe she had, and she sensed—*felt*—his honesty, his compassion, his pain. Like her, he did not want to see her people move. But a move would be best for everyone. She hoped.

"I'll stay with you through this," he murmured.

Would he? Yes, she thought he would. She wanted to cry with relief. *But afterward . . . after my people move he will go to his true home.* And she would not try to hold him; she did not want him to hate her.

"I need your help," he said. "Your father and most of the townspeople trust and like me. But if we divorce . . . They want us to be married, and I don't know whether they would be as friendly if we divorce. I don't know whether they would still be as convinced that they should move. They might decide to retaliate against the settlers. Then soldiers *will* come, but they won't ride up to settlements to protect the Indians, they'll ride up to kill them."

She lifted her head and stared up at him, her heart quickening. "You *want* me to be your wife?"

"For now," he responded honestly. "Until the relocation takes place."

"Is that not tricking my people, as you accused me of tricking you?" There was no anger in her voice. She was just not sure that they should deceive the people.

"It's for their good, Danagasta."

She glanced down at the mat-lined ground, considering his words, then she looked up. "You are right."

He released a long breath, appearing relieved. "I'll help

you move your things in here. I won't live in your old cabin. Your husband's there."

What was he saying? "Losi is gone, buried in the mountains. His spirit rests in the Nightland," she said, confused.

"His memory is in that cabin. You've saved his things. Unless you're ready to part with them—"

"No," she blurted out. She wrinkled her brow, surprised by the force behind the word. She truly did not want to part with Losi's things. She wanted to ask Tlanuwa why her keeping the belongings troubled him—he did not love her and he only intended to stay with her until her people moved. Perhaps he had feelings for her then, but he did not wish to admit them. She would not demand to know his feelings; she would spend her time with him, patiently loving him and hoping that someday he would return that love.

"We will move my things here," she agreed.

"Only *your* things."

She nodded. "Only my things."

He tilted his head, studying her, perhaps wondering—and worrying—more about whether she would think of her first husband whenever she was with him.

She moved around him, intent on the door. Reaching it, she lifted her coat from the floor and draped it about her shoulders, then paused with her hand on the door's leather latch. "I did not think of Losi when I laid with you," she said, glancing back at him. He had turned and was watching her. "You are a powerful lover, Tlanuwa. You do not allow thoughts of another man between us."

Turning back, she lifted the latch, opened the door, and stepped out into the glow of the Sun.

People still stood about, as if they had been waiting to learn what had transpired inside the lodge. Danagasta spotted Sali, Kayini, and Ewi, stern-faced, sitting and talking with children on stumps outside of Sali's lodge. Danagasta felt Grant step up behind her.

She turned, a question on her lips, and he swept a buffalo skin around her, then lifted her hair over it. He pulled the hide together beneath her chin. *To show everyone that he has accepted me as his wife,* she thought.

Part of her wanted to cry with relief, and another part wanted to laugh with joy.

They walked together through Big Water, drawing a small crowd behind them. As they made their way between cabins, more and more people looked up from various tasks and joined the gathering, chattering excitedly.

"They speak of having a feast and dancing," Danagasta told Grant.

He nodded, gazing at her, trying to appear happy. But his eyes were dull. His jaw and the area above his upper lip were peppered with whiskers. His hair had grown a great deal since his arrival in the town, and it waved gently over the coat he had apparently donned before joining her outside his cabin. His dark brows and thick lashes added to his handsome look, a look of which Danagasta was proud.

Chapter Fourteen

An hour or so later, while carrying an armful of Danagasta's folded buckskin garments toward his lodge, Grant heard someone shout something in Cherokee. Numerous townspeople pressed toward the palisade gate, and a Cherokee man pulled it open. In rode two white men, both heavily caped, snow dusting the shoulders of their woolen garments. One man's hair was gray, the other's was pure white, flowing about his face in soft waves.

"Agent Meigs and Reverend Blackburn!" Danagasta whispered from behind Grant.

He glanced over his shoulder, a brow raised.

She pursed her lips, sighed, and promised, "I will not be a shrew."

He nodded.

"Chief Doublehead liked the reverend. When the men who were to kill Doublehead only wounded him, the chief ran and hid in Mr. Blackburn's mission near the Hiwassee settlement. But the appointed men found Doublehead."

Grant's father had told him about last year's Council-ordered assassination of Doublehead, who had once been considered a great leader by his people. Grant had stated that the Council's action seemed rather barbaric, but Charles, his father, had merely shaken his head and said the Indians had their own system of justice, that Doublehead had apparently committed some terrible crime.

"Chief Doublehead agreed to secret articles in treaties negotiated by Agent Meigs," Danagasta said.

Grant turned a look of disbelief on her. She nodded. "It is true, Tlanuwa. Meigs offered Doublehead his own tracts of land if he would give up large pieces of land owned by our people. Doublehead did a dishonorable thing."

"It sounds as though Meigs did, too," Grant commented under his breath.

"That is why many of us do not trust him."

"Your father likes him."

"My father likes peace."

"I thought Blackburn's mission school was located with the agency in the Tellico Blockhouse," Grant said, watching people mill around the two visitors as the newcomers reined in their horses. Meigs, a tall, thin man, slid down, then the reverend dismounted, a robust giant in comparison to the agent.

"The mission is at the Blockhouse now," Danagasta responded. "Blackburn was frightened by Doublehead's murder and was granted permission to move the school. Not many of the people send their children to him. He at first agreed to teach the children reading and writing, but some parents learned he was teaching them his religion, too. If he has come for more children he will not get them!"

Grant shot her another look of warning and reminded gently, "Your temper, Danagasta."

"I will stay in the cabin if I must. But know that the reverend feels the only way to teach the children properly is to take them from the influence of their parents and house them at the school. You have been among my people for some time. Tell me what is bad about the parents? The children are happy. Why take them from Big Water?"

She swept past him, carrying a large bowl filled with

personal items—wooden combs, woven belts, beaded bands, a wooden tool with a thin sharpened stone attached, a stick wrapped in buckskin, strips of leather, the small bowl containing ointment she applied to her skin, a fan of what looked like turkey tail feathers sewn to a deerskin handle, and two small, dried cakes.

Grant hurried after her. "You'll come out if I need you?"

She inhaled and exhaled deeply, looking straight ahead.

"Danagasta, we agreed to work together toward moving your people. I'm sure Meigs is here to talk about the land."

"I did not know he would bring the reverend with him."

"But he has, and if you believe so strongly that Blackburn is here to take some of the children to the mission, don't hide in the lodge. Stay with me, stay among your people and don't let him convince the parents to send their children with him."

"Should I shoot arrows into him or stab him with my knife?" she inquired sweetly.

"Danagasta . . ."

"I sometimes think fighting is the only way to force whites like Meigs and Blackburn from our Nation."

"Words can be weapons, too. Use words."

"I cannot. I become too angry. Then my words spill out and create more anger."

"Then stay by my side—I need you—and let me do the talking. I care about the children as much as I know you do. I won't let Blackburn take any back with him."

She took another deep breath and released it in a rush. "I know you care about them, Tlanuwa. I know . . . and I trust you. I will be by your side when you need me. But first permit me some time alone to calm myself, as you say."

Agreeing, Grant walked with her to the cabin, where he placed her things near the foot of the bed. Then he withdrew from the lodge with the intent of introducing himself to the two visitors.

He stood beneath the overhang of a cabin roof, observing Meigs's powerful and erect bearing as the man greeted some of the people by inclining his head. Grant knew that Meigs had participated in the Revolutionary War, serving under Benedict Arnold as a major, and that a few years later he'd been promoted to colonel. Meigs was considered a minor hero of America's battle for independence, having led a gallant and successful attack against the British on Long Island.

Wrapped in a heavy buffalo coat, Hanging Basket stood beside the door to his lodge. Sequatchee and George Dougherty stood near him, looking serious and not necessarily friendly. Grant went to stand with them, drawing a nod of approval from the old, sharp-eyed chief. While Hanging Basket might like Colonel Meigs, Grant wasn't sure the chief wanted the reverend in Big Water. Hanging Basket's obsidian gaze kept landing squarely on Blackburn, watching the man closely as he stooped to speak with a group of children. Grant felt an urge to rush forward and stand between the reverend and the little ones—Cullowhee was among them, he noticed—but he suppressed the urge, telling himself that he'd unwisely allowed Danagasta's words about Blackburn to influence him. He should watch the man, then decide for himself whether or not the reverend was good for the children.

Agent Meigs and Reverend Blackburn slowly made their way toward Hanging Basket's lodge. The chief said something in Cherokee, and both George and Sequatchee nodded. With a jerk of his head, Sequatchee indicated that Grant should follow him and George, who was already walking toward the visitors.

As Sequatchee, George, and Grant approached the two men, Grant's gaze caught Meigs's. The colonel smiled, but Grant didn't perceive the smile as being genuine. Distrust lurked in the agent's eyes, distrust Grant didn't appreciate since he'd single-handedly convinced many of the Indians, Danagasta included, of his honorable intentions. He didn't relish having to convince another person. Of course, he didn't quite trust Meigs, either, so he supposed the colonel's scrutiny of *him* was fair.

"Mr. Dougherty. Sequatchee . . ." Meigs greeted when he reached the two delegates Hanging Basket had sent. His blue-gray eyes turned to Grant. "And you're Mr. Claiborne, I presume?"

"That's correct." Grant offered his hand.

The colonel shook it. "So the Chickamauga chiefs are willing to talk about exchanging land . . ." The sparkles in his eyes indicated that he'd like to know how Grant had managed that.

"They already spoke with me," Grant responded. "They want to meet with President Jefferson."

"We will speak more in the Council House, where Hanging Basket waits," Sequatchee said. Meigs nodded, and Sequatchee and George turned to lead the way.

"Should the reverend come, too?" Grant asked, remembering his vow to Danagasta.

George stopped, turned back, and fixed a cool stare on Grant. "Rev'rend's not welcome in the Council House. 'E's 'ardly welcome in Big Water," he remarked, turning to walk away again.

Meigs walked slowly, and Grant fell into step with him, walking between lodges. Soon they were some seven paces behind George and Sequatchee, and Meigs asked if there was anything pertinent he should know before they went in to talk to Hanging Basket. "I came because I should take part in any negotiations. I'm surprised by your success."

"They haven't traded yet. They've requested military protection."

Meigs sighed. "I see. Anything else?"

Grant started to say "Nothing," then thought better. "I've married Hanging Basket's daughter."

If Meigs had been eating, he would have choked. His face reddened, and he coughed. "A bit of a conflict, don't you think? You work for the United States government." Long seconds of silence ensued. "Hanging Basket approves of the marriage?" the colonel asked.

"I believe Hanging Basket wanted the marriage from the beginning. It's a long story, one I'll relate later. But you should know that I believe that almost everyone in Big Water wanted me and Danagasta to marry."

"Are you saying your *marriage* helped convince them to relocate?"

"It may have. They learned to trust me. I frightened off some white men who attacked the women and children. Danagasta's husband died last summer, and I believe the people have wanted another husband for her."

"And here I thought you were being accused of bringing in whiskey to sell," the colonel said with a smile. "Sequatchee sent a missive to the agency. Then, of course, I received Hanging Basket's note that you would be meeting with him and some other chiefs and I decided they must have either forgiven you or chosen to overlook what you did."

"I didn't bring whiskey in to sell," Grant responded angrily. He had only a few seconds to glare at Sequatchee's back, knowing why the man had tried to discredit him, then he and Megis reached the Council House.

Danagasta sat near the fire in her new home and lifted a dress of white deerskin from a small trunk her new husband had brought from her old cabin. The dress had belonged to Cornsilk, Danagasta's mother, but Danagasta had worn it the night she had given herself in marriage to Losi. She had not yet worn it for Tlanuwa since her marriage to him had not been planned, but she would. This night she would.

The dress was fringed and decorated with porcupine quills. From the trunk constructed of pieces of wood bound together with strips of buffalo hide, she removed long hairpins carved from bone and turned them over in her hand. Then she rose, placed the dress and the pins on the bed, slipped from the dress she wore, and returned to the fire, near where she had also placed a bowl of water and a piece of softened skin.

She squeezed the excess water from the skin and began washing herself. She did not have time to go to the river or to the creek. So she bathed here, beginning with her face and neck and traveling down. When she finished she again strode to the bed, where this time she lifted the wedding dress, slipped it over her head and arms, and smoothed it down over her body to where it ended just below her knees.

She combed her hair and worked a small amount of grease into it until she knew it appeared glossy. Then she lifted it, twirled it, and fastened it to the top of her head with the pins.

Finally she closed the trunk and pushed it to one corner of the lodge. Smiling, she returned to the fire and lifted a nearby pan, thinking she would cook for her new husband.

Much later, with the buffalo hide he had given her draped about her shoulders, Danagasta emerged from the cabin carrying a hollowed gourd containing water and a bowl filled with food: an ear of roasted corn, frybread, and dried venison. In the distance, she heard many voices, but she saw no one near her and Tlanuwa's cabin, so she walked through Big Water to the field used for playing stick-ball and lacrosse, and for large gatherings such as festivals.

A number of unlit torches had been lodged in the ground around the square. Much of the snow had been brushed from the grass. The people mingled, conversing and laughing, while some tied onto their legs turtle shells fastened to pieces of buckskin. When the person danced, the shells would rattle. Children shouted and giggled, playing the basket-dice game and chasing dogs that had wandered onto the field. From the opposite side of the square, drumbeats rose and part of the field cleared so the lead dancers would have room to shuffle. Danagasta scanned the gathering for Grant but did not see him. She was just beginning to wonder if he was still meeting with her father and Agent Meigs when she felt a tug on her covering. She glanced down at Awe-ani-da, who stared up at her with wide eyes.

The girl popped the thumb from her mouth and spoke softly in Cherokee: "Tlanuwa say if I see you bring you to him. He say you not mean. You not hurt me."

For a moment Danagasta could only stare down at the girl in surprise. Then, delighted, she hunched before Awe-ani-da so she could peer into the child's dark eyes. "Do you believe Tlanuwa?" she asked in their language, hoping . . . She had never wanted to frighten any of her people, especially not the children.

"Yes," Awe-ani-da responded without pause, nodding firmly.

Sighing heavily with relief, Danagasta smiled. "He is right. I will not hurt you. You will take me to him now?"

The child nodded again, popped the thumb back into her mouth, then turned to lead the way through the crowd. Danagasta spotted Ewi and was pleased when her aunt's gaze went to her hair and the woman smiled proudly. Danagasta returned the smile, almost losing sight of Awe-ani-da. She hurried to catch up with the girl.

They had nearly traveled the length of the field when Danagasta finally saw her husband, seated cross-legged with Hanging Basket, Sequatchee, Tsatsi, Agent Meigs, and Reverend Blackburn on a number of skins spread on the ground before a fire. Sequatchee was the first to see her, and he came slowly to his feet. Danagasta wondered at his stare, then she realized how different she must look with her hair swept up and away from her face.

She sought her husband's intense gaze, finally finding and holding it. He, too, appeared startled as he stared at her with appreciation, making her blood warm and her heart skip. All sounds faded in her ears—the drumbeats, the turtle-shell rattles, the many voices, the laughter . . .

As her father, Tsatsi, Agent Meigs, and Reverend Blackburn rose, she lowered her lashes and eased the covered bowl of food and the gourd from beneath the hide she wore. Then she approached Grant.

Scrambling to his feet as if he had suddenly awakened from a dream, Tlanuwa glanced around at the other men. Danagasta had not seen her husband act so uneasy, and she could not help a smile, knowing her appearance was the reason. She felt curious people press forward behind her, saw Awe-ani-da join Kayini to the right, and she saw Sali step up beside Kayini to watch.

"I have brought you *agisti* and *ama*," Danagasta told Grant. She stepped onto the skin that had been laid for him, and offered him the food and water. She lifted her lashes and gazed into his eyes again.

"You look beautiful, Danagasta," he murmured, taking the bowl and gourd. He turned, put them on the ground to his left, then faced her again. "Please . . . sit with me."

Nodding, she sat and snuggled deeper into the buffalo hide. He sat beside her, and Sequatchee, Tsatsi, her father, the agent, and the reverend settled again, too, pulling their legs beneath them. Tlanuwa brought the bowl onto his lap, lifted the cover of woven cloth, tore a piece of frybread in two, and bit into it.

"*Wado,*" he told her. "It's good."

She smiled. "There is no need to thank me."

Gourd rattles began keeping time with the drumbeats, rising wildly, fading, then rising again. Murmurs started in the crowd as people began wandering away; the murmurs soon rose to full conversations.

A child scurried close by, and Reverend Blackburn caught him around the waist and pulled him into his lap, teasing, "You're going to hurt yourself, boy. Run smack into someone and hurt yourself." He tickled the boy—Wadigei, Cullowhee's friend—and Wadigei giggled. Then the reverend bent and whispered something in the boy's ear. Danagasta wanted to jump and snatch Wadigei from his arms for fear that Blackburn might be trying to lure the child to his mission school. Instead she looked at her husband, who smiled gently, seeming to understand how difficult controlling herself was while she watched Reverend Blackburn and Wadigei together.

Grant could only take his eyes off Danagasta for a few moments at a time. In the white dress decorated with tassels and quills, with her hair swept up and pinned to the top of her head, she looked elegant and regal. She looked like exotic royalty, if there was such a thing.

The flames from the many torches made of pine knots lodged in various locations around the square gave her skin a satiny copper glow. Orange light danced in her slitted eyes when she turned them on him and smiled. She looked so utterly different from when she left her hair fall loose and when she glanced at him, sometimes fearfully, sometimes seductively, around the curtain it formed. Whenever she tipped her head and peered at him around her hair, he wanted to ravish her, right then and there. But the way she looked at him right now, the way she *looked*, made him want to delicately lift one of her hands and bring it to his lips, where he would gently kiss the back of it.

He ate some of the meat, corn, and bread so she wouldn't think he didn't want it, then he offered her what was left. She took a mound of bread and began tearing off small pieces and eating them slowly, in ladylike fashion. Almost oblivious to the men seated nearby and the many townspeople having a merry time, he handed her the gourd.

She drank from it, then lowered it, and lifted a hand to wipe away water that trickled from one corner of her mouth. He suddenly longed for a white handkerchief to offer her; since he didn't have one, he swept her hand aside, stopped the water with two fingertips, and looked into her eyes. He wanted to reverently kiss her, then touch her cheeks, nose, forehead, and hair. He shook his head, wanting to laugh in disbelief at himself. He was awestruck.

"Something is wrong?" she asked.

"Only you, Danagasta."

She frowned. "I—"

"You're the grandest lady I've ever seen."

She ducked her head, smiling. "A lady is a good thing to be."

Chuckling, he nodded, remembering what he'd said to her last night about being a lady not a shrew. He sobered, still wanting to touch her. More than ever he wanted to touch her. But he didn't exactly want to disturb her appearance. "I could waltz with you all night," he murmured.

"Waltz?" She looked uncertain.

"It's a form of dance. Your people have many dances. So do mine."

She nodded, understanding. "I will teach you many dances if you teach me many dances."

He grinned. "Oh, for an orchestra—a group of people with different instruments! Instruments . . . like the drums and rattles are instruments."

"You are an odd man, Tlanuwa," she said playfully.

"These instruments, do they sound like drums and rattles?"

"No. When played right, they give off sweet, wafting tones. We play them at the same time, like your people do the drums and rattles, and the sounds blend and create harmony, like when two people sing the same song together."

"You make me wish to know more of your world."

He put a forefinger to her lips to silence her. "Don't, Danagasta. We'll simply enjoy what time we have together."

Her hand stole up his arm and covered the back of his hand, moving it and pressing it to her cheek. She kissed his palm, withdrew, drank more water, then turned to watch the writhing dancers.

From where he sat beside Tsatsi, Sequatchee watched Danagasta kiss Grant Claiborne's hand. He was not close enough—being five people away, with the chief and the two visitors between Tsatsi and the deputy agent—to hear the words Danagasta exchanged with Grant. But judging from the expressions on their faces, he knew they were intimate words, words spoken between lovers. He wanted to growl, rise up, and toss Grant Claiborne from the town. He wanted to battle the man with poles, but unlike Kaloquegidi, he would not let the intruder win. He had dreamed of seeing Danagasta dressed as a bride again—but dressed as *his* bride.

"The girl is in love with the man, can you not see that?" Tsatsi asked quietly in Cherokee.

Sequatchee stiffened. "I see only that he has taken her from me."

"When will you realize that you never had her? When will you realize that the time has come to end your devotion to her?"

"I had her. She almost let me kiss her one night, then *he* appeared from the shadows."

"Did he force her from your arms or did she leave willingly?"

Sequatchee clenched his jaw. "She left willingly."

"You have tried for nearly three seasons to convince her to let you court her."

"I will drive him from Big Water! From our Nation! She was my brother's bride. Now she should be my bride!"

"Do you want to kill him, Sequatchee?"

Sequatchee did not answer—he only glared.

"You want to murder a United States diplomat . . . You would risk the lives of your people to possess a reluctant woman when another waits willingly? Think hard and long. Think beyond your selfishness. Think about Danagasta's happiness. I did not want her involved with the deputy agent, either, but I knew she would not marry you, so *I* offered her marriage. I was concerned . . . But now I see the way she loves this man and I can only hope that he will be a good husband for her."

"A good husband?" Sequatchee spat. "He wants the land. Only the land. Once he has it for his government, he will be gone! What will Danagasta have—"

"He does not want only the land, my friend. He wants her. Perhaps he will be gone after the trade is made, but until then Danagasta will be happy." Tsatsi leaned toward him, his gaze hard. "You would kill her second husband, too?"

Sequatchee's eyes flared. "I did not kill my brother! I did not pour the drink down his throat!"

Tsatsi's gaze persisted.

Sequatchee started to turn away. Tsatsi grabbed his arm and said over his shoulder: "Do *not* kill the man. Somehow, cleanse yourself. See the healer."

Sequatchee jerked his arm free, got to his feet, and walked off, away from the crowded field.

Not far away, Kayini was dancing, smiling, and laughing with Awe-ani-da, Cullowhee, Wadigei, and a few other children. From the corner of her eye, she saw Sequatchee hurry off, and, as her smile faded, she lowered the foot she had lifted. Wadigei jerked on her arm, urging her to dance more, but she could only stare at the darkness where Sequatchee disappeared, wondering what had made him rush away from the chief's gathering.

Somewhat breathless from her rapid movements, she glanced at Tsatsi, wondering if he knew. The man inclined his head to her, then jerked it in the direction of the deep shadows Sequatchee had slipped into. Torches flashed light on the many people, some seated on and huddled inside hides surrounding the field, others dancing, oblivious to the wintry air, coverings cast aside.

Tsatsi wanted her to follow Sequatchee.

She wanted to—how she wanted to! Something had disturbed him, and she wanted to comfort him.

But she could not bear the thought that he might turn away from her. She had seen him watching Danagasta and her husband, and she feared he did not accept the marriage. He would, in time—she hoped. But right now he did not, and if she went to him she would risk more heartache for herself.

She turned her gaze back to Wadigei and smiled. Then she eased back into the dance, shuffling and lifting her arms and legs.

She danced and danced, laughing with the children, forcing her mind from Sequatchee and from wondering where he had gone, and why. She noticed Danagasta smiling and talking with her husband, and soon Danagasta stood, reached for his hand, and urged him to join the dance with her. He let her lead him onto the field, where he awkwardly followed her movements. Cullowhee hurried over to tease him, and Kayini raced after the boy to snatch him back.

"You are very mischievous," she said sharply, taking the boy by the arm. "Leave them alone."

"You dance like the Terrapin, Agent-man," he taunted before she could turn him away.

"Have you seen a terrapin dance?" Tlanuwa shot back playfully.

"I see him—in my head!" Cullowhee called.

"Your mother will make you stay in the lodge for days," Kayini warned the child in Cherokee. "You disturb Danagasta and her new husband."

He wrinkled his nose and lips. "They are not trying to be alone. I do not disturb them."

"No, they are not trying to be alone, but they do not want a child between them, teasing them."

"I was only having fun."

"Have your fun here—with me," she said, returning him to the spot where she had danced with the children. "Or have it tomorrow if Tlanuwa wants to shoot arrows or play a game with you."

He cast her a dark scowl, then, instead of joining in the dancing again, he marched off in the opposite direction of Danagasta and her husband.

"I will watch you, Cullowhee," Kayini called, warning him. Not looking back, he soon disappeared in the crowd of people.

Grant danced—or tried to—until his feet hurt, until he thought about playfully begging Danagasta to let him sit back down. But he didn't want to disturb her smiles and laughter or the happy sparkles in her eyes. So he danced until *she* suggested they sit back down.

She ate more bread and drank more water while he talked to Hanging Basket, Meigs, and George. Sequatchee had long ago wandered off, and now the reverend was gone, too.

Grant looked around, searching the crowd for the missionary, finally finding him with Kayini, Awe-ani-da, Cullowhee, and Wadigei. Remembering Danagasta's warning that Blackburn was only here to take the children from Big Water, Grant rose to go join the minister's little gathering.

The man was talking to them about English letters and adding fingers, about learning to read and write . . . about visiting a place "that's especially for children." Grant heard the word "mission," and he stepped forward.

"Just a visit, is it, Mr. Blackburn?"

The giant of a man turned on him, one eye squinted. "A visit . . . then the children and their parents may decide the rest."

"And what is 'the rest'?"

"Well now, we have children who stay with us. Makes for better learning."

"You could bring teachers here—if the townspeople want to learn to read and write English," Grant said.

"You're interested in tutoring the adults, too? Surely you don't have room at your mission for the entire town."

Blackburn squinted both eyes now, studying Grant. "Believe we need a private conversation, boy."

"Deputy Clairborne," Grant corrected, folding his arms. "Perhaps we do . . . Reverend."

The man jerked his head in agreement, then glanced back at the children as if deliberating whether or not to continue talking with them. He finally brushed by Grant and walked off to again sit near Agent Meigs.

Kayini flashed Grant a smile. Grant returned it, then went to resume his position near Danagasta.

She hadn't moved from the skin. He'd thought she might follow him, or at least press up behind him if she spotted him talking to Blackburn. But she had remained seated on the hide, behaving herself, exactly as she'd promised she would.

"What was he saying to them?" she whispered.

"You don't want to know."

"I do."

"Danagasta, I think it's better if I don't—"

"He wants to take them away," she said, watching him. "I told you." She shut her eyes briefly. "You do not know how many times I have watched my people be torn apart. I cannot remain silent while the enemy plots to snatch our children."

With that, she stood and hurried off, disappearing into the darkness between lodges.

"Your first quarrel?" Hanging Basket asked in English, leaning Grant's way.

"Hardly," Grant responded dryly. "And I don't imagine it will be the last."

Hours later, he entered his lodge and found Danagasta seated on the bed, the drapes tossed up over the canopy, Cullowhee's chess game on the tick before her. A small fire crackled in the center of the cabin. She held a knight in her hand, and she dropped it on the board when Grant neared.

"I did not mean to bother your things, my husband. I was curious. I am sorry."

He sat on the edge of the bed and began unlacing and removing his soft leather boots. "It's not mine. It's Cullowhee's. And you don't need to apologize." One buskin dropped, then he worked at the other one. "Blackburn's retired."

Her brow tightened.

"He's gone to bed. To sleep," Grant explained.

She nodded.

The second moccasin slipped to the ground, and Grant rose and moved to sit behind her. He reached around her and lifted the red playing piece she'd dropped. Holding it by its round base and leaning over her shoulder slightly, he turned the piece between a thumb and a forefinger. "A knight. A very brave man. A man-at-arms . . . a warrior. Or . . . a man devoted to the service of a lady," he said, glancing at her face.

She smiled at him, then went back to looking at the knight's intricately carved face and armor; even the little nose was chiseled to perfection. The wood had been smoothed.

"The game is called chess," he explained. "It's a battle of skill between two sides—two kingdoms, if you will. Each side tries to capture the other's men. Usually the pieces are black and white. But for some reason one entire kingdom here is painted red."

"My people believe red is good," she said softly. "It is the color of success—and war. Black is death."

"Ah. Perhaps that explains it. A white man's game adapted a little to fit Cherokee beliefs."

"The red will always win."

He smiled. "Each piece has certain powers and moves. The knight can leap two squares in any direction, then one square forward or backward, or left or right—north or south, or east or west, whichever direction the board faces," he said, putting the piece on the board and showing her what he meant. He left the knight and picked up another piece. "The rook can only move north, south, east, and west, and the bishop moves across corners." He reached around her with the other arm and pushed the bishop back and forth diagonally over red and white spaces on the square piece of wood. She nodded, understanding.

"The king," he said, touching the crown on the head of the fierce-looking character with a royal robe draping to its base, "is only allowed to move one square at a time in any direction. But the queen . . ." He pressed his cheek against Danagasta's and shifted his hand from the king's crown to the queen's base. "The queen is strong and poised, and calmly makes her moves along straight lines as far as she can go. The queen can very often win the struggle for her people."

He slowly moved the queen forward, eliminating two white pawns and a bishop, then backward, pushing aside a white rook. He moved the queen to the right, where there was nothing, then to the left, eliminating the white king. That wasn't exactly the way the game was won, Grant knew, but for his purpose at the moment, gently pushing the king aside was effective.

"Between two skilled players, the game is played slowly, with much thought. Every move must be carefully considered. The pawns," he murmured, fingering one, "are the little people—the weakest—who can be bumped easily. They must be cautiously protected. They can move only one square at a time, forward, or across a corner. But they can also be of great help in trying to catch the enemy."

She sat very still, staring at the board and the pieces. "It is a difficult game," she said finally.

"Yes, it is."

"You are wise about it."

"Not exactly wise. I've simply played it many times."

"You will teach me?"

"Yes. If you're patient."

"I will be patient."

He withdrew his hands from the pieces and the board and ran them up her arms to her shoulders, feeling the softened skin of her dress, the tassels decorating the sleeves. He lifted his head and stared at her hair. "You look so beautiful, I'm almost afraid to touch you. When you walked up to me with the food and water, I almost didn't know you. But when you smiled, I did. I like seeing you smile."

That prompted another smile and a glance at him from the corner of her eye. Her coppery skin glowed, shimmering in the firelight. He skimmed the fingertips of his right hand back down her arm, over the tasseled deerskin and her silky forearm. He splayed his hand over hers, and he kissed her jaw, admiring its strength.

"Tlanuwa," she whispered, suddenly breathless.

He lifted the chess board and lowered it to the floor. She turned on the bed and faced him. Both of them sat with one leg folded beneath them, and the other hanging over the edge of the frame.

Grant touched her cheek; then her lips, running his fingertips over the bottom one. He caressed her jaw, then lifted her chin and bent to kiss her tenderly. She leaned toward him, but he caught her by the shoulders and gently held her back. He felt her arms start up, and he pressed them down, lifting his head to stare into her hazy eyes. "Patience, Danagasta."

Her tongue darted out to wet her lower lip. He leaned forward, kissing her with a little more force this time—and again he pressed her arms down, holding her inches away from him. "Patience," he said again.

She inhaled deeply, then slowly released the breath.

He kissed her again, watching her . . . waiting. She sat unmoving except for the rise and fall of her chest. He nipped at her bottom lip, kissed the top one, then gently parted both with his tongue. She tipped her head up to his, welcoming his slow ravishment, and her tongue met his, lightly frolicking. Raising his folded leg, he brought his knee up, planted his foot on the bed, then slid his hand around her back and urged her toward him.

He cupped one of her breasts, feeling her nipple harden through the deerskin. Danagasta groaned softly, arching into his touch, surrendering to his attention.

Earlier, while watching her dance, he'd noticed the ties on the back of her dress. He reached for them, pulling both free while slowly pushing the hem of the garment up around her thighs. She lifted her bottom, and he eased the dress up over her hips, waist, and breasts, urging her arms up so he could slip the deerskin off. Then he moved forward, forcing her to lie back.

Her thighs parted, and he glimpsed the tender flesh that made her a woman, but he swept up past it, kissing and massaging her swollen breasts. He suckled, drawing first one, then the other nipple into his mouth, murmuring how sweet she tasted, like the richest wine. Withdrawing back between her legs, he slipped a hand down across her tight stomach, to the light sprinkling of hair below it. He touched her woman's place, sliding two fingers up and down the dampness, then pushing them gently into her. She groaned, arched her back, and began moving her hips against him.

Grant slipped his fingers in and out of her, kneading one hip and inhaling her sweet, thick scent. It wafted around him. Desire had already settled in his groin and in his shaft, and now it grew intense.

Danagasta reached for him, wanting, needing more than his fingers inside her. The fingers drove her wild, teased her; they were a cruel sample of what awaited. She whispered his name, pleaded, but he swept her hand aside and continued the torture. Finally he withdrew his fingers, but only to lower his head and kiss her throbbing feminine flesh. She cried out at the feel of his lips there, and she buried her hands in his hair, unable to control the rocking of her hips as he suckled.

By the time he lifted his head and moved up between her legs to kiss her breasts again, she was gasping and writhing. Her hands slid down to his chest. He caught one and brought it to his mouth, nipping at the back of it, then turning it over to kiss and lick the palm. Fire flowed through Danagasta's veins. Heat scorched her lungs. "*Uyehi,*" she whispered. "*Tsilvquodi.* Love me!"

His lips traveled down her arm, pausing to lick lightly on the inside of her elbow. She caught the edge of his woven belt with a trembling hand, grappled her way to his waist and tried to loosen the knot that held his shirt closed. He again pushed her hand aside. She groaned in frustration. He untied the knot himself, tossed the belt over the side of the bed and let her sweep his shirt down over his shoulders and arms and off his hands. She ran her hands over the thick hair on his chest, finding the nipples that hid beneath, taunting them between her fingertips, drawing the first groan from him and loving the sound of it.

His mouth claimed hers, taking her breath. Her hands found the belt that held his breechclout and leggings, and she pulled free the thong that secured it. He helped her push his clothing down . . . down to his thighs, nearly to his knees, then he pressed himself against her, into her; he filled her.

He shoved his hands beneath her hips, lifting her to him, and he began a quick rhythm in and out of her, a rhythm as steady as the beat of the drums outside which could barely be heard now. Her whimpers and moans mingled with his ragged breathing. She ran her hands up his muscled arms, over his shoulders, down his back, over his buttocks, pressing him down, urging him deeper into her with each thrust.

He changed the pace, slowed it, grinding his hips against hers. He kissed the bottom curve of one of her breasts, drew his tongue lightly around the nipple, caressed the other breast and caught its hard peak between two fingers. Wrapping her legs around him, she tossed her head back, baring her neck. He devoured it, biting and kissing, again quickening the rhythm of his thrusts. Her body tingled, surged to meet his . . . then pleasure rippled through her.

Shuddering, he groaned, releasing . . . and laid his head upon her shoulder.

Chapter Fifteen

"A FINE AFTERNOON, DON'T you think?" Meigs said, standing in the doorway to Grant and Danagasta's cabin. They'd been sitting near the fire they'd built, eating corncakes and some roasted pork Sali had sent Cullowhee to deliver to them. Then a knock had sounded on the door, and Grant had risen to go answer it.

"Yes, it is," Grant agreed, wondering why Meigs had shown up at his lodge.

"Spring will be upon us soon."

Grant nodded.

"Am I interrupting something?" the agent asked.

"We were just eating. Come in." Grant stepped to the right, allowing the man ample room to enter the cabin.

Megis stepped inside and immediately began assessing the surroundings. His gaze went to Danagasta, and he nodded a greeting. Then, with his hands clasped behind his back, he looked around at the walls and the meager furnishings.

"That's a rather small bed for two people, isn't it?" he asked, glancing at Grant.

"We don't mind," Grant responded.

Meigs studied him for a long moment, then smiled and gave a quick nod. "Yes, well, during the first few months of marriage the couple notices little beyond each other."

He walked around a bit, then hunched near the fire. Danagasta stared coolly at him from the opposite side. "You're Danagasta, Hanging Basket's daughter. We met several years ago. I don't know if you remember—it was in Chief Doublehead's village."

Grant watched her eyes glitter, and he held his breath, waiting for the explosion.

"I remember," she said, lowering her gaze to the bowl resting in her lap.

Grant released his breath, feeling a surge of pride. She had wanted to lash out verbally, perhaps even physically, at the man. But she hadn't.

Meigs observed her longer. Grant felt an urge to tell the man to stop staring at her—staring was rude, didn't he know that?—but Danagasta was getting a fine lesson in patience and restraint, so Grant held his tongue.

"Mr. Claiborne," the agent said, standing and moving away from her finally, "I was rather hoping we might spend the afternoon conversing—coming to know each other better. Perhaps we could take a walk in the forest or near the creek or river."

"I will go," Danagasta said, standing. She and Grant had spent the morning lazing in bed and near the fire, and though she was dressed and her hair was combed to a blue-black sheen, she still looked sleepy. Grant knew she hadn't rested well, probably because of the reverend's and Agent Meigs's presence in Big Water.

"We'll go walk, Danagasta," Grant said. "You don't have to leave."

She put her bowl down, lifted the buffalo skin he'd given her the morning they had agreed that their marriage would be beneficial to her people, and draped it about her shoulders. "I had planned to talk to some of the other women today. I will do it now."

She actually managed a stiff smile for both him and

Meigs, then she approached the door and soon stepped outside, closing the portal behind her.

Grant approached the fire—and the colonel. "Coffee?"

"Yes, thank you. They've set you up quite well here," Meigs commented, glancing around again as Grant reached for a mug and the tin pot he'd removed from the fire only moments before Meigs had knocked on the door. The agent removed his cape and tossed it over a stool placed near the far wall.

"They appreciated me driving off those ruffians," Grant said, pouring coffee into the mug. He stood, handed the mug to Meigs, and with a flick of one hand indicated the skins at his feet. "I can fetch stools or chairs if you mind sitting on these hides."

Sipping coffee, Meigs regarded Grant over the rim of the cup. "Now why do you think I would mind sitting on hides, Mr. Claiborne?"

"I don't know that you would or wouldn't. I'm only trying to be—"

"Ah! Therein lies our problem. We really don't know each other at all. I made assumptions about you yesterday, and I see suspicion in your eyes when you look at me. You've been listening to your wife, no doubt. Danagasta's distrust of me is no secret. Her first husband was friends with Chief Doublehead, a man who eventually agreed to some very satisfactory treaties."

"I know about the treaties. What I didn't know was that secret articles were included in those treaties. Apparently the Cherokee Council learned of them and ordered Doublehead assassinated."

Meigs sat on one hide. Grant sat on another, reaching for a second mug in which to pour coffee for himself.

"There were some . . . *separate* articles," Meigs admitted.

Grant glanced warily at the man, unsure if he wanted to hear this. He wondered if his father knew about the articles. But how could Charles not? Surely he reviewed every legal document that came to him. "Was the chief lured into agreeing to them?" Grant asked.

The colonel sighed. "There are times, Mr. Claiborne,

when a few amenities must be made on the side. Doublehead was a force in the Chickamauga faction during the late Cherokee wars, and convincing him to remain peaceful was no easy task. As a means of security, he wanted land he could call his, and that is precisely what we gave him. He knew he risked being called a traitor by his people. He knew he risked death."

"Did you know?" Grant chilled. He thought he already knew the answer, and if he was right, he didn't know if he could work with Meigs.

A moment of thick silence ensued.

"I knew," the agent said finally.

Dammit. Grant's hand tightened around his mug. He was right. If Danagasta heard this conversation, she would want to kill the agent.

"Did my father know?"

"He was informed. Like you, I was told to negotiate for land, and that is exactly what I did."

"By making a traitor out of a man who was apparently a great leader." Grant's voice was tight and strained.

"He was a war chief—savage and brutal. He—"

"As I was told all the Chickamaugans were? He was human!"

"He was not forced to sign."

"No—he was *bribed* into signing. And my father knew . . ."

Tiny nerves twitched around the agent's eyes. "For a man who married Hanging Basket's daughter to secure an exchange of land, you're incredibly self-righteous."

"I'll be blunt—and brief, Colonel Meigs. I believe a westward move is in the best interest of these people. I accepted this appointment for personal reasons. I came here willing to do what I was informed needed doing, but since my arrival things have changed . . . my feelings have changed. Living here . . ." With a wave of his hand and a glance around, Grant indicated the cabin. "Living in Big Water has given me a different perspective. I'd never seen an Indian before I came here. I had preconceived notions of an unintelligent, lower form of people. Instead I found a devoted, loving, proud people."

"This is no place for personal feelings," Meigs said.

"Have you considered how difficult it was for the Indians to order the death of one of their chiefs? I hate to think that if our government had stayed out of the Cherokee Nation—out of these people's lives—it might not have happened. I lay awake most of the night thinking about that."

Meigs's gaze narrowed. "The land is here. It's ripe, and our settlers want it."

"So no matter what you have to do . . . No matter if you have to lie or cheat or offer private *amenities*, you'll do it because you want to look good to your superiors. The first of those you must impress, of course, is my father. Have you considered the ambiguity of our positions falling under the secretary of war's supervision? I thought about that for the first time last night. If I were an Indian, I'd look with suspicion on the 'white man's government,' too. We've signed peace treaties, yet we send delegates from what is, in essence, our *war* department."

The look in Meigs's eyes was full-fledged distrust now. The man sipped coffee, but never took his gaze from Grant. "Why don't you resign your post if you find its duties so distasteful?"

"I thought about doing that, but I've decided to use my position to help these people."

Meigs tipped his head back. "I might remind you, Mr. Claiborne, that you fall under my command. That you are my deputy. If I were to ask for—"

"Yes—under your command . . . under the command of a man who seems to have no conscience," Grant responded softly, knowing he was about to draw a dangerous line. One that frightened him because he wasn't sure what, besides trepidation, lay on the other side. "Well, thank God I mistakenly landed here instead of at the Tellico Blockhouse. Thank God I met these people before I met you. If I'd known of your unscrupulous dealings, I would never have agreed to accept the appointment, and if I'd learned of your dealings shortly after my arrival, I would have promptly left the Cherokee Nation and not have become involved in any of this."

Moments passed in which Meigs looked quite taken aback—he flushed pink, then the color drained from his face. His lips parted, then snapped together. Grant half expected to be called out.

Meigs leaned forward. "Mr. Claiborne, you are employed by the United States Government. You could be accused of insubordination and even of being a traitor if you persist with these outrageous statements. Under United States law, traitors are hanged."

"At the moment, you won't accuse me of anything," Grant responded, staring straight at the man. "Right now, you're well aware that one negative word from me about the land exchange might induce the Indians to change their minds."

More nerves jumped around the colonel's gray eyes. "I don't believe your wife is aware of why you married her . . ."

Grant tossed what coffee remained in his cup at the flames. The fire sizzled and popped, and Meigs jerked back, looking startled again. "You're wrong," Grant snapped. "Not that my relationship with my wife is any of your business."

Meigs started to retort, but shut his mouth instead and sat quietly for a time while watching Grant. "All right, Mr. Claiborne," he said presently. "I came here peacefully, wanting to get to know you. But you've made your position clear: Instead of a having a deputy, I have another person to battle. For now I'm forced to overlook the conflict of interest in which you've embroiled yourself, the matter of an Indian agent marrying a Cherokee woman. You will stay in Big Water until I lead a delegation of chiefs to Washington. Once the delegates and I leave the Cherokee Nation, you will be relieved of your duties. A detailed report of this incident will be sent to the secretary of war."

"I'll be going with you to Washington," Grant informed him, not dwelling long on what his father was going to say about this "incident." "I'll be inspecting any treaty before it's put before the Indians. And believe me, Colonel, I'll know what I'm looking at. I have a law degree from the

College of William and Mary. After I'm satisfied that everything is as it should be, *then* you may relieve me of my duties and even have me arrested if you wish."

Meigs's jaw fell open. "Why, you pompous, overbearing—! Do not assume that anyone in Washington will take you seriously when you demand to—"

"To not take me seriously would be a big mistake."

The agent got to his feet, smoothed his coat, grabbed his wrap from the stool, and headed for the door. *The meeting is adjourned*, Grant thought caustically. "When you write to my father, don't forget to mention that the Indians need military protection," he reminded.

Meigs tossed a glare over his shoulder, then flung the door open and disappeared outside.

Grant lay back on the hemp carpet and stared at the poles overhead. He would lie just so for a while. If he sat up too soon before his stomach stopped churning, he'd become ill. He couldn't believe his father had known that if Chief Doublehead agreed to those articles, he risked death.

He didn't want to believe.

The following day, in an effort to put his mind on something besides Danagasta and the deputy agent, Sequatchee collected a long poplar log from the forest, rigged it with twine to a horse, and made the animal drag the log to just outside the palisade. There Sequatchee had Catolster help him lift the log and position both ends on stumps. Using fire and an adze, a tool with a thin blade secured to a wooden handle, Sequatchee began the long, time-consuming task of hollowing the log into a canoe. Working just outside of Big Water, he was available if Hanging Basket needed him, but he could not see Danagasta and her husband.

He worked and worked, burning out the wood, chipping bark away, pushing the adze along and slowly peeling away poplar. He did not want to think about anything but his task. But thoughts crept from dark corners of his mind anyway, and images appeared over and over inside his head: Danagasta as a young girl he wanted to court properly, but he was so flustered by just the sight of her that he did not have the courage to ask. Kayini, looking at him with adoration and love in her eyes. Losi telling him that he and Danagasta would marry. Losi eagerly drinking the first flask of whiskey Sequatchee provided him, and wanting more . . . learning to love the drink—so much so that he frightened Sequatchee at times. Again and again, Losi went across the river to the whites and traded them trinkets for flasks . . . He could no longer live without whiskey.

The adze slipped, and Sequatchee winced at the blood that appeared on his other hand from a small cut. He dropped the tool and pounded the log, wanting to chip and chip, cut and cut . . . wanting Losi's blood to be his own.

Danagasta and Dougherty were right: He had killed his brother. He had put the poison that eventually made his brother crazy into Losi's hands. *Sge! Ha!* If only he could take back what he had done! If only . . . He wanted his brother back—and he wanted Danagasta to be happy.

He was not sure the deputy agent would stay with her, but Tsatsi was right in saying that Danagasta was in love with Grant Claiborne; the love shone on her face. If the man left her when his task among the people was complete, Danagasta's heart would be broken.

Sequatchee picked up the tool and went to work again. Despite the cold wind that rattled the tree branches, perspiration beaded his brow. He wiped it away now and then, peeled more poplar, fetched a pine torch from where he had lodged it in the ground beside the fire he had built, and burned more wood out of the log. The work was tedious enough that by the time the Sun began lowering in the Skyland, he had succeeded in chipping away all of the bark but creating only a shallow curve from one end of the log to the other.

From between logs forming the palisade, Grant and Cullowhee watched Sequatchee off and on. This afternoon Cullowhee had chattered about how Sequatchee had brought a log from the forest, propped it on stumps and begun cutting and burning the wood that Cullowhee knew would eventually be a canoe. Watching Sequatchee work excited Cullowhee; he would like to learn to make a dugout.

Watching excited Grant, too, and made him want to go outside the palisade and offer to help. Carving a canoe wasn't like fitting planks, beams, and spars together to build a schooner or some other such vessel, but the simplicity of the canoe and the artistry that went into creating it fascinated Grant no less.

Some four cabins to the east along the palisade, Kayini, too, peeked between logs now and then while weaving a basket. She sensed that Sequatchee worked because he was troubled, and she longed to go to him. But what good would going to him do if he did not want to accept her comfort? She saw him drop the adze and she started to run out. But when she turned, there was Sali, shaking her head.

"His arms are not yet open to you," Sali said in Cherokee.

Disconcerted, Kayini sat back down on the little stool she had brought from her family's lodge and went back to weaving her basket with trembling hands.

Runners sent to towns and villages along the river and farther up the creek brought chiefs to Big Water the following day. There were four in all, and they, Hanging Basket, Sequatchee, and George Dougherty met with Grant and Meigs in the council house. The chiefs insisted on talking to "the white chief in Washington," and Meigs told them that he and Grant would lead a delegation of them to the United States capital during the upcoming summer. That seemed to please the Cherokee representatives; they nodded solemnly at each other, then passed a pipe to the colonel.

That night Grant stepped from the palisade gate and wandered between dark trees, as was his habit when he needed to relieve himself. He was just reaching for the thong on his belt when he heard low singing. He stepped between more trees, moving forward, more deeply into the forest, hearing the voice a little more clearly, though many a word was slurred. The lyrics were from an old English song Grant thought he recognized: ". . . wanton in her eye! Her arms white, round, and smooth, breasts rising in the dawn . . . Then did her sweets impart, when e'er she spoke or smiled."

There was a grumble, then the singer launched into another tune, something about passion being a source of all delights. Grant couldn't help a grin. Obviously one of the white men had stepped from inside the enclosure, perhaps to do the same business as he, and apparently felt lonely for female company. The voice and the lyrics were a surprise, a little slice of the world Grant had left months before. He moved forward, intending to get a peek at whoever was in the trees with him.

Twigs snapped beneath his buskins. The voice stopped singing. An owl hooted, filling the silence. "Who's there?" the man demanded. "I've got a pistol. Don't do anythin' you wouldn't want to die doin'."

Blackburn. Grant now recognized the deep, gravelly voice, though the man couldn't seem to form his words well.

"Grant Claiborne," Grant said, stepping forward. He barely made out the missionary's shadowed form propped against the trunk of a tree.

"What the devil're you doin' wanderin' out'n this wood, boy?"

Grant narrowed his eyes, now hearing a definite slur in the man's words. "Attending personal business. I might ask the same of you."

"Attendin' a little personal business o' my own."

Grant moved closer to the man and caught a whiff of whiskey; the sour smell wafted on the cold air. "Quite an . . . indelicate song, coming from a reverend," he half teased. "And when did a man of the cloth take to tipping a whiskey tin? You might be a little more discreet. Since the death of a certain townsman last year, the people of Big Water have an aversion to whiskey. *I* know."

Grumbling something, the minister struggled to get on his feet. "That so?"

"That's so."

"Well . . . I'll be takin' it a ways from here, then." Blackburn turned, started off, then turned back, stumbling slightly. "Wouldn't, uh . . . wouldn't want to join me, would you, Mr. Claiborne? We could talk 'bout the children. Only way to make civilized people of 'em is to teach 'em somewhere where there's no evil Indian beliefs an' heathen practices. All that dancin' the other night! Teach 'em a few Christian ways an' their bad habits'll go by the way."

Annoyance prickled the back of Grant's neck. He took three steps, reached for the flask Blackburn held in his right hand, uncorked the container, and flipped it, staring straight into the missionary's widening eyes as the whiskey gurgled and trickled, soaking the grass near Grant's feet.

The reverend groaned. "What're you doing? It's all I had left!"

"If you expect to talk intelligently to the people of Big Water, if you expect me to give you a moment of my time . . . don't talk about evil Indian beliefs and heathen practices while you're drunk. I've been here for months—moons—and I've seen nothing I consider evil. I've met no heathens." Grant dropped the tin, then smashed it with one foot.

Blackburn stared at him. "What're you . . . Dressed like 'em, talkin' like 'em—an' not just so you can convince 'em to trade land! You're one of 'em!"

"If you dislike them so much, why are you here?" Grant had to wonder aloud.

"Got a callin', that's why I'm here."

"A calling . . . From whom?"

"Why, from—"

"It doesn't matter. Everyone has demons to fight, Mr. Blackburn," Grant said. "You should see about getting rid of yours."

With that, he slipped back between the trees, hearing Blackburn grumble again.

Several mornings later, Grant took a mug of coffee and joined Danagasta outside the lodge where she was grinding dried corn into meal with a large wooden mortar and pestle. He set his mug on the ground and came up behind her to playfully reach around and help her grind.

"What are you doing?" she asked, smiling as he placed his hands above hers on the pestle.

"Helping." He pressed down at the same time she did, twisting the pestle, feeling and hearing the kernels break up. "Grinding corn is harder than it looks. How do you keep at this for long?"

"It is not so hard."

"Are you going to tell me it gets easier with practice?"

They pressed and twisted again. "It does," she said. A second later, she went still. "Look."

Grant glanced up and saw Meigs and Blackburn heading this way. They were accompanied by Hanging Basket, George Dougherty, and a small crowd of townspeople.

"I wonder what they want," Grant said.

"I do not want to think about that."

"We've come to say goodbye, Mr. Claiborne," Agent Meigs said, nearing.

Grant inclined his head in acknowledgment. "I'll send a message to the agency if there are any new developments."

"That would be an appropriate thing to do," Meigs responded, and Grant didn't miss his slight emphasis on "appropriate."

"Mr. Claiborne," the reverend said, stepping forward to extend his hand over the mortar. Grant shook the hand, all the while wondering at Blackburn's flickering eyes. He suspected the man wanted to say something more to him but didn't feel he could in the present company. He didn't seem resentful of the fact that Grant had poured out his whiskey the other night.

"By summer we will be traveling toward Washington," Meigs remarked.

Nodding, Grant stepped around Danagasta and her mortar and joined the gathering as it began moving in the direction of one of the palisade gates. He glanced over his shoulder just as she resumed grinding the corn.

Outside the gate, Meigs and Blackburn mounted their horses, which someone had brought from the pen. As the two men took their reins in hand and turned the animals, only the reverend bothered to tell Grant goodbye again.

Agent Meigs wasted no time riding away. Seconds later, Blackburn followed.

Afternoon arrived in Big Water, and Kayini was surprised when Danagasta joined a group of women and men bound for the river to collect water; usually Danagasta unwisely went by herself. But perhaps she had decided to start being friendly again.

The women carried hollowed gourds on their hips, and some had settled the straps of deerskin water bags between their breasts at an angle. The bags themselves dangled near the womens' waists. Danagasta filled her containers, then stepped back from the river, stumbling once. Kayini's older brother carried Kayini's bag, so Kayini approached Danagasta and gently took her gourd.

Danagasta looked startled. "Why are you helping me?"

"Because you are my friend," Kayini answered, giving a quick smile. She started off, seeing that many of the women had already climbed the hill. "Come, or they will leave us. I do not like being caught alone at the river anymore."

Danagasta moved up behind her, finally falling into step with her.

"Spring is not far away, I think," Kayini remarked. "Listen to the birds." They sang sweet songs, chirping overhead, alighting on bare branches. A mass of them fluttered up from a tall pine, making the boughs sway. The air held a light freshness.

"It is good to be able to hear the birds again," Danagasta said softly. "For so long I could not. I could hear only the voice of sorrow. My sorrow."

Kayini glanced at her. "Your love for Tlanuwa has made it possible for you to forget that sorrow."

"I did not think I could love another man. I am sorry for being mean these past seasons. To say that does not seem to be enough. I . . . when I think back, when I remember how I shouted at people, how I was mean . . . I am ashamed."

Kayini reached over and squeezed Danagasta's hand, drawing a stare once again. She smiled, then a slow, uncertain smile moved across Danagasta's lips. After a moment

Kayini sobered and inhaled deeply, summoning courage. "I have something to ask of you."

"What?"

"I have loved Sequatchee for a long time. Before Losi's death he asked to court me, and I accepted. But he has not looked my way since his brother died."

Kayini stared at the trees on the hillside. She and Danagasta reached the peak and started down. Up ahead, the other women and the men talked and laughed while carrying their water. "Sequatchee admired you, Danagasta, and when Losi died, he felt he should marry you and take care of you. He still feels that way. I believe he does not trust Tlanuwa—your husband—as many of us do. I believe he feels that the deputy agent will leave once the land exchange is made, and so he feels he must stay free because you will be sad again and will need to be taken care of. Perhaps Tlanuwa *will* leave. No one can be sure. Perhaps you *will* be sad again. But you do not love Sequatchee, and if you feel you cannot ever love him as a wife should love a husband, please speak to him and somehow free him of his duty to you." She made the request in a rush, then stared straight ahead as she walked, not wanting to see anger in Danagasta's eyes. Surely Danagasta did not think to keep Sequatchee waiting for her always.

More birds chirped, alighting then fluttering away. The water sloshed in the gourd. Sprinkles of it dampened one side of the colorful robe Kayini had woven for herself.

"I have never wanted Sequatchee to feel he must take care of me," Danagasta said finally. "I will speak to him."

Kayini released a breath of relief. "I ask one more thing—that you look inside your heart and try to forgive him. He has not drunk any whiskey since his brother's death, I feel certain. He blames himself, and you make his guilt worse. I risk your anger by saying this, but I love Sequatchee and I want his happiness. I want him to stop blaming himself. He did not force Losi to drink the whiskey while they were hunting. He did not force his brother to run out in front of the arrows. Losi killed himself." Kayini looked at Danagasta, who stared at her with wide eyes, and repeated quietly but succinctly: *"Losi killed himself."*

"I must not be a shrew anymore," Danagasta mumbled as her startled gaze slipped from Kayini.

Kayini was not sure what Danagasta meant, and why Danagasta was saying such a thing to herself, but she did not comment.

"I am trying to become a nice person again," Danagasta said. "I want my people to love me again. I do not want anyone to be afraid of me."

An unseen force gripped Kayini's heart. "We all love you. We have understood your anger and bitterness, though at times it has been difficult to tolerate. I am glad Grant Claiborne came to Big Water. None of our people would have scolded you the way he did. He is your healer."

Danagasta nodded, agreeing. "I will think about Sequatchee. I will talk to him."

"If you consider how much you love your husband, you will know how much I love Sequatchee," Kayini said. "We are not so different. We would die for the men we love. I know that in my heart." She squeezed her friend's hand again, and Danagasta stopped between trees to embrace Kayini. Kayini returned the affection, and both women laughed as water from the gourd splashed them. When Danagasta lifted her head to stare down at Kayini, Kayini saw tears, like those she felt sliding down *her* cheeks, in Danagasta's eyes.

"I do know how much you love him," Danagasta whispered. "I do. And I know how frightening it must be to worry whether or not he will return your feelings. Anything standing in the way of him doing that must be removed."

Rejoicing in her heart, Kayini turned with Danagasta to continue on to Big Water.

When they neared the palisade, they saw Sequatchee, again working furiously at making his canoe.

Chapter Sixteen

THAT NIGHT, THOUGH SNUGGLED warmly against her husband, Danagasta could not sleep. She turned onto her left side, heard him mumble something in his sleep—"death" and "wife"—and she turned back, propped herself up on an elbow, and smoothed the hair from his brow.

She could not see his face—right before he had fallen asleep, he had lowered the buffalo hides around the bed to keep the warmth inside—but she felt the tautness of his forehead and she whispered soothing Cherokee words to him. She began chanting softly, a combination of words her mother had taught her, syllables meant to comfort the soul. Blowing the smoke of remade tobacco over him would help, too, she knew. Perhaps she would weave some cloth, take it to the healer, and watch him wet the tobacco with his saliva, lift it, and speak sacred words—remake tobacco. She would explain the ritual to her husband, then explain that together the smoke from the great leaves and the words could help him.

Grant stopped mumbling and slipped into deep sleep again. But she still could not sleep, despite having lain in the bed a long time. Kayini's words to her after they had gathered water still weighed on her mind.

She was touched that after all this time, after all her anger and lashing out, Kayini still considered her a friend. Kayini was sweet and good; her heart was the size of one of the large mountains, it seemed. How could she say no to anything Kayini asked of her? She understood Kayini's love for Sequatchee, she thought as she listened to Tlanuwa's heavy breathing. Kayini deserved to lie in peace like this with the man she loved, and if Kayini felt so strongly that only Danagasta could release Sequatchee from his feeling of duty, Danagasta would talk to him and try to do that.

She wondered if Sequatchee really had not drunk whiskey again since Losi's death. For the first time since that horrible day, she wondered what exactly had happened during the hunting venture. She wondered what Losi had been thinking, *if* he had been thinking, and she wondered who had shot the arrows that killed him.

Does it matter? a voice whispered in her head. *You keep wanting to live in the past, keep wanting to relive the past when the present matters so much more. You have a new husband. He is good and wise. For the first time, you feel whole again, and it is time to help others feel whole again, too. It is time to help those who have suffered because of your bitterness.*

Through the buffalo skins and the lodge walls, Danagasta heard a wolf howl. Another answered, and the howls continued back and forth for some time. They were long, haunting wails, drifting on the wind, and as always, they captured Danagasta's interest. She was part of her mother's clan, the Wolf clan, and her ears had always perked whenever the animals she felt akin to called to one another.

Hoping she would not wake Tlanuwa, she sat up and eased from the tick, slipping silently between the bed hangings, taking a buffalo hide with her to drape about her shoulders. She had slipped a chemise on after she and her husband had made love earlier, and she felt its hem brush her calves as she walked to the cabin door.

Though the thin snow was cold to her feet, she stood outside the lodge, leaned back against the logs near the door, and listened to the mountain creatures. There were other noises, a baby crying in the distance and a dog barking, most probably at the wolves. Stars twinkled in the dark Skyland—they were dancing boys, Cornsilk had often told Danagasta, naughty boys who had not come home when their mothers had told them to, and so they had been lifted to the Skyland and would be there forever.

The Moon is the Sun's brother, Cornsilk had explained, a ball thrown up in the sky in a game played long ago. Two towns were playing against each other. One of the leaders of the game picked up the ball with his hand, something that is not allowed, and threw it toward the goal, but it struck the sky vault instead, and became stuck. There it remained, reminding ballplayers not to cheat.

The cabin door brushed open. "Danagasta?"

"Here," she replied, unmoving.

Tlanuwa moved from the door to her and complained about the cold snow on his feet. "What are you doing? I woke, and you were gone."

"Listening to the wolves and watching the sky. Listen."

He quieted. A howl echoed over distant hills to the north, then moments later one came from the east. The dog barked again.

"They were talking—the wolves," she said. "Perhaps they are planning how to get the dogs from the town's warm fires so they may return. Long ago the dogs were in the mountains, and the wolves were beside the fires here. The dogs were cold and ran down and chased the wolves from the fires so they could sit near them. The wolves went to the mountains, where they prospered and increased and have lived since. But sometimes they are cold and would like to come down again, so they howl."

"Well, I must be a wolf. I'm cold," Grant said, then he leaned near her ear and howled softly. She laughed. "I'm going back to bed," he grumbled. "I don't know how you tolerate standing in the cold."

"My feet are just now becoming cold—and I have been outside for some time!"

"They've adapted."

She cocked her head. "I do not know 'adapted.' "

"Your feet are used to the cold. Mine aren't. Mine like warmth."

"I will warm them for you," she said, smiling seductively. "I will warm *you*."

He chuckled. "I'm sure you will. But first you have to come back to bed."

Nearing him, she slid her hand down to meet his while tipping her head back and kissing him. She let him tug her gently back into the cabin.

Seconds later, they slipped behind the bed hangings.

The following day, Grant and Cullowhee stood near the palisade again, watching Sequatchee work furiously over the canoe—peeling away more and more wood, creating a deeper and deeper hollow. Grant had always felt Sequatchee's dislike of him. They'd even had words the night Grant had seen Danagasta in Sequatchee's arms. So Grant was reluctant to approach Sequatchee with questions about making a canoe.

"Why do you watch him through the logs, Agent-man?" Cullowhee asked.

Grant glanced at the boy. "I'm curious."

"You are afraid to go out."

"I'm not afraid."

"Then why do you not go talk with him? Like me, you would like to know more about dugouts."

"Why don't *you* go talk to him?"

"I am not permitted beyond the palisade alone."

"It's not like you to honor a rule," Grant teased.

"I know the reason for this rule. Many rules—I do not know the reason for them."

"Ah, the logical mind of a child!"

"I will ask to go out with you if you agree to go," Cullowhee said.

Grant drew back, giving a short laugh. "And what if I don't want to go?"

The boy turned from the logs and started off. "You want to go. If my father, Talalah, Shutegi, or one of the other men were making the canoe, you would have gone when they began," he tossed over a little shoulder.

Grant couldn't fault Cullowhee for his perception. He caught up with the boy and walked with him to his family's cabin, where Cullowhee pulled the oak door open, allowing him and Grant to enter the lodge.

Grant had been inside the large cabin before, where Sali and her husband lived with their three children. He waited in the main room, what might have been called a parlor in the white man's world, while Cullowhee called for his mother and scurried down a hall formed by stitched-together skins hanging from overhead beams. Sali appeared in the hall, her brow knitted as she spoke to her youngest son in Cherokee. Cullowhee answered, pointing to Grant, then Sali looked up, smiled, and nodded. Cullowhee hurried excitedly back down the hall.

"I promise to return him before long," Grant told Sali. Cullowhee said something in Cherokee over his shoulder, and Sali nodded at Grant again.

Back outside, Grant and Cullowhee cut between lodges, spotting Kayini and Danagasta working at a finger loom near Kayini's family's cabin. Both women looked up, and Grant approached, with Cullowhee at his side, to explain that he and his little friend were about to go outside the palisade to talk to Sequatchee.

"I need to speak with Sequatchee soon myself," Danagasta said.

Grant had hunched near where she sat on a stool before the loom, and now he peered curiously at her.

She glanced down at the white belt she was weaving. "I need to tell him I no longer blame him for Losi's death. I need to make peace with him."

Grant couldn't control the smile that pulled at his mouth. Yesterday afternoon he'd been pleased by the sight of Danagasta and Kayini walking back from the river together; they'd entered Big Water some distance behind the other women and the men who had accompanied the group in the event there was more trouble with the Tennessee settlers. Weeks ago, Sali had told Grant that Danagasta and Kayini had once been friends before Danagasta's bitterness toward Sequatchee had driven the young women apart. Kayini loved Sequatchee, Sali had explained, and Kayini—and many others—did not feel Danagasta should blame Sequatchee for his brother's death. So Grant had been surprised, but delighted, when he had seen Danagasta and Kayini conversing pleasantly.

"You really don't blame him anymore?" Grant asked Danagasta.

"I do not. You and Kayini, even Sequatchee, made me realize all the reasons I should not. But I have made Sequatchee feel more guilty than he already did, and I must think of a way to help him now so that he does not keep blaming himself."

Grant couldn't help himself; he reached up to caress her cheek. "I'm glad you realize that Sequatchee didn't kill him," he said. Then he stood and turned with Cullowhee to go see if Sequatchee would talk to them about the canoe.

Danagasta said something more, in Cherokee this time and in a louder voice, ending it in English: "I should not have scolded you about the broken cane, Cullowhee."

Cullowhee dipped his head, glanced at Grant, then tossed Danagasta a shy smile. Grant ruffled the boy's hair, letting his hand fall to rest on Cullowhee's shoulder as he and his little friend advanced on the palisade gate.

Sequatchee looked up as the deputy agent and Cullowhee approached, and he lowered the lit pine knot he held over the length of poplar. These past days, he had noticed Grant Claiborne, Cullowhee, and even Kayini watching him but he did not think they knew he noticed them. Cullowhee had always been fascinated by any sort of wood work, and many times Sequatchee had answered the boy's numerous questions, had even shown him how to carve a bow. Cullowhee did a fine job of that now.

Sequatchee had made only four dugouts in his adulthood, because the four he made were sturdy, and he did not have frequent need of a canoe since he was content not to wander far from Big Water. During the Chickamauga wars, he and others had not traversed the Tennessee often because the white soldiers watched for them on the great *equoni-geyvi*. But because the making of a canoe took many days, Sequatchee had used the craft these past days to occupy himself so he would not have time to wander Big Water and see Danagasta and the deputy agent together. He understood Cullowhee's interest in the shaping of the dugout, but he wondered at Grant Claiborne's.

"*Osiyo,* Sequatchee," Cullowhee said as he and the deputy agent neared.

"*Osiyo,*" Sequatchee returned, gripping the torch as he regarded the boy. He asked in English: "Your mother said you could go beyond the palisade?"

"*Vy.* I am *equa.*"

Sequatchee grinned. "Yes, you are big, but you also have an adult with you, one who protects women and children very well." He had not wanted to admire the way the deputy agent had protected the women and children by the river that day, but he had—and he still did.

"We've come to look at your canoe, if you'll allow us," Grant Claiborne said.

Sequatchee met his gaze and nodded, though he wished Danagasta's new husband would go observe someone else. He had started making the dugout outside the palisade so he did not have to see the man. Now he was faced with him, and with the prospect of having to be around him for as long as the man wanted to look at the *tsiyu*.

"We can watch closely as you burn and chip away the wood?" Cullowhee asked excitedly in English.

Sequatchee shifted his gaze from the boy to Grant, though he spoke to Cullowhee: "The white man has an interest in knowing how the *tsiyu* is made?"

"Tlanuwa is my friend," the child said, looking apprehensive, his nose and lips wrinkled. "I know he has Danagasta and you do not, but—"

"We will only talk about the canoe," Sequatchee said gruffly, turning away.

The white man cleared his throat. "I'm interested in any water vessel."

"I have put sticks here in the part I have already carved," Sequatchee said, nearing the center of the length of poplar. "Now I will put fire to them, as I watched my father and uncle do many times, and burn out some of the wood. Then I will dig out more and more, and shape the inside and finally the outside."

Stepping up beside him, Cullowhee and Grant Claiborne peered down at the pile of sticks laid in a crisscross pattern. Sequatchee held the lit pine knot out to Cullowhee and said, "Put it to the sticks."

The boy did not hesitate; he took the torch and lowered it, holding it to the sticks until they began to glow like embers. Then he handed the torch back to Sequatchee, who nodded his approval.

"You have seen the tool—an adze," Sequatchee said, taking one from the leather sheath tied to his left thigh. "It is used to carve and shape. You push it along the log, and it peels the wood away. My father sometimes used a hatchet."

"Why don't you use a hatchet?" the deputy agent asked.

"Because I like the feel of the wood beneath my hands—and because the adze is slower."

"Why must you go slow?" Cullowhee inquired.

"I work better when I work slowly. And when I work slowly, the digging and shaping takes longer. It keeps me from inside the town, where I do not need to be right now."

From the hollow he had made in the log, Sequatchee lifted another adze and turned and handed it to the white man. "I do not understand why you want to learn how to make a dugout. You will leave Big Water once the land exchange is made. In the white man's world, one does not need to know how to make a canoe."

Grant tipped his head, regarding Sequatchee harshly. "I didn't come out here looking for a quarrel with you," he said, taking the tool. "I told you—I'm interested in any water vessel. Looms and plows were introduced in Big Water by whites so your people would have an easier time farming and weaving. Perhaps I can take something I learn here back to my people. Learning from each other benefits all."

Sequatchee studied him a little longer, then leaned over the log and began scraping. The deputy agent moved a short distance down the length of wood and began scraping, too.

Much later in the day, Danagasta approached the cabin she had shared with her first husband. Among the Cherokee, the lodge and most everything inside of it belonged to the woman. If the husband and wife divorced, the man simply packed his belongings, left, and went back to his parents' home or built himself a new lodge. It was the ancient way still observed in Big Water, though Danagasta knew that in many settlements, new ways and customs, introduced by incoming whites and liberal Indians, were rapidly replacing the old.

She paused outside the cabin, glancing at the structure she had watched Losi build. She remembered him carving the ends of the logs, fitting them together, then securing them with strips of wet buffalo hide that would shrink while drying. She remembered him working clay and grass together to fill in cracks and holes so the cabin would be warm during winter and cool during summer. She remembered the day he had finished, how he had climbed down from the strong roof upon which he had secured many pieces of bark. He had approached her where she sat on a wolfskin nearby and he had held out his hand, beckoning her, then leading her into the lodge where she had given herself in marriage to him. They had been happy in their home, and she had delighted in the knowledge that they would soon have a child. Then he had died.

Thinking about him and the baby she had miscarried soon after his death did not hurt the way it had as little as two moons ago. Losi would always occupy a place in her heart, though he had had a weakness for the white man's poison, a weakness she did not find admirable. She now realized that she should have objected more to him filling himself with whiskey, that in a way she had made drinking it easy for him. How sad that he had not had the sense to know that something that weakened his mind so much could not be good for him, that it might even bring sorrow to those who loved him.

"What were you thinking when you poured the poison

down your throat that day?" she demanded aloud, again envisioning him working on the roof. For the first time, she was angry with him for being so careless, for being so foolish. "I loved you, but you did not consider me—and so you are not worthy of my devotion. I have spent seasons blaming other people, and I will no longer do that."

She still loved him, but she would make no more excuses for his behavior—and she would no longer put the blame for what he had done to himself on Sequatchee. If she had known that fateful day what she knew now . . . if she had felt as strong inside, she should have packed Losi's things when he refused to leave his whiskey flask in the lodge, handed him his belongings, and told him to leave, that since he obviously did not care about what happened to her and their child, she would take care of herself and the *usdiga*.

"You could have tipped your flask and poured out the whiskey. Instead you chose to drink it," she said, entering the cabin.

She began gathering his things, many belts she had lovingly woven for him, the lacrosse sticks, several balls made of animal hair and hide, two breechclouts, buckskin breeches on which she had stitched with black thread the image of an eagle; beaded and tasseled shirts, a small cane-pouch that held tobacco, cloth used to make a turban, and a feathered stick he had often inserted in his head-covering for decoration. She gathered his bow and arrow, his blowgun and darts feathered with thistledown, his set of turtle-shell rattles and three pipes he had carved from stone . . . She piled everything on a large wolfskin, rolled the hide and secured it with three leather strips, one at each end and one in the middle.

Then she started from the lodge.

At the deerskin flap, she turned back, thinking she had forgotten something. She had: his water drum—a small keg with a groundhog-skin head—which rested in a far corner. She crossed the nearly deserted cabin, bent, snatched up the drumstick and tucked it under her arm. Then she lifted the drum and settled it on her hip.

Outside, she walked past rows of lodges and past children playing ball on the town square. Some of them stopped to stare at her, and she shocked them by smiling and by saying *"Osiyo."* Two lifted their brows, while others whispered to each other. Danagasta's smile widened as she walked on, toward Sequatchee's cabin.

It was a small lodge, tucked between two large ones. Sequatchee had been a young man when he and Losi's parents had died of smallpox, and the two brothers had lived here alone until the day Losi finished the new lodge for his bride. A bearskin was tacked to the outside of the cabin. A hide hung in the entrance.

Danagasta paused near the hide, breathed deeply, and spoke loudly in her people's language: "Sequatchee, it is Danagasta. I have come to speak with you."

Soon the flap was pushed aside, and Sequatchee stood in the doorway, his hair mussed and his eyes slightly swollen as if he had been asleep. He wore dark blue breeches and a shirt of red and blue cloth. His calves and feet were bare. "Danagasta," he said in a tone of great surprise.

"I have brought things . . . Losi's things. May we talk inside?"

He stepped aside from the door and with a flick of his hand indicated that she should enter.

The inside of the cabin was dim and cold. More skins, and feathers collected on twine, hung on logs that formed the walls. A small trunk held an array of pots, bowls, spoons, and other utensils. Mats covered the floor some distance from a dark spot where a fire had obviously burned. Two stools were pulled closely together. Pieces of flint, some chipped into arrowheads, rested atop one.

"There is the Sun outside, Sequatchee," Danagasta said, surprised at the feeling of loneliness and desolation the lodge stirred in her. She turned and met his gaze and realized the feeling of loneliness and desolation came from him, not necessarily from his surroundings. "I am sorry for what I have done to you," she whispered, feeling a surge of anger at herself. How could she have been so selfish these past seasons? So much so that she had made him more miserable than her?

"You have not done anything—"

"No. I have, Sequatchee. Do not tell me I have not. I am only beginning to realize that no one should be made to feel guilty for what another person has done. Losi's death disturbed both of our lives, but I am sorry that I have made his death worse for you to bear. I cannot imagine . . . it was hard for me to bear. I cannot know how I would have felt if someone had blamed me for it. I know such blame would have hurt me inside, worse than his death and the loss of the baby hurt. You did not kill him, Sequatchee. My husband killed himself, and you and I need to forget and find happiness."

He stood with his back to one side of the wall near the entrance, and stared at her, his eyes shimmering.

Smiling gently, she approached him. "You do not know what to think of me coming here and speaking of such things. I am sincere. I have not come to yell at you or trick you. I have brought some of Losi's things that we should sit and look at together. If you want to keep anything, you may. Anything that is left I will take somewhere and bury as we buried my husband's body. Please understand—I must. And I think you must."

"Your face," he said finally. "It has a glow it has not had since before Losi died."

"I have found peace, Sequatchee. And I want to help you find peace. I know that you have cared for me for a very long time, but you must try to understand . . . I care for you, too, but not in the way a wife should love a husband. I do not feel you should spend your life worrying about what will happen next in mine, worrying about who will take care of me. I want to see you find happiness with a family you help create."

"Danagasta, I do not feel the deputy agent will stay—"

"It is not for you to worry about. It is my problem, my difficulty, my marriage. Much of your devotion to me is guilt, and the time has come to bury that guilt. Before Losi's death you had started to go on with your life. You had asked to court Kayini—you had asked for permission you did not need, but felt getting was important. There are many things to admire in you, but you are wasting them by waiting for me."

She lowered the drum and stick, then kneeled, placed the rolled skin on a mat before her and untied all three strips of leather. Glancing up, she noticed that Sequatchee had pressed his back to the wall and that his gaze darted between her and the hide. She unrolled the skin, revealing Losi's breechclout, breeches, and the stick that he had often used to decorate his turban. The tobacco pouch came into view, and Sequatchee released a long breath and a soft cry that sounded like that of a wounded animal.

"No!" He started across the cabin. "I do not need to look at more of his things! I have enough!"

From a corner he yanked forth a chest, threw the lid open and pulled the trunk toward her. Near her partially unrolled hide, he dumped the contents of the chest: a flageolet of cedar wood, a beaded neck band, small woven and beaded tassels that were sometimes pinned to a turban, a stick wrapped with buckskin and used to buff silver ornaments, cakes of dried deer brains mixed with fiber and roots, used to tan skins. There were moccasins and shirts . . . even a chungke stone. Losi had loved playing chungke, a game of stones.

"Sequatchee," Danagasta whispered, staring at the many things, "you are like me. You have tortured yourself by keeping his things with you."

He rubbed his forehead, then made a fist and kicked at the items—kicked and kicked. He breathed rapidly through his mouth, demanding, "Why? Why did he . . . Why did he do it? Why did he run out in front of the arrows? Stupid, stupid Losi! He thought he could not die! Stupid, foolish, crazy . . . ! He left me and he left you, and I am angry. I am *angry*!" He gave one last kick, scattering his brother's belongings. Then he dropped to his knees, lifted some of the items to his face, and wept, his body trembling with the force of his grief.

Though Danagasta was angry with Losi, too, she could find no more tears to shed for her first husband. She had shed so many right after his death and so many since. She felt stronger inside now, but Sequatchee did not yet, so she laid a hand upon his back and spoke soothing words to him; she began singing a soft Cherokee song to help calm his soul.

They sat on the floor mats for a very long time, until Brother Moon shone down from the ventilation hole in the roof, until Sequatchee's every tremble ceased, until every sob left his body. Until he lifted his head and stared at her with glistening eyes.

"I will make a fire," he mumbled, wiping his face with his hands. "Then we will look at these things."

She nodded.

He gathered wood from near a far wall and built a fire in the center of the lodge. Then he sat beside her, asking wearily, "Do you love Grant Claiborne?"

"Yes."

"You are sure he was not bringing whiskey into the Nation to sell?"

"He told me he was not. I must trust him. He is my husband."

"I would have been a fine husband for you, Danagasta."

"You will be a fine husband for Kayini." She picked up the flageolet, ran her fingertips along the smooth wood, and traced several of the holes in the instrument. "Losi taught you to play this?"

"No, he never did. But he could make beautiful songs come out of it."

Smiling, she nodded. "Yes, he could. I have not seen this since the morning before we were married, when he approached me in the forest where I was gathering plants to cook. He climbed up into a tree and played it for me the entire time. All the women teased him, telling him he was a fool in love. But they thought him cute."

"He planned to teach me how to play it." Sequatchee inhaled deeply. "So I could charm my own female, he said."

Danagasta's smile broadened. "Catolster knows how to play it. You could ask him to teach you."

He managed a weak smile. "Perhaps I will . . . in time."

She placed the flageolet and picked up the silver buffer, turning it in her hand.

"He liked ornaments," Sequatchee said. "He made many for our mother when we were boys."

"He liked *decoration*," Danagasta remarked, amused. "Feathered sticks and tassels in a turban when he wore one. Losi . . . he had his special ways, did he not?"

"Yes, he did."

Sequatchee reached around her back and pulled the drum toward him, tapping the taut groundhog skin with a forefinger. Then he picked up the stick and tapped the head with it, creating a soft, hollow beat. "He liked to make music."

"And he liked to dance."

Danagasta dropped the silver buffer, unrolled her wolf-skin the rest of the way, and lifted the buckskin breeches on which she had stitched the image of an eagle. She stared at the great bird. "I did not tell him, but I used strands of my hair for this," she said glancing up at Sequatchee.

He lifted his brows. "Your hair?"

She nodded. "You and Losi and others were going hunting for a bear, and we know how fierce the bear can be. I wanted to go, but Losi said no, so I stitched these breeches for him and used strands of my hair to make the eagle. That way part of me went with him. It was deceitful of me and—"

"But that was what Losi loved about you the most, Danagasta. He never knew what to expect from you. You never bored him."

She smiled, and he smiled back. "Part of me went on the bear hunt," she remarked, lifting her chin.

He laughed, a good sound.

Sequatchee reached for the turtle shells, into which Losi had put small stones to make rattles, and he began tying them on his calves. Danagasta fastened the lower ties, while he fastened the upper ones. When they were secure, he stood, and she took up the stick and began beating out a rhythm on the drumhead, a fast rhythm Losi himself had beat out many times.

Sequatchee began chanting and dancing, shuffling and lifting his legs and arms in rapid succession. He closed his eyes, squeezed them shut, and she thought she saw tears ease between the lids. She looked down, sensing that wearing Losi's rattles while dancing and singing comforted him, forced him to face his grief. Afterward he would begin to heal.

Much later, the rattling and chanting ceased. Danagasta stopped beating the drum, and she sat in silence while Sequatchee removed the rattles, finally tossing them aside. He took up the tobacco pouch and one of the pipes she had brought. Moving away, he rummaged through his trunk and returned with a long hollow pipe handle which he fitted on the pipe. Then he stuffed tobacco into its bowl and advanced toward the fire to light it. Soon, the sweet, pungent smell of *tsalu* wafted in the cabin.

He touched her arm, and when she looked up, he offered her the pipe. She had smoked sometimes with Losi. She took the instrument, put the stem to her mouth and drew deeply from it, coughing when the smoke entered her lungs. She closed her eyes and forced herself to breathe deeply. Before long the tobacco's soothing power drifted through her body.

Sequatchee sat beside her, and together they continued to smoke, passing the pipe back and forth. Finally, he said, "I loved my brother. I will always love him. But you are right—we must bury all these things. We must keep our good memories of him and try to be happy now."

Danagasta nodded, agreeing.

Chapter Seventeen

WINTER FADED WITH THE last of the snow, and spring began with much rain in the great mountains. The mist came again, rising every morning from the trees, making distant hills and snow-topped crests appear hazy. Kayini sometimes saw Sequatchee watching her from afar, but he never held her gaze for long. Still, he was at least watching her sometimes . . .

One afternoon she gathered a group of children around her in the town square, which was rapidly turning a vivid shade of green. She sat on a stool, surrounded by Cullowhee, his friends, and many other precious children, both small and large. As she often did, she began telling them the stories she had loved hearing as a child, stories they, too, loved.

"The buck has not always had horns," she said, leaning forward to capture the children's interest. "His head was once smooth like the doe's. Deer was a great runner, and Rabbit was a great jumper, and the many other animals were curious to know which one, Deer or Rabbit, could go farther in a race. The animals talked about their curiosity and finally arranged a match between Deer and Rabbit, offering a nice large pair of antlers as the prize for the winner. Deer and Rabbit were to start together from one side of a thicket and go through it, then turn and come back. The one who came out first would get the horns.

"All the animals—Possum and Wildcat and Turkey and Mole and Bear and many, many others—came to watch the race. The antlers sat on the ground at the edge of the thicket to mark the starting point. Everybody admired the horns. Rabbit said, 'I don't know this part of the country. I want to look through the bushes where I am to run.' The animals thought that was all right, so Rabbit went along, into the thicket. After he was gone so long, the animals suspected he must be up to a trick. They sent a messenger to look for him. In the thicket the messenger found Rabbit gnawing down bushes and pulling them away to clear a road nearly to the other side.

"The messenger did not let Rabbit see him. He turned quietly away and came back to the animals, telling what he had seen. When Rabbit returned to the gathering, the animals accused him of cheating. He denied it until everyone went into the thicket and found the road he had cleared. They agreed that such a trickster had no right to enter the race at all, so they gave the horns to Deer, who was proclaimed the best runner, and Deer has proudly worn the horns ever since. The animals told Rabbit that since he was so fond of cutting down bushes, he might do that for a living always, and so he does."

Some of the children smiled and talked excitedly among themselves, putting their hands to the tops of their heads and playing like they were Deer. After a time, some pleaded for another story, and Kayini began another of the many that she had learned as a child. She began telling how, after the animals awarded the antlers to Deer, Rabbit bore a grudge and resolved to get the horns. Rabbit tricked Deer into letting him sharpen his teeth, but instead of sharpening them, Rabbit got a hard stone with rough edges and filed and filed away at Deer's teeth until they were worn down nearly to the gums. When Deer tried to bite a branch, he could hardly bite at all, and Rabbit laughed and said, "Now you have paid for your horns."

Wadigei, one of Cullowhee's close friends, wanted to hear how Deer had gotten revenge on Rabbit by daring him to jump a certain stream, and Awe-ani-da wanted to hear the tale of why Mink smells. Kayini told both stories, then told some Snake legends.

Sequatchee had slept very late because he had enjoyed working on his canoe by the light of the moon last night. Three days ago, he and Danagasta had journeyed a ways from Big Water to bury most of Losi's things. He had kept the drum and its stick, however, and Danagasta had kept the tassels Losi had sometimes used to decorate his turbans.

Sequatchee rose, dressed, and tucked his carving tools into the sheaths dangling from the belt he wore. Then he emerged from his lodge, thinking to again work on the canoe. But this time he did not necessarily wish to avoid anyone; he simply wished to finish what he had begun. He felt better in his heart today than he had since the day of Losi's death, when he had begun blaming himself so much, when the obligation of taking care of his brother's widow had begun to gnaw at him. He felt lighter, free of shame and much guilt, though he would always regret introducing Losi to whiskey. But at least now he could lift his head whenever he walked through Big Water. At least now he could look Danagasta in the eye and not feel the urge to fall to his knees at her feet and beg her forgiveness.

He neared the town square and paused beside a cabin at the sight in the field: Kayini with children gathered around her knees. She, too, had been hurt by circumstances surrounding his brother's death, he thought. Before that terrible day, he had begun to court the girl who had grown into a woman before his startled eyes; after that terrible day, his guilt had been so intense he had resolved to convince Danagasta to marry him so he could take care of her, so she would not be lonely, and so she might have the children he knew she desired.

But now . . . Now, for the first time in nearly four seasons, he paused to allow himself the pleasure of looking upon Kayini again. She was a woman who had always thrilled and charmed him in little ways. During the seasons he had pined for Danagasta, Kayini could have married someone else, but she had not. He could not help but wonder if she had been waiting for him, hoping he would come to his senses.

With hand motions and facial expressions, she emphasized parts of the old stories. Some of the children stood and wandered off, but most were spellbound. She had braided her long hair to one side, and the plait draped over her thin shoulder and full breast, and ended at her waist. He recalled how excited she had looked the morning she had collected the bowl of hominy he had placed on her family's doorstep, an indication, properly given, that he wished to court the unmarried woman within the house. From where he had stood watching some distance away, he had seen her smile, clutch the bowl to her chest, then withdraw into the lodge—an acceptance of his request.

She felt his gaze; she glanced up from the children, and her eyes scanned the cabins located near the square, finally landing on him. Their gazes locked. Her lips parted, her hands stilled, and after a moment, her eyes skittered back to the children. If she had been a white woman, a pink flush would have stolen across her cheeks. Sweet Kayini . . . He suddenly longed to apologize for ignoring her for so long.

His feet seemed frozen to the spot, but he forced them into motion. He walked onto the square, approaching Kayini and her group of children. She glanced up as he neared, and she paused in telling how the Sun had become angry at the people and so had transformed a man into a monster snake, which the people called Uktena—or, the Keen-eyed.

"No one tells the legends better than you, Kayini," he said softly. "I am sorry for the way I have ignored you."

After stating the apology, he walked on, not tarrying, for he knew the children wanted to hear the story, and he would not be responsible for keeping it from them. But he felt Kayini's gaze on his back until he passed between, then beyond, two lodges.

Sequatchee's first words to her in so long made Kayini's heart leap, and she almost could not continue the story she had begun. Had Danagasta talked to him? Had she forgiven him, released him from the guilt he bore over Losi's death so that he could see that his devotion to Danagasta and his desire to marry her was not so much because he loved her, but because he felt he owed her something? Kayini could not be sure, of course, why Sequatchee had crossed the square to speak softly to her then continued on, but she could hope, as she had for so long.

When the ground had adequately warmed enough for spring planting, Grant watched many a ceremony, enacted by the "priest." Danagasta explained that the ceremonies were performed to ensure good and abundant crops.

Each family was assigned a section of the large town garden. Grant and Danagasta were given an area, and though tilling it and removing all the roots was hard work, it was satisfying. Grant found that he longed to see the final result. As small as his and Danagasta's garden seemed, he took great pride in it. He almost couldn't wait for the plants to spring up, lush and green, and he told Danagasta how he felt, how excited he was.

During the corn-prayer ceremony, single grains were deposited in a number of small dirt hills formed within each family's section, and the priest spent days "blessing" each area—sitting near it, smoking what Danagasta called "sacred tobacco." He scattered more grains of corn, shook a rattle, and sang songs. Near the end of the blessing sung for Grant and Danagasta's lot, a breeze rustled the branches of the few trees located within the compound. When Grant looked up, Danagasta explained that it was the spirit of the Old Woman bringing the true corn. Now they must leave the field and not return for many days. When they returned, hopefully they would find young stalks.

They did.

More crops were planted, and as the days passed, as tree

buds opened, as rhododendron bloomed pink and white and azaleas began blazing the hillsides with color, Grant and Danagasta's section of garden flourished, as did many other lots. The creek and river had thawed, and water rushed down from mountain streams. Birds populated the trees and the azure sky.

They hunted together one day, walking a good three miles from Big Water, spotting a number of deer. But she had her eyes on a certain one, she said, a fine buck with a broken horn, and they tracked the animal another mile, until Grant was ready to collapse. She began singing a song she called the deer-hunting song, and he began to seriously doubt that she knew what she was doing. Then she brought the buck down with one arrow.

"I've, uh, practiced some archery," he said in amazement, "but I've never seen anyone do that!"

She was going to carry the animal back across her shoulders, but Grant insisted that he should. By the time they reached Big Water, he was exhausted, and she laughed at him.

"Stop that," he scolded lightly.

"I told you I should carry him."

"How do you do this?" he asked, spotting the palisade. "Hunt deer miles from Big Water and carry them back?"

"The men sometimes make litters."

"Why don't you?"

She shrugged.

"We'll make a litter next time," he grumbled.

The next day, using an ax that one of the men had made for him, Grant chopped down a poplar tree, cut away the branches, then had Catolster and Kaliquegidi show him how to rig the log to horses. Once the length of poplar had been dragged near Grant and Danagasta's cabin, Grant began chipping away bark and wood, using an adze he'd fashioned himself from carved oak and sharpened flint.

One afternoon while he was working, pushing the adze along the slight hollow he'd formed in the log, he noticed Danagasta seated on a stool and milking a cow not far away. He took the stool he'd placed near the log and quietly approached her. He plopped his stool behind hers, settled on it, and peered over her shoulder, watching her hands squeeze milk from the udders into a wooden pail. The milk foamed and frothed.

"That looks interesting," he teased. "Why did you bring this animal here?"

"Milking her here is easier than milking her around the other cows and bulls in the pen." She smiled and squirted milk at him. The warm stream hit his forehead, trickled down over one eye, dripped onto his cheek, and rivered down from there. He caught some of it with his tongue. Danagasta stopped milking to laugh.

"Funny, is it?" he said, tickling her ribs. She laughed more and wriggled on the stool. The cow's back legs shifted, and she glanced up and around from the pile of corn husks Danagasta had put down for her. Grant let go of Danagasta's ribs, not wanting to spook the animal.

But he didn't intend to let Danagasta get away with squirting him. He reached over, grabbed an udder and gave it a yank. Nothing happened. "You couldn't have milked her dry already," he said, mystified. "You haven't been sitting here that long."

Danagasta laughed again. "That is not the way to milk her. You cannot just pull. Watch . . ." She took the udder between her thumb and forefinger and pressed down, squeezing gently. Milk streamed into the bucket, creating more bubbles and froth.

Grant copied her action, but only produced a trickle of milk. He frowned. "This is more difficult than it looks. How did you learn to do that?"

"I did it again and again, until I became better."

He pressed down and squeezed again, and this time produced a weak trickle. Glancing around, the cow raised her back leg nearest Danagasta, threatening to kick them and the bucket.

"She doesn't like me," Grant observed.

Sighing, Danagasta tried to look serious. "Perhaps not."

"Very well." Grant rose and gathered his stool. "I'll go back to making my dugout."

"You pout better than Cullowhee," she said, smiling.

He grumbled playfully as he walked toward his length of poplar.

That evening, she invited him to bathe with her in the creek. At his request—he didn't want her exposed to danger—she'd stopped bathing in the river. Now that the water had warmed somewhat, he didn't mind joining her now and then.

The sky was a mixture of red, orange, blue, and purple, and the colors reflected on the water. In the distance, trees rose gently up hillsides and mountains, creating a blend of deep green and blue among many colorful flowers and plants. Once Grant and Danagasta were in the water he couldn't seem to take his eyes off her for more than a moment at a time. The cool water flowed around their thighs, and droplets clung to her breasts as she tipped her face toward the setting sun, breathing deeply. Her eyes flickered orange and red when she met Grant's gaze and smiled.

Uninvited, Awe-ani-da came charging into the creek, her naked bottom shimmering. Grant heard a shout and spotted her father, Catolster, lumbering this way; the child had apparently wandered from him. Wondering if he should toss Danagasta her dress, then remembering that none of the women were modest to the extreme, Grant watched as Danagasta caught the girl up in her arms and twirled her around, drawing a shrill giggle from Awe-ani-da. Grant smiled, and for a startling moment he wondered what a child conceived by him and Danagasta would look like.

The thought caught him by complete surprise, as did the notion that he was growing at least as fond of Danagasta as he was of the child she was holding, and he shook his head in an attempt to force the disturbing thoughts away.

A little later, he entered the lodge before Danagasta and built a fire, knowing she'd want to dry her hair over it. He always tried to give her time alone right after she bathed, so he gathered his pipe and the tobacco pouch she'd woven for him, and turned, planning to visit Hanging Basket for a while.

Danagasta entered the cabin, her eyes still glowing, her sleek hair draped over one side of the wolfskin coat she often wore until she was warm and dry.

"*Osiyo,* my husband," she murmured in her richly seductive voice.

Turning her back to him, she pushed the coat from her shoulders, and let it fall softly to the planked floor. The sleeveless white chemise she had donned upon stepping from the creek flowed gently around her. Firelight danced on her skin and her hair. Grant couldn't take his eyes off her.

I'm falling in love with my bewitching Cherokee wife, he thought.

He ought to leave the cabin quickly. But it was too late . . . Desire stole over him as she turned slightly and he glimpsed the shadow of one breast. He forced himself to loosen his grip on the tobacco pouch before he crushed it. Danagasta glanced at him over her shoulder, then leaned over her basket of personal belongings. He dropped his pipe, stick and pouch on top of a stool and approached her from behind, telling himself it wasn't love. No, it wasn't love—it was lust. That was all.

She straightened, holding a comb carved from bone, and he brought his hands up to rest lightly on her hips. He ran them up over her waist, then around to cup her breasts.

She gasped, then laughed. "Tlanuwa . . . You are very hungry this night, and not for food."

He dipped his head and kissed her shoulder, neck, and jaw, nipping at them. "Tell me how you know."

She laughed again, a low, breathless sound. "I saw much hunger in your eyes while we bathed. And now . . . your touch is fierce."

His hands stole back down to her buttocks, then lower, to her thighs, then back up, easing the chemise up as they went. He dipped and pressed himself against her, eliciting another gasp.

"My husband . . . *Sge!* You are already ready."

He nipped at her earlobe. "Does that surprise you? You have a simple but unnerving way of greeting me. But tell me—how do *you* feel?"

Tipping her head back, she closed her eyes and breathed deeply. "I will not be able to stand up much longer."

"Mm. Exactly the response I'd hoped for."

She spun around, smiling mischievously, and stepped away from him. Her hands clutched either side of her chemise, lifting it slowly to mid-thigh as she tipped her head and regarded him around her curtain of wet hair. A throaty noise escaped him as he viewed her shapely legs, wishing she'd keep lifting the chemise . . . wondering if she would.

She dropped it, letting the garment flow back down around her calves. Then she approached him. He grabbed her upper arms, tugged her toward him, and claimed her mouth, parting it quickly and ravishing it with his tongue, groaning in satisfaction when she pressed herself against him. His hands stole around to the back of her thighs, raising the chemise and parting her legs.

He lifted her, and she wrapped her arms around his neck, her legs around his waist. Her tongue darted out to meet his, then quickly traced his lips and slid into his mouth, exploring. He couldn't believe that before getting her in this position he hadn't thought to free himself of the leggings and the breechclout he'd slipped on after leaving the water.

He lowered and released her so he could escape the clothes. She sank down onto the coat she'd shed upon entering the cabin, and on her hands and knees she turned to straighten it, to smooth the bunches.

Unable to resist the temptation, Grant kneeled behind her, and worked at loosening the belt securing his breechclout. He slid a hand under her, caressing her breasts, then he eased the hand toward her stomach, and finally between her thighs.

Again she gasped. "Tlanuwa! You are a male hungry for the female."

He growled low. "That's exactly it. Come here." He eased her back against him, and when her buttocks touched his groin, he made little movements, as if thrusting in and out of her.

"Tsigataha!" she murmured, giving up smoothing the robe in favor of lifting her knees, one at a time, so she could raise the chemise.

He finally loosened his belt and pushed his own garments down, freeing his erection. Withdrawing a bit, he moved his shaft up and down the back of one of her thighs, then slipped it between her parted legs, searching for and finally finding her wet female slit. He grasped her hips, thrust, and entered her.

She gave a startled cry and stiffened. He stilled, wondering if she would withdraw . . . hoping she wouldn't. Leaning over her back, he reached beneath her again and tenderly kneaded her breasts, actually feeling thankful for the pause because it allowed him a moment to get his body under control. He didn't want to give two or three thrusts then explode inside her. While that might be intensely pleasurable for him, it would leave her unsatisfied.

"It's all right, Danagasta," he assured softly, kissing her between shoulder blades, then moving up to speak near her ear. "This position just feels different. It will feel better for you. Very pleasurable."

He nudged her hair from her cheek and watched for any other sign that she objected. If he saw one—a firm shake of her head, a grimace—he would back away, withdraw, turn her over and have intercourse with her in the traditional position.

Instead of showing a sign that she objected, she pressed back against him, then she moved forward, silently urging him to begin moving in and out of her.

Straightening, he ran his hands back down along her back to her hips, and began a slow, deep rhythm. Her soft moans, gasps, and cries of pleasure enthralled him, urged him on. He leaned over her again, whispering her name as he continued to move. He pushed the chemise to her shoulders, and she fiddled with the drawstring, then reached back to pull the garment over her head and off, one arm at a time, and toss it aside. He tucked his head beneath her arm and kissed the outer curve of a swollen breast, then licked at the dark peak.

He slowed his pace and pressed deeply within her, drawing a thick groan of pleasure from her. He braced his body with his hands spread flat on either side of her on the coat and pumped quickly in and out, in and out . . .

Her breathing became short and shallow. Between pants, she uttered Cherokee words, always reverting to her native language whenever emotions and sensations became intense. Some simple words he recognized—his Cherokee name, "love," "husband"—words he didn't *want* to recognizc, but words that drove him nevertheless.

He kissed his way up and down her back, felt her go rigid, catch her breath, then issue a series of moans as pleasure shot through her and she tightened around his length.

He slowed the pace again, released the mental hold on his body, and let physical sensations take over. He inhaled the sweet essence of their joining, withdrew, and rubbed his shaft against her swollen flesh, reveling in the tender feel of it. Then he slipped back inside her, and set a rhythm again. He felt himself swell to near bursting. Finally he groaned and spilled into her, mumbling her name. . . .

Chapter Eighteen

DAYS LATER, KAYINI SAT in the square again with children gathered around her knees. Just across the way, Sali was milking a cow, and Ewi was weaving on a loom. Some of the townsmen had gone off on a hunt, insisting on taking the reluctant deputy agent with them. But Kayini had noticed that Sequatchee had stayed behind. He was now leaning against one corner of Sali's cabin, carving something and glancing up at the gathering in the field now and then.

Kayini had already relayed to the children how the *Nunnehi*—the Immortal Ones—had come to the defense of the old town of Nikwasi when an unknown tribe had invaded the country, burning and destroying settlements. Now Cullowhee wanted to hear about *Tsulkalu*—the slant-eyed giant.

Kayini began the story, though hesitantly, because it started with a girl who was of age to marry and who was now faced with the sometimes difficult task of choosing a husband—and because Sequatchee had pushed off from the side of Sali's dwelling and was nearing.

Kayini told about the widow who lived with her daughter in the town of Kanuga on the Pigeon River. Sequatchee sat on the dry grass near Cullowhee's friend, folded his legs, and continued carving the piece of wood in his hand.

"The mother advised the daughter a great deal," Kayini said, "telling her to choose a good hunter so they would have someone to take care of them and always have meat in the house. One night a stranger came to the dwelling wanting to court the girl, but she said that her mother would let her marry no one but a good hunter. She—"

" 'Well,' said the stranger, 'I am a good hunter,' " Sequatchee interrupted.

Kayini's gaze shot to him. He had said that—and he was looking straight at her! Her heart skipped a beat. From her position on the stool, she shuffled her feet back and forth once, then silently ordered them to be still.

"The stranger was a man the girl had once known," Sequatchee continued slowly. "He had gone away, and she had forgotten him, but he regretted the way he had cast her aside, and he wished to renew their courtship. The man and the girl . . . the woman . . . talked and talked, then he invited her to the lodge he and his brother had built. Soon she stayed the night with him and became his wife . . ."

Kayini understood Sequatchee's implication. A soft sound tore loose from her throat. She glanced down at her hands.

"That is not how the story is told!" Cullowhee objected, and Kayini was glad that all attention was now fastened on Sequatchee. Unnerved, she watched him from beneath her lashes. He took a moment to grin and laugh with the children, then his gaze returned to her. It was an imploring gaze that seemed to ask "What will you do now? Accept my rather improper request—or turn me away?"

Kayini swallowed the lump in her throat, then forced her gaze up to meet his. "The girl . . . the—the *woman* told the stranger—the man—that coming to her and asking such a thing was not the usual way. She told him that she should take time to consider his request, but that because for nearly four seasons she had waited for him to come back to her, she would wait no longer. She told him that she . . . that she accepted his invitation." Kayini looked down, then up again, and she added quickly: "That is—was—if her mother or her aunt approved of the match."

"That is not how the story is told, either!" Cullowhee objected again. More giggles went through the small gathering of children.

As he unfolded his legs and got to his feet, Sequatchee mussed the boy's hair. Cullowhee grumbled playfully that people always made him look as though he had been caught in a great wind.

"I would not be surprised to learn that a great wind had given birth to you," Sequatchee teased. "You are very often as troublesome as the wind."

Cullowhee grumbled more, and Sequatchee approached Kayini.

He pressed the wood he had been carving into her hand, gazed into her eyes, and murmured, "You are beautiful—as graceful as the deer. I will go speak with your mother *and* your aunt."

As he walked off, she glanced down at the object he had given her. It was a deer.

Kayini told herself that he had changed his mind once about her, and he might very well do so again. Therefore she should not get overly excited and wish for something that still might not happen. But she could not help but feel the familiar flicker of hope. She had not dreamed Sequatchee's words. She was certain she had not. She had heard him twist the old story to fit his need. And while she ordinarily would not appreciate someone doing that, his changing of the story had charmed her—and unsettled her.

She managed to finish the real story for the children. She told how the mother had discovered that her daughter's husband was really a great giant with long slanting eyes, that when the man realized the old woman had been spying on him, he went off very angry. But the girl wanted to be with her husband, so she followed him.

The children, possessing the discipline to sit attentively for only so long, began wandering off. When only two remained, Kayini begged off telling another story. She stood and forced herself to walk, not run, to her family's lodge.

She knew that Madi, her mother, very much liked Sequatchee and had been disappointed when, after Losi's death, he had turned his eyes back to Danagasta. She did not think her mother would disapprove of Sequatchee courting her. She did not think that Saloli, her aunt, would disapprove, either. But for a reason she did not know, she worried that the elder women *might.* If they disapproved, she, being a devoted daughter and niece, would not go against their word.

New concerns seized hold of her: Could she be a good wife for Sequatchee? Yes, she could cook and clean, but would he be pleased, truly pleased, when she lay with him? She had never been intimate with a man, not in a physical way. Oh, she had heard many women talk about lying with their husbands, but she did not truly know what lying with a man would be like . . . and not knowing how to please Sequatchee frightened her.

She reached her family's dwelling, pushed the door open, and stepped inside.

Saloli, her aunt, lived in a lodge located five cabins away, but she was here now, sitting with Madi, Kayini's mother, near a fire where they were roasting corn. Yudi, Kayini's small brother who was now three winters, lifted two small pots and banged them together, making a terrible racket. Their older brother was probably off roaming the town. Gogisgi, Kayini's father, sat on a trunk near where his young son frolicked, and he leaned forward, playfully scolding Yudi by shaking a pointed finger at him. Giggling, Yudi banged the pots again.

Madi and Saloli looked up at Kayini at the same time. They exchanged warm glances, then turned them on her and smiled. Suddenly Kayini knew that Sequatchee had been here, and she knew that he had received the approval of both her mother *and* her aunt.

Kayini sank down onto a nearby stool and fought tears of relief and apprehension. They came despite her efforts, and she bowed her head to hide them. She heard the elder women's voices murmuring softly, though she did not try to make out their words. Then a gentle hand touched her shoulder. "Sequatchee coming here and gaining permission does not make you happy, my daughter?" her father asked.

She brushed a tear from her cheek. "It is not that. I am happy. But I am frightened. He has not just asked to court me. He has asked me . . . he has asked me to stay the night in his lodge. He has asked me to marry him. Unlike Danagasta, I have not been married. I have always *wanted* to marry Sequatchee, but the arrangements are suddenly happening very fast."

A pause ensued. Yudi banged the pots again, and Madi and Saloli's fire crackled. "You are afraid of him—as a man?" Gogisgi inquired.

Kayini spread her hands and pressed them against her face. "I know, but I do not know! I have listened to talk . . . What if he is not pleased with me? What if he is not sincere? What if he simply wants a female to lie with him? So many things . . . So sudden. All of a sudden!"

"Ah, Kayini," Saloli said softly. "He *is* sincere. He will be your husband. He *will* be pleased with you."

Kayini's father gave her shoulder a firm squeeze, then he moved away. Saloli and Madi came over to sit on the floor beside Kayini.

"You will make him very happy, my daughter," her mother said. "He now realizes that—that is why he is ready *now.* That is why this has happened so fast. You are a good cook, a good housekeeper, a good storyteller for children . . . You will bear Sequatchee's children and love them and care for them as no mother has ever loved and cared for her children."

Kayini heard the cabin door creak open, then shut. The lodge was suddenly quiet, and she knew her father had taken her brother outside so the older women might talk to her in private.

"It is not so frightening to lie with a man and make him your husband," Saloli said. "Sequatchee is gentle. He will not hurt you. You have already pleased him by accepting and asking that he seek our approval in the old way."

Kayini rubbed her eyes. "I should not cry like a child. I finally have what I have wanted for so long."

Madi touched her hand. "That is true."

"And soon you will have *all* that you have wanted," Saloli remarked. "Children—and a home that is truly your own. If you really want all that Sequatchee offers, you must dry your tears and find the courage to go to him."

Nodding, Kayini breathed deeply in an effort to do exactly that.

Sequatchee lay awake most of that night, waiting for Kayini. She did not come.

The next afternoon, he watched a group of women, Kayini included, gather in preparation to go draw water, and he volunteered to be one of the men to accompany them. No one liked the women going beyond the palisade alone anymore, and so some men always went with them whenever they had to go.

As he joined the group of men, his bow slung over a shoulder, his gourd of arrows resting on his back, he caught Kayini's eye and smiled. She lowered her head, then glanced up, giving him a faint smile in return.

He wondered why she had not come to him. She had accepted his offer of courtship and marriage, but she had had a condition: that he gain the approval of her mother or her aunt. However, he had more than met that condition by getting the approval of *both* women. So why had she not followed through with her acceptance of his invitation to stay the night with him? This could not be her bleeding time, or she would be in the menstrual hut. Had she decided not to marry him? Had she remembered his devotion to Danagasta and decided that she did not wish to be his wife because he had given her no assurance that he was free of what had held him to Danagasta? He did not know. He had thought he had fixed everything between himself and Kayini, but the long night had brought new worries.

The palisade gate creaked open, and the group moved outside Big Water.

The people passed between trees and stepped over and around bushes and low-lying scrub, heading toward the great river instead of to the creek, preferring to take their water from the Tennessee. Danagasta walked close to Kayini, and the two of them shared low conversation.

Though the mountains had warmed, Danagasta still sometimes wore a wolfskin coat, and she tugged at part of it as she spoke to Kayini. Sequatchee longed to hear her words and Kayini's response.

"My daughter fears lying with you."

Sequatchee glanced over at Madi, Kayini's mother, who had stepped up beside him.

"She fears that she will not please you," Madi said.

Sequatchee wrinkled his brow, then let it relax. "She has never lain with a man?" He knew that some women did, without considering themselves wed. More was involved in becoming married than just lying together. Blankets and food were involved, too. Sometimes words.

"Never," Madi answered. "I assured her you would be gentle."

Sequatchee thanked her, then told her he *would* be gentle—if the opportunity arose. "Do you think she will come to me tonight?" he asked.

"I do not know. That is Kayini's decision."

Sequatchee nodded, and the woman moved on.

At the river, Sequatchee stood on the bank looking out over the water for possible danger while the women approached the Tennessee's edge and dipped their gourds and water bags to fill them. They did not tarry—many now greatly feared white settlers. Sequatchee spotted five white men watching the women from near trees and brush, but he said nothing. Catolster and Shutegi had come along, too, and Sequatchee glanced over at Catolster, who jerked a nod, indicating that, yes, he saw the whites watching. Sequatchee and Catolster would say nothing for fear of alarming the women. They would simply watch. If the white men drew close, however, they would be forced to act.

The group started back toward Big Water—up the hillside overlooking the sparkling *equoni-geyvi.* The men fell behind the women until the gathering reached the peak, started down the other side, and were well removed from any threat. Sequatchee saw Kayini and Danagasta conversing again, and curiosity gripped him.

"Go to her," Catolster said from nearby.

Sequatchee glanced over, grinning slightly. "How do you know what I am thinking?"

"You have watched the two of them since we left the town. And only this morning, Gogisgi bragged that you had arranged to marry his daughter. Go talk to her."

Sequatchee did not need more prodding. He quickened his steps, and soon moved up beside Kayini and Danagasta.

"I will carry that for you," Sequatchee said, looking at the gourd Kayini had filled with water and that now rested on her hip.

Her eyes shimmering, Kayini slowly handed it to him.

"I need to speak with Sali and Ewi," Danagasta said, and she hurried off to catch up with the older women. Sequatchee told himself to remember to thank her later. He did not believe Danagasta really needed to speak with Sali and Ewi. She was merely trying to give him and Kayini a chance to speak.

Sequatchee and Kayini walked in silence for a while. Then they both started to speak at the same time. Snapping their mouths shut, they looked at each other and smiled.

"After you deliver the water to your family's cabin, will you walk with me in the forest?" he asked.

She hesitated, then nodded.

Once inside the palisade, the group dispersed. Sequatchee walked with Kayini to her family's cabin, meeting Madi along the way. Kayini's mother saw them together and smiled. When they reached the lodge, Sequatchee placed Kayini's gourd just inside the door, then stepped back outside, offering Kayini his hand. Without hesitation, she took it and let him lead her from Big Water.

Once in the forest, Kayini paused here and there to pluck little flowers that mingled with the grass. She twirled them, brought them to her nose, closed her eyes, and inhaled their scent. Smiling, she continued collecting them. She and Sequatchee passed many trees, and she playfully rounded one very thick trunk, showing herself on the other side just as Sequatchee reached the tree. The length of a short arrow separated them. Pausing and growing serious, she looked down at the ground.

He lifted a hand and touched her jaw, then moved his fingers beneath her chin and raised it. She was forced to look into his eyes.

"You fear the love I want to give you, sweet Kayini?" he murmured.

She did not answer; she stared at him, her breasts rising and falling rapidly.

He ran a thumb over her tender bottom lip, then leaned forward to lightly kiss her mouth.

He lifted his head and waited, fearing she might withdraw. But she seemed unable to move; she simply stood staring at his lips. He suddenly wondered if he was the first man to kiss her, and he felt a thrill at the suspicion. "Just kissing you brings me great pleasure," he whispered.

He moved his hand over one side of her jaw again, then eased it to her neck, marveling at the smooth feel of her skin. He touched the shoulder of her rough, woven dress, then slowly ran his hand down to the upper swell of one breast. She looked down at his hand as it massaged gently, then she sighed, tipped her head back, and closed her eyes, seeming to enjoy his caress.

He stepped closer and kissed her neck, licking hungrily, restraining himself from tugging her to him. "How did I ever ignore you? How did I ever turn my back on you and devote myself to another? I will not lie to you," he murmured near her ear. "There will be brief pain for you when we first come together. But then . . . then our dance will bring pleasure."

He kissed her again, but this time he probed the tender, innocent inside of her mouth with his tongue as he lowered his hand to the curve of her hip. He stroked her jaw, then lifted his head to look down on her closed eyes, on the splays of black lashes against her smooth cheeks, on her dark, parted lips . . .

"Have I hurt you, Kayini?"

She opened her eyes. They were hazed with passion. "No . . . No. You have made me feel things I have never felt."

He caressed her jaw again. "You saved yourself for me? All these moons while I devoted myself to another, you were saving yourself for me?"

She nodded. "I have always loved you."

"I am honored," he said truthfully. "I do not want you to fear me. I do not want you to fear that you will disappoint me. That is not possible."

She lowered her lashes. "Forgive me . . ."

He smiled. "There is nothing to forgive. If you wish to marry me, come to me when you are ready in your mind. I will be a good husband, worthy of your devotion. I asked you to walk with me so I could show you that my touch is not such a terrible thing. So I could show you that you already please me."

Kayini returned his smile, though nervously, then she hesitantly lifted a hand to touch his jaw.

"Things are much different between us than when you were a child," he commented, kissing her fingers. "One day you were a girl, the next you were a woman. *You* frightened *me*."

She laughed.

As he took her hand and led her from the tree, the birds sang cheery songs. Overhead, tree branches rustled excitedly and the Sun shimmered down.

Kayini glanced shyly over at Sequatchee, and when he smiled again, her heart threatened to burst with joy.

Days later, as the pink and purple glow of evening lit the Skyland, Kayini roasted two ears of corn over the hearth outside her family's lodge. Once back inside the cabin, she rolled the corn and some personal belongings in a blanket she had woven some time ago. She kissed her baby brother, smiled shyly at her older brother and at her parents, then left her family's lodge.

As she walked through Big Water, people nodded happily at her, seeming to know where she was going and what the night would mean for her. She nodded back, excitement and nervousness fluttering through her body.

Sali's lodge was located only a short distance from Sequatchee's, and he was seated with Catolster and

Whitetree, Sali's husband, outside the dwelling. As Kayini approached, her head lowered humbly, Sequatchee came slowly to his feet.

Ordering her heart to slow, she walked up to him and said softly, "I am still invited to your lodge?"

"Kayini," he whispered. "Yes. That will not change."

"Do you still wish to marry me?"

"I would not have asked you to come to me if I did not."

"I am coming to you." Her words were short and terse because she felt such disquiet inside. Trembling slightly, she glanced at Sequatchee from beneath her lashes.

Rubbing an open hand on his thigh, Sequatchee looked at Catolster and Whitetree, who both grinned and jerked their heads as if to say silently "What are you waiting for? Take her to your cabin!" It was the first time Kayini had seen Sequatchee act nervous, and she could not help a smile. His nervousness helped calm her somewhat.

"Should I go there and wait for you?" she asked.

He shook his head, then stepped forward. "Tonight, Kayini? You are sure?"

"Yes." She wanted to tell him that since he had returned her to Big Water after their walk in the forest, she had longed to feel his touch again. His hands were soothing as well as exciting; they had taken much of the fear from her and stirred intense physical feelings. She very much wanted to feel them on her body again. She still felt some fear when she thought of engaging with him in the most intimate physical act—joining their bodies—but he had assured her that the discomfort would not last long, and she believed him.

They turned together and walked toward his cabin. Kayini heard shouts of joy go up behind them. Knowing they came from Catolster and Whitetree, she fought laughter. Sequatchee tossed the men a playful glare over his shoulder.

When they reached the cabin, Sequatchee pushed aside the skin hanging in the doorway, allowing Kayini to enter. She stepped into what would be her new home, and went to a spread of soft bearskins where she assumed he slept.

From hooks on a nearby wall, he removed his bow, then took up a gourd filled with arrows.

"I will return soon," he said, and she knew he was going to hunt: It was not uncommon for a man to bring his bride meat to show that he was a good hunter, therefore a good provider. She knew Sequatchee's pride and his respect for traditional ways, so she did not object to him going. She also knew that if he wanted to bring her meat, he must hunt before darkness settled on the forest.

Still, once he left, the lodge was very quiet. She unrolled her blanket, placed it on his bearskins, lay down on the coverings, and waited.

It was not long before he returned, holding a rabbit by its hind legs. He asked if she wanted to join him outside where he planned to clean the animal. Answering yes, she rose from the coverings and followed him.

Outside, Kayini and Sequatchee settled on tree stumps to one side of the lodge. Children played around nearby cabins. Adults mingled in the distance, conversing and casting pleased looks at Sequatchee and Kayini. As Kayini watched Sequatchee clean the rabbit, he began talking casually about the day, so long ago, that she had wandered from Big Water and become lost in the forest. "I was a curious child," she said, smiling shyly.

"You were sweet even then," he teased. "Kayini . . . who wanted to know many things. Your little brother will be the same way. He will have to be watched closely."

"Yes, Yudi will roam. We will find him outside the enclosure one day, I am certain."

Only a faint amount of light remained in the Skyland now. Several dogs lurked in the shadows cast by the overhang of the cabin roof, waiting for Sequatchee to finish cleaning the rabbit so they could come and eat the remains.

He finally finished, and stood, giving a sharp whistle to call the scavengers over. They bounded toward him, panting, and began greedily eating what he had left for them.

Back inside the cabin, Kayini returned to the bear hides. Sequatchee approached and knelt before her, his hands still soiled from his work. He had wrapped the meat in the rabbit skin, and now he offered the small bundle to her, saying, "I give you this, Kayini, to show that I will be a good provider. To show that, if you allow me to be your husband, I will take care of you."

Her heart quickened as she took his gift, but she did not lower her lashes this time. He leaned forward and planted a kiss on her mouth, then he withdrew, stood, walked across the cabin to a large gourd, and began washing his hands.

"Do you have stones so that I may build a fire?" Kayini asked. "I want to cook the meat."

He jerked his head toward a stool. Leaving the meat on the bearskins, Kayini rose and neared the piece of furniture, seeing the many pieces of flint and stone resting atop it. She selected what she needed, collected wood from the small pile near the door, then set about building a fire in the blackened area in the center of the cabin. She used her hand to fan the sparks into flames, then she fetched the meat just as Sequatchee neared, holding forth a long skewer. Kneeling, she pushed the stick through the meat and held it over the fire.

Sequatchee sat behind her, stretched out his legs to one side, gently rested a hand on her back, and stroked her upper arm with the back of his other hand. Kayini turned her head and smiled at him.

"I am happy that you came," he said sincerely. "I was very lonely and confused after my brother's death. Now I will not be."

"You have much faith in me, Sequatchee."

"No. I have faith in us. In our marriage."

As the meat heated, its juices dripped into the fire and sizzled. Sequatchee's large warm hand on her back moved slowly up to her neck, caressing her. His fingers reverently touched her long braid, lifting it over her shoulder toward him. She felt him work at the end of the plait, and she wondered if he was undoing it—untying the leather strip at the tapered end and easing the three sections of braid apart. She glanced back at him just as he rubbed his cheek with the lower part he had unplaited.

It was her turn to tease him, though she did so nervously: "You have never given me so much attention, except when we walked in the forest."

"I want to give you more." His eyes were darker than they had been a moment ago.

"We will share the meat," she said, a mild tremble in her voice. "I brought corn, too."

Nodding, he continued unbraiding her hair. He played with the many strands—smoothing them, bringing them to his face, running his fingers through them—the entire time she cooked the meat. She was aware of not only the smell of the roasting rabbit, but also of *his* smell, a thick manly scent mixed with the saltiness of perspiration. She withdrew the skewer from the fire, and he rose and strode to the chest where he kept many of his personal things. He returned with a large bowl, held it out to her, and she dropped the meat into it.

They sat on their coverings. She put the bowl between them and fetched the roasted corn from where she had left it in her rolled blanket. They began eating slowly, tearing off pieces of meat, bringing them to their mouths, biting corn from the cobs. Sequatchee's gaze on her was constant and unrelenting—why had she ever worried that he was not sincere?—and twice her own gaze wavered, falling to the bowl.

She glanced up after looking away the second time and found him smiling. She smiled back, though nervously. He licked corn and meat juices from his lower lip, then placed his cob in the bowl, reached across the dish, took her cob, and placed it atop his. Then he pushed the bowl aside, rose up on his knees, and moved toward her.

He slid a hand to the back of her neck, then to her upper back, finding the ties to her dress. He pulled them apart quickly, almost effortlessly, and eased the dress over one shoulder and down. Kayini closed her eyes and breathed deeply, trying to calm herself.

"Sweet Kayini . . . open your eyes," he murmured. "Let me see their fire."

She forced them open. He smiled, and she knew he was trying to make this less difficult for her. As he leaned forward to kiss her lightly, she sat very still.

He kissed her again, and this time his lips lingered. His soft tongue touched her mouth, urging her lips apart; his arms slid around her back to draw her closely to him. He kissed her deeply, lovingly, gently, as if afraid of hurting or frightening her.

A spell began stealing over Kayini; it was as if her soul were rising up to mingle with his. The crackling of the fire faded, the barking of a dog became so distant she might have been dreaming it. Sighing, she tipped her head up to Sequatchee as the last of her fear became buried beneath the thunderous gallop of her heart.

He lifted his head and whispered, "Your people and mine are one. Your heart and mine are one. Never forget that I walk about, Kayini."

She shook her head, indicating that she would not—how could she, even if she tried? Forgetting him would be like ripping away a piece of her heart. Even thinking of trying such a thing was painful.

"I will make you my wife . . . my love," he said, and his lips stole down to her shoulder.

Her hands seemed to lift of their own accord to smooth his hair and touch his strong, sinewy back. She wanted to move against him, touch the length of her body to his, satisfy the throbbing need that had begun in her breasts and between her thighs.

He pushed her dress down farther, baring a breast, and he kissed his way down to it, finally drawing the tip into his mouth. Kayini gasped. So soft and warm, his mouth! No—it was hot . . . He suckled and kissed, and she arched against him, bringing a hand up to press against the back of his head, shamelessly and silently pleading for more of this sweet torture. He stroked the other breast, wrenching soft moans from her, then he lifted his head to push the dress from both shoulders.

He stared at her breasts, then lifted his lashes and locked gazes with her. She caught her breath at the undisguised heat and appreciation she glimpsed in his eyes. This was not the first time he was seeing her nakedness; he sometimes saw her in the creek or in the river. But Sequatchee had never looked upon her with such hunger in his gaze, with the flames of want leaping so unrestrained in his eyes.

"Remove the dress," he said raggedly. "Ah, Kayini, remove the dress . . ."

Without hesitation, Kayini stood and pushed the garment down over her hips and thighs. It slid over her calves and pooled at her feet. She stepped out of it.

He rose up on his knees, running his hands up the outsides of her legs. He stroked her thighs, drew his head closer, pressed it against her stomach, then withdrew and kissed her just below the navel. His lips scorched a trail down . . . down . . . A hand slipped between her thighs to urge them apart, then he kissed the feminine flesh at the joining of her legs, parting her lips there with his fingers.

Fire shot through Kayini. She cried Sequatchee's name and squeezed his shoulders. Though the intimate play shocked her, she did not withdraw—she could *not* withdraw. She wanted more . . . oh, so much more! And he gave more; he licked and kissed until her legs trembled weakly.

He lifted his head, grasped her wrists, and tugged her down to him. She dropped to her knees, and from there he pressed her onto her back.

His hands began whispering over her body, leaving heat in their wake. He touched his groin to her leg, and she felt him . . . How hard he was! How hard and demanding, touching her, probing for entry she longed to give him.

"Sequatchee!" she cried in a hoarse whisper, her hands on his hips urging him up.

He reached between them and worked at his breechclout. A long time seemed to pass before he finally tossed it aside, before he rose to his knees and she saw how very much he desired her.

He settled atop her, smoothing back her hair, whispering that the pain would not last long. "Not long, my sweet Kayini . . ."

A thrust of his hips embedded his length in her. Pain ripped through Kayini, and she could not help the cry that tore loose from her throat. She bit her bottom lip to stop a whimper, and she squeezed her eyes shut, fighting the tears that swelled in them.

"No shame, my wife," he murmured, lifting his head. He stroked her jaw, then kissed her mouth. "There is no shame in tears. I know you hurt. It will feel better, I promise you."

He urged her to bend her knees, part her legs more, and he lifted her hips to his. Soon the waves of pain began to seem distant. He suckled at her breasts again, and the want—the need—began again, low and deep inside her.

He began moving in and out, slowly at first, then quickening the pace. The pain was completely gone now, replaced by a pleasant storm that rushed in her ears. She heard him groan and cry her name, then the clouds burst and brightness shimmered down on them, on their joined bodies. Colors filled the Skyland, and the mist of their souls danced in the distance.

Chapter Nineteen

SHOUTS AND CLAMORING VOICES outside the cabin woke Grant and Danagasta. But before either of them could get out of the bed, someone hammered on the cabin door.

"Open up, Master Claiborne! I know you're in there. These folks led me right to you."

Grant rubbed his eyes. *Luke?* No, he was dreaming.

He rolled off the tick, stumbled to the portal, and flung it open.

There stood Luke, dressed in fringed and beaded buckskin. A length of beard was braided and the plait dangled to about three inches below his chin. His thick hair, tied back with a strip of leather, reached well past his shoulders. His ruddy countenance had deepened since Grant's last glimpse of him on the flatboat. His green eyes sparkled with mischief.

"Where the bloody hell've you been?" Luke bellowed. Townspeople pressed up behind him.

Grant reeled back. "Don't shout. It's too early in the morning for shouting. I might ask where the hell *you've* been."

Luke squinted one eye beneath a bushy brow. "Well, now . . . invite me in for a cup o' coffee or a little tea brewed from some weeds I'm sure the women get from the forest, an' just maybe I'll tell you. Or if you're wantin' a bigger word . . . I'll *enlighten* you."

A snort issued from Grant. "When did you become a 'learned' man?"

"Always had po-tential," Luke said, looking wounded. When he didn't move from the doorway, Grant asked impatiently, "Aren't you coming in?"

"Maybe you might want to think about puttin' some clothes on first."

Grant looked down, suddenly realizing he was stark naked. Giggles rose from the gathering behind Luke.

"Well, what're you waitin' for?" Luke grumbled. "That dip in the rapids must've taken your sense. Or don't you wear clothes anymore?"

Grant grinned. "I wear clothes."

"But there's damn sure nothin' modest about you. Go on," Luke said, pulling the door toward him. "I'll wait. Just give me a shout when you're dressed, an' then I'll come in."

The door shut, and Grant went back to the bed to lift the clothes he'd dropped on the floor beside the frame last night. Danagasta peeked curiously from between the bed hangings. Grinning, Grant explained that they had a visitor, his friend from the flatboat who had apparently finally been found.

Once Grant was dressed, he returned to the door and pulled it open. "Do come in, Mr. Williams, and tell me what sort of adventures you've had these past months." He had half a notion to give Luke's braided beard a flip and tease the man to no end about it. But then, Luke could very well tease him about wearing a breechclout and leggings.

Luke stepped inside and pushed the door shut. Grant began building a fire so he could make coffee while Luke surveyed the inside of the lodge. His and Luke's friendship had been forged over the ribs of a vessel in a Baltimore shipyard, and the friendship had flourished in a few taverns over cards and tankards of ale. Grant's father had never approved of Grant mingling with the "wharf riff-raff," but Grant had enjoyed many of the wharf people.

"Who would've thought?" Luke commented, obviously amused. "Look at you make that fire! An' you not havin' built one in a *fireplace* the whole time you lived at Claiborne House! Shoo . . . Looks like you've gotten right comfortable here."

Grant grinned. "So where have you been? Surely you didn't find those clothes in our flatboat trunks."

Luke glanced down at his elaborately decorated shirt. "No . . . I've been with the Creek—"

Grant followed Luke's gaze to the bed, where Danagasta had emerged from behind the buffaloskin drapes. She wore her chemise, and her loose hair flowed about her shoulders and down her back. Her skin glowed with morning freshness. Her eyes were still slightly swollen with sleep and held an uncertain look.

Luke turned a sly grin on Grant and said under his breath, "You always did have a way with the ladies, Master Claiborne."

Grant rose, crossed to Danagasta, took her hand, and led her toward his friend. "Danagasta, this is Luke, my flatboat companion," he said, choosing not to mention the fact that he and Luke had also been drinking companions. He'd have to make it very clear to Luke, right away, that he wouldn't drink with him while they were in the Indian Nation. "Luke, this is Danagasta . . . my wife."

Luke's grin slumped into a frown. "Wife? Now, what'd you go an' do—Beggin' your pardon, o' course, Dan-Dana—"

"Danagasta," Grant said, amused by the man's shock.

"Dana-gasta. There. Well, now, you see, I just never thought him the marryin' kind. Not again anyways. He . . . But it's nice to meet you, ma'am, er, Dana-gasta." Luke took her hand and bowed his head to kiss the back of it while Danagasta looked down on him with great surprise.

Grant's brows shot up. "I never thought *you* capable of manners, Mr. Williams," he quipped.

Luke straightened. "Pah! Mr. Williams! I've learned a few manners 'long the way, I'll have you know."

"If you'd like to go sit by the fire, I'll prepare the coffee."

"Believe I'll do just that. Long as I can take her with me, that is," Luke said, still holding Danagasta's hand. He led her to sit near the flames.

Grant collected the tin coffee pot from near the fire, measured coffee from a leather pouch in which he stored the ground beans, and collected water from the gourd placed near the door. While he worked, Danagasta asked Luke if he had started to say that he had been staying with the Creek Indians. Not many Cherokees were friendly with the Creeks, she said, though Big Water's people and most of the Cherokees settled along the Tennessee River were. Luke told her how the battered floatboat had been uncontrollable once a storm and the rapids together had beaten many a leak in its hull. He and the men from Virginia he and Grant had hired had finally gone over the side, choosing to swim to safety rather than drown in the "floating contraption."

Upon hearing Luke call the flatboat that, Grant laughed. He'd cursed at the boat, calling it exactly that right before he went down in the rapids. But the truth was, the vessel had held together well despite what it had gone through before reaching the rapids. Luke laughed good-naturedly with Grant.

"What happened to the Virginians?" Grant asked.

"Well, see . . . we swam up to the riverbank an' collapsed there, pretty worn out after tryin' to manage that boat. Bit o' time passed, an' when we got up, not precisely knowin' where'n the hell we was—beggin' your pardon again, ma'am," he said, leaning toward Danagasta. "We'd done been through two not very kind rivers, you see . . . an' there were Indians everywhere on the Tennessee's bank, lookin' like they wanted to kill us. We were white intruders on their land, an' they didn't take too kindly to that."

Danagasta smiled. "The Creeks take less kindly to white intruders than my people do."

"Well, I ain't got no way o' knowin' that, 'cept if the

master there's got some stories of his own to tell," Luke said, giving Grant a curious look.

"Perhaps I'll keep you wondering," Grant teased, pouring coffee into mugs. He handed both Luke and Danagasta cups, then settled near Danagasta with his.

Luke scowled. "Mother o' Mary! What kind o' hospitality is that? Keep me wonderin' . . ."

"The kind of hospitality I give someone who's made me worry for a good six months."

"Just what was I supposed t'do? Spent weeks tied to a pole 'fore the Creeks decided they wouldn't burn or scalp us!"

"They can be terrible enemies," Danagasta said.

"I worried 'bout you, too," Luke told Grant.

"Did you?" Grant inquired nicely over the rim of his mug.

"Sure I did."

"I do have stories to tell, as a matter of fact," Grant said. "A madwoman pulled me from the rapids . . ."

Danagasta dipped her head, trying to hide an embarrassed smile.

"That so?" Luke asked, eyeing her, then Grant. "An' what'd she do to you?"

Grant sipped more coffee. "Finish your story. You were tied to a pole for weeks, during which you wondered if the Creeks planned to scalp and burn you . . ."

"They fin'lly cut us down an' made us work for 'em. Had to bring 'em their food an' water for a time. Virginians escaped one night. Woke up in the mornin' an' they were gone—just like that. A woman took a fancy to me, an' I . . . well, I had to work for her for a spell."

"Doing . . .?"

Luke twisted his lips. "This an' that—'lot of *that* in the cabin—beggin' your pardon *again*, ma'am," he said, sighing. "Don't know a delicate way to tell this."

Danagasta and Grant both laughed. Grant could have told Luke that he needn't worry about offending Danagasta.

Luke managed a laugh, too, then he sobered, shuddered, and continued: "The woman died in her sleep one night.

After that, I was left alone. Was makin' plans to leave an' search for you, then I took a likin' to a couple of young women down there. Have been livin' with 'em ever since."

Grant had just taken a drink from his cup. He coughed, sputtering coffee at the fire, not, thank goodness, at Danagasta or Luke. He caught his breath, managing to recover. Danagasta's eyes widened. She clapped a hand over her mouth in an unsuccessful attempt to stifle laughter.

"Two women?" Grant blurted out incredulously. "You've been living with *two women*?"

"What's so bad 'bout that?" Luke demanded. "Ain't like I'm forcin' 'em. We're all happy. Time spent down in the Creek lands has been good for me. For one, I've sworn off whiskey. 'Course, I didn't have a choice in the beginnin', but I feel a bloody sight better now that I'm not drinkin'."

"Have you married the women?"

"I'd say we're married in our own way. It ain't the Christian way, but we're happy."

Grant considered his own marriage, how it had come about—not in "the Christian way," either—and decided he shouldn't be too hard on Luke. But he couldn't resist teasing, "You must be quite a man to, uh, manage two women."

Danagasta had lowered her hand, but it flew back to her mouth, and she laughed uncontrollably, swaying against Grant. Grinning, he took the mug from her hand to keep her from spilling the contents. Luke couldn't help a chuckle. He breathed deeply, puffing out his already stout chest, and Danagasta laughed harder. Grant shook his head, still in disbelief, all sorts of questions going through his head, none of which he would ask Luke because the answers were none of his business. Though Luke's situation was amazing and even shocking, Luke and his women were happy, and that was all that mattered.

As Grant and Luke drank the last of their coffee, Grant asked if Luke had met many of Big Water's people.

Luke shook his head. "Two Cherokee men who came knockin' at my door weeks ago askin' if I was your friend didn't bother to introduce me when we arrived. They'd been all over the land, asking questions . . . 'Course, I didn't give 'em time to introduce me to anyone here. I wanted to see you."

Grant clapped a hand on Luke's back. "Lord, I'm glad to see you, too. I worried. I have to be careful how I tell my story. I don't want to anger anyone," he said, tossing a teasing glance at Danagasta.

"I was a shrew," she admitted with a shy smile. "Now I sometimes wonder why he did not shoot me with Cullowhee's bow and arrow."

Luke looked confused. "Cullowhee?"

"One of his friends."

"You learned to handle a bow and arrow?" Luke asked Grant.

"Halfway" came the response.

Danagasta's smile widened. Sparkles lit her eyes. "He has learned how to plant a garden and build a canoe, too, but he cannot yet milk a cow."

"Hah! The cows don't like me," Grant grumbled.

"You yank on them. Do not yank! Squeeze gently," she advised. "Then they will not try to kick you."

"I'd rather chase the hogs from the gardens."

To the sound of her laughter, Grant set his mug down and got to his feet. "What are your plans now?" he asked as Luke stood, too.

"What d'you mean?"

"Exactly what I said. Are you going back to Baltimore or staying here? We had talked about building a few more ships together."

Luke grimaced. "You're not meanin' to hold me to that, are you? I've got obligations now, y'see. One of the wives is . . . well, she's in the family way."

Grant stared at him, then shook his head. "Luke's going to be a father?"

"That's right, I am. Thought I was too old for havin' little ones, did you?"

"I never said that."

"You didn't have to, my friend."

"I'll get cleaned up," Grant said, stretching. "Then I'll take you outside and introduce you to people. Did you bring your wives?"

"No, no. They like stayin' at the cabin, an' I wasn't goin' to force them 'long. Figured I'd come, spend a bit o' time with you, then go home."

"Home?"

"Aye . . . home. Like this is your home now."

Grant didn't respond.

"Well—ain't it?"

Danagasta rose near Luke. In silence she met Grant's gaze, then said softly, "He is still deciding. Know, my husband, that the door will always be open for you." With that, she swept past him and walked toward the bed. She slipped behind the hangings, probably to dress and to comb her hair.

Coughing, Luke shifted from one foot to the other. "Believe I'll wait outside," he said, turning away. "You prob'ly ought to take some time an' . . . Well, I'll be outside."

Once he left the cabin, Grant approached the bed and lifted a hand to draw back one of the hangings and flip it over the canopy. Just as he expected, Danagasta was sitting on the tick, her legs folded beneath her as she combed her hair. As she tipped forward, it spilled over her thighs. She glanced up, smiling.

Grant took the comb from her, sat behind her, and began tending her hair. He stroked it, smoothed it, admired the way it spilled about her shoulders. He dipped his head and kissed her neck, feeling an urge to ask why she wasn't asking questions about his future plans. Didn't she care?

Of course she did. How many times had she cried his name while they made love? How many times had she come into the circle of his arms and given herself to him? How many times had she happily cooked for him and straightened their lodge? He'd once known that she still loved Losi, her first husband, but she loved *him* now.

He didn't know why he wanted her to ask questions.

She started to move away from him. He tugged her back, a touch of alarm surging through him. *Why?*

He was being ridiculous, or so he told himself, but almost in the same second he realized how big a part of his life she had become. He realized that he'd been more proud of her when he had introduced her to Luke than he was of the garden they had planted together or of the canoe he was slowly but surely carving. He was more proud of her than he had been of anything in a long time, in what seemed like forever.

He had told Luke that she was his wife, and certainly no one had stood over him and threatened him to make him admit that. He had loved the way she had looked emerging from behind the bed hangings, sleep still glazing her eyes, her hair slightly mussed, her skin glowing. He had been pleased to introduce her as his wife.

He had fun when he was with her. Yesterday he had helped her fish; two days ago he had helped her make bread, and she had playfully taunted that he was doing woman's work. The day before that, they had gone hunting again, and this time *he* had brought down a deer—because she had been giving him archery lessons. He loved watching her bathe, loved watching her frolic in the water. He loved the way the sun shimmered on her skin. He loved listening to her soft breathing as she slept.

"Do you love me, Danagasta?" he asked, swallowing.

She went very still; she seemed to almost cease breathing. "Yes, I—" Her voice broke. "I love you, Tlanuwa. With my soul."

A large knot formed in his throat. "With your soul . . . And yet a person can't know what turns life may take or what the outcome will be. Nothing is certain."

"You say this to a woman whose life once seemed crushed."

She was right. He couldn't claim to be any more frightened now, because he had fallen in love with his Cherokee wife, than she surely must have been when her first husband had been killed.

"I have asked nothing of you," she said. "You asked if I love you. I answered."

For some reason he had needed to know. *Why?*

He was still determined to go home. Home to Baltimore to sit in a wing chair with a book on his lap and a glass of Madeira at his fingertips. He would sleep in the huge tester bed in the upstairs chamber of the small house he had purchased shortly before he and Emily had been married. He'd wear real clothes again—silk shirts, breeches, neatly tied cravats. He would go to the wharfs and oversee the building of ships in the yard his family owned, and he would set up a small law practice in the city and start utilizing his law degree. While he moved about Baltimore conducting his business, he would think of Emily now and then, but not imagine that he could see her on every street corner and in every shop. He could go *home* now and stop running from the memories there. He could go home and finally apologize to her parents for blaming them for her death. He felt better inside, stronger than he had when he had first set out on this adventure.

And yet he was frightened by circumstances and emotions and questions he wouldn't allow himself to think about for long. *(Where is home now, really?)* No, he wouldn't think about Emily and see her everywhere. He might see someone else . . .

"Danagasta," Grant whispered against her hair. "I want you to know that I love you, too. That I never meant to fall in love with you. But I have and . . . Danagasta, I already have a home somewhere else, a father and a mother, a brother and a sister. Please understand . . . I don't want to see you hurt but . . ." He released a ragged sigh. "I already have a home and I miss my family."

She inhaled deeply. He thought she was crying and he silently cursed himself because he *was* hurting her.

She twisted in his arms, took his jaw in her hands, and lifted it. They looked into each other's eyes.

"Go home, then, my husband. I will always know you in my heart and soul. I would have died without you to help me, but now I am well," she said, though tears ran down her cheeks. "Do not worry that you will anger me. I understand. *Vv*—I understand that you must go to your true home."

She shifted her position, putting her back to the wall, and she drew his head down to her breast.

Chapter Twenty

DANAGASTA WATCHED LUKE DRAW an arrow back in a bow and squint at the target before him: a white circle painted on the trunk of a hickory tree. He released the shaft and it flew through the air, embedding itself just above the circle. Excited shouts erupted from Cullowhee, Wadegei, Inoli, and other boys who had gathered behind Luke, Grant, and Danagasta. The boys agreed that Tlanuwa's friend was a fairly good shot.

"Here," Grant said, handing Danagasta the bow that Cullowhee's father had made for him only days ago. He grinned. "Show Mr. Williams how to hit a target."

Danagasta shook her head, giving him a slow smile. "That would not be polite, my—"

He put an arrow in her hand, then took her by the shoulders and gave her a gentle push so she would step up beside Luke, who was chuckling at the boys' praise.

"*Vv*, Danagasta!" Cullowhee said excitedly, seeing the bow in her hand. "You will hit the middle."

"I will not. Cullowhee, you—"

"C'mon up here, lass, an' have a try at it," Luke said in

a tone of great accommodation. He stepped out of the way, bowed slightly, and made a sweeping motion with one hand.

Grant's grin widened. "Yes, Danagasta, do have a *try* at it."

That was all the prompting she needed. She lightly settled the feathered end of the shaft against the sinew, pulled the string back, took quick aim, and released the arrow. With lightning speed, the shaft whizzed toward the tree and hit the target dead center. Cullowhee and his friends whooped again, but twice as loud this time.

Luke's bushy red brows forked as he stared at the tree. "How did . . . You'd think . . . An Indian woman? I've seen warriors miss targets larger than that!"

Danagasta smiled. "Then they are not very good warriors, Unodati. That is not even a *moving* target."

"She's not your usual Indian woman," Grant remarked, his eyes sparkling.

Luke scowled good-naturedly. "So I see."

She handed Grant his bow. "But now I will go and be a usual Indian woman, as you say. We have spent the morning and part of the afternoon going about Big Water so Luke could meet our friends. Now I must make bread and *wissactaw* so we have something to feed Unodati this evening."

"*Wissactaw?* Unodati?" Luke said, looking confused.

"*Wissactaw* is a drink made from parched and powdered corn," Grant explained. He folded his arms across his chest and narrowed his eyes at Danagasta. "Unodati . . . I don't know. She's using it in place of your name, so I'd be apprehensive. She concocts some rather unfavorable names."

She laughed. "Unfavorable, my husband? I could have called you worse than Tsuwa. I could have called you 'the beast that could not swim.' "

"Those rapids were vicious!" he objected.

"Doubly vicious for someone who does not know how to paddle."

"I know how to swim. I grew up near the ocean. I *know* how to swim."

"Do not become indignant, Tlanuwa. The river grows warm. One day soon we will go there, and you can show me that you know how to swim."

"I've swum in the creek."

"It it not high like the river. Before you journey north again, I want to make certain you can swim very well."

His mouth twisted. "I can swim."

"Very well. You can swim. Then you will not be afraid of the water during the river journey."

"We'll go on land."

"Because you do not wish to get into another boat?"

"Say there, Grant, she may have a point," Luke said. "You really don't know—"

"I know how to swim," Grant said loudly.

"Less than I know how to shoot a bow, my friend! When a person is afraid o' water, the best thing he can do is jus' get in it—"

"And paddle," Danagasta said.

"I'm not afraid of the water. I know how to swim," Grant insisted.

Behind Danagasta, the boys giggled. "Tsuwa and Unodati . . . A weak Waterdog and a big Bushyhead," Cullowhee said. He pointed to Luke's thick, wild hair, laughed, then twisted around and ran into Inoli, then Wadigei. Luke made a heroic effort to comb his hair down with his fingers. Grant scowled beneath his dark brows and muttered, "You little scamp. I'll dunk you in that river."

"Do not go in, Agent-man. You will drown."

"Cullowhee," Danagasta admonished. This teasing had gone far enough. She knew by now that a scowl from Luke did not necessarily mean the man was irritated; he merely liked to play at making people think he was. But a scowl from Grant very much meant her husband was irritated. "You have attractive hair," she told Luke. "Beneath Grandmother Sun its many colors shimmer. I was playing with you. Unodati . . . Bushyhead. It is not so unfavorable."

He gave her a rather shy smile. "Think you could, uh, well, teach me to shoot an arrow like that?"

She smiled back. "You are my husband's friend. I would be honored. But now I must bake the bread and grind the parched corn. I will feed you then teach you." She would also be more than happy to teach her husband to swim better if he decided that admitting that he did not know how to swim well would not wound his manhood.

Luke's smile blossomed into a grin just before she turned to walk away.

She strode leisurely through Big Water, stopping to speak with people here and there. In the square a group of men were preparing to go hunting. Bows were tucked through straps on the outer edges of arrow-filled gourds resting across the men's backs. Sheathed knives and flasks filled with water dangled from the hunters' belts. *Gahawi sita*, dried seeds and meat, no doubt filled the pouches that rested on their hips. Sequatchee, Whitetree, Catolster, and Shutegi were adjusting each other's provisions and weapons as Danagasta neared.

Sequatchee was the first to look at her. He smiled, but it was a rather weak smile, a rather unsure smile. He had taken Kayini to wife, and since Kayini had gone to him many days ago, no one had seen very much of the newly married couple. Danagasta smiled at him, fairly certain she knew why . . . The same pleasure that had kept her and Grant busy since she had become his wife was also occupying Sequatchee and Kayini.

She halted before the men. "A hunting party . . ."

They all looked at her, and she was reminded of the day Losi had died, the way the men had looked then. Their eyes had been filled with apprehension and fear then, too.

"I am not going to shout and scream," she told them in Cherokee, tilting her head. "I only came to say that you must be careful, that I love all of you like brothers. That I do not blame any of you for what happened. Do you have enough food and water?"

They all nodded, some at the same time, some at different times.

"We should have a small festival, those of us who live in our cluster of cabins. Shutegi, I hear you have a new son, and Catolster, during the winter your wife will give birth again—Awe-ani-da will have a sister or a brother. Cullowhee will someday become a fine man, Whitetree; he will make you proud. Sequatchee is now married, and so am I. We all have reasons to be happy. I will speak with your wives and plan a celebration."

Their expressions were still guarded, but not so much because they feared her, she thought, as because they worried about whether she would *remain* happy, whether her husband would stay with her. She could not promise them that he would but . . . "I will never again allow grief and sadness to rule me," she said softly. "Know that. There is always something to be happy about. I feel as though I missed much of the sweetness of one summer and the color of one fall, but I will not miss another season until the day my soul passes. My husband is good. I love him, but I will find other things to be happy about if . . ." She glanced down at her hands, then back up at the men. "I do not want him forced to stay with me. He has a family—parents, and a brother and sister. We should trade the land only if we see that trading will benefit us all, not only me. The land should not be used to make my husband stay with me. I see no honor in forcing him. I see honor in the way he commits himself to working honestly for his people. I do not think he knows the many bad things we have endured at the hands of his government. I do not think he realizes how much land has been taken and taken, how many promises have been broken. If he wants to return to his people, we should not stand in his path. His leaving me to return to his white world should not affect our people's decision to go live in the Arkansas land."

She studied the men to measure their reactions to all that she had just said. They looked at each other, then back at her, then at each other again, then back at her . . .

She felt certain that Sali, Whitetree's wife, had persuaded her husband to let Grant believe the Indians would not trade their land if Grant left her or divorced her. Whitetree had strong feelings about the white settlers, but keeping Tlanuwa here for her would have driven him, too. He would have talked to Catolster, Sequatchee, Shutegi, and others. Danagasta strongly suspected that the men and

Kayini, Ewi, and Sali had spoken to many people within Big Water, perhaps telling them to keep the land talk alive so Tlanuwa would remain in the town. Her father was surely involved in the plot, too, and . . . Danagasta shook her head. "I am honored that everyone cares about me, but we cannot force my husband to stay. We *cannot.*"

"He has made you happy again, Danagasta," Catolster said, "but that is not the only reason we have talked about trading land."

"White settlers are closing in on all sides, planting, hunting, building the iron place that brings more whites," Whitetree said. "We once had complete control of the great river. Now we must fear pushing even one canoe out into the water."

Sequatchee jerked a nod. "Kayini is my wife now, and I do not want to fear for her life every time she goes to gather water or cane. But Danagasta . . ." He paused, as if unsure whether he should continue. "There is also division in our country that has become very bad. The National Council blames all the Chickamauga chiefs for the land that was signed away by Doublehead and Tahlonteskee, his brother-in-law. Tahlonteskee fears for his life, and our own chief, your father, could be put to death because he has been speaking with the agents about selling our land—land the Council says we do not have the right to sell. If we defend him, *we* could be put to death. But we *will* defend him. We are not afraid to die."

Danagasta's eyes widened. "No!"

"Yes. It is sad and it is frightening, but it is true."

"We must go . . . move. Soon!"

"Yes, we must." Sequatchee moved close to her. "Do not look or speak as if you are alarmed. The other women do not know of this threat, and we do not want them knowing," he said in a low voice. "We do not want them to worry. You are the chief's daughter and you are like a warrior at times. Now, more than ever, we need you to act like a warrior."

"You are going hunting," she accused. "You cannot—"

"We must or butcher cattle we will need for food during

the journey west. Men are posted in the forest not far from the palisade. We will be gone only a day."

"Cherokees killing Cherokees," Danagasta mumbled. "That cannot be. Doublehead's murder was shocking, but this . . . Tahlonteskee . . . my father!" She shook her head, unable to put her outrage into words.

"We will move so that it will not be. Your father will leave soon with your husband for Washington to sign a treaty, and he will be removed from danger. While he is gone, we will begin traveling west with wagons and horses provided by Meigs. Your father will go from Washington to the Arkansas land, where we will be waiting."

Her eyes widened more, if possible. "So soon? The move will be so soon?"

"It must be, Danagasta. Your father's life is in danger—possibly our entire town is in danger. If Meigs comes tomorrow telling Chief Hanging Basket that the time has come, then the time has come."

"But the women will wonder."

"When we order them not to question, they will understand how serious the matter has become."

"I will protect them . . . all of them," Danagasta said, glancing around.

"Protect them now by ridding your face of worry. You will not help them by alarming them."

She struggled to do as he said, but once she succeeded, her stomach still felt tight and sick. Forcing a smile, she touched his forearm affectionately. "Kayini must be proud. You will someday lead what will soon be our western nation."

"Kayini is *tired*," Catolster remarked, trying to make a joke to lighten the mood after the startling thing Sequatchee had just revealed to Danagasta. She was grateful and managed to laugh along with the men. But she still felt terrible inside. Sequatchee dipped his head and made a sound of exasperation in his throat.

"She is happy," Danagasta assured him. "I *know* she is happy. Marriage to you is what she has always wanted."

Sequatchee lifted a crooked grin to her. "I hope she is as happy as I am. Go now and plan that festival. Smile and do the things you always do. Do not make anyone suspect that anything is wrong."

Nodding, Danagasta left the field, left them to their preparations while her stomach felt twisted in knots.

She breathed deeply to calm herself as she moved through Big Water. She passed the hot house, in which the people gathered around many fires to warm themselves during winter. Small children played nearby, laughing and squealing, and when their skin-covered ball rolled up to her toes, she scooped it up and tossed it back to them. A little girl named Meli batted it down with a hand, then giggled when a boy grabbed it, ran, and other children chased him with small, netted ballplay sticks in hand. They were playing their version of the game their fathers sometimes gathered in the field to play, only they had no posts to put their ball through; they had made two lines through the grass and whenever the ball crossed either line, some children cheered while others groaned. Three girls were playing the game, trying to ignore the calls of their mothers to come back to basket weaving and working beads onto clothing. Danagasta smiled, remembering that she had been the same way as a girl: more interested in ballplaying and in learning to shoot an arrow straight than in weaving, stitching, and other duties delegated to women.

She continued on, passing the Council House, passing cabins and people who glanced up from a variety of occupations—molding pottery, weaving thread into cloth, sharpening sticks and knives, making butter, tanning hides which were tacked to the ground . . . She reached the cluster of cabins in which her home was located and she walked between Shutegi's and what was now Sequatchee and Kayini's.

Kayini sat on a stool placed near the door, stitching a shirt cut from cloth, a man's shirt. Her pretty hair was braided to one side. She wore a red and brown dress, and her feet were bare.

"A shirt for your husband?" Danagasta inquired. She knew who it was for, but she could not resist teasing her friend. Besides, the teasing made her feel somewhat better.

Kayini glanced up. Her eyes were brighter than they had

been since last summer. "Danagasta!" she whispered, her voice filled with girlish excitement. Except that she was no longer a girl. *Tla no* . . . the glow in her cheeks was that of a woman. "I was just thinking of going to see you. Why did you not tell me how wonderful it could be? How I would want to be with him again and again? There was always much talk to hear, but I never knew I would want to lie with him every day! Now he will be gone hunting. I will miss him."

Laughing, Danagasta sat on the ground near Kayini's feet and fingered the shirt. It was only halfway sewn together. The two unstitched edges draped over Kayini's right thigh. "I did not tell you because there is no way to tell how wonderful it is to be with the man you love," Danagasta said. "I could have said 'it is wonderful,' but that would not have told you anything. I hope you gave him much food to take on the hunt. There will need to be more of him if this shirt is to fit him."

"It is not so big!" Kayini held it up, looking unsure suddenly. She sighed. "You are right. It *is* big."

"He will wear it proudly."

"I hope."

"He will."

Kayini resumed her stitching. "I think that Sequatchee's devotion to you was not the only reason our friendship changed," she said thoughtfully a moment later. "A girl becomes a woman one night, and her thinking and other things become different. She no longer lives in her parents', or her aunt's, lodge—as with you when you married Losi. She gains responsibilities that are truly her own, and she suddenly needs more than food and water. She needs the man she loves. You became a woman when you married Losi, but I was still a girl. We were still friends, but you had knowledge I did not. You changed while I stayed the same."

Danagasta nodded. She had felt the difference in their closeness after her first marriage, but she had said nothing to Kayini about her feelings because she had clung to the hope that Kayini and Sequatchee would marry soon. Then Kayini would understand why she did not always have time anymore to romp through Big Water with her, why she could no longer spend entire days talking and laughing with her. She had a husband to cook for and a lodge to keep. Kayini had not always understood the fact that marriage had brought Danagasta new responsibilities. Though she did not pout when she came to visit Danagasta at her new home—Kayini would never pout—she had often grown very quiet, and soon she would make an excuse and walk away.

"I do not suppose Sequatchee would be content with having his aunt stitch his clothing anymore?" Danagasta said, though she knew he would not be. No man would be happy with that sort of arrangement after he was married.

"I would not think of having her do it," Kayini said, looking taken aback.

"I was not telling you to ask her. I was teasing you."

"He has only one bowl," Kayini confided. "No pestle and mortar to grind nuts and corn. He hardly has a cup from which to drink! Two pots, but no spoons. But he has ballplay sticks and knives and arrows and *four* bows. Why four bows? And why has he been making so many arrows these past days? All the men have, in fact. They say for hunting, but it has been a long time since I have seen them make so many arrows." She searched Danagasta's eyes—for an answer, Danagasta thought. But it was an answer she would not get.

"He lived here, but he hardly ate here. He ate with Catolster's and Whitetrees's families much of the time," Danagasta explained with calm she did not feel inside. "He did not like living alone. But even when the brothers lived together the house was kept—or not kept—the same. If you need help . . ."

"No. I am not overwhelmed, just surprised. I did not expect that it would be so obvious that he had not had a wife."

"You started a bowl," Danagasta said, glancing off to a low table near the side of the house where some clay lay half formed.

"Yes, but I could not concentrate enough to get it right. I feared it would be lopsided. I worry that my husband is going hunting." She gave a soft, short laugh, then tossed up a hand. "I checked his flask," she whispered, her eyes watering. "I am a bad wife because I do not trust my husband. When he stepped from the cabin to relieve himself, I checked his flask to see what it held. Can you believe I did such a thing? When he returned, I fought the urge to ask him if he had whiskey stored anywhere."

Danagasta shut her eyes, then opened them as memories of the morning of Losi's last hunt flashed through her mind. She had checked his flask, too, then she had had words with him about taking whiskey along. "Oh, Kayini, you are not a bad wife. You were just remembering the day Losi died. You were remembering what I said to you. The worry will pass. I am surprised that Sequatchee did not take his own life after his brother's death. He grieved more than I did. He blamed himself, and I made his guilt worse. He will never again touch whiskey. Believe me—never again."

"Yes. I was remembering the words you said just before we realized that the men were returning early. You said—"

"No, do not repeat what I told you in the river that day. Those words are in the past, Kayini. We go on now. We forget. We do not open old wounds. We go forward . . . to wherever the path leads."

Kayini studied her. Finally she brushed away a tear and glanced down at the shirt she held. "You are right, but I am still frightened. This is the first time he has gone hunting since we wed. The night will be long."

"I will stay with you," Danagasta said. "We will roast corn and laugh and talk while we eat. We will sneak from the lodge and run around other dwellings, hiding from each other."

Kayini laughed, despite her tears. "But your husband . . ."

"His friend is visiting. He will not notice."

"He will! When you go to the menstrual hut to spend your days, he wanders at night. I have seen him."

"Does he?" Danagasta asked in surprise.

"Yes. He loves you. It is obvious when he looks at you. He will not go back to his people. He will stay with—"

"I do not want him forced to stay." Danagasta repeated what she had told the men in the field only a short time ago.

"Do you think he will really go back?" Kayini asked, her brow furrowed.

"Kayini, I think he *must* go back."

"But, Danagasta! How do you not cry over this? How do you not wring your hands and . . . How do you cook and sew and . . . How do you *continue*, knowing he will leave someday?"

"I have cried. But I will shed no more tears about him leaving. If he sees me crying, he will feel he cannot leave. I think he already feels he should not, that I will suffer if he does. I will not show him sadness. I will not make him feel that he must stay. I love him—and I want him to be happy."

Kayini stared at her. "You are amazing! I do not know that I could be so brave."

"You were brave for some very long seasons," Danagasta said, standing. "I follow your path, Kayini. I must go cook now. Then I will find my husband and explain that I will be staying with you this night."

"My path? I was not so brave."

"That is not true. You were very brave."

Danagasta walked away, thinking that, before she went to cook, she would go see Sali and Ewi about planning the festival.

Two days later, Danagasta, Sali, Ewi, Awi-gadoga—Catolster's wife—and Dudi, Shutegi's wife, gathered to clear the children's play area, located on the far side of Danagasta's old cabin, of twigs and anything else that might hurt bare feet. The small celebration would be held here tonight. The men would soon bring unlit torches and lodge them in the ground at various points around the small square, and later the women would bring the food they had spent most of the morning preparing.

Only yesterday afternoon the men had returned from hunting with a bounty of meat, and most everyone who lived in Danagasta's cluster of cabins had gathered behind one row of lodges to scrape and tan the hides beneath a tentlike structure—poles over which were stretched already tanned skins—that could be taken down on sunny days and put back up on rainy days. Some of the meat would be eaten tonight, but some would be dried on racks and eaten in upcoming days. Danagasta had asked if Catolster would bring his flageolet this evening and play a song for Kayini and Sequatchee. Catolster had grinned and quickly agreed.

Dudi's infant was but one moon old, a boy-child who slept strapped in a sling against his mother's chest instead of on her back. Many women bound their babes to cradle-boards soon after the infants were born in order to flatten the backs of childrens' heads, but Dudi had not done so with her first infant and apparently did not mean to do so with this child, either.

"He is more content when he hears my heartbeat," she told Awi-gadoga when Awi-gadoga asked why he was strapped to her chest instead of to her back.

Awi-gadoga said something about that not being the usual way, but Dudi ignored the remark and bent to pick up more small sticks and put them in a pocket she had stitched onto her woven dress. Unbalanced, she almost fell forward, but she steadied herself with an outstretched hand. Awi-gadoga said something about how that would not have happened if the baby were on Dudi's back, then she walked off. Dudi continued her task in silence.

Danagasta approached Dudi. "I and the others will gather the sticks. There are corncakes in a bowl on a small table beside the door in the cabin. You could go fetch them, if you would like."

"But, Danagasta, you have done so much work already! You and the others cooked while I slept the day away with my young son."

"You were tired. No one minded."

"Here," Dudi said, shifting the babe to the crook of her

arm and working the sling over her head with the other, "you can hold him while I find sticks."

Hold the infant . . . the *usdiga*? For some reason the thought alone nearly paralyzed Danagasta. He was so tiny, and she was so large. Also, she would be reminded of what she had lost. She already was reminded. She had caught herself watching the boy-child many times since Dudi had come out to help clear the field. "No, Dudi, I cannot. I should not. I will—"

"Yes. You have wanted to hold him since you saw him," Dudi responded emphatically, pressing the stirring baby against Danagasta's chest. The boy's face wrinkled. His clean black hair shimmered in the light of Grandmother Sun. His tiny fist touched Danagasta's breast. His precious little mouth twisted, then opened wide in a yawn.

"No," Danagasta said again. "Please . . . Take him away. I cannot." But her arms lifted, and she cradled him against her. "Oh, Dudi . . . he is beautiful!" she whispered.

"Go sit on the stool," Dudi said, tossing her head toward the stool that rested against one side of Danagasta's old home.

Danagasta did not need more urging. She took the *usdiga* and went to sit on the stool, just as Dudi had suggested.

Inside the sling, the baby's body was wrapped in a piece of wolfskin. No doubt the hide would be his throughout his childhood, and he would grow into a strong, courageous, bold, and stealthy man. Beneath the animal skin his lower half was lightly swaddled. He yawned again, then opened his slanted eyes and gazed around. The longing for a child of her own surged through Danagasta, and she kissed the infant on the forehead, then turned her eyes to the Skyland, silently praying that someday she would hold her own baby in her arms. She would carry it against her breasts just as Dudi did, so she would always have it near her heart.

She felt that she was being watched. Yes—Sali, Ewi . . . all the women were watching her, but she felt a familiar intense gaze and when she turned her head, she caught sight of Grant standing very still not far from the play area.

Luke Williams had left Big Water only yesterday morning to return to his Creek wives, and last night Danagasta had shared a savage, desperate passion with her husband. Three times they had made love—each time just as fiercely as the time before. She sometimes thought he did not want to go back to the place called Baltimore, but other times she felt that he very much wanted to go live with his white family again.

Last night he had gone back and forth. He had made love to her, then talked about ships, particularly ones called clippers that could outrun larger ships used in the white man's ocean battles. He had made love to her again, then talked about his younger sister, who had become "engaged" just before he had left Baltimore. Being "engaged" before getting married was important to many white people, he had said. He had made love to her again, then talked about the months and even years of work and worry that went into planning a wedding in his world. The actual marriage sometimes cost a lot of money for the bride's family, he had said. Then he had grinned and remarked that he respected the Cherokee way of forgoing pomp and circumstance. She had shaken her head when he had fallen asleep before explaining "pomp and circumstance."

Now he stood holding a piece of what George Dougherty often called foolscap, or paper. The Cherokee called paper "talking leaves." She had told her husband that she knew how serious the Chickamaugans' situation had become, that she knew her father's life was being threatened, and that rather than be separated from their beloved chief, the people of Big Water would move. She knew that the people of at least three other settlements were moving, too.

Tlanuwa stared at her, then his eyes darted between her and the baby. He opened his mouth as if to tell her something, then clamped it shut. His hand clenched around the talking leaf, and suddenly she knew . . . She *knew*.

The foolscap said the time had come to take the chiefs to Washington. There, a treaty would be signed. He had told her that Washington was his world, or part of his world, just as Big Water was only part of the Cherokee Nation. She saw in his eyes that once he was back in his world, once the treaty was signed, he would stay there.

And her people would soon travel to the new land.

Chapter Twenty-one

Between Shutegi and Catolster, numerous dances were pounded and rattled out with drums and gourds. Danagasta strapped on a pair of turtle-shell rattles Kayini loaned her, and beneath the silver and orange glow provided by the *Nunda sunnaheyi* and the many torches, she danced and danced. She pulled in children to join her, and once she tried to pull in her husband. But he was distant this night, far away and very quiet. Once he smiled and laughed while speaking with Kayini and Sequatchee, and Danagasta watched him, trying to capture his gaze. She began dancing for him, imagining his hands on her body, between her thighs, sliding up over her belly, and then over her breasts. She imagined him thrusting into her, but still she could not capture his gaze.

Frustrated and breathless, she finally marched over to him. "Why do you not even look at me, Tlanuwa?"

He twisted a blade of grass, worked his jaw back and forth, and finally lifted his glittering blue eyes to her. "Don't you realize I'm leaving soon, Danagasta?"

"You are not gone yet," she said, her hands on her hips.

"You said in three days. Three suns. For three days you will pout and keep yourself from me? You will ignore me? You have made the decision to leave. It is done. Do not pout. And do not ignore me."

"Come with me," Danagasta," he said so softly she barely heard him. His voice was strained.

Come with me . . . She closed her eyes, and the words sounded over and over in her head. They seemed to take on the form of something real; they seemed to put hands on her shoulders and urge her toward him. But she could not go . . . she could not.

"I am told that this Washington is at least three moons away," she responded quietly. "I am told that my father is in danger. I know the people's devotion to him, so I know that most everyone in Big Water is in danger as well. He will be safe while he is with you, but the people . . . There will be those who do not want to leave, who will remain somewhere in this Nation. But I will stay with the others. I will help lead them to the new land. I will help build homes for them and care for their children. I cannot go with you, Tlanuwa. Many whites hate Indians. I could not find a place in your world. Please do not ask this of me."

He thrust the blade of grass away. "I know there's no way. The prejudice would be unbearable. I was trying to figure a way to have everything I want. But there is no way. You'll be careful? You'll watch out for Awe-ani-da and Cullowhee and—I can't expect you to watch out for everyone. What the bloody hell is wrong with me?"

She smiled gently, dropped to her knees before him, and placed an open hand on one side of his jaw. "We will all watch out for each other. Now come and spend these last days happily with me. It is all I ask. Come and dance."

"I don't want to dance," he said raggedly. "I want to make love to you."

And how she wanted him to! She was suddenly breathless again, and this time the rapid rise and fall of her chest had nothing to do with her dancing. Her smile turned seductive. "Right here, my husband? Before everyone?"

That brought a smile to his lips. "I couldn't possibly

take you north. You'd shock the women into swoons, and the men . . . they wouldn't know what to make of you."

She pushed her fingers between his, brought her lips close to his, and murmured, "Take me to our cabin."

He issued a throaty chuckle. Then he sobered, and his nostrils flared. "Damn, Danagasta. I smell you already."

"I smell you, too. But I want to smell you more." She lifted his hand to her breast.

"Come on," he grated, scrambling to his feet. "We probably shouldn't leave the celebration so early, but if we don't, I *will* be reduced to making love to you right here on the grass in front of everyone."

She stood and turned to walk off. But she was quickly swept off her feet and into his arms, and then *he* walked off. She pressed her face to his chest, hearing the strong beat of his heart above that of the drums and rattles. She smelled the wild scent of him and his mountain-lion shirt, and she burrowed her face in his chest, parting the vee more deeply so she could better smell him, so she could taste him. She kissed and licked his chest, feeling the coarse hair beneath her wet tongue. She inhaled deeply, never wanting to forget his heady, masculine smell. She nudged the shirt open more and drew a nipple into her mouth, skirting it with her tongue, kissing and suckling it.

"Danagasta," he whispered. "If you persist, I'm not going to be able to walk. I'll have to drop you somewhere and just do what needs doing."

"*Tlugvis,* Tlanuwa. There are trees to the left," she murmured persisting.

"They'll hear us! I—"

"Do you think the people do not know what we do every night in our lodge? No . . . outside, wild and free. With the dew clinging to our skin. We'll breathe the smells of the trees and leaves—and each other. We'll listen to the summer breezes while we move together."

He laughed, a low, rich sound that vibrated through his chest. "You bring forth the animal in me."

"What are we but animals?" she responded, smiling against his skin. She slid a hand beneath the other side of his shirt, grazing the nipple there.

"Devil take . . . ! All right." He headed for the trees.

Once among the whispering oaks, elms, hickories, and chestnuts, he lowered her to the damp grass. His mouth fell on hers, claiming her lips with a swiftness that made her heart pause. She turned her head and pushed him away. His glittering eyes held questions, and his ragged breathing told her he would not wait long to take what he desired, that he had no patience for whatever game she was playing with him. He rose up onto his knees, wondering aloud what the hell she was doing. "You tempted me in here," he said, glancing around as if still worried that they would be discovered. "Now what are you thinking?"

Her skilled hands found the thongs that secured the belt holding his breechclout and leggings. Seconds later, she pushed the clothing down and took his hard shaft in her hands.

"You have tasted me many times," she whispered. "But I have never tasted you . . ." She dipped her head to do so.

"What? Mother of . . . Danagasta!" he grated as her lips closed around his length. His hands slid into her hair.

He stiffened, groaning as she withdrew her mouth, ran her tongue over the smooth tip, then took at least half of him deep inside her. Trembling, he pleaded for her to stop even as his hands pressed her head to his groin. She caressed his sac, felt him draw up tightly, felt his shaft swell to what must be an almost painful intensity . . . then she withdrew her mouth again and kissed his lower belly, feeling his manhood press against her throat. He whispered her name over and over, and she could tell by his tone and by the way he flung back his head and groaned low and deep that he was struggling to hold back his seed, that he loved what she had done to him. That he wanted her to do it again.

She moved her lips down over his belly to where his hair thickened.

"No—wait!" he cried. "Not yet. Oh God, I've never felt anything so good. Wait."

She gazed up at him in wonderment. "You have not . . . No *agehya* has done this for you?"

"Some women have, but oh, Danagasta, your mouth is hot. It's torturous. Wait."

She touched the end of his shaft, then lifted her fingers to her lips and licked away the dampness that had gathered there. "My *tsilvquodi*," she murmured, looking up at him, "you are sweeter than honey."

He pushed his hands deeper into her hair, then slid one around to touch her lips. She sucked two of his fingers into her mouth and drank their saltiness. Overhead, branches rustled. The music of the drums was now a quick two beats, a brief pause, then one beat. Then two, pause, one . . . over and over. The rattling had died down.

She took him into her mouth again, and she began a rhythm, sliding her lips back and forth, over his smooth end, and once, clear to the hilt where his hair tickled her face. Her hands caressed his firm thighs and buttocks as his groans and whispers filled her ears.

He squeezed her shoulders, saying, "No more. No—no more." But she knew he wanted more—he was only afraid he would not be able to hold back much longer.

She uttered no objection when he urged her to her feet and pushed her back against a nearby tree. He lifted her dress, but only enough that he could get where he wanted to go, and he pressed his body against her, breathing rapidly. She parted her thighs as he lifted her and drove up into her.

He was more swollen than she had ever felt him. He filled her completely, and when he dipped his head to her shoulder and began thrusting his hips back and forth between her legs, the pleasure was deep and sweet. She heard her cries and his groans as he plunged again and again, erratically, speaking her name against her neck.

He moved their joined bodies to the ground and drove in and out of her, but there was now no rhythm to his movements, only a frenzied pace as his skin began glistening with sweat. She tried smoothing his hair to gentle him, tried kneading the taut, bulging muscles of his shoulders, upper arms, and back. But there was no soothing him, there was no stopping this desperate mating. So she spread her thighs as wide as possible and let him go. The force of each thrust was almost painful, but when his seed came it came in powerful bursts that made her cry and whimper with pleasure greater than any she had known.

Still struggling to catch her breath, she ran her fingers through his hair and skimmed them over his shoulders. His breath was irregular and hot against her neck, but she did not move from beneath him, did not even try to shift the load of his weight. She bore it, wanting to always remember it.

Presently he lifted his head. "Did I hurt you? Danagasta, I'm sorry. I've never—"

She put a finger to his lips. "You did not hurt me. You are my fierce *asgaya* this night, more fierce than the most painted warrior just cleansed with fasting and with the black drink."

"What's the 'black drink'?" he asked, turning their bodies to one side.

"A drink prepared by Pretty Women or Beloved Women—select women within the tribe—for men about to go to war. The men fast, then drink, and they are cleansed and strong."

He glanced around. "I've never made love out in the open like this. Here we lie, nearly naked. Someone could walk up and see us."

"White man's modesty," she teased. "We have some modesty but . . . why hide from each other?"

"I don't suppose I'd be so modest if I'd been allowed to run around naked as a child."

"The animals wear no clothing."

"Animals are animals."

"Why wear anything more than an animal skin or some other light garment except during winter? Why always lie together inside a lodge when everyone knows what we are doing? We are not really hiding anything."

"I'd rather not feel as though I'm on a stage," he said, fighting a grin.

"A stage?"

"A place . . . a platform where people act out stories."

"Act out? They pretend to be in the stories? They pretend to be *part* of the stories?"

He nodded. "An audience—a crowd of people—watches from seats inside the building, or theater, in which the stage is built."

"That is an odd thing, Tlanuwa."

"It's odd to you."

"It is odd to me. You would like to be part of an audience again?"

"Yes, I would," he said softly, sobering.

"Do not grow sad again, my husband. During the last days, be happy. Help me gather the corn, squash, potatoes, and beans that grow in the garden we planted together. Help me hunt for meat in the forest to wrap and send with you. I will cook much food for you and for my people to take on the journey. We will work together, side by side, and be happy."

"How do you keep from hating me?"

Her brows drew together. "What reason do I have to hate you?"

He fell silent. An owl hooted in the distance. Crickets' songs filled the silence between drumbeats.

"The chirpings of the *talatu* are many this night," she observed. "I smell the *natsis*—the pines—above the horses and the white man's buffalo."

He smiled. "The cattle. Cullowhee calls them that—'white man's buffalo.' "

"Are there buffalo in the Arkansas land?"

"I honestly don't know."

"I will pray for them. We have not seen buffalo for many seasons now. The *yunsu* skins you have—they are old, sacrificed by the people because they love you."

"I had no idea."

She nodded. "I knew as soon as I saw you wearing one that I would not succeed in trying to make you leave Big Water. I knew you had somehow earned that *ganega*. Soon afterward, I heard talk that you had defeated Kaliquegidi with the poles, and *sge!* I feared you. I knew you were worthy of respect—and of adoption into the tribe."

"Considering how much you didn't want me in Big Water after you learned who I was, I can understand why you became so mean after seeing me wearing the skin."

"Why I became a shrew . . ."

He laughed lightly. "You'll never forget that word, will you?"

"*Tla no.* It affected me. When you stood up and said the word in my face and told me its meaning, I realized that you were right. That I *had* become a shrew, and that if I did not change, people I loved would soon turn away from me."

"I'm proud of you," he said, caressing her face.

She felt tears burn the back of her eyes, and she blinked, fighting them. What had she said to him—do not be sad? And she had vowed not to cry. "Tell me about your white family," she said, wanting to keep the conversation light. "Their names, what they look like . . ."

"All right." He raised his head, settling it in a cupped hand. "My mother's name is Jeanne. She's half French—"

"I have heard of the French people. Tsatsi has spoken of them."

He nodded. "Very willful. My father and I—we seem to have an eye for willful women."

"What does this mean? *'Willful.'* "

A smile crossed his lips. "A willful woman is a woman who will do whatever the hell she wants to do, no matter who or what stands in her way."

Danagasta laughed. "Until someone calls her a shrew."

"Now . . . Willfulness is only irritating sometimes. Hatefulness is intolerable—no one should deliberately be mean. As I said, my mother is half French. She has blue eyes and black hair, and she thinks I can do no wrong. My father . . . Blue eyes again, but they're hard. He has auburn hair—"

"Auburn?"

"Red, brown, copper . . . like fall."

"Ah! You have a mix of your parents' hair."

"My father's name is Charles. He has pride like my mother—however, hers and the king of England's together might not do his pride justice. But he doesn't have as much as you do," Grant said, almost as an afterthought. "You have as much as the English and the French put together." He laughed. She furrowed her brows. "That's a lot, Danagasta. A mighty sum."

"Your father is mean?" she asked.

"No—not mean. Just . . . dignified and noble. Proud. Devoted to the people in his life."

"Like you, my husband."

He kissed her. "Yes. I suppose I'm like him. He's patient, too. He was ready for me to take over the shipping business my family has owned for years just about the time I decided I needed to leave Baltimore for a while."

"Can he not take care of the ships himself?"

"In my world, some fathers tend to hand their businesses and interests to the eldest son when the son reaches a certain majority—age—or when the father feels the son is competent enough to take over. My father is very much a product of old ways. His father came over from England shortly after my father's birth, and he never supported the colonial revolt. But neither did he make trouble for himself and his family by declaring himself a Tory. I'm sorry," Grant said, flashing her a sheepish smile. "I'm probably talking about things that confuse you."

"*Tla no.* As with the chess game, I want to learn. I know England. I know that nation once claimed ownership of what is now the United States."

"Well, England once owned what is now *part* of the United States. Five years ago, France sold President Jefferson a huge tract of land called Louisiana. The Arkansas land was part of that purchase."

She shook her head. "It is all this buying and selling of land that confuses me. My people claim farming and hunting grounds, but we never bought and sold land before whites came. My father once told me that the Maker of the Human Family put the land here for us all to live on. Why can we not all live on it in peace and respect, then? My people would not plant on fields or hunt in forests claimed by the white man. They would not kill the animals only for pelts to trade. Over many seasons, we only asked to be left alone. And yet white men would come and come, asking for more land, wanting to 'buy' it, and when we would not sell, we were attacked and the land was taken in treaties. If the Cherokee Council had not agreed to let the whites build the iron foundry at the mouth of our creek, soldiers would have attacked again. That is bad—and *that* is what confuses me."

She put a hand to her mouth and smiled. "Now I am sorry. You were talking about your father and how his father came to this land shortly before your father's birth. But what does 'colonial' mean? What is a Tory?"

" 'Colonial' relates to people occupying land to which a mother country claims ownership. A Tory . . . How to explain this?" He struggled for a moment, obviously thinking. "A Tory is ordinarily a member of a group of people in England who believe laws and principles should be a certain way in that country. Years ago, Tories in this country were often referred to as Loyalists because they were devoted to the king of England, who was determined to put an end to our revolt. My grandfather was a Loyalist, but he played both sides in order to feed his family. He felt the colonies owed allegiance to the king, but he helped bring in items for the colonies from other countries when English ships tried to keep goods out."

"*Sge!* I mean no disrespect, but what is honorable about that?"

"I didn't say I agreed with what he did. But that's how my family got its start in America. My father fought with my grandfather for years because, shortly after the revolution, my father began working for the government the people of the freed colonies struggled to establish. Only we're not called colonials anymore . . . Well, I shouldn't say that. We don't call ourselves colonials. The English call us that, and they mean it disrespectfully. My father was never a true Englishman, but socially he thinks like my grandfather and he expects me to take over the shipping business. Not that I'll mind. I've always loved designing and building ships. I just don't always like my father standing over me, telling me that as the eldest Claiborne son I have obligations. That I have to do certain things."

"He is a difficult person?"

"Set in his ways is a better description. It's irritating sometimes. The world changes, and rules change along with it. America isn't part of England anymore."

"The colonials are like my people. They are like the

Chickamaugans," Danagasta said thoughtfully. "The Cherokee Nation is our mother, but we must part from her because things have become difficult."

"That's a good comparison—putting things side by side and seeing how they're the same."

"This revolt, and becoming free . . . It was not easy?"

"No. Not by any means. In fact, during the years right after the war was won by the Americans, England—or any other country, for that matter—could have stepped right back in and taken over. For a number of years the new government was weak. There was little organization and there was some rebuilding to do. You'll have to build new homes—an entire new settlement, in fact, and Big Water's men will be the leaders. None of you will be ruled by a National Council that sends out assassination parties."

Danagasta shuddered. "I am glad you are taking my father from here. When I think of men chasing him with tomahawks the way they did Doublehead . . ."

"They won't. If there's any trouble, we'll leave immediately. We won't wait."

"I wish you would not wait so long. Three suns . . . That is much time."

"It will take Meigs that long to secure enough provisions. We'll travel at night to the agency, and from there we'll go to the river."

"You spoke of a sister and brother, too," she said, refusing to allow fear for the men's safety to grip her heart.

"My sister. Colette." Grant smiled and looked off at the trees. "The *chérie* of Maryland, of Virginia, of Washington . . . My *chérie.* My little sister has dark hair, dancing eyes, and a mischievous, flirtatious nature that's charmed many a man. But only one stole her heart."

"Chérie?"

"A dear. A darling. A delightfully charming person. *Chérie* is a French word."

"You love this sister," Danagasta said, unable to help her own smile at the obvious emotion on his face.

"We're very close. We talk a lot. She comes to me when she has trouble, only I haven't been there for her these past months—since late last summer when I left Baltimore. My younger brother . . . who knows if he'll be glad to see me? He's always resented me because I'm the oldest, and our father has always favored me over him. I'm not saying that out of arrogance or conceit—that's just the way it's always been. My father sent Randolph to the finest schools. He's given Randolph all the educational support a son is due from his father, but the favoritism was always there. He'd buy new horses, and the most well-bred would always go to me. I'd be allowed to listen to the men's conversations in . . . Well, our father's preference for me was obvious, so I don't fault Randolph for resenting me."

"That would be difficult—having a brother who does not like you."

"It has been difficult, but I don't feel sorry for myself. I feel sorry for Randolph. I've talked to my father about showing Randolph more attention and respect. As I said, however, he's a product of my grandfather, who very much adhered to primogeniture—the right of the eldest son to inherit his father's holdings."

The tree branches stirred. The drumbeats quickened again. The gourds resumed their rattling. Danagasta's skin had grown cool from the dew-damp grass and the light breeze that swept over it. Grant touched her breasts, molding them gently. He planted a light kiss on her lips, drew back to study her, then he kissed her more deeply, easing his tongue into her mouth and touching it to hers. His manhood was still inside her, and it began to stir and swell with life. He turned onto his back, taking her with him. She straddled his hips, and he pushed her dress up, over her breasts, then up and off her arms.

They began moving together as the wind moved through the trees, with soft whispers and sighs, and now and then there was a moan. She reigned proudly above him, thrusting out her breasts for his touch, controlling the rhythm, and this time when they reached the peak, it roared around them, then became a blissfully sweet pleasure. It was like a summer storm, exploding . . . then calming to a mild and gratifying rain.

Chapter Twenty-two

FALL 1808

"Tsuskwanun nawa ta!"

Danagasta glanced sleepily around, trying to locate the shouting person who complained of having a worn-out blanket. Through the crowd of people gathered before the three tents belonging to some of the soldiers who had helped lead the Chickamaugans to the new land, her gaze finally fell on a crippled old woman: Walini.

Many lines marked Walini's face. Her hair had long ago turned gray, and now it was nearly white. Danagasta knew that the woman was nearly blind, though Walini's clouded eyes were locked on the soldier as he stood gazing angrily down at her.

"Tsuskwanun nawa ta," Walini said again.

"Go away, old woman. I don't have any—"

"Tsuskwanun nawa ta!"

"I said go away! That means turn around and get away from here! Now!"

Danagasta fought her way through the crowd, apologizing along the way to anyone she pushed aside. She finally reached Walini, whose face was covered with a thin film of dust. The woman was shivering. Danagasta turned to the soldier. "You dare to shout at a Beloved Woman?"

He drew back, startled, then anger sparkled in his green eyes. "She was shouting at me. Besides, I don't give a damn *who* she is. I don't have any more blankets."

"What do you cover yourself with at night?"

He inhaled deeply. "Ain't none of your business."

Danagasta remembered her husband's words about patience, about going slowly while trying to accomplish something. These past moons, his words about patience had been hard to remember. The people had arrived in this new place only yesterday. The long journey had been difficult, made on flatboats through rough rivers while a group of Cherokee men followed along the riverbank, driving the livestock. Every evening the flatboats had stopped so the people could go ashore, eat meat taken from butchered cattle, and gather around fires to rest. Despite having enough food, a number of young and old people had taken ill and perished along the way. Only this morning, Danagasta had seen Dudi and her infant, both alive and well, and her heart had nearly burst with relief. How many sick had she tended along the way? How many people had she seen buried on strange riverbanks? But not once had she cried. Not once had she shown anyone that she had doubts that most of them would reach the new land where they would once again plant and hunt and be happy. She had vowed to help her people through this difficult time. They would survive to see many Suns rise and fall. Right before he had left for the Tellico Blockhouse, her husband had again promised the people of Big Water that Grandmother Sun rose even in the west—and she did. She was shining brightly right now.

"Please," Danagasta said to the soldier. "She is old and does not have much longer to live. She is a sacred woman. Please search about and try to find a warm blanket for her. I gave mine to the children. Some of them are sick and cold. Please . . ."

The soldier eyed her, but his look was not lustful, as some of the others' had been during the journey. He was weary himself; his eyes were dull, and dark circles prevailed beneath them. His clothes were dusty and dirty. Even his yellow hair was not as bright as it had been days ago. His gaze dropped to her slightly swollen belly. "Woman with child shouldn't ought to be giving away her supplies. You ain't got a blanket?"

She had realized shortly after the journey began that near the end of the winter she would have a child . . . a precious *usdiga.* The discovery had increased her faith, had made her realize that the Maker of the Human Family would not allow such a thing if He did not want her people to continue to populate the world. There was no stomach sickness with this pregnancy; not once had she felt nauseous. There were no bad feelings, no sense that something terrible was about to happen. This baby would be born alive—she knew that in her heart.

"I have a buffalo skin," she answered. "That is enough. If you cannot find this woman a blanket, I will give the skin to her."

"No . . . No, now don't go doing that. I'll find her something. Do you have food?"

There was honor in the man before her, even though he had shouted at Walini. "The blanket, please. She is shivering. The old grow cold very fast."

He jerked a nod, withdrew behind the tent's flap, and a few seconds later, Danagasta heard the other soldiers teasing him. He grumbled something at them, then reappeared on this side of the tent, a folded blanket and a bulging cloth bag in hand. "Mackinaw," he said, handing Danagasta the blanket. He pressed the bag into her hand. "Beans. Now if you'll just find a way to keep her away from here. She ain't let us have any peace for the last two hours. You're all here!" he called to the crowd. "Spread out and start settling." His gaze went to Walini. "I'm, uh, sorry. I'm bone-tired—like all of you. Tempers start flaring after people get so tired."

Danagasta translated his English words into Cherokee for Walini. Walini dipped her head in understanding and forgiveness.

"*Wado* . . . Thank you," Danagasta told the soldier. "I

will warm her and cook for her. Please understand that this is a new place for us. Many of the people are frightened. Others are sick. Our cattle, corn, and other food is nearly gone. We need provisions to help us through the winter—the planting season is over already. By next summer no one will be begging at your tent. But for now we need your patience. If you look into the forest," she said, motioning to where the trees thickened not far back from the Arkansas riverbank, "you will see our men cutting wood to build lodges. Others will gather grass and clay—if clay is to be found here. Some men went off to hunt and will hopefully bring back much meat. Then the women will build fires and cook, and we will offer you and the other men fresh food."

It was a gesture of peace. Some of the people had resented going to the agency and finding soldiers there, waiting to accompany them on the journey, and they had had nothing but sharp words for the white men. Grant had explained that the men knew the country, that they knew the best routes and trails to follow. Still, the Chickamaugans had never liked the sight of United States soldiers, the soldiers did not like them, and many quarrels had erupted during the journey.

Apprehension flared in the eyes of the white man standing before Danagasta. "I don't . . . I don't know about that. Some of the men might not like . . . might have a problem with—"

"Taking food cooked by Indian women?"

"*I* don't mind, understand. But—"

"I understand that if you are hungry and our food smells good you will want some. You were kind to give me a blanket for Walini and beans for myself. I was only offering kindness in return."

He nodded. "And I thank you for it. Your husband's cutting trees with the others?"

"No. My husband has gone to be with his family in Baltimore."

His brows lifted. "A white man?"

"Yes," she answered, placing a hand on Walini's shoulder. She turned away with the old Beloved Woman and started off through the crowd. A number of children and old people followed, wanting her to cook the beans. She settled Walini on her buffalo skin, pulled the thin, scraggly blanket from the woman's shoulders and replaced it with the thick woolen blanket the soldier had given her. Then she set about gathering wood to build a fire. Afterward, she would take a pot from her bundle of belongings, dip water from the river, and boil the beans.

While the beans were cooking, she took the last of the ground corn she had carried in a pouch during the journey, drew more water from the river, and made corncakes. There were only twenty, but she broke them up and handed each person a bowl of beans and a portion of corncake. For cooking, the Arkansas River would do, but it was filled with much sand; so she took several large leather-encased flasks and set off in search of a stream. She would find one somewhere so the people would have good water to drink.

She began walking, trying to ignore the weariness she felt. She had hardly slept for days. Feeling the flutter of new life low in her womb, she touched a hand lightly to her belly and turned her eyes to the Skyland.

"*Wado. Asga-Ya-Galun-lati,*" she whispered, thanking the Great Spirit for the child she carried.

She only wished her husband could know this—that he would soon be a father. She wondered how he was, if he had made his journey safely; if he was well and strong and happy. She wondered about her father, who had devoted his life to his people and who was now exiled from his ancestral home. Having to leave had been heartbreaking for all the people, but Danagasta knew that her father had not taken the departure well. She had stood beside him near the agency and had watched him drop to his knees and kiss the homeland. Then, with tears in his eyes, he had turned in silence and boarded the boat that would take him away. Once his boat had rounded the river's curve, she herself had cried—because he was gone.

But that is done, she thought, lowering her hand and continuing her search for a stream. *Now we go on. We make this place our home. I will bear this child and my fa-*

ther will smile again when he returns from Washington and learns that he is a grandfather.

She stepped around thickets, studying the trees and scrub. There were oaks and hickories here; there were berry vines and herbs and wild potatoes and onions—things she had gathered many times from the ancestral forests. She could gather acorns and nuts . . . Though the berries were drying and the herbs would be bitter by now, and the potatoes and onions might be shriveled since the ground was growing cold, she would still gather them. Bitter and shriveled was better than starvation.

She had no more corn to grind, and she doubted if any of the other women had any. She had set out with pouches of hickory nuts, but those were gone, too, consumed during the long journey. The last time she had looked, there were no cows left, only four bulls, hardly enough meat to feed the people of Big Water throughout the upcoming winter, let alone to feed the other Chickamaugans who had joined them. Most of the others had arrived at the agency without provisions of their own. They had relied on what food was supplied by the soldiers, and that had been precious little.

But here . . . here was food! A turkey raced through the brush ahead, and three squirrels scurried up and down trees to Danagasta's left. Fish leaped in the river, in water that was ugly, but at least it harbored food. The people would eat. She would tell the healer where she had spotted herbs, and he could make medicine to help the sick. They would survive the winter to see spring and summer in this new land.

Shouts sounded from up ahead. Someone called her name. She listened closely, heard her name again, and then—oh, sweet sight!—Kayini and Sali broke through trees and brush up ahead and raced toward her. They had been put on a different flatboat than she, and she had not seen them for at least one moon. She had begun to wonder if they, too, had perished. But *tla no* . . . they were here, not buried in some faraway place. They were here, alive and well!

She ran toward them, feeling the flasks twist and hit her

hips again and again. But the bouncing flasks did not stop her. Nothing would have. She wanted to embrace her friends, weep joyously with them. Then she would ask them many questions.

She and Kayini flew into each other's arms, nearly knocking each other down. Danagasta held her, enjoying the solid feel of her friend. Though she had shown much courage during the journey and since her people had arrived yesterday, she had been frightened and apprehensive deep inside. But knowing that Kayini and Sali were alive brought her renewed strength, hope, and faith.

"Ewi," she said breathlessly, drawing Sali into her and Kayini's closeness. "Where is my aunt?"

"There," Sali managed, glancing in the direction from which they had come. Danagasta saw only the riverbank and the forest. "Beyond the trees. Our boat stopped upriver a ways. We were looking for food. We walked far. She was sick for a time but she is well now. Nuts . . . look!" She held up two full pouches. "It is here, Danagasta. There is food all around. This land is rich!"

"Yes, I was just discovering that," Danagasta said. Relief poured over her that Ewi was alive. She had not thought she could feel *more* relieved than she had felt when she had spotted Kayini and Sali moments ago. "When we finally stopped yesterday, I was so tired I could hardly walk. I noticed nothing, only that the ground provided a place to sleep that was not so crowded. I just made corncakes with the last of my meal and I was worrying about whether or not the men would find meat. But I just saw a turkey, and there are squirrels."

"Rabbits, quail, ducks . . . *Deer*," Kayini said excitedly. "Danagasta, we have seen many deer!"

"And look at the mountains. Oh, look at the mountains!" Sali turned. They all turned. They had observed the mountains from the flatboats, of course, but standing together looking at them was exciting.

In the distance, colorful crests rose gracefully. The purple and blue deepened in the valleys, but the many autumn trees lent splashes of orange, red, yellow, and green to the slopes. Only three clouds floated lazily in the Skyland and they did not look even mildly threatening. The air was crisp, but the bright Sun promised much warmth for the day.

"Not one white settlement," Kayini said. "I have not seen one white settlement."

Sali smiled. "I saw one, but it was far upriver. Long before we stopped. It was small."

"Look," Danagasta said, pointing to a flock of geese that rose from trees and soared over the breathtaking mountains.

Sali nodded. "Our men will hunt well."

"Some men from my group are out now," Danagasta said.

Kayini embraced her again, unable to help herself. "Sequatchee and Catolster are going later."

"Awe-ani-da and Cullowhee . . . How are the children? We have become so separated. Dudi and Shutegi are in my group. And Walini, the old Sacred Woman, is there. But so many others . . . There are many boats, and finding familiar people has not been easy."

"Awe-ani-da and Cullowhee and most of the others are well," Sali told her. "Inoli . . ." She shook her head.

Inoli had been one of Cullowhee's close friends. "Cullowhee must feel bad," Danagasta said.

"He understands that Inoli's spirit did not want to be here."

Nodding, Danagasta looked off at the mountains again. "We must help our men clear land for new settlements. We must gather what food is around us and store it. We must help the people grow strong again. We will begin a new nation, here in this western land where light, not darkness, lives. This is a white path, a good path."

Kayini and Sali whispered agreements.

"But for now, I am in search of a stream—clean water," Danagasta said, lifting a flask.

Her friends smiled and beckoned her to follow them. They would lead her to the stream they had found yesterday.

* * *

She gathered her water, then told Kayini and Sali she would find them again later. She must return to the people she had left. She had promised them water, and she meant to gather acorns, grind them, and make bread. Hopefully the men who had gone hunting from her group would return soon with meat.

When she arrived back at the encampment, they had already returned. She whooped when she spotted three deer dangling by hind legs from overhead branches. The men had hung them up and were skinning and cleaning them. The people gathered around were talking and smiling, though many stayed back, either still sick or weary.

Danagasta set to work building another fire and grinding acorns. Other women came over to help, and the men soon built more fires. Presently the smell of roasting venison filled the air, making Danagasta's mouth water. She had not had venison in so long, in what seemed like forever. Her stomach growled, but she somehow waited until everyone had food before she sat and eagerly ate the meat and bread someone handed her.

Later she told a group of women about the herbs, berries, and nuts she had seen in the forest. If they looked closer, they might find even more, she said, and the women agreed to search the forest the following day and gather food.

Once everyone was fed and resting comfortably, Danagasta returned to the buffaloskin where she had left Walini earlier. The Beloved Woman had wrapped herself in her blanket, lain down on the ground beside the hide, and now slept soundlessly.

Danagasta lay down on her side on the buffaloskin, always thinking of and smelling her husband when she snuggled against it.

"You're something, you know," a white man said behind her. It was the soldier with whom she had pleaded to give Walini a blanket. "Cooking, gathering water, wiping sweat off people, helping the old and sick around, holding babies and children until they're asleep . . . All day you were about to drop yourself, but you kept on. I ain't seen anything like it—like you. I ain't seen anyone act so unselfish."

Danagasta turned over, sat up, and brushed strands of hair from her face. "I help them because they are my people."

"I've heard of dedication, but you beat all I've seen. I've heard of being committed to your own blood—your own kin—but I'd sure like to see you stay on that hide the rest of the night and sleep. If you don't, you won't be much good to any of them when you're laying dead under a few feet of dirt. That is, if you don't mind me giving you advice."

She shook her head. "I do not mind. I will stay here. But only if you forgive my people for not being nice to you during the journey. We did not expect soldiers to lead us."

He nodded. "You might not have gotten here without us. Some of you ain't never been out of those mountains back East."

"I understand."

"I don't know your circumstances fully," he said, shifting his weight from one boot to the other. "Why your husband went back to Baltimore and you were left to get through this alone. I, uh, wanted to let you know that if you're ever of a mind to send him a message . . . I talked to my commanding officer and I've the means to get it there. Your husband could send one back, and the two of you could communicate that way."

Her gaze held his. Send a message to Tlanuwa? Make him feel as though she missed him? She did, but she would not make him feel bad about going to be with his white family.

She turned away and lay back down. "Perhaps he does not wish to . . . communicate with me, as you say. No message."

"Ah, now, don't be stubborn. He'd be a fool, even I can see that. Good woman like you—"

"You forget the color of my skin. You forget that I am an Indian."

"No, ma'am—I ain't forgetting that at all. I'm standing

here looking at you, and I can see the obvious for myself. Does he know there's a baby on the way?"

He did not know. But telling him would make him want to come. He was an honorable man, and he would come, whether or not he thought he could be happy living with her and her people.

"No message," she said, firmly this time. Then she softened her tone. "Please, no message."

The soldier sighed. "My name's Sergeant Cross. If you change your mind, just come to the tents. We'll be cutting trees and helping build cabins tomorrow, so we'll be out in the forests most of the day. But I reckon we'll be back to rest and eat now and then."

"*Wado,*" she said softly.

She shut her eyes, fought memories of her husband, and soon fell asleep.

The next afternoon, after much thinking, she approached the soldiers' tents. The sergeant was seated on a stool to one side of a tent, eating something. He glanced up as she neared. "It's good, this bread you and the others made from those acorns."

"I am glad you like it. You said you could send a message to my husband."

His chewing slowed. "That's what I said. I'll get it there."

"Tell him . . ." She glanced off at the mountains, wanting to tell Grant a lot, wanting to tell him more than anything that she loved him and missed him. "Tell him we arrived safely. All of us."

"But some died along the—"

"We arrived safely. That is what I want him told."

He squinted at her. "Could I leave off the 'all of us'? You don't want to lie to the man. If we leave that part off, you're not lying."

She saw no harm in his request. "You are right. Leave it off."

He nodded.

She told him her husband's full name, then said, "I will bring you more bread."

"You ain't got to do that."

"Do you like it?"

"Blazes! I told you I did."

"Then I will bring you more." She turned away, meaning to go fetch more for him.

"If it's a girl, what do you mean to name it?"

She turned back. "I don't know. Why do you ask?"

"I'm partial to little girls. I have two of my own, one I ain't seen. She's oh, eight months by now. I was just interested."

"I have not thought of a girl's name," she said quietly. "But if it is a boy, I will call him *Tlvdatsi*—Panther, Son of the Mountain Lion."

He nodded. "Reckon that's a fine name for a boy."

She smiled, agreeing. Then she walked away.

Chapter Twenty-three

BALTIMORE
FEBRUARY 1809

SEATED IN A WING chair near the hearth in his library, Grant lifted a water glass to his lips and watched the back of the stately man who had entered the room not five minutes ago, softly but forcefully demanding to know where his eldest son had been last night. "You were supposed to have been attending a supper party at the home of Alexander Bickham," Charles Claiborne had said.

"I forgot about the supper," Grant had answered calmly. "I apologize."

"You . . . *forgot*?"

"That's right. I forgot."

"As you forgot to contact Thomas Ashton about representing his interests?"

Grant scowled. "That was an oversight. I'll contact him—"

"Save your breath. He's gone elsewhere."

With every graying hair combed neatly in place, Grant's father gripped his hands behind his back and began pacing slowly. Even his steps were refined and carefully calculated. His head was held erect and at an aristocratic tilt above a perfectly arranged white cravat. His eyes were as sharp as ever, assessing, never missing a thing. They settled on a table situated in a far corner of the room. Only a half hour ago Grant had brought in some wood he'd been whittling on out in the garden. He'd placed the smaller pieces of wood atop a large square slab and had placed the slab on the table.

Charles approached the table and lifted a piece of wood. "What is this?" he asked, turning back. "You *carve* while you should be at the shipyard?"

"It will be a chess set," Grant answered.

"You have a chess set. Made from the finest ivory. If you want another, any merchant can order you one."

"I'm content making my own."

Charles dropped the piece of wood and crossed to the mantel, where he picked up a pipe bowl Grant had only recently finished chipping, sanding, and polishing. He'd ordered the stone through a merchant who had looked at him curiously, then said he'd be happy to find Mr. Claiborne some fine stone. Grant had managed to create some semblance of a wolf's head on the pipe bowl. He was proud of it.

"So while I arrange meetings for you to discuss ships and investments . . ." his father began in a tone of growing impatience. "While I send to you friends and acquaintances looking for legal representation . . . While I suffer the indignity and embarrassment of being told that you simply do not turn up for certain affairs that I arrange for your good . . . While shipwrights and other artisans wait to talk to you, you are carving wood into chess pieces and working stone into pipe bowls. *Indian* pipe bowls, no less."

"It's something I like to do," Grant responded.

"And is your other great interest building campfires in your formal garden?"

Grant's eyes narrowed. "Who told you about that?"

"Does it matter? I know. People are watching you, saying things about you. Is it not enough that you had the audacity to defy Colonel Meigs, to question the man's judgment and tactics—"

"His *tactics* are unforgivable, and I was horrified to learn that you knew about them."

"They are effective. It is not enough that you waltzed into Washington dressed like a savage?" Charles continued, undaunted, his voice growing tighter and sharper with each word. "That you slept on the floor of that inn room with those chiefs?" He paused to shake his head and toss up his hands, looking more discomposed than Grant had ever seen him. "My son . . . Is it not enough that Colonel Meigs claims you married an Indian woman, and friends and relatives are asking why. Must you shoot down every attempt I make to help you slip back into a normal life? You're a Claiborne, but the name will only take you so far. I unwisely let you go down to the Cherokee Nation. *I* appointed you and sent you—"

"I asked you to send me."

"Yes, you did. And I should have said no. But at the time I agreed that you needed to go away. Why not to Boston or New York? I asked. But no, you wanted adventure, something quite unlike what you had done all of your life. So I sent you, knowing you were more than competent to help Colonel Meigs negotiate a treaty. I could have chosen from a number of men, but I chose you. I chose my own son because he *asked*. You see, Grant, contrary to what you sometimes think, I do care about you. I care about you very much."

"I've never said you didn't. I've never thought that," Grant responded quietly.

Charles returned the pipe bowl to the mantel and clasped his hands behind his back again. "So I sent you. I thought you would be safe with Colonel Meigs, a man I greatly respect. You would be at the agency for the most part. Other times you would be out speaking with the chiefs, but you would not be living among the Indians. You would get this idea of doing something of a different nature out of your head. You would have your adventure, tire of it as all boys do sooner or later, then return home and resume your life."

"I'm thirty-one years old. I'm not a boy."

Charles didn't seem to hear. "You insisted on hiring that riffraff from the tavern—"

"Luke Williams is my friend," Grant snapped, placing both hands on the arms of the chair, and rising. "He is not riffraff."

"Yes. Well . . . you hired Mr. Williams, then, to be your guide. He seemed incompetent from the beginning. He burst in here—"

"With maps in hand!"

"He took my son, my *eldest* son, straight to the Chickamauga Creek settlements and deposited him in the rapids!"

"I slipped on the deck of the flatboat and *fell* into the rapids! We were driven south by a storm!" Both men had stepped forward to glare at each other.

Grant looked away first. He moved toward one of the windows flanking the fireplace and stared out at the snow-covered lawn that unrolled gloomily to where it met the street. The garden where he had built the fires these past evenings was located behind the house. "I'm sorry."

Charles sighed heavily. "We've done nothing but quarrel since you came home. Come. Sit back down. I'll pour you some wine. Madeira. It's always been your favorite."

Grant started to object; he started to tell his father that the last thing he wanted to do was drink Madeira, that he'd look down into the rich dark wine and see Danagasta's lips. They had always reminded him of fine Madeira. Lush and sweet and tempting and—

He squeezed his eyes shut, leaned forward, and touched his forehead to a pane. Lord God, he was miserable. The house he'd bought after his marriage to Emily now seemed so *large* and unnecessary. He couldn't seem to eat a meal without thinking of having bread baked on a stone hearth outside, without wanting a mug of *wissactaw*, made by Danagasta's hands. He had done more than build a few fires out in the garden, he'd removed a sapling and fashioned a rather weak bow. For the string, he had used hemp bought from a female peddler at the docks. Then he'd gone to the nearby Patapsco River where he found reeds to fashion into arrows. The merchant who had obtained the stone for him had also found him some flint, and Grant had soon chipped pieces of it into arrowheads. During the last two days, he'd shot arrows into every tree in the blasted garden and had snapped at the gardener when the man dared to object. Damn the man—whose garden was it anyway? Every time an arrow had flown and hit its mark he had thought of how proud Danagasta would be of him. The outraged look the gardener had given him had been nothing compared to the valet's shocked expression when Grant told *him* only yesterday that he no longer preferred hot baths. He wanted them cold.

Grant's father soon brought him a goblet of wine from the small sideboard nestled between tall shelves of thick, leather-bound books. "Have this," Charles said. "You'll feel better. In time you will be yourself again."

Grant closed his eyes and drained the glass so he wouldn't have to look at the wine. Then he placed the goblet on the windowsill. Be himself again? Yes, he needed to be himself again. He felt like a stranger in his own home. Everything here felt alien . . . the smooth crystal of the glass he held, the leather of the wing chair in which he'd sat. The smell—old books, tobacco that was too richly sweet, not wild like the Indians'—it was all too foreign.

He had left part of himself somewhere—and he suspected he knew where. Right now it was somewhere along the Arkansas riverbank, in the hands of a woman he couldn't seem to forget.

"I'll get more wine," his father said, and started off.

"No!" Grant drew a hand over his mouth. "Please—no. It—it reminds me of her."

He felt Charles's eyes on his back. "You surely aren't going to tell me that the Cherokee have wine with their meals," he finally said, laughing a little. "Madeira, at that."

"No. She . . . Her lips are the same color."

Charles was quiet for a long moment. Then, very softly he said: "My God, perhaps Colonel Meigs was right in saying that you married her to secure the trade. But you fell in love with her along the way. You fell in love with an Indian woman."

There was no need to tell Charles every detail of what had happened during his stay in Big Water, so Grant elected to tell only the important parts: "I didn't realize that I was marrying her. When I discovered that it was done and that I could divorce her if I wanted to according to their custom, I chose not to. I had realized that the Chickamaugans weren't as cold-blooded and brutal as everyone thought. I had made friends among them and I suspected that if I divorced her, they might not trade the land. You and President Jefferson wanted it, so I did what I had to do to get it. I—"

"That's barbaric," his father seethed.

"I know, and now I'm deeply ashamed."

"No. I'm not talking about what you did. They blackmailed you. They cannot hold a man that way."

"They didn't hold me. In the end, they saw that the move was entirely necessary. Doublehead had been assassinated, and a cry for the deaths of other Chickamauga chiefs rose from the Council." Grant sighed heavily. "I weighed my every decision. I could have divorced her before leaving. I don't think I wanted to. The land wasn't the only thing holding—"

"Did you speak vows? Was there a priest or minister present?" Charles demanded.

"No."

"A Bible of any sort?"

"No."

"Then there's nothing to fear. The church won't recognize a heathen wedding. I've worried that excommunication might be considered, though."

Grant turned and settled a hip against the frame. "There was nothing heathen about it. And the last thing I fear is being excommunicated. I fear memories more," he said under his breath. "You don't seem to understand how easily I slipped into honoring their customs. They seemed strange for a time, but now they don't seem strange at all. I consider myself married. And I feel as though I've deserted my wife."

"Do not be ridiculous. There's no need for guilt. Once

you put the matter from your mind, these bad feelings will be gone."

"You don't understand. Guilt is only a small part of it. I love her. She has become a part of me—a part I thought I could live without. Now I'm finding out that I can't. I thought I'd slip back into life here, but . . ." He ran a hand through his hair. "I need her. I need to make love to her, hear her soft breathing while she sleeps. I need to eat the food she cooks for me. I need to watch her mold a bowl, dance . . . I need to hear her greet me in the way that only she does: '*Osiyo,* my husband.' "

Charles stared at him in utter shock, his eyes glittering, his jaw set. The man finally tore his stricken gaze away and neared the sideboard. He turned over a second goblet and filled it with wine. Grant stared at the dark liquid.

"Blast it all!" his father blurted out. "It's for me. Stop looking at it."

Glancing up, Grant found his father's glare darting between him and the wine. "I—" Grant shook his head, then turned back to looking out the window.

"What will happen now?" Charles asked in a strained voice.

"You want me to become a distinguished Baltimore attorney and shipbuilder. You want me to enter politics one day . . . I don't know what the hell comes next. I want you to be proud of me, but I'm alive and I had Emily for so short a time. Now I've walked away from a woman I've fallen in love with, and she's alive! Just walked away. I can't believe I did that. I thought I was doing the right thing at the time, but I don't know anymore."

"You had to get the chiefs to Washington. They trusted *you*, not Colonel Meigs. I think you did a fine job despite Meigs's report about your conduct. I want you to know that."

"Thank you," Grant whispered, though the praise did nothing to raise his spirits.

"You had to return. You had to come back because you knew I would expect you to. And because you had to find out where you belonged."

Grant turned around to find his father watching him closely. "What are you saying?"

"That maybe trying to force you into the life I want for you is wrong. That maybe you belong with her, not us. That no matter how much saying this and letting go hurts me, it must be said and I must let go because even Charles Wentworth Claiborne can be wrong." He tossed back the glass of wine, drained it as if it were a shot of whiskey, then plopped the glass down and started for the library door.

"Where are you going?" Grant asked, startled.

"Home. To gather my composure. Try not to forget Colette's first supper party tomorrow evening. I have no political agenda for you. I just know that having you there is important to your sister since you missed her wedding."

A second later, Charles pulled the door shut with a soft click. Grant stood staring at the portal for a long time.

Numerous candles lodged in a beautiful chandelier cast a soft glow on the long table in the elegant dining room of Colette's relatively new home. The table was set with the finest silver, crystal, and china, and flanked by a number of important Maryland citizens. Even the governor had arrived, and he was conversing with Leigh, Colette's husband, at the far end of the table.

Seated ten chairs down on the opposite side, Colette talked easily with a man on her left, smiling her charming smile, tilting her head of dark Grecian curls, laughing, then turning to speak to the man on her right. Grant finally caught her bright gaze, grinned, and lifted his goblet to toast her; her first *soirée* was already a huge success, and the evening was not half over.

In the eyes of the Claiborne men, Colette could hardly do anything wrong. Grant spotted Randolph and Charles watching the Claiborne *chérie*, their faces aglow with pride. Mother was often hard on her—as she was on everyone—but even Mother would be proud tonight. She already was. Grant tipped forward and spotted her watching Colette, too, a beaming smile on her face. The political ambitious Leigh would be ecstatic. Right now he seemed perfectly composed, but Grant knew the man—Colette had met him nearly ten years ago—therefore he knew that beneath the calm exterior, Leigh was trembling with excitement. Grant could hear him already: "The governor!" he'd say. "How did you manage it, Colette?"

Well, she hadn't exactly managed it through her father's mighty influence, though being the daughter of the President's secretary of war most certainly had helped. She had told Grant only this morning of the surprise she was planning for Leigh—and that she had arranged it simply by calling on the governor, finding him in, and asking if he would like to attend. She had doubtless smiled and conversed just the right way, too, Grant thought, still grinning. He knew his little sister was an *expert* at charming people.

"Scandalous, I tell you. It was absolutely scandalous!" Fae de Louvois said from her place to Grant's left. "First that duel in which he killed Mr. Hamilton, then the business of treason." Her eyes glowed. She spoke excitedly with a heavily accented voice that would have revealed that she was French even if her name had not.

Fae had been planted at this gathering. Grant knew . . . Colette was up to more mischief than just springing the governor on Leigh. She and Mother knew about his Cherokee marriage, but he suspected they had put their heads together anyway, found the French delight who had been talking incessantly since supper began a half hour ago, and placed her at his elbow. If he didn't know that making an ocean voyage could be disastrous at this time of the year, he would swear they had shipped Fae de Louvios from France for the sole purpose of putting the woman in his bed. Supper was merely the prelude. The mademoiselle had started hovering near him shortly after his arrival, and Grant didn't doubt that she would crawl into his lap if he gave her even one inviting look.

Colette and Mother were simply trying to take his mind off his wife. Surely they weren't trying to marry him to the lovely but overbearing French creature. Still, he wondered . . . He had spent much of his life trying to gauge his mother and sister's next move, and had been unsuccessful enough times to know that he should worry.

"Do you not agree, monsieur, that the business involving Mr. Burr was quite exciting?"

Political talk. Fae had gone from prattling about Napoleon's remarkable achievements to talking about Aaron Burr, who had killed the great Alexander Hamilton in a duel, and had been accused of plotting treason on an island in the Ohio River soon afterward. Apparently Fae found scandal exciting.

"Mr. Burr was declared innocent," Grant remarked.

"But he is not. There are those who say he is not. He could have accomplished it, some say. He had many boats and guns. Like the Emperor Napoleon takes Europe, Mr. Burr could have taken the United States. *Oui?*"

Grant turned a hard gaze on her. "You should be advised that you sit at a table with at least two men—the governor of Maryland, and my father, the secretary of war—who feel that Aaron Burr should have been found guilty of high treason. You may think that what he apparently tried to do is exciting. I consider it an affront. While we fight to keep both France and England from impressing our seamen into their service, Mr. Burr thinks to overthrow our government. What, in the name of the Father, is exciting about that?"

She flinched, then eased away the slightest bit.

"I may have French blood in me, but I am very much American," Grant said. "Napoleon seeks power and glory, not freedom. Not liberty. There is nothing right in what he has done and continues to do."

Her voice was soft: "You forget that France aided your revolution with—"

"Wrong. Our colonials couldn't have won the revolution without the aid France provided. But, Mademoiselle de Louvois, Napoleon was a boy at the time of our revolt. The France that aided us is not the same France that exists today."

"It is a better France."

"Only time will tell. If you find it so desirable, why aren't you there?"

Her eyes widened. Color flushed her pale complexion. She lowered her dark lashes. "You do not enjoy my company, monsieur. You have snapped at nearly every word I have said, every attempt I have made at conversation!"

He studied her. She was very pretty, adorned in an empire gown of burgundy satin. The color of the dress enhanced her dusky lips and provided a striking contrast to her ivory skin. Colette and Mother had chosen well, but they shouldn't have chosen at all.

"I apologize for my rudeness," he said softly. "You're very attractive. If I weren't so in love with my wife I might find you even more attractive. But—"

She gasped. "Wife?"

He nodded slowly. "You didn't know?"

"I do not make a habit of throwing myself at married men!" she whispered. "I do not think to become a *maîtresse*."

"And I'm not looking for a mistress."

"I did not know . . . I cannot believe!"

He laughed lightly. "I can. You don't know my sister and mother very well. They'd like to see me married to someone right here—tonight."

"But you are already married! You said—"

"I don't think they've realized that yet."

"How can they not? If you are married, you are married."

"I was married . . . in a different way. A way they can either accept or not accept. I've been miserable enough that it doesn't make a whole hell of a lot of difference to me anymore. If they love me, they'll accept the marriage."

"Forgive me for saying so, but you are an odd man, monsieur."

"Yes, I've been told that. Your food is getting cold."

She began eating, and he began asking her questions, trying to make polite conversation, trying to be a gentleman. He asked where she was from, and he was surprised to learn that she was visiting from her beloved France, that she had relatives right here in the city, that she had been in Baltimore since last fall. When he asked how his sister and mother had talked her into the scheme of trying to win his attention, she said that they had told him he would someday be a very wealthy man, a powerful man in the American government.

"Ah, you thought to be crowned an empress someday?" he teased. "Like Josephine?"

Her glittering eyes told him that, yes, that was exactly what she had thought, what she had dreamed of for a short time.

"You're in America, not France," he reminded her gently, silently cursing Colette and Mother. When he cornered them . . .

"How well I know, monsieur." Grimacing, she placed her goblet on the table. "Your sister holds a fine *soirée*, but the wine . . . the *vin* is terrible!" she whispered.

Grant tossed his head back and laughed.

"Beautifully done, little sister," Grant said, stepping into the richly appointed drawing room. Colette stood near a window, looking out at the carriage house where, only moments ago, their parents had stepped into their conveyance, waved goodbye, and set out for home. Leigh was with the governor in the library down the hall. Grant had followed Colette in here. "I have only one suggestion," Grant said. "Next time be a little more considerate of my feelings. What the devil makes you think I want any woman but my wife?"

Colette turned a sad smile on him. "You are going back, aren't you? Papa told us—Mother and I—but we did not want to believe. Oh, Grant, she's an Indian woman, for heaven's sake! I believe they call them squaws."

Grant inhaled deeply. "White men call them squaws," he said, releasing the breath. "It's a derogatory name, one I don't want anyone calling her."

She crossed her arms, hugging herself. Her eyes glistened with unshed tears. "You just have to go back and live with her? Father has talked Mother into trying to understand, but Grant, I'm having a difficult time with this. This . . . this *marriage* you claim—"

"I love her. I enjoyed living with her. I want to live with her again. She's my wife, Colette, and I won't argue about the validity of our marriage."

She glanced at the hearth where a fire blazed. "When?"

"What? When what?"

"When will you leave?"

"In April. I have to arrange the sale of my house and belongings. If you want anything . . ."

"You'll let me look through things?"

"Yes. Some books and keepsakes . . . I'd like to leave them with you."

"Of course. Oh, Grant, you could have so much here."

He cocked his head. "Colette, you've no idea what I'll have there."

She turned away.

"Don't be distant and cool. I'm your brother, remember?" he said. "Where's Randolph? He came late, and I didn't see him leave."

"Walking in the garden."

"The paths are covered with snow!"

"I had them cleared. He doesn't want you to leave, either, you know."

Grant lifted a brow. "No, I didn't know. I thought he wanted me to stay gone. He's hardly had a friendly word to say to me since I returned."

She turned back to him. "You've always stood to gain what he has always wanted, Grant. You cannot blame him."

"I never have. He can have it all now. He'll no longer be the passed-over son. We'll both be happy. Maybe he won't hate me."

"He does not hate you. Do not leave for that reason."

Grant shook his head. "Oh, Colette. How many times must I tell you that I love her? That no matter what anyone thinks of what I've become, I know I can be happy with her. I'll come back and visit every few years. Two years from now, I'm sure I'll be an uncle—if the way you and Leigh fawn over each other is any indication. An uncle . . . now, that's a thought."

She smiled, blushed prettily, and turned back to the window.

Grant walked up behind her, put his arms around her

and propped his chin on her shoulder. "What are you staring at? The carriage-house lanterns? What a boring view!"

She laughed. "I'm not really staring at anything. I'm thinking about you. You'll always be my brother, you know. Do not forget that."

"I don't plan to—*I* just reminded *you* of that fact. Make me an uncle, will you?"

"You know I'll try."

"Ah! I know you will. The gleam is back in your eyes."

They watched the distant lanterns in silence for a time.

"What if you had set out on a journey, had been captured by hostile Indians, and Leigh had been one of them?" Grant said softly. "At first he might not have been receptive to you, in fact, he might have hated you for some reason. Then during your months spent with his people, something special began growing between the two of you. Something unequaled in emotion and intensity. You shared some incredible days and nights together. Magical hours. Your feelings grew and grew. You became afraid of them because you knew they were strong, but you didn't know exactly how strong they were until you found yourself back among your people. You had told yourself that was where you belonged, that you and Leigh couldn't possibly have a future together because you were of different races. You began missing the simplicity of the life you had led while with his people. You had experienced many new and different things, and you had found something special and refreshing about them, too. You missed Leigh and his way of life with a heaviness that seemed unbearable. You wanted to—"

She twisted in his arms and pressed her face to his chest. Her tears wet his waistcoat. "Stop! I've never heard anything so beautiful! So passionate and heart-wrenching. Oh God, how you love her!"

He kissed her hair. "I don't want to hurt or embarrass anyone, Colette. Not Father, Mother . . . not you. But I have to go back. Actually, not back. Instead of to Tennessee, I'll be going to the Arkansas River. Lord, how I've wondered if they arrived there safely, if she's well, if she misses me the way I miss her. I thought I could do this. I thought I could forget and go on. I can't."

She lifted her head. "She must be incredible. To have won my brother's heart the way she has, she must be incredible."

He smiled. "She is. Perhaps someday I can bring her here, and you can see for yourself. A short visit wouldn't be impossible."

"Oh, Grant. She'd be the talk of Maryland. And the talk might not be kind."

"It might not be. But it would die in time. Maybe you could visit us there. They would welcome you—you're my sister. Indians aren't such frightening people. They value family and home life. They have a vast respect for all living things. They're like us—if our homes were threatened, we would feel angry, too. We would fight, too."

"Maybe I can," she said wistfully.

"The conditions are far different," he warned.

"I'm sure they are. But I would get to see you. That is all I care about. I'm going to miss you—again!"

He brushed tears from her face. "Stop crying now. Leigh will wonder what I've done to his lovely wife. Besides, you'll truly be the *chérie* of Maryland after your success tonight. People will be scrambling to get invitations to any event you plan. You have every reason to feel happy."

She tipped her head and smiled. "You are proud of me?"

He saw the mischievous gleam in her eyes. "I'm very proud of you—you know that!"

She laughed. "Yes, I know."

"Now dry your tears. Look beautiful and happy for Leigh. I'm going to go find Randolph and see if he'll talk to me. I'd like to spend the next few months establishing a friendly relationship with him, if not a brotherly one. I've never wanted him to feel threatened by me."

"Be patient with him, Grant."

He kissed her forehead, then withdrew. "My dear sister, I am the teacher of patience—sometimes."

She gave him an odd look as he turned to leave the room.

Chapter Twenty-four

Unmoving, Danagasta stood in the river up to her knees and stared down. These waters were not so clear as those of the Tennessee, but she could still see the *atsadi* that swam close, not knowing that danger lurked nearby. She stabbed with her sharpened stick, twisted her wrist, and lifted a wriggling fish from the river. She opened the pouch that rested near one hip and dropped the *atsadi* in it. Then she lifted her face to the Skyland and whispered her gratefulness to the Spirits who had been so kind and generous to her people.

They had survived the winter, though they had had to bury more dead during the long months. Still, they had not buried many—only ten, Danagasta thought. Ten deaths were more than enough reason to grieve, but there was much to be happy about, too: the bounty of fish to be found in this river, the many animals that roamed the forest, the rich land the people had found when they had turned the soil and blessed it during spring planting, the strong, healthy crops that grew in the gardens . . . the birth of her son three moons ago.

His struggle to be born had been a long, difficult one. Ewi and Sali had been with her for many hours, then the healer had come. The old turbaned holy man had spoken words: *Little one, hurry, come out. There—a bow, a bow!* He urged a boy-child to "jump down." Then he blew a medicinal extract on Danagasta's head, breasts, and the palm of each hand. Sali propped her up from behind, and she pushed and pushed, finally delivering the infant into Ewi's outstretched hands. The baby had cried almost immediately.

"Is it a bow or a sifter?" Sali had asked excitedly.

"Ball sticks or bread?" Danagasta had asked breathlessly.

And finally Ewi had smiled up at them and answered: "A bow and ball sticks. It is a strong boy."

"A boy," Danagasta had whispered, lying back. "A boy . . . just as I dreamed. Just as the healer said. Panther, Son of the Mountain Lion. Of course he is strong!"

The women had laughed together, and soon Ewi had put the wet, squalling *usdiga* on Danagasta's chest. Danagasta had comforted him with the nipple of one breast, and she, Ewi, and Sali had laughed with joy because he was so eager and powerful for a newly born infant; his forceful suckling had nearly taken Danagasta's breath.

After a time, Ewi had helped her clean herself while Sali had warmed water to bathe the baby. Later, Ewi had taken her new nephew to see his grandfather. When she returned with Panther, she had told how Hanging Basket, whom Agent Meigs had delivered along with the other chiefs to the new land near the end of winter, had held the boy and wept with joy. He had called other important men in the tribe to see his grandson: Sequatchee, Whitetree, Catolster, Shutegi . . . Then he had sent them all away. He had even sent Ewi away for a few moments so he could spend time alone with the boy. When he called for Ewi to come back, it was to place the child back in her arms and ask about his daughter, if she would recover to be well and strong again, and Ewi had answered yes, that Danagasta had her father's strength.

Danagasta walked through the water toward the bank. She had caught ten fish, enough to feed the families of her close friends. Ewi sat on the lush green riverbank, cradling the crying Panther, trying to soothe him by dipping her finger in a bowl, coating it with mashed hominy, and letting him suckle the food from her finger.

"He is very hungry," Ewi said. "With his appetite, he will grow tall and big. Sit and give him a breast. He will eat the hominy, but his mother's milk will feed him better."

Danagasta lifted the pouch over her head and dropped it to the ground. She placed her stick beside her catch, then sat down, and took her little one. He smelled the milk; he opened his mouth like a baby bird and turned his head toward her. She lifted her deerskin shirt—she had sewn shirts and skirts for herself to wear after Panther's birth because lifting the shirt so he could nurse was easier than freeing the ties on a dress and lowering one shoulder of the garment at a time. He found a nipple without her guidance, and she smoothed his jet hair. But was it so black? Sometimes when Grandmother Sun shone down on him just right, she thought she glimpsed strands that were not quite so dark . . . that were more brown than black. His eyes were brown, but they were a shade lighter than a full-blood Cherokee's.

He coughed as milk warmed her breast and then poured into his mouth, and she pulled him away for a moment, put her hand behind his head and sat him up until he could catch his breath. "Slow, my hungry boy. Be patient or I will one day be forced to teach you how to play Cullowhee's chess game."

Ewi gave her an odd look. Danagasta laughed and put Panther back to her breast. "Cullowhee's chess game. My husband began teaching me how to play it. It requires much patience."

Ewi smiled, understanding. She took Danagasta's pouch and said that she, Kayini, and Sali would begin cleaning the fish. Then she rose and headed toward the row of cabins that stood just above the bank. All the people who had once lived in Big Water were scattered in cabins all over this new land. That did not sadden Danagasta, for everyone seemed content, and she was happy knowing that smiles had returned to many faces. She often rode about to visit people she knew. She frequently visited Walini and sometimes called on Kaliquegidi, who had chosen to settle farther back in the foothills near a small stream. Catolster, Whitetree, Sequatchee, and Shutegi had built cabins for her and her father, and she was grateful. Life along the Arkansas River was good.

A fish splashed in the river, and when she glanced up to watch the water while her son fed, a vessel coming downriver caught her attention. It was a flatboat. Only during the journey here had her people traveled on flatboats, and the soldiers had long since taken the floating cabins away. Now canoes populated the shore.

Someone shouted behind her, racing through the trees, calling an alarm that whites were passing through. Though her people were not hostile and no whites had troubled them since their arrival, some came through occasionally. When they did, the Cherokee men sat close to their weapons until the whites passed. It was a habit learned long ago and not easily put aside.

Danagasta should have risen and walked back to her cabin just in case these whites were hostile. But she stared at the flatboat and froze. Her heart quickened. She blinked. *Tla no.* The Sun was in her eyes. *Sge!* The man who stood, bold and proud, on the front of that boat was not her husband. Could not be . . . He was not. Tlanuwa was in Baltimore with his family.

"Danagasta, come!" Ewi said sharply. "Remove the baby from danger!"

"There is no danger," she mumbled as her aunt took her by an elbow and urged her to her feet. Though Danagasta went with Ewi, she cast a long look back at the flatboat. The man had disappeared . . . she had been imagining. She blinked again. "I danced too long last night. I will rest with Panther," she said, knowing the boy-child usually fell asleep after nursing in the afternoon. "I will rest, then I will not imagine things that cannot be."

She felt dizzy . . . faint. As soon as she reached her cabin, she placed Panther on the bed the men had built for her, and she lay down beside him and shut her eyes. She heard many voices outside, but they were not shouts of alarm. Some children were shouting something that sounded strangely like "Agent-man."

Danagasta lay very still, not allowing herself even a shred of hope. Her baby stirred, and she brought him back to her breast, where he nursed contentedly again while she struggled to block all noise from her mind.

They were on the flatboat before Grant and the men he had hired to help him guide the thing could even moor it to trees on the riverbank: Cullowhee, Awe-ani-da, Wadigei . . . other children and a number of men and women. Kayini hugged him. Sali and Ewi grinned and kept nodding. Catolster said, "It is good to see you," then proceeded to help moor the boat.

A laughing Whitetree offered Grant a mug of *conutche*, a drink made from pounded nutmeats. "The Sun rises very well in the west," he said.

"Thank God," Grant responded dryly. "I might not have my hair if it didn't." The men laughed together.

Sequatchee, as always, regarded Grant apprehensively from where he stood near Chief Hanging Basket beneath a tree on the embankment.

Grant had been told they had all arrived safely. A man stating that he carried a message for him had arrived on his doorstep in Baltimore one March day with the good news. Still, Grant was relieved to see his friends. He couldn't begin to tell them *how* relieved he was. When he'd left them at the Tellico Blockhouse, not one of them had been in good spirits.

"Where's Danagasta?" he asked Ewi.

She stared at him, still smiling. He wanted to shake the information from her. He wanted to see Danagasta, hold her, make love to her, and he knew Ewi understood English.

"Where is my wife?" he demanded.

Ewi's smile broadened. "Your *wife* is in her lodge."

"Will you show me where her lodge is?" he asked impatiently.

She glanced at Hanging Basket. "First you must see my brother."

Grant studied Hanging Basket, wondering if the chief's reception would be a warm one or a cool one. The man had not said one word about his daughter the entire time they had been in Washington. But Grant knew Hanging Basket had not approved of Grant's return to Baltimore. From the moment they had departed with Meigs and the other chiefs from the agency, Hanging Basket's manner toward Grant turned cold. Now the chief looked just as angry as he had then.

Grant began to feel a bit sick in his stomach. These people loved him. But he couldn't help but wonder if they would put him right back on his flatboat and loosen the lines from the trees if Hanging Basket told them he didn't want Grant here.

"Fine," Grant told Ewi. "I'll go talk to him." He had fought his family and traveled for months to be with his wife, and damn if he'd be put off by a severe look from Hanging Basket.

He leaped from deck to shore and climbed the slight embankment, finally planting himself, feet apart, right in front of the chief. Behind him, the clamoring Indians fell silent.

"I've come for my wife," Grant said.

Hanging Basket's eyes flashed. "My daughter will stay with her people."

"I haven't come to take her away. I've come to be with her. To stay with her."

"To leave again one day?"

"Only to visit my white family. Perhaps every two years—every eight seasons. I'll make my home with her."

The chief's obsidian eyes flashed.

"Please," Grant said. "I've never lied to you. I love her."

A moment passed. Grant held his breath. What would he do if Hanging Basket said no? What would he do if Danagasta's father turned him away? God, he didn't know . . . He'd give serious thought to searching every cabin until he found her. Then he'd claim her. She was his wife, and he would claim her, by God. He had come too far, waited too long, endured too many lonely nights. He had dreamed of this day for too long to allow himself to be turned away.

Her father nodded slowly. He spoke to Sequatchee in Cherokee, then Sequatchee stepped forward, saying, "Come. I will take you to her." Though the expression on Sequatchee's face was serious, there was no tone of hostility in his voice.

"*Wado,*" Grant told Hanging Basket. The man dipped his head in acknowledgment.

Sequatchee led the way across the gentle slope overlooking the river. Cabins rose up ahead.

"She's well?" Grant asked as he fell into step beside Sequatchee.

"She is well."

Grant eyed the man. "You and I have never gotten along well. But I think it's time we put our differences aside, don't you think? Danagasta thinks highly of you now, and I won't have us being—"

"We have no differences, Tlanuwa. You made her no promises, yet you have come back to her. You plan to stay. You are right—you have never lied to any of us. You have much honor."

They reached the lodges and stopped near the third one.

"She is inside," Sequatchee said. "There is someone with her. You will not want him to go."

"Like hell I won't," Grant muttered, wondering who the devil had the audacity to be in the cabin alone with his wife.

Sequatchee grinned. "I tell you—you will not want him to leave."

"I thought you said we had no differences. I thought you said—"

"Stop complaining, Agent-man, and go inside. You will like what you see." With that, he walked off, chuckling more with each step. "I would like to stay and see your face, but it is a private moment," he called over his shoulder. "Stop staring at me and go inside."

Grant faced the lodge, feeling another sensation of unease in his belly. What was waiting inside? Who would greet him when he opened the door? Sequatchee's final revenge: letting him open the door on Danagasta and the lover she had taken because he had been away for so long and she had thought he was not coming back. He didn't think he could bear the hurt, the heartache.

Sweat beaded his brow as he took a deep breath and pushed the portal. It creaked open.

She lay on a bed that had been built against the far wall, and her back was to him. Clad in a shirt and skirt, her feet and legs bare up to her calves, she was lying too still. Grant's first thought was that Sequatchee had lied. Sequatchee was playing with his mind. She didn't even seem to be breathing. She wasn't with a lover, she was dead.

Grant approached her, his boots touching lightly on the cane mats lining the floor.

In a few swift movements she was off the bed, had a knife in her hand, was crouched and snarling Cherokee syllables.

He laughed aloud with relief. "Well, I see you haven't changed too much since I've been gone. Are you going to cut me again or put that knife down and come here? I'm here to stay, Danagasta."

Her eyes widened. She drew a few quick breaths, and released them in a rush. She whispered his Cherokee name, but she didn't move.

"I can see you're not going to do either. So I'll just have to take the knife from you and *take* you in my arms."

He did exactly that. Then he dipped his head and kissed her, long and deep, the way he had dreamed of kissing her for a year now. A blessed year. They had left the Chickamauga settlements last year in the middle of summer. And the middle of summer had arrived again. He tasted the rich honey of her mouth, whispered that he loved her and that he planned to be her husband forever, that he would hunt for her, provide for her, protect her . . . That he hadn't done much but think of her while he was in Baltimore. That he couldn't live without her.

His hands went to her breasts, and he thought they felt fuller and heavier. She arched into his touch. He bent to scoop her into his arms, meaning to place her on the bed and make love to her right now, this instant. But she stopped him, pushing his hands away, and stepped back and to one side of the bed.

"Danagasta, what . . . ?" His gaze followed hers to the tick, and then he saw *why* she hadn't let him continue, why she hadn't let him lower her to the bed: A baby lay fast asleep on what looked like a panther skin.

The infant's skin wasn't as coppery as that of most Cherokee babies he'd seen. The hair was dark, but not so dark that it resembled coal. The child was clad in a sleeveless buckskin garment that just touched its knees. Grant stared and stared at the infant, and as he stared, a slow realization began to dawn.

He dropped to his knees beside the bedstead and reached a trembling hand to touch the child. He had stopped breathing, it seemed. But when his hand touched the chubby face, when it traveled up and touched the silky hair . . . when it traveled down one small arm to touch the amazingly tiny fingers . . . when it touched a plump thigh, a knee, a calf, a foot, and precious toes . . . when the child stirred and opened its eyes and stared silently up at him, Grant inhaled deeply.

"God . . . Oh, Danagasta . . ." He sat back on his heels and turned his startled gaze on her. "Oh, Danagasta." It was all he seemed capable of saying.

Danagasta lifted the baby from the tick, dropped quietly to the floor before her husband, and placed the child in his arms. "I named him Panther," she said when he glanced up. "But we can change his name if you want. The naming of a boy-child is usually left to the father. I . . . you were not here. *Sge!* Have you really returned to me, or do I dream?"

He shook his head. They laughed together. He looked down at his son, who lifted one arm and yawned.

"There's no need to change his name. I saw you holding Dudi's baby that day, and I thought of this," Grant whispered. "Do you know I thought of us having a child? It scared me to death because I knew I was about to leave."

"But now we have a child, and you are here . . . *Osiyo,* my husband," Danagasta said through her tears. "Welcome to our new home."

AUTHOR'S NOTE

With all due respect for the Cherokee Indians, I must make note of some historical points, as well as a few fictional liberties I took during the writing of this book.

Colonel Return J. Meigs: Though there is plenty of documentation that suggests that a large number of Cherokees respected the agent and were grateful for his assistance, one cannot ignore the fact that whenever the United States government felt it needed more Cherokee land, the colonel was all too willing to bribe the chiefs to obtain the land. In 1805 he negotiated for three valuable tracts, and in 1806 he arranged the treaty that led to Chief Doublehead's assassination. He continued to serve as the United States agent to the Cherokee Indians until his death at the agency in 1823.

In 1808 Meigs did indeed lead a delegation of Chickamaugan chiefs to Washington to meet with President Jefferson about exchanging land. Tahlonteskee certainly feared for his life, and a number of other Chickamaugan chiefs did, too. No treaty was signed during the ensuing meeting, however, as other Cherokees discovered the Chickamaugans' desire to sell more land and were angered. The federal government encouraged emigration, and even paid the transportation costs of those Indians wishing to settle around the Arkansas River in what is present-day northwestern Arkansas. Approximately 1500 Cherokees moved in the years 1808–1811, calling themselves the Cherokees West or Old Settlers. Efforts at encouraging more Cherokees to move were stopped because President Monroe feared the Indians would side with the British during the growing crisis between the United States and England. The War of 1812 followed.

One final note, an interesting one: Under the United States Trade and Intercourse Act, it was illegal for any United States citizen to sell whiskey to Indians. "Parson"

Blackburn, however, was discovered to be operating a distillery in nearby Maryville, Tennessee, and selling whiskey to the Cherokees. Reverend Blackburn was "disgraced" in the Indian Nation, and by 1810 his once successful school at the Tellico Blockhouse had gone to ruin.

Sometimes justice does prevail.

TERESA WARFIELD
April 1993

SOURCES

Berkhofer, Robert F., Jr. *Salvation and the Savage.* New York: Chicago: Greenwood Press, 1976.

Bowden, Henry W. *American Indians and Christian Missions.* Chicago: University of Chicago Press, 1981.

Eaton, Rachel. *John Ross and the Cherokee Indians.* Chicago: University of Chicago Press, 1921.

Mails, Thomas E. *The Cherokee People.* Tulsa: Council Oak Books, 1992.

McLoughlin, William Gerald. *Cherokees and Missionaries, 1789–1839.* New Haven: Yale University Press, 1984.

Mooney, James. *Myths of the Cherokee* and *Sacred Formulas of the Cherokees.* Reproduced 1982 by Charles and Randy Elder-Booksellers, Nashville, Tenn., in collaboration with Cherokee Heritage Books, Cherokee, N. C.

Woodward, Grace. *The Cherokees.* Norman, Okla.: University of Oklahoma Press, 1963.